WEST BOUND

MAGGIE RAWDON

CONTENT NOTE

A list of content information you may want before reading can be found on maggierawdon.com/content-information

PROLOGUE

L evi

"DROP IT!"

The muzzle of the gun presses against my temple, knocking my glasses askew, as my fist tightens around the bag in my hand. I close my eyes, focusing only on my breathing. The sound of the air filling my lungs and slipping back out again into the night.

In. Out. In. Out.

For now, at least, my lungs work like they should. Like they always have. The way I hope they will for a long time to come.

The barking demands of the masked man robbing me at gunpoint are a garbled hum. The deafening alarm that's sounding through the whole room is a distant buzz. The gallop of my heart slows to a more predictable rhythm.

"Give him the bag." My brother's voice breaks through. I open my eyes to glance at him in my peripheral vision. He mirrors my stance, frozen in place, fists balled and jaw tight.

We took this job off my father's plate. He'd planned to do it himself, argued with us about this alternative, but his heart's been weaker than normal lately. A scene like this one would have killed him, and for all his perceived faults, my father is a good man. My mother couldn't bear a world without him. And my family is everything to me.

Which is why I don't argue when my older brother gives me a command. We could hash it out behind closed doors later. Right now, I don't flinch. I drop the bag of stolen objects at the robber's feet, just like he asked.

The smack of the fragile artifacts against the Carrara marble underneath our feet echoes in the sterile hall. The robber's eyes narrow, and he presses the muzzle against my skin until it forces my head to tilt at an angle. My sweat parting like the Red Sea around it as it makes its way from my forehead to my cheek.

"You son of bitch!" the man snarls. He sounds like he's all bark and no bite. If it were just us, I'd test my theory. But I won't put my brother's life at risk to sate my curiosity.

"You have what you want. Now fucking leave us alone." My brother doesn't bother hiding the fury in his tone. I imagine he's having similar fantasies about ending their lives.

"The fuck did you—" We're spared another round of needless yapping when the wail of police sirens pulls around the corner.

"Let's go!" the robber's coconspirator shouts as he takes off for the exit.

My would-be murderer lets out a frustrated sigh of discontent. Disappointment that he doesn't get to see me die if I had to guess. He pulls the gun from my head, grabs the bag off the floor, and takes off down the hall after his friend. I hear the sound of relief in my brother's slow exhale for half a second before the police sirens get too close for comfort.

"Down the stairs. Out the back entrance. I stashed it under the steps. Out the black door with the red sign. Over the fence to the left, across the alley, turn right, through the gap in the second fence, and right down the street." I repeat the instructions for how to get to our getaway car in case I don't make it out with him.

"Smart," he remarks, a hint of admiration, as we take off for the stairwell. When I suggested we stash the reliquary that brought us here before we filled our bags with some other opportunistic finds that might muddy the waters of a future investigation, Grant had been annoyed at the extra time it took. Now, it's going to save us. If we manage to get out before the cops find us, that is.

The sirens are close now. Just outside the building as we take the stairs down three or more at a time. I duck under the stairway, grabbing the black bag I'd stashed with the reliquary inside, before we bust through the black door.

The rain batters my face and forces me to duck my head down as we take off for the fence. If we can climb it before the police come around the building, we have a chance in hell. That's a big fucking if as I watch Grant's boot slip off the rung almost as soon as he puts it on. I glance backward, checking to make sure the coast is still clear.

I stop to boost him, shoving him upward. He's strong, but I'm stronger. We both need more time in the gym and less at the bar drinking whisky. That's going to change in the future. I heave the bag over the fence without the time to be more delicate, and he catches it.

"Go!" I yell. We don't have time to play heroes right now. We'll both die. But this is my brother we're talking about. He's not about to leave me, even if it means he gets shot too.

I'm lucky when I don't have the same trouble as him. I haul myself over the top of the fence and land in the alley with a thud before we take off running. It's his turn to look back when we turn right.

"So far, so good," he mutters as we slip through the gap in the fence.

I can see the car in the distance. We're almost there. So close and yet so far. We have to walk this stretch quickly. A slight jog might even be warranted given the rain. But we can't run like we've just stolen something.

This kind of work isn't our strong suit. It's not our usual line of business. Far from it. The Quiet Horsemen are a lot of things, but cat burglars aren't one of them. Or at least they weren't before today. I'm not even sure why we're doing this or who we're doing this for. My father never gave a shit about collector's items or reliquaries before today.

Our father has been cagey with the details, and the way he fidgets when he talks about this deal makes me think he's doing it under pressure. Maybe to protect us. From who or what, I'd love to fucking know. The fact that he'd put not one, but two of his sons at risk? That he didn't trust anyone who wasn't blood right now? It's bone-chilling if I stop to think about it too long.

Grant's got the doors to the car unlocked, and we slip inside. I'm grateful for the tinted windows as I toss the bag in the back and pull my glasses off to wipe them free of raindrops. Grant revs the Shelby's engine and tears out of the parking space as quickly as he can without hydroplaning.

I check the link to the building's security system. The looped footage covers our tracks. I'd double—no, triple—check it when we get to our safe house. But so far, so good. Just like he said.

We're several miles down the road before either of us dares to speak. The windshield wipers are our only soundtrack besides the slowing of our pounding hearts.

"I thought today was it," Grant admits. I grunt my agreement.

"I hope whatever this is for, it's fucking worth it," I mutter, wiping my glasses again when the condensation fogs them.

ONE

L^{evi}

"FATHER, forgive me for I have sinned." Her voice is soft and sweet as it comes through the divider of the confessional. I'd recognize it anywhere after months of stalking her every movement through her phone and weeks of observing her here on the grounds of the convent, even if the swath of copper-spun hair wasn't visible through the grate as I pull it back. "It has been one month since my last confession."

I slip two fingers under my white collar, attempting to buy myself breathing room. But it won't budge. The heavily starched fabric is like a vice, scratching against my skin as I flip through the notes I quickly scribbled down about the sacrament before I entered this medieval cage of secrets. I just have to hope I have enough of an outline to get me through. If hell exists, I'm certainly going after this.

I was only able to gain extended access to the remote island in the middle of an alpine lake by pretending to be a priest on pilgrimage. The convent is famous for its numerous reliquaries and shrines established behind the towering stone walls that seem more like a fortress than a home for a religious order. When I arrived, I claimed that I was on sabbatical, practicing reflection while I researched a book I was writing on the lives of saints. The massive archive in one wing of the convent had proven to be the perfect alibi while I tried to make sense of everything I knew about her so far.

The only problem with the plan is that on days like today, when the priest who usually takes English speakers' confessions is out sick, I'm politely asked to take over the duty—with no good reason to say no. So now, I'm trapped here right along with all the salacious details and inner workings of the penitents' personal lives. The confessions run the gamut. Taking extra desserts on a bad day. Laziness when it comes to the recitation of prayers because they hadn't slept well. Anger at being made to clean the toilets for the fourth time this month. There's a long list of supposed sins that seem more like an account of the human condition. It hadn't occurred to me until just now that she'd be one of the penitents. I have to bite the inside of my cheek to keep my smile at bay.

She shifts on the kneeler, unclasping her steepled hands to a laced and folded position, and clears her throat before she speaks again.

"And lastly, I've been having impure thoughts about someone. Someone I shouldn't." She pauses, taking a breath before she finishes her confession. "A priest."

"A priest?" I finally speak, wanting to be sure I heard her correctly. Thankfully, it comes out more strained than I intend and masks the sound of my real voice.

"Yes, Father. I know how it sounds. I *know*," she laments.

"It's been weighing on me. I've been praying. But I have dreams." She sounds flustered, and I can imagine the creep of a blush spreading over her cheeks. I've seen it more than once in the archives when I've caught her off guard. I only regret not being able to see through the privacy screen well enough to watch her color change now.

"Dreams are out of our control. You can't sin in your dreams. Have you acted on them?" I do my best to mimic the altered tone I used before.

There's a long pause. One that makes me feel like she's about to admit to the sin of betraying her vows. But I haven't done anything with her. Not yet. And if it's not me, which priest? Is there someone else she's seeing that I don't know about? The drip of panic enters the back of my mind as I try to figure out who might have that kind of hold on her. I need it to be me. *Only me.*

"Not with him."

Not with him? My brow furrows and I shift on the worn cushion as I try to make sense of it.

"Without him?" I ask, gritting my teeth when I realize I spoke in my normal voice.

"Alone," she answers so softly I can barely hear her. "At night."

Oh.

Oh, fuck.

I clear my throat and then shutter my eyes. I'm already imagining her hands moving under the sheets of her dormitory-style bed in her tiny room. It's not like I haven't heard her before, making those little noises when she thinks no one is listening in. But now I'm wishing I'd been able to watch too.

Fuck. I'm making this awkward for her by leaving her in silence. If I were a real priest, this would be a run-of-the-mill, if not a little extra-spicy, confession, and I sure as fuck would not be imagining it.

"Is there anything else?" I cover, trying to pretend like I was waiting for the end of her confession.

"No."

"Then for penance, say three rosaries." I've been doling out rosaries left and right today. It's the best I can remember from the few times my mother took us when we were children. Two was the highest I'd given all day, but three felt fair given her sins. "A day. Until the dreams stop or for a full month. Whichever is longer," I tack on at the end.

I hear the sound of her nodding behind the wall, the rustle of her hair, and the soft whoosh of movement, and then she begins to recite the act of contrition. Her voice is beautiful. I could listen to her talk for hours, repeating prayers, talking about the archives, giving a tour of the reliquaries on the convent grounds—the content doesn't matter much. She has a soothing voice and an almost melodic laugh. One I've grown rather fond of while I've been getting to know her better over the last few weeks as she served as my personal archivist, guide, and occasional lunch companion.

We've managed a few walks alone through the garden, too, when I volunteered to help her gather ingredients for dinner. A chore she seems to get assigned more often than not around here. She loves to cook, and she lamented the fact that she can't make some of her favorites from back home in the States. It was nice, she said, to have someone else who could relate to her cravings.

She finishes her recitation of contrition, and I repeat the words of absolution from the notes in front of me that I've been practicing all day, trying to slow them in a way that makes them sound more profound and to buy myself some more time in quiet reflection.

A few moments later, we share the sign of the cross, and she scurries out from the darkness of the confessional back into the bright light of the church. A stream of stained-glass-soaked sunbeams floods through the small grate, and I shut the window to block it out, shrouding myself in darkness again. I lean my head against the wooden wall behind me. I can't think too hard about what she confessed. My mind would wander to places my body would follow. Things I can't act on while I keep up with the ruse of confession. I'll save that for later.

Instead, I focus on the job I was sent here for. Reconnaissance. First, to get to the bottom of her role in her father's business, and then, to get as much information as I can on the reliquaries housed here. I'm running through the remaining list of archives I need to cover.

I've been photographing pages whenever I can get a moment alone and sending them back to Charlotte, the art and archives expert on our team, for translation and dictation. She's been doing her best to make sense of the piecemeal bits I'm able to give her. It's rare that I'm left completely alone. If I'm lucky, I have the company of the redheaded sinner from a few moments before, and if I'm unlucky, I have one of the older German nuns who glares at me from across the room and shushes me in broken Bavarian. The kind I'm half-sure are curses. At least, that's what I have to assume they are given the harsh inflection. Either way, I wasn't about to test my luck. It means that this is all taking much longer than planned, and my brother and his associates are growing impatient with my progress.

I press the light on my watch and check the clock. Five more minutes, and then I can go back to my room and fire off a text message to my brother about the irony of me handing out penances and absolution. I'm sure it'll give him a much-needed laugh.

I could tell him about her confession. I should tell him. It means my plan is working. She's falling for my act and growing more vulnerable by the day. But I'd rather have her little secret all to myself for a little while longer. At least until I can get her to act on her desires.

I step out of the confessional a few moments later, trying not to groan as I stretch my legs. These things were built for much shorter men, not my six-feet-four frame, and the tips of my shoes had been shoved against the door, with my knees folded at an awkward angle just to try to keep myself inside.

I take in the detailed woodwork of the door—appreciating the craftsman's work from hundreds of years beyond his grave. There's a scene of a conscience-stricken man on bended knee in the forest, hands clasped as he begs for a chance at salvation. We all could use some right now. I turn the latch, locking the secrets within, and step back into the vestibule.

The wind sweeps through, stirring the hem of my robes, as someone opens one of the massive abbey doors. It catches for a second too long, slamming shut. The sound echoes through the church, and the nun at the door gives me a sheepish look of apology before she proceeds toward the altar, carrying a fresh armful of ivory-colored candles to replace the ones that are rapidly approaching their end. I follow her movements down the aisle only to catch another set of eyes. Bright blues that are locked on me. Ones that belong to Sister Mary Anthony, previously and much better known as Zephyrine Schaefer, the penitent I just absolved, and the governor of Colorado's daughter.

Her full, rosy lips are parted, and her eyes are wide. Even from across the room, I can see the pink flush racing up her neck at her realization that I'd been the voice on the other side of the confessional. Her head swivels back toward the crucifix before she presses her forehead to her folded hands. Her knuckles whiten as she grips the rosary beads, while her lips try to keep pace as she prays faster, like it's an incantation that might rid her of the demon at the center of her wicked dreams.

I can't say I blame her for them. She's been at the center of mine for the last few weeks. Ones where I get revenge for all the hell her family has put mine through, and ones where she's on her knees just like this, her hand gripping just as tightly as she works toward a different sort of absolution. They're just that though—fantasies. The reality is grim. If she knew just how much torment I intend to rain down on her loved ones, she might be saying a different prayer altogether.

TWO

Zephyrine

MY HEART HAS BARELY SETTLED in my chest when I collapse onto the bench in the garden next to the closest friends I have on this island, Sister Ulrika and Sister Teresa. When we're alone, though, I still call them by their given names, Aria and Tamara. To me, that's who they are. We're all here out of necessity rather than some sort of calling, and while I do my best to follow all the convent's rules, sometimes old habits die hard. I miss hearing people calling me by my old name instead of Sister Mary Anthony, and we still talk in English when no one else is around.

They're taking a short break from cleaning up the weeds and pulling in some of the fresh veggies and fruit from the walled plot. It's a sort of potager's garden for the convent's kitchen, which serves the residents and the relic seekers all the same. This time of year, we always have a flurry of new guests, and we're kept extra busy keeping food on the table and fresh sheets on the dorm beds as the tourists make their way through.

The relics are the convent's biggest draw. Thousands of years of saints' bones, blood, and tears are locked up in beautifully ornate reliquaries that are as stunning as they are grotesque. We have a series of small museum halls and shrines that wind through the convent's ancient corridors. Places where relic seekers spend hours visiting and praying as they learn about the saints' lives and the miracles they're purported to have worked in their lifetimes. Some come just to take in the view, a quick stop on their way to the grand palace across the lake, but others come in the hopes of cures for rare illnesses and the end of personal misfortune by touching a miraculous piece of the past. The abbey serves as a kind of last resort for people desperate for one final chance at a different sort of life. One better than what they've had, and the three of us are no exception to that rule.

"Something wrong?" Aria squints into the sun and shifts the fresh basket of basil leaves in her lap to the side as she studies me.

"He took confession today." I let out a soft sigh of frustrated embarrassment. I can't believe I didn't recognize his voice beyond the divider.

"He?" Tamara's nose scrunches up in confusion as she stands and brushes the garden dirt from her knees.

"Father Levi."

"Still struggling with the near occasion of sin?" Aria does her best not to smirk as she asks.

"I just wish he'd go home. He has to be close to finishing his research, right?" Father Levi reminds me too much of things I can't have. Ones I'm desperately trying to come to terms with giving up forever. If I were ever going to settle in here—really make this place my home—I need to let go of the hope right along with the vice.

"He's too pretty to be a priest." Tamara gives her thoughts on the matter. We were all in agreement on that at least.

"And too young," Aria adds. "What happened to them all being old and gnarled? A mess of liver spots and patchy gray hair? I liked it better like that."

"And I personally can't trust a man, priest or no, who wears long sleeves all the time. It was 25°C the other day. You can't tell me he wasn't melting in that black shirt out in the sun." Tamara raises a brow.

"Oh yes. That tight black shirt." Aria raises a brow at me, and I close my eyes, trying not to imagine it. This is what happens when you spend so much time hiding away from the rest of the world. Long-sleeved black shirts suddenly become too sexy for your imagination to handle.

"Now *you* need to go to confession." I match her raised brow with my own.

"I'm tired of confession." She sighs. "It's not like we can get into real trouble here. I'm always confessing the same three things. Jealousy of people who get to leave this place at the end of the week. Anger at Abbess Frances for always giving us more chores in a few days than I think she's ever done in her life. And laziness for not wanting to go to church twice on Sundays." Aria pouts a little.

"Well, you can add being tired of confession to the list next week," Tamara teases her.

"At least it'll add some variety." She huffs.

"We're probably the world's worst novices." Tamara reflects on our lack of composure.

"I'm sure there were others. King's discarded daughters.

Mistresses. Revolutionaries. The archives are full of mentions of them." I feel the need to defend us. There were plenty of interesting women who ended up here just like we did—compelled against our will or for lack of better options.

"Mentions of their punishment too. At least Abbess Frances prefers tours of kitchen duty rather than outright torture," Aria admits.

We fall into silence for a moment as a bird lands and steals one of the strawberries Tamara dropped on the pathway between the berries and the basil. I imagine a million down-trodden feet have passed through this walled garden. Some seeing it as a bastion of safety, others as a cage meant to clip their wings. They'd be deprived of the ones that let them soar too high and replaced with the weight of chastity and temperance.

"So what did you confess to?" Aria glances up at me again before she returns to picking the stems off the leaves.

"That's between me and Father Levi." In more ways than one. I start to blush again, less prominently than when I discovered he was my confessor, but enough that my friends would know it was something shocking.

"Something bad then," Tamara observes as she looks over me like she might find the answer written somewhere.

"Something I'd prefer Father Mark had heard rather than him." I run my lower lip between my teeth. I have no idea how I'll face him again, and given the amount of time he spends in the archives, there will be no avoiding him for more than a few hours.

"Something salacious then?" Aria's eyes brighten with the possibility.

I press my lips together, and she lets out a low breath.

"Not about him?" she presses, her eyes lighting with amusement.

"It was a dream," I answer defensively.

"You confessed to a dream?" Tamara looks at me like I'm strange.

"It was a dream I liked." I'm not about to repeat my confession in the broad light of day. It's bad enough that he knows. I feel dirty. Like I've sinned all over again by telling him. The long lectures from the abbess were getting to me.

But I needed to get it off my chest and somehow be absolved for thinking of a priest that way. Thinking of another man, one who doesn't have those kinds of vows and responsibilities attached, is bad enough, considering my own circumstances. But the two of us? Together? It's an impossibility. Sacrilegious, if I'm being honest with myself. I can only imagine how his opinion of me has altered. The new friend I've been making is now likely lost to awkward avoidance. Or at least I could hope. I'm not sure which I'd hate more, him dodging into a row of the archives to avoid seeing me, or him smiling knowingly when my cheeks heat under his gaze the next time he asks for my help. Either way, I'm in for torture.

"Ah, I see." Aria tries not to grin, but her eyes betray her all the same.

She struggles with the rules as much as any of us. I'm half certain she's broken them with visitors. Somewhere, a man is sharing a pint with a friend, bragging about how he's so good in bed he managed to bag a nun.

"He's a priest. I'm sure he's heard worse." Tamara, ever the pragmatist, offers up a distraction.

"He's a man. I'm sure he's *done* worse," Aria adds, reveling in her own assessment.

I could see her point. Father Levi is too handsome and clever not to have had a youth that was filled with at least some measure of iniquity, or at least the temptation. Another flash of his wicked smile outside the confessional returns.

I try for a moment to imagine him as a naive young virgin and draw a blank. In my mind, Father Levi definitely had a past, even if he doesn't have a present, and for that, at least, he can't completely judge me. He knows what it's like to be human. At the end of the day, whatever orders we take, whatever vows we swear to uphold, we're human underneath it all.

"Aria," Tamara hisses, using only her name as a reprimand, snapping me out of my thoughts.

"You know it's true. All priests probably get it out of their systems before they join the seminary." Aria shakes her head.

"Father Mark did say he had a girlfriend before," Tamara admits.

"That's a hard one to imagine." I think of the graying old man who's always discussing the principles of the gospels and reciting the beatitudes to us.

"Did you tell him it was him in your dream?" Aria asks.

"No. But I doubt he thinks I'm having dirty dreams about Father Mark or Father Peter."

"How dirty was it?" Aria always wants the juicy details when it's something more interesting than our daily chores.

"Three-rosaries-a-day dirty."

"Oof." She grits her teeth and then gives me a sympathetic look. "For how long?"

"Until the dreams stop or for a month. Whichever is longer."

They're stunned into silence, and I can feel the creep of embarrassment returning.

"There were other sins too," I try to explain.

"Are you still working with him in the archives?" Aria twirls a leaf of basil between her thumb and forefinger, no doubt plotting how she might get me out of my situation.

"I don't know. He might not want my help now." I bury my face in my hands and groan. "I can't believe I didn't realize it was him. I was so focused on doing what was right and getting this guilty feeling off my chest that I just made a bigger mess."

"Don't get too in your head. Maybe he found it endearing, and he'll let you do some extra credit in the archives to get back in good graces," Aria counters, and both Tamara and I snap our heads in her direction, eyebrows raised. "Oh wow. Okay. I did not mean it like that, and now I'm seeing why you have dirtier minds than me."

"Impossible." Tamara rolls her eyes. She's the best of us for sure. I might wear a better mask than Aria does, but I fear that if Tamara knew any of my real thoughts, she'd be dousing me in holy water on the daily.

"Mädln!" Sister Maria Teresa shouts from across the garden. She calls us girls like we aren't all in our twenties. I suppose compared to her seven decades toiling away on this earth, we still seem like children in comparison. "Wir müssen Abendessen machen! Schnell!"

"And onward to the next chore we go." Aria moans, gathering the basil and her gardening gloves. I help clean up the small harvest by picking some of the peppers and tomatoes, filling another basket before I follow them inside.

Maybe I can stay in the kitchen all night tonight instead of having to serve tables. I don't love sweating over the stove, but piping the whipped cream on the cakes and making the schnapps-spiked vanilla sauce that the convent restaurant is famous for wouldn't be the end of the world. It would give me a few more hours of reprieve from seeing him in person.

But it still wouldn't stop the way I'd spend half the night back in my room, doing my best not to think of him, and having him appear unbidden anyway. Sometimes, I remember him debating the complexities of reliquary records while pushing his glasses up his nose and flashing me a bright grin. Other times, I imagine a future that doesn't exist. One where he sweeps me off this island, onto the one across the lake, and we dance the night away in the half-finished palace's mirror room under the light of a thousand candles. At least in my head, there's a world where there's a happy ending and not the reality I've chosen for myself or the one fate dealt me back home.

THREE

L evi

"OH MY FUCKING GOD!" A whiskey-rich laugh echoes from the other side of the line as I explain the day's events to my older brother, Grant.

I'm wandering on the far edge of the lake, a good distance from the convent's walls along the shoreline, where I have a clear line of sight to make sure no one has followed me out here. Not that anyone would. They're all convinced I am who I say I am, to the point I start to wonder myself until I get a dose of reality through the phone again.

"Fucking hell. It's funny, but I don't know if it's *that* funny." I curse as I pick up a rock to skip across the lake as the sun sets. I miss the lake back home. The falls that pour into the river that leads to its basin. The feel of the Colorado sun on my face and the sight of ponderosa pines and aspens rising out of the red rocks and scrub brush. The memory is such a contrast to the hint of Alpine chill here and the broad linden trees and edelweiss. They're beautiful in their own right, but they aren't home.

Speaking of beauty, this lake is breathtaking when you're alone. It's so much quieter out here at this hour when the sailboats and the kayaks have gone home for the day, the tourists are tucked in their beds, and the wildlife has simmered to a dull hum as they nestle down for the night. I took a walk once after dinner with Zephyrine, and I hadn't known where to put my eyes, on her or the sunset. I could see why the convent was built here. Why the king was designing a castle to rival Versailles on its shores.

My brother's renewed laughter knocks me out of my daydream.

"Oh. I'm not sure there's anything funnier than that. You as a priest taking confessions from nuns?" He cracks up again, and I hear the distant tinkle of a woman's laughter in the background. I suspect it's my future sister-in-law, and he confirms it a moment later. "Even Dakota can't stop laughing."

"Laugh it up. Both of you. Real funny when you're not the one sweating it out in a tiny box trying to remember whatever the hell we learned at St. Martin's when we were kids."

"I'm sorry. I just... Did anyone confess to anything spectacularly devious?" he muses, no doubt rattling ice around in his lowball glass.

I can see him now, like he's right in front of me, leaning back in his worn leather chair behind his massive oak desk in the offices above the Avarice. Grinning at the way I'm being forced to play a man of the cloth in these austere conditions halfway around the world while he runs the floors of the casino from the safety of his cushy executive suite.

When I'm not moonlighting as a priest, I co-own a luxury

casino resort in Purgatory Falls, Colorado with him. It's a small mountain town that my family has run behind the scenes for decades from our home at Bull Rush Ranch. My youngest brother owns the ranch and inn now with his once-and-future wife, and my oldest brother and I have taken over the largest family business outside of it. Ours turns a much bigger profit than the ranch could ever hope to, thanks to a never-ending supply of lust and greed, but they're both formidable family businesses.

"I couldn't tell you if they did. Confessions are private." I play the reverential role assigned to me on this mission.

"Oh fuck. You have been there too long." He groans, and I hear the squeak of his chair as he sits up straight again.

"I just want a decent fucking burrito, smothered in green chili. I would give my soul for one right now. That and an endless supply of cold ice water. I don't know what the fuck these people have against good Mexican food and water that doesn't fizz," I grumble. The food here is good. The little cakes Zephyrine makes are even better. But it doesn't stop the rumble in my gut that can only be sated with familiar flavors and a glass of ice-cold water from the mountain runoff.

"At least you get to enjoy the beer." Grant attempts to remind me of the benefits of being here. There's one particular upside I've enjoyed more than I should, and I wonder if she's been using her rosary all day to atone for her part in it.

"Fair." I launch another rock across the water, but it dips below the surface after three mediocre skips.

"Did you get any more research done in the archives? The stuff Charlotte wanted?" His tone turns more serious, and we shift back to the business at hand.

"Not today. I was practically snatched out of my bed by Sister Maria Teresa, politely instructing me I would take the English confessors today. She's a fucking battle-ax. I don't know how these women deal with her every day. A lifetime of it. Can you fucking imagine? I could barely handle dad telling us what to do as kids." I scoff.

"I don't think they have much of a choice. Isn't that the whole deal with them when they take their vows? Something-something poverty and obedience and all that?" My brother sighs on the other end of the line, and I can hear him filling a whiskey glass, the slow trickle of the pour, the click and roll as the cap slips back into place. Just another thing I miss. There's plenty of good liquor around here, more than enough. But I miss the taste of home at this point, regardless of how irrational it is.

I have to focus on priorities. I can do my job from here, and what I'm doing right now is worth ten times what I could be doing in an office at the Avarice. Besides, it's not like I have someone waiting for me. My brothers are both engaged. Grant runs our empire, and the other plays professional football when he's not running the family ranch. My sister's marriage might be on the rocks, but she has a wildly successful career as an archaeology professor and a teenage daughter that's smart as hell. Then there's me.

I'm floundering by comparison. And in my thirties, floundering feels a hell of a lot like failing, even if there's plenty of money and all the worldly possessions I could ever dream of. Not that I particularly wanted love either. That shit burned me before, and I'm more than happy to watch my brothers walk down the aisle while staying well clear of the mess it creates in your life. But it still feels like there could be something more than this. Especially now that I'm watching these women who have dedicated their entire lives to simplicity and service. They seem, at least outwardly, happy to be living out their days that way. I've been trying for the last several weeks to make sense of it.

"I suppose that's true. I can't fathom it. But good for them," I mumble when I realize I've been lost in my thoughts while he takes another slow draw from his glass.

"And what about her?" My brother brings us back around to the real subject of the phone call, the one who brought me to this island in the first place.

"She's good. She's warming to me. I'm making progress with her." I keep my assessment perfunctory.

She's another little conundrum because, from all my observations of her, with and without her knowledge, she seems like a good person. Every bit the perfect little nun she appears to be. Minus a few indiscretions in the middle of the night. None of which match the ruthless roots of self-interested pricks on her family tree.

"Still keeping an eye on her via the phone?" he asks, the jovial brother gone and the ruthless head of our family back on the line. I installed specialized spyware on her phone through a zero-day exploit on one of her apps when we first discovered her. It gave me access to everything, even the ability to activate her camera and microphone. Features I might have taken advantage of once or twice.

"Yes, lots of interesting data." I stare out across the lake to where the shadows of the mountains start to fade into the dark horizon. Flashes of her dance through my vision. That melodic laugh of hers, followed by her sweet smile. The way her nose scrunches up when she studies a book in the archives. The breathless sighs in the middle of the night as she works herself up to—

"Like?" My brother interrupts again by pressing me for details.

I usually share everything with him. In a case like this, I always would. I'm not just his business partner; I'm head of his security team. There's a trove of confidential information I have on her now from the things she's shared with me, Father Levi, the priest, on our walks to the things she unknowingly shares with me, the watcher, who installed spyware on her phone. But the intimacy of some of the things I know about her make me hesitate.

I'm guilty of cherry-picking the things I share. If it's pertinent to the investigation I'm conducting—anything to do with the madman she calls a father or his unhinged quest to obtain Caroligian relics—I'm an open book. I've been quick to give them every single detail I find and spending long nights helping comb through datasets to find anything that might help us turn up answers. But if it's just her, the private would-be college student turned nun? I leave her privacy intact. For now, at least.

"Nothing of use to us. Just gossip with her friends. Pictures of the lake. Searches to identify bugs in the garden. Tickets for the Vienna Boys' Choir performance for Christmas. Some notes about Christmas markets." Late-night jam sessions through her favorite playlists and, on a good night, searches for adult content she's curious about into the wee morning hours when she panics and deletes it all. But only after she hides her favorites in a secret folder labeled "Recipes." I'm busy smiling to myself about that when I hear Grant calling my name through the phone.

"What? Sorry. I was distracted by something on the lake." I toss another rock, and it doesn't even skip, just disappears below the surface of the cold, rippling navy waves, down into the depths.

"I asked if you have a timeline in mind?"

"Not really. A couple more weeks maybe. I imagine I'll have anything Charlotte could possibly use by then. It might be enough time to soften her toward me, but I don't know how much she's going to confess to an outsider. The priest thing helps me as much as it hurts me. She thinks I'm too fucking holy to tell me any of her dirty family secrets or anything that would be particularly helpful in twisting Daddy's arm." At least unless I'm behind the mask of the confessional. I should try to arrange that again, but how I'd keep it a secret from her next time, I'm not sure.

"She might twist his arm for us. Or even if he knew just how easily we could snap her neck..." My brother sounds like me now. Cold and calculating. Her father tried to kill all of us, including my brother's bride-to-be, and that simply couldn't stand. But I wasn't keen on the idea of harming her.

"She's never even mentioned him. Not even in passing." It's the truth.

"Does that mean anything though? You said yourself she might not want you to know about him." Grant knows as well as I do.

"It's possible. Like I said, I'm hopeful with a little more time, she might crack open." Especially now that I know she's been fantasizing about me late at night. That's an opportunity I can exploit.

"We might not have that kind of time." My brother points out the obvious. We'd gotten a reprieve when we foiled the governor's plan. We had a loose eye on him in the form of our uncle, our very own mole in his establishment—not that he's trusted with many details. If he folded under our pressure, I can only assume the same would be true of the governor. Pragmatically speaking, it really seems only a matter of time until he tries to kill us again. There's a real possibility we don't have time to figure out the why before it all collapses in on us.

I need these reminders. The ones that keep me grounded when I get distracted by her and the pull I've created between us.

"I'll press her tomorrow when I see her in the archives. See if I can't ask some questions about her life before that puts us down the path where she might start talking." It was high time to make some decent headway with her. Something I can't quite put my finger on has been holding me back, and I worry that it might grow if I don't start putting a tighter leash on my imagination.

"Good. Don't go soft on me, drinking all that German beer and spending your days on vacation." Grant's brotherly tone has returned.

"You know I'd much rather spend my vacations at a cabin in the Rockies, drinking some decent whisky and kicking your ass at a couple of rounds of cards."

"Then let's get you back here to do that."

"I'll call you in a few days. Let you know how it goes," I promise.

"Oh. I almost forgot. Rowan's in Munich on business for the next few days. Acting as a courier for one of Charlotte's projects. He said to see if you wanted to meet up." Rowan is one of Charlotte's many paramours and Hudson's head of security. The Kellys and the Stocktons share business and many of the same passions and problems—one of them being the governor. I could pass some discoveries from the archives off to him by hand and relieve my mattress of the storage.

"Yeah. I can take the train in. I'll text him."

"Good. Good. I'll talk to you soon. Light a candle for my immortal soul, will you, Father?" Grant jokes.

"I don't think there's much of one left to save." I laugh. "Talk soon."

I hang up the phone and start to make my slow, meandering walk back toward the convent. I'll need to be quiet entering the gates. They have a curfew and quiet hours they like to maintain since so many of the walled inhabitants prefer the crack of dawn to the dead of night. I'm not ready for bed quite yet. Too curious about what she's up to.

I pull up the app that lets my phone mirror hers, and I see that she has a playlist pulled up. It's always an eclectic mix. New music and old. Country and rock. Rap and pop. Love songs and rage songs. It looks like a little window into her soul. Whether it's the echoes of her past life she's found in those lyrics or just the pleasure of living vicariously through the melodies, I'm not sure yet.

I came here expecting someone completely different from the person I found—boring, plain, carrying out her father's orders like a good soldier, with very little *real* good in her. I'd been sure, given the evidence of her support for his campaigns in the past, the seemingly picture-perfect family, and her proximity to a treasure trove of relics—one that might include the final piece to the collection he was creating. It was all a sure sign of her involvement with him. But she seems to genuinely care about the other nuns here and always seems to make the sightseers smile when she tours them around the abbey. All of her interactions with me leading up to today have been nothing short of innocent goodwill. So much so that I almost feel guilty for stalking her like this. Almost but not quite.

It means I'm missing something, potentially the key piece we need to make the whole puzzle come together, and I can't afford to waste much more time trying to figure it out.

FOUR

L evi

I'M TOO busy scrolling through the playlist as I walk down the pier to see the person standing on it, and I have to quickly tuck my phone away when I finally notice her. She's clueless to my presence even as I get close, too used to the safety of the small community here. She's humming along to the song and dancing her way over the worn-out old boards.

When she spins around, her eyes widen, and she starts to scream, but it's quickly silenced as she chokes on it instead. Then she stumbles backward toward the edge of the pier. I lurch forward, grabbing her upper arm through the oversized cable-knit sweater she's wearing, and pull her forward before she can stumble back into the dark waters behind her.

She blinks for a moment, taking me in and confirming I'm not a mirage before proceeding to pull her headphones down around her neck. She fumbles around her pockets, frantically searching for her phone when the sounds of the risqué pop song come blaring through the speakers. I grin as she works to turn it off, her cheeks blazing with heat and her fingers deftly flying over the screen to try to silence her late-night dance party.

"Sorry. Sorry," she apologizes as she finally gets to the screen she needs, and silence falls between us.

"I don't think I've ever met a nun with a playlist quite like that," I say. There's no way I could have seen the whole list from her quick fumble with it, but she's too embarrassed to realize, and I'm too dishonest to admit I already know every song on it for a different reason.

"Oh, um. It lets me unwind a bit from the day. I just need to let loose sometimes after all the cooking and cleaning. I'm sure you know what it's like. There have to be hard days. Giving last rights, taking confession—" She stops abruptly when she realizes what she's walked into.

"No hymnals?" I frown slightly as though I'm disappointed in her lack of devotion.

"I, uh, have another list with those on there." It's an obvious lie. One I'd see straight through even if I didn't know it for certain. She did have a playlist of Gregorian chants and one of the Boys' Choir for Christmastime. Maybe she was counting those to skirt the falsehood. But I'd rather pin her to it, let her squirm a little. After all, I need answers.

"I'm starting to see why you end up in confession so often." I cant a brow skyward as my eyes drift over her skeptically.

Her lips press together, and her eyes dart down. It's hard to believe this mild-mannered nun is the daughter of the man I hate so much. She barely seems like she could hurt a fly, let alone be part of a politically corrupt, empire-building family. But maybe I haven't applied the right pressure yet.

"I thought we weren't supposed to talk about that?" She steals a glance at me, but then her eyes hit the floor again.

"Talk about what?" I pretend to have no idea what she means.

"About the confessional today—" When she looks up, she stops abruptly, realizing I'd been trying to give her the out. "Oh. Sorry. I... I'm so bad at this." Her cheeks brighten.

"What's this?" I ask using air quotes and trying to soften my countenance enough for her to relax.

"Awkward things." There's a long beat of silence, and then she shakes her head, her face marred with mortification. "I had no idea it was you. I would have never confessed to that if I'd known it wasn't Father Mark. I'm sure it was awkward for you too."

"What you tell me in the confessional stays there. Between you and God." I reassure her, and she nods her understanding, but her eyes drift to the horizon in thought. "Unless you feel like you need to talk about it more to alleviate your conscience," I add.

Every single bit of information I can squeeze out of her means a little more data. The more weaknesses she reveals, the more opportunities I have.

"Well, given that we're already discussing it... I could use your counsel, I think."

"Of course."

"I just wanted to say I know it's wrong. I know what I did was wrong. I'm sorry for how it must make you feel."

"Why is it wrong?" I want to hear her say it.

Her eyes meet mine again, and she studies them like she's trying to root out whether or not this is a test or something else.

"I shouldn't have those dreams. Or those thoughts. But the closer I get to my final vows, the more doubts I have. I think the dreams—it's my subconscious manifesting those doubts."

"So you're not out to seduce me then?" I tease her.

A small smile flits across her face and fades.

"We all have those doubts," I continue. "We question whether or not our choices really make sense. If it's the right thing or the wrong thing. Sometimes, our subconscious works through it in unusual ways. All of that is normal."

"It's normal to have those kinds of thoughts about a priest?"

"You'd be surprised what I hear in the confessional," I lie. I wouldn't know, but I imagine it happens often enough to younger priests. Her smile returns at that admission, and she nods her understanding.

"Ah, yeah. That doesn't surprise me. Aria says you're too pretty to be a priest."

"Should Aria have been at confession?"

"I wasn't trying to get her in trouble. In her defense, I think it's hard to look at you and not have an opinion." She hedges her bets.

"You're blaming me for it then?"

"Well, if you represent the temptation of sin, we should all stay away from you, right?" She posits a fair conundrum, teasing me back in the process.

"It's only the near occasion of sin if I'm likely to let you act on it." I take a step closer to her, closing the distance between us. "If you think I have the same kinds of doubts. If I'm vulnerable to sin as well." I reach forward and sweep a lock of hair out of her face, daring her to make a move in return. "Do you?"

She stares down at the small space between us and then looks up at me, surprising me with her next act of bravery. She takes the smallest step forward, leaving the Holy Spirit with so little space to move between us that I wonder if we won't just catch fire right here on this dock. Her for breaking her vows and me for tempting her into it.

"Are you?" Her eyes lift to meet mine, fighting to hold

steady despite the deep blush I can still see in the moonlight, the thrum of her heart at her pulse point, and the steadying breath she takes to calm her nerves.

"The collar doesn't create a force field to protect me from the same sorts of base cravings any man might have." Neither does the long wool skirt nor the high collar of her conservative clothing. If anything, it's made them worse. I fantasize about peeling every layer off her. I dream about what confessions she might make with my tongue on her clit.

"So you have impure thoughts too?" Her brows lift with the honest inquisition.

I roll my lower lip between my teeth, doing my best not to smile at her description. Impure doesn't begin to cover it.

"I think about it sometimes, yes. My mind wanders. Especially at night."

"Would you ever act on it?" Her words are a soft temptation, and if she weren't a mark and a nun, I'd already have her on her knees. I've got to remember I'm playing her and not the other way around.

"There's always the temptation. Under certain circumstances, I think it'd be hard to resist," I admit.

She takes another step forward, erasing any distance between us, and her head tilts upward as she holds my gaze. I don't flinch. She's practically begging me to kiss her. And fuck, for a second, I want to. I want to know what she tastes like. I want to feel her lips on mine.

Which is exactly why I can't. My brother was right about me going fucking soft out here. I have to remember what the fuck I'm doing. She's a means to an end. A pawn I need to bend to my will. Seducing her but not fucking her was part of that plan. If I kiss her out here like this, I'll be at risk of fucking up everything. I've been on this island too damn long, unmoored from the things that really matter and letting myself indulge in too much of the things that don't.

"But what kind of priest would I be if I acted on every temptation? We have to hold ourselves morally accountable, or all of this is for nothing." The last bit comes out sharper than I intend. A reminder to myself as much as her that acting on every impulse is the kind of base vulgarity that got me into this situation in the first place. It's why I was out partying a thousand miles away instead of at home on the ranch when my parents needed me the most.

She snaps out of the spell she's been under. The one where she thought this ended like a fairytale, where I'm ready to give up everything I believe in for one taste of her. Her lashes flutter, confusion and a hint of betrayal behind them, quickly followed by another flood of embarrassment at having misread the situation.

"Oh. I didn't. I wasn't." She takes a step back, and another, rapidly trying to reestablish the space between us as if she wasn't the one who closed it. "I'm sorry. I wasn't trying to imply that—" She doesn't get the last word in because the next step she takes is over the edge of the pier. This time, it's too quick for me to catch her, and she plunges into the watery void beneath, the dark waves lapping over her face and silencing her scream.

FIVE

Z ephyrine

I'VE BARELY HAD time to register the pier disappearing
from beneath my feet before I'm plunged into icy water, the
sapphire sky disappearing behind wave after wave. I start to
sink almost immediately, the weight of my skirts increasing by
the second as the water soaks through the heavy fabric.

*This can't be real. I'm asleep. I'm just tired and imagined
everything that came before this too.*

It's my first thought, however illogical given the circumstances. The very real version where I'm fading into the
oblivion of a deep lake in the middle of the night.

*I'd wanted to die for so long. To be erased just like he was.
And now, when I least want it, I'll get my wish.*

Worse yet, I'm going out like this. Drowned by my skirts, a
nun in training, so lonely and pathetic that I just threw myself

at a priest. If I'm lucky, I'll get a tiny cross on the shore like the mad king across the lake did when he drowned. Except I don't have a half-finished castle to show for it. I have nothing to show for anything in my life so far.

I can't let it end like this. Not like this.

My adrenaline kicks in a second later, and I start to kick and flail, reaching skyward and fighting the sinking anchor at my waist and the brutal cold that already feels like it's wrapping its frigid fingers around my bones. There's another invisible but heavy hand at my throat that feels like it's simultaneously crushing and corroding my windpipe.

I can't breathe.

It's the next thing I register. It should be obvious that I'm drowning, but I'd been so focused on sinking that my mind had failed to register anything else. The little bit of air that I'd sucked into my lungs as I fell is already running low. The burn intensifies, and every moment that passes feels like an eternity.

I'm a terrible swimmer. I could barely manage a doggy paddle on a good day. I always joked that I didn't need to know how to swim the dry climate of a landlocked state like Colorado growing up. Now I'll die because I never practiced the skill.

Hopeless and useless.

At least until I feel arms wrap around my waist, tightening around my middle. I struggle at first, thinking it's my imagination—my mind playing tricks on me as I lose consciousness—or worse yet, a third danger, a monster from the deep ready to drag me to my watery grave. But then, on my next upward kick, I feel myself get a little closer to the surface. A second kick, and it really feels like progress. I don't trust it until the third and fourth seem like real momentum too. Somehow, through the blurriness of my fading vision in the water, I see it's his hands wrapped around me, his body helping to propel us upward.

Father Levi makes another powerful kick, and another, and

we're moving faster to the surface. The twinkling stars in the sky are reappearing over my head through the waves, and despite the burn in my lungs and the black halo starting to appear around the edges of my vision, I feel hope.

One kick. Two kicks. Three kicks. I start counting to force myself to stay conscious. I'm uselessly trying to help him, but somehow, it's working. We're so close, and my lungs feel like they might bleed from how much they're burning. We breach the surface of the lake as I choke on the water, desperate for air.

"Breathe," he shouts. "Breathe."

He circles around me, coming face-to-face with me in the water, and holds me steady as he kicks to keep us at the surface. His normally serene face is stormy with a mixture of concern and anger, his brow heavy. I try to breathe just to satisfy his demands. He looks furious. For the almost kiss or the drowning, I have no idea. I'm too frazzled to make sense of it.

I take in a shallow breath at first, shaky and spluttering, but it's more oxygen than I've had in what feels like an eternity. Then another less shallow one, and another. Until I can finally take a deep enough breath to feel the panic slowly recede, even as I cough and struggle to kick and paddle.

I'm desperate not to be useless. For my own sake as much as his. It feels like salt in the wound to almost drown and then not even be able to help rescue yourself. If I manage to get out of this lake, I'm taking swimming lessons as soon as the abbess will let me arrange them. I'll go twice a week. Say an extra rosary after Mass on Sundays. I just want out of this alive with some shred of my dignity intact.

"I've got you. Just make sure you can breathe." His voice loses its demanding edge, concern bleeding through instead. His arm wraps around me again, securing me before he starts to move us toward shallower water.

It's impossible to get back up on the pier again from our

position beneath the waves, but he takes us toward the beach. Slowly but surely, we make progress. My breathing has steadied, and I cling to him like a rag doll, anxious not to be carried back out to the depths.

The realization of how cold I am starts to seep in, and I feel the chill through every bone in my body as my feet finally touch the murky bottom of the lake. He holds me steady, even as I stumble in the shallow waters. I try to right myself, hoping to seem less pathetic, and only manage to catch my ankle on a submerged branch. My wet skirts wrap around my legs, and suddenly, I'm tumbling forward and nearly landing face down in the water again if not for his strong grip and the way his arms wrap around me, snatching me from that fate to drag me up.

The tears hit hard, clawing at the back of my throat as I work to choke them down. I feel ridiculous for not even being able to walk to shore properly. A sob heaves out of my chest, and I'm embarrassed even at that—for being such a mess in a moment when I should be thanking him for saving me.

"I'm sorry. I'm just so—" I can't even get the words out as my teeth start to chatter, and my lips feel stiff.

His eyes search mine with worry, and without another word, he stops in the ankle-deep water. His hands go to my waist as he rips at the buttons on the back of my skirts, dragging them off, and then my sweater follows. It feels like an anchor lifted off my body, but my legs are still unsteady as I take my next step.

I don't take another one. I'm lifted off the ground and into his arms as he takes charge. Another round of tears bubbles up, but I manage to bury my face against his chest before they become audible. I can't remember the last time I let someone help me, let alone carry me. I'm not sure anyone ever has. But I don't have the will to fight him in this moment, and I'm even less excited about the prospect of another stumble. So if this man wants to help me, I'll just let him. I'll worry about making apologies tomorrow.

He makes the trip back to the convent seem inconceivably short, especially while carrying a soaking wet mess. He makes quick work of the doors and has us marching down the hallway toward the dorms.

"Wait!" I press my hand to his shoulder when my brain finally catches up as the warmth of the interior hallways knocks the worst of the chill off my body.

We can't possibly go into the dorms like this, even if we do look like drowning rats. Sister Maria Teresa will have my head. She'd single-handedly reinstate the gallows and put me up on them herself. He halts, turning a skeptical eye on me.

My eyes catch on his neck before I can speak again, distracted from my original warning. The thick, cordlike muscles in it are taut from the strain of carrying me, but there on his skin, inches away from mine, is what looks like a tattoo. It was covered deftly with some kind of cover-up, makeup, or otherwise, but the dip in the lake has left it partially revealed. It looks like the tip of a horseshoe.

My stomach drops at the sight of it, and my mind starts to race. I've never seen a priest with tattoos. It's not criminal on its own, but it speaks to a longer life between reaching adulthood and joining the seminary—a life marked by tattoos and maybe women. It would make sense. He's too pretty to be a priest, maybe even a touch too clever and charming.

"What's wrong?" His tone doesn't leave room for any disagreement, and he starts marching down the hall.

"They could see us go into my room." My voice is rough from the combined strain of coughing and the cold. I'm glad I have an excuse for it. It's an easy lie to cover up my nervousness.

"Let them. I'll explain you nearly drowned. Now tell me where your room is."

He carries me through the halls like I weigh nothing, winding around corners and moving like he wasn't in the icy water right alongside me as I direct him to my room. He opens the door, setting me down on the chair at my desk and flipping on the light in the dark room. It's blinding, and I squeeze my eyelids together against the fresh intrusion.

"Towels?" He gives a truncated demand. I nod to the drawer as I work to unbutton my blouse with frozen fingers. He charges on while I struggle to manage one button. My icy hands are still thawing and refuse to cooperate.

"Here." He appears with scissors he must have taken from the sewing kit I have perched on my shelf. I suck in a deep breath as he makes contact with my skin, and my self-preservation instincts kick in, capitalizing on my paranoia for half a second until I realize his intention.

He moves my hands out of the way and cuts through the fabric. It falls to the sides, revealing my simple white cotton bra underneath. I blink up at him and place a hand over my chest, which does nothing at all in the way of achieving modesty in these conditions.

"Take that slip off unless you need me to cut it too." It's another rough demand. I stand slowly, hooking my fingers under the elastic waistband, and manage to pull it off without taking my underwear with it. He averts his eyes, sparing me more humiliation.

He wraps me in the fluffy white cotton, giving me an ounce of my dignity back and the slightest promise of warmth around my core. He moves us to the small bathroom attached to my room, cranking the hot water on. His eyes dart over my form, less in the interested way I've seen him do when he thinks I'm not looking, and more like he's studying a specimen under a microscope, making sure I'm all in one piece and nothing too much is out of sorts. I catch a glimpse of myself in the mirror and immediately regret it. I'm even paler than usual, my soaking red hair is plastered to the sides of my face, and my cheeks are bright pink as my body attempts to bring me back up to temperature.

"What about you?" I manage to chatter out the question while pulling the towel tighter around me. He's still drenched, and his clothes are sticking to every inch of his skin. I've never seen a priest with this kind of body, but given that most of the ones I've known have been headed for retirement, maybe I just didn't have the right sample size. I don't have time to dwell on it. I'm too busy just trying to feel my fingers again.

"I'm going to my room to clean up. Then I'll come back to check on you." He's already on his way out the door. Apparently, now that I'm no longer near death, he can't wait to get away from me.

"Careful with how much noise you make on the way back. It's late, and the abbess hates being woken up," I remind him, as if he doesn't already know about the rules. I would just hate to see him get reprimanded for the trouble I caused.

He nods and disappears out the door to my room. I finish undressing in the bathroom, feeling another round of chill coming on before I hurry to climb into the shower. The water is a blessing and a curse, feeling scalding hot against my chilled skin but finally providing the real warmth I've been seeking. I close my eyes and lean against the tiled wall as it hits my body and shoulders.

I have no idea how I'm going to make up for this mess. I can imagine the looks on Aria and Tamara's faces when I tell them I nearly kissed the man and then forced him to jump into a dark, watery abyss just to keep me from drowning. And that's after today's earlier incident, where I confessed that I think about him in the middle of the night. I feel like crying at how pathetic it sounds when I hear it laid out like that, but I only manage to force a weak and wretched groaning sound from my chest, my tears still too frozen to fall.

But as Abbess Frances would say, time marches on, and so must we. So I reach for the soap and start to lather it up slowly, almost too tired to move. Nights like this, I almost miss home. Almost, but not quite.

I'd hit my bed early, and then I'd sort out this mess in my head about Father Levi's priestly credentials and my greatest embarrassment yet. But I can't stop myself from thinking back through every interaction we've had, every word he's spoken to me from the moment we met until just now on the pier.

Was he a priest with a past? I couldn't judge him for that. Mine is one I'd leave at the bottom of the lake if I could. The fewer people who know about who I was before I crossed the convent threshold, the better. But for him... why hide it? He couldn't possibly have such a dark past, could he? If he did, it would paint everything about our budding friendship in a different light. I swallow a shallow breath as I stare at the tile of the shower.

SIX

L^{evi}

I NEED the trip to Munich this weekend. I'm texting Rowan the second I get out of this shower on the backup burner I have stashed away. It's an emergency. Anything to get off this island and away from those big, blue, needy eyes staring at me like I'm the best thing she's ever seen. I can't take much more of it. Not in my current state.

The fact that I'm standing with my hand wrapped around my cock in this tiny convent dorm room shower where I have to duck to even get my hair under the water to wash it, seriously considering jacking off to thoughts of a nun, tells me my time here needs to come to a close. A vacation from it at least. I've exceeded my tolerance for a lack of vice, and now my dick is settling for whatever vanilla fucking fantasy it can conjure up.

One where she's in her white cotton granny panties and T-shirt bra, asking if there's any possible way she can thank me for saving her life.

I tighten my grip and take one long stroke of my fist, grinding my teeth at the way it lights up all my nerve endings. I'm dying for the real thing though—for the warmth of her thighs straddling my lap while I listen to her breathe fast and heavy. A chance to listen to her voice tell me how good my cock feels while she grinds over it. Watching that perfect little body of hers chase an orgasm. I could give her that much, couldn't I?

"Fuck," I curse, tearing my hand away from my dick.

I'm not giving in. Not until I can imagine someone else in her place. I don't need that tacked on to the ever-growing list of embarrassing shit I've done on this work trip. I'm better than this.

If I wasn't just back from the brink of hypothermia, I'd douse myself in the icy water that's always readily available from these faucets. In lieu of that, I rush to finish my shower and put on a fresh set of clothes. I snatch my glasses off the table and clean them one more time. I'd shoved them in my buttoned shirt pocket before jumping in after her, and managed not to lose them in the water, but they're still ice-cold and fogged up.

I'll check on her, say my goodnights, and starting tomorrow, I'm going to begin treating her like a mark again. I shove my glasses back onto my face, adjusting the temple tips on my ears. They're slightly bent and a little worse for wear. Just like me. Exactly the reason why I have to get back to brass tacks. No cutesy conversations about her favorite things or watching her dance to her favorite songs in the middle of the night. From now on, it's business. Nothing more, nothing less.

TWENTY MINUTES LATER, I'm headed to her room one last time. I just want to make sure she hasn't frozen to death and check her ankle isn't swelling. I tell myself I'm not worried about her. It's just that the last thing I need is for her to be booked off to a hospital where I don't have access to her. I have to wrap this job up quickly, get what I need from the archives, see if she's a dead end, or has something we can use, locate a relic if there is one, and get the fuck back to Colorado.

I rap my knuckles lightly on her door, not wanting to make enough noise to wake her neighbors. We don't need suspicious eyes on us at this hour of the night. She's right about that much. I don't even know how we'd explain it either, since the truth seems almost as implausible as a lie.

"Hi." She answers the door quietly, cracking it open.

"Just wanted to check on you and make sure you're all right. Warmed up?" I give her my best priestly look of concern.

"Yes, come in." She opens the door and steps aside, urging me in as she eyes the hallway suspiciously.

I get a better look at her little dorm room now that I'm not worried about stripping her out of cold clothes and avoiding hypothermia. It's small, with bare stone walls and a few alcoves for religious items. There are no photos, no mementos, nothing that might give me more clues about her. The small lamp in the corner bathes the room in a yellow-orange glow, and her bed is still neatly made, not a wrinkle to be seen, like she hasn't even sat down yet.

"Can I get you some tea? It's really helping me warm up," she offers, nodding to her own glass. I don't really want tea, but Father Levi would probably take what he was offered. Accepting Christian charity and all that, like the abbess was always going on about. I can't speak German for shit, but the time I've spent on the island has me understanding a lot more than I did in college. Even if half of it is Bavarian. I could thank the abbess for that.

"Sure. Sounds good." I nod, and she immediately sets to work getting me my own cup.

"Coming right up." She glances back and gives me a small half smile for my cooperation in this awkward dance we're doing. It turns out that a missed forbidden kiss and a near drowning don't have much of a playbook to follow.

"How are you feeling? Still cold?" I ask as I sit gingerly down on the edge of her bed and watch her pour herself another cup of tea at her desk. It's littered with ceremonial items she appears to be cleaning, some I recognize, some I don't. All of it glittering in low light and casting prisms on the ceiling and walls.

"I fear it's going to take a little bit to get the chill off completely, but the shower and tea helped. Are you cold?" She's bundled up with a wool blanket draped over her shoulders as she walks toward me with the tea. Thank fuck. The last thing I need is to see her in some sort of nightgown. I'm getting to the point I might find her bare ankle enough. Speaking of...

"Understandable. How's the ankle?" I ask as I take a few small sips of the tea to test the temperature.

"Sore, but I don't think it's broken or anything. Maybe a little sprained." She presses her lips together and looks at it doubtfully.

"Good. Those branches are dangerous. Biting when you least expect them." I try my best awkward humor, attempting to play the role I'm assigned instead of slipping into the real version of myself. I'm tired, bone-deep exhausted really, and it's hard to stay in character right now. I take another long sip of the tea, hoping it's caffeinated, and it'll help keep me awake a little while longer.

"As is the lake, apparently. I'm so sorry that happened. I'm so clumsy, and I just wasn't thinking out there. I should have been more careful. You're a hero for going in after me. I'll be sure to tell everyone that tomorrow." She gives me a soft smile, and my eyes are drawn to her lips again. They're so beautiful. A perfect shade of rosy pink; the cupid's bow like the arches of two stained glass windows side by side, kissing each other just as they meet in the middle. Like we might have. The urge to kiss her returns. I have to close my eyes to shut it out. I take another swallow of the tea to buy myself time before I set it aside on the small nightstand.

"You don't have to do that." I try to reassure her. I'd rather not give the rest of the nuns fodder for gossip about us. It'll hurt my mission. "I'm sure you'd rather not tell them details any—" A yawn breaks my explanation.

A wave of tiredness comes over me with the weight of a tsunami. I have to struggle to keep my eyes open, and I blink rapidly to try to clear it, yawning wide again and pressing my fist to my mouth to cover it.

"It was a long day." She gives me a worried look. "Did you want some more tea?" She holds up the thermos in her hand.

"Yes. I can't believe how tired I am. It's hitting me out of nowhere." I'm annoyed with myself. Tonight is the perfect chance to have a heart-to-heart with her. We're completely alone in a way we rarely ever are, and she's vulnerable. Grateful too. I want to press some of the questions I've been meaning to ask about her past before the convent. I just need to be awake enough to ask them without making it feel like a sloppy interrogation.

"In case you want more." She pours me another cupful and sets the thermos beside it.

I don't notice the nervous tremble of her hand and the

careful way she studies my face until I've already downed the second cup.

"You're cleverer than I took you for," I manage to mumble before everything goes black.

SEVEN

Z ephyrine

OUR POSITION IS AWKWARD. He's lying on my bed, each arm sprawled out in the direction I tied it, and I'm straddling his lap as I look over the tattoo on his neck. I had a suspicion, one that wouldn't stop haunting me in the shower, but I needed more evidence to confirm it. This was the only way.

My eyes follow the curve of the horseshoe down as it dips under his collar. I catch a peek of more just below it. I slip my fingers under the material to get a better look, lifting it until I see the hint of other tattoos down his chest. They might have more answers about who Father Levi is. Maybe he has entirely valid reasons for his tattoos, a life before he committed to his vows, but I need to know what story they tell. If he's even a Father at all, or if the tingling nerves at the back of my neck that I can't seem to shake are warning me about danger instead of attraction.

These little peeks of skin won't do. I'll have to strip him down, and the faster I work, the better. In an ideal world, I'd have him untied and tucked in with an alibi when he wakes up. I plan to tell him he passed out from exhaustion. I'll say I just let him sleep it off not wanting to disturb him after his heroic effort. A tinge of guilt slips over me for repaying him this way. But I need answers.

My fingers work over the buttons, still slower than usual but with none of the egregious trouble I had before. The further down the shirt I go, the easier it is, and the more of his privacy I feel like I'm invading. I'd been curious, even imagined what he might look like with his shirt off in the wee hours of the morning. But even my wildest dreams hadn't been this creative.

He's a work of art—even more beautiful in sleep where I can take it all in. The sharp curves of his cheek and jaw, the scruff shadowing the valleys of his face, his thick lashes covering his normally strikingly pale blue-green eyes, and his lush, full lips are pressed together in sleep-bound silence. His neck contracts as he swallows, his Adam's apple bobbing with the movement, and it draws my eyes down over his throat and chest, back to the tattoos and the job I'm supposed to be doing.

Undressing a priest. I don't know what I did to get myself in this position.

That's not true. I know exactly what I did. I was born into the wrong family, and with it, I inherited the mess that is my family, for better or worse, with all the consequences of a politician for a father who will do anything to ensure he stays in power for as long as humanly possible. In my former life, I agreed to be whoever and whatever he needed me to be. There was a time when I was young that I even wanted to live up to that family name, make him and my mother proud of more than just my brothers. At least until the convent changed everything.

But as I sit here, I can't help but feel like I've absolutely lost the plot at this moment in my life. The black-and-white truth of what I'm doing stares back at me. Me, months away from final vows as a nun if things go my way, with a priest wedged between her thighs, tied up on her bed while she undresses him after she poisoned him. A man who may very well be innocent.

But I don't have time to question my morality or my ethics right now. I only have time to act. Because if I'm right, and he's not a priest, I have a precious few minutes to find out who he is and do something about it. I get back to the work of undoing his shirt. I make easy work of revealing more skin with each slip of a button from its hole.

Until I push the fabric aside. My fingers stop. My heart skips. There's a thick, raised scar, one that starts in the middle of his chest and spreads out in both directions.

It's a brand. He's been *branded* like he's cattle. It's well healed, and the ridges are a pale pink, just a few shades off his regular skin tone. The trauma was something he experienced years ago, but I can't imagine the pain it must have caused. The weeks, maybe months of healing. I hold my breath as I touch it. My fingers trace the edge where the skin is glossier and smoother, following the soft borders of the healed wound.

"Who did this to you?" I ask out loud, looking up at him while he's still unconscious but steadily breathing. The rise and fall of his chest brings the ridges up to the pads of my fingers and then drops them away again.

I study the brand, pulling back from my close-up view. There are distinct letters. A *B* and two *Rs* that merge together to form what looks like an upside-down cattle skull. I spent summers in cattle country, but I grew up in the city. I have no idea what ranch it represents. But I know it does. If I can find that out, I can likely find out where Father Levi came from, and with it, more information about his past.

I pull my phone from under the mattresses. It's a burner I keep for emergencies. Considering I lost my real phone in the lake and have a man tied up in my bed, I feel like this counts. I barely get to bring up the search for cattle brands before I stop dead in my tracks.

I hear a low groan that's barely audible, followed by the sound of Father Levi licking his lips. There's a deep sigh, and I look up just in time to watch his tongue dart out and run over his lush lower lip.

Lord, help me.

I'm distracted by it, and I can't afford to be. The pull this man has on me, despite everything that should stand between us, it's like he knows me. Like he can see past the blushing innocent facade I try to keep up around here, to the parts of me that are still left over from my past life. A flash of how close we were before I fell to my near-watery grave. The dare in his eyes. I shake my head.

Maybe I couldn't handle this investigation on my own. I might need to call for backup, see if someone can come here and help me deal with him. Assuming it is what I think it is, and he's not some innocent priest. I want him to be. But too many puzzle pieces about him weren't fitting right. And if I'm wrong about him, things could get complicated fast. Way more than I can handle as just one little old nun. But who would I even call to help me?

No. I can't think like that. I made it this far. *I can handle this.* I'm a little rusty from life at the convent. It's worn down my sharper edges, but I can absolutely put them back to rights. I was a Schaefer. This was supposed to be its one benefit. The ruthlessness. I can handle one man. I'm not about to let some cattle hand who's escaped the pasture and wandered too far from home put all my hard work to waste.

I can't, and I won't.

His lashes flutter, and I ditch the phone, quickly tucking it back under the mattress and shoving the corner of the comforter back down. There's another soft groan, and he starts to reach for his forehead before the rope stops his movement.

"Fuck..." He lets out a low curse.

Fuck is right. Definitely not a priest. How could I have been so dense not to see it?

His lashes flutter faster, and he tugs on the binds again. Then he rolls his hips until he's restricted by my weight. He wiggles underneath me. But I don't budge. He's not at full strength yet, still too dazed to be formidable, and my thighs hold him in place.

"What the fuck?" He groans, and his lids slowly slide open, blinking and trying to focus on me before his eyes dart over to one of the restraints around his wrist. I hope the knots hold. I was in such a panicked hurry; I don't know if I tied them tight enough.

There's another roll of his hips, like he's absently testing to see if he can buck the weight of whatever's on him, and I press my hands to his chest to keep from being thrown to one side or the other. It unnerves him. The muscle in his jaw ticks in response. His focus drifts back to me, slower than it should, thanks to the drugs. He tries to make out my form through what I assume must be bleary vision, given the way his lashes flutter irregularly under his glasses.

"Fucking hell is this? What are you doing?" he grumbles.

He says it almost like he recognizes me and is perplexed by the fact that I'm straddling him. He shifts underneath me again, and this time he's stronger. I lose my purchase on his chest, slipping back slightly and square onto...

Oh hell. He's enjoying this a little too much.

I can't think about that right now.

"Who are you?" I ask sharply.

"Sister Mary?" he mumbles. His eyes go to where our bodies meet, and his brow slowly rises higher. "What are you doing?" The accusation lies thick in his tone.

"Tell me who you are. I know you're not a priest, *Father Levi.*"

That gets his attention. His body goes rigid for a moment, and then it's like a switch flips. He's trying hard to clear the fog now. Blinking and shifting. Tugging on the binds around his wrist. Trying to sit up while I press down on his chest, my nails biting into this skin.

"Did you tie me up?" He asks a question that has an obvious answer. "And take my clothes off?" An even more obvious answer as we both stare down at his bare chest.

"You seem to like it well enough," I taunt him, blustering my way through this with more confidence than I have.

I need him to believe it though. He doesn't know that I'm out of practice and a little too soft to deal with a problem like him on my own right now. I should have run the second I realized he wasn't a priest. But now I'm committed.

His brows slam down, and his mouth twists. His hips shift upward, and if his hands weren't occupied, I know he'd have them wrapped around my throat by now. A thought that sends a flutter of fear and awareness through my body.

"What are you doing?" he demands.

"What are you fucking doing here?" I snap back.

The curse sends his brow skyward again before it slants back down, and a wry smile appears. His wits are back. He studies me for a long, silent moment.

"Mask off then? *Good.* It's about time. Nice to finally fucking meet you, *Zephyrine.*" He says my name like it burns his tongue, and the fact that he knows it confirms just how much danger I'm in.

"What do you want?" I sound scared even to my ears.

"You're doing all this, and you don't know what I want?" He's amused. He's tied up and pinned down, and it's amusing to him. He has zero interest in taking me seriously now, and it makes my mind run wild with panic.

"I can call the abbess. Report you for impersonation. You won't like the consequences." I try a threat in the absence of any real power in this situation.

"What will she do? Give me a stern talking-to? Tell me I'm not welcome back here to enjoy the stiff mattresses and the ice-cold showers?"

"She'll report you to the order. I'll report you to someone even worse," I warn him.

There's a sharp snorted dismissal in retort.

"Ah. There she is. Daddy's little girl. I was surprised she didn't come out to play sooner. Only when you're feeling threatened then?"

"I don't feel threatened. You should be the one worried." I nod to the rope around his wrists to remind him—and me—that he can't do much in this position.

"Should I?" He lets out a dark laugh, and it's the only warning I get.

He rolls his hips hard and fast, bucking me up, and I have to scramble to hang on to him and avoid being tossed to the tiled floor. I let my nails dig deep into his skin, punishing him for the act, but he doesn't flinch. In fact, his wry smile grows into something more devious.

"You like this," I blurt out loud because it's a revelation. I'm used to dealing with men who are blatant assholes. I've got plenty of experience with them. It's how I ended up here. But I've never had one this good at pretending. He deserves an Emmy. "I don't know how I ever thought you were a priest."

"I don't know either," he agrees easily, and I feel a flush of embarrassment.

He's not scared of me or my threats. Not even a little bit. If I'm going to get him to admit to anything, I'm going to need some bite to my bark. I push away from him and move from the bed, quickly glancing around for something to make him talk.

I spot the thurible I'd been getting ready to clean earlier today on my desk. There are still coals inside, and I grab matches out of the drawer. I flick one against the striker. The flame rises from the tip, illuminating the corner of the room. I press it to the little black lumps, and they quickly catch fire. I blow on the matchstick, extinguishing the flame, and try to steel my nerves as I look back at him.

"Going to try to hold an exorcism? It won't work." He continues to taunt me from the bed. Not a single care or worry in the world. It must be nice.

I grab the aspergillum out of the pile of other things I meant to polish before I was sidetracked by the night's events. I stuff it into the thurible and then glance back over my shoulder.

"Tell me why you're here," I demand.

"Why do you think I'm here?" He glances behind me, and then his eyes come back to mine, unbothered by the threat he must see brewing there.

"I don't know. I'm here on this island with nothing but nuns, and you come all this way to put yourself in the middle of it."

"That's odd, don't you think? That a normal college girl just suddenly drops out. Moves to Europe not long after. Then ends up joining a convent. Would you consider that normal behavior? Do the nuns know about your family?" He knows far more about me than I would have imagined. I wonder if he already knows why I ran away and is just playing me to see if he can rattle more information free. A chill runs down my spine.

"I think people have all kinds of reasons to do what they do. It doesn't make it odd." I didn't have a choice—it was this or the end of my life, and I wasn't ready to go out just yet. Not like that.

"I suppose not for someone like you."

"Like me? What am I like?"

"A con woman, for starters. Don't you worry about how you've lied to all these poor women?"

"Don't you?" I hit back when the blow lands exactly as he intends. This was rich, considering he's a blatant liar.

I'm always reminding myself that this is a means to an end, that it's not personal. I never intended to hurt any innocent bystanders. But the friendships I've made here weigh heavily on my heart in the middle of the night when I think about how they'd view me if they knew everything.

"Not a bit."

I rip the aspergillum out of the coals, sure that it's hot enough now, and make my way back to him. I climb onto the bed again, crawling over the top of him and pinning him down, using my thighs to squeeze his legs together as I hover the hot metal over his abdomen. The glow from the lamp reflects off the patterned surface and creates a spray of light over his skin.

"Tell me what you want from me," I threaten.

He merely grins in response.

"You gonna burn me with that?" He scoffs like he doesn't think I have the guts.

"If I have to. Or you could tell me what I want." I'd rather he keep this simple. I'm not a torturer by nature. I just don't know what else to do, and I'm terrified of any possible reason I can think of for him being here.

"Guess we'll see what you're made of then." His eyes are focused on the spot where my palm wraps around the handle, shaking as I try to work up the nerve to sear his flesh with it.

His unflinching calm rattles me. He's completely unmoved. Disinterested almost. I have to make him see things from my perspective. My eyes search over the tattooed skin for a spot.

"Tell me," I demand again, but I'm met with silence. Nothing but a mocking smile comes from his lips, and I take a deep breath of frustration. "Which tattoo do I ruin? This one with the pretty scenic view, or this one with the cowboy? Maybe we can set this whole field on fire." I run my fingertips over the grasslands etched into his surprisingly soft skin and then look up to meet his eyes. "What do you think?" I'm hovering a half inch from unleashing agonizing pain. He glances at it and then up at me, unimpressed and unmoved. The devious look etched on his pretty face only grows darker.

"I think you should do it and see what happens next," he taunts me.

The bait works because I take it, pressing the aspergillum to his flesh and watching as his skin reacts even as he tries not to. He barely flinches, but his muscles contract slightly, and he inhales sharply, letting out a slower than a normal breath in its wake. Those are the only signs at all that he even felt it. No screaming. No passing out. I pull the metal tool away from his skin to see the white and red marks it left in its wake, the intricate gothic detailing making a mirror pattern over his flesh.

"What do you want? Tell me," I demand. "I'll do it again."

He doesn't answer. His eyes, temporarily shuttered, reopen, and he looks at me like he can see through me. His lips don't move, and his jaw doesn't shift. He might be more determined. I toss the aspergillum to the stone floor in frustration.

"Tell me what you want!" I'm louder than I should be,

given the late hour, and my eyes instinctively dart to the wall where I worry I'll hear a sharp knock from my neighbor.

"You." I barely hear the word before his legs shift underneath me. He spreads them, and mine in the process, until I fall forward like I had before. This time face-planting onto his chest because I've been too distracted. His legs wrap around me, and his arms follow. Somehow, he freed himself from the binds I put them in.

He flips us in such a rapid fashion that I barely register what's happening before I'm underneath him. He has me pinned to the mattress, his thighs pinning my hips and both of my wrists in a vice grip above my head. My mind struggles to catch up with the sudden swap of power until I try to free myself and fail. My heart sinks.

It was a trap.

He reaches above my head with his free hand, grabbing the thermos I'd made him drink tea from. It's still uncapped. The one I'd spiked with the drugs that had knocked him out. He holds it up to my lips with an expectant look, but I shake my head.

"Drink," he demands.

I press my lips together. There's no way I'm letting him drug me. I have no idea what he'll do to me. Rape me. Kill me. Cut me into tiny pieces. Burn every inch of my skin in retribution. I have no idea what he's capable of, and the scars on his own skin tell a violent story. Even as I refuse him, my eyes are caught on the snake that hovers over my head, encircling his forearm and wrist, frozen in time like it's about to strangle its victim.

"Open up and *drink,*" he repeats, his countenance growing stormier by the second.

I shake my head, too scared to use words for fear he'll take the opportunity to pour it down my throat.

"You won't like it if I have to force you."

I press my lips tighter in answer.

"Have it your way." His patience snaps, and he pours the drink into his own mouth, holding it there as he sets the flask back on the desk.

His hand goes to my jaw, his forefinger and thumb pressing at the spot where it hinges. I move to thrash underneath him, but his body pins me in place. I shake my head and do everything I can to try to resist, but it's fleeting at best.

As the pain and pressure mount, I lose the battle. My mouth opens just enough that he has access. He seizes it, squeezing tighter and forcing my mouth open wider. He leans down, his lips practically touching mine, and spits the drink into my mouth. It douses my tongue and rushes to the back of my throat. I start to choke and sputter, but his hand moves to my chin, pressing my jaw upward and forcing my mouth shut again.

"Swallow," he orders.

I shake my head, fighting him with every fiber of my being. Tears well in my eyes. I wish I'd made more noise earlier. I wish the abbess had spotted us on the way in from the lake. Anything would be better than this.

"There are worse things I could do to you. Don't make me." He threatens like he can hear my thoughts. He takes another swig from the poisoned flask. The look in his eyes makes my heart rate double. He's serious. Deathly so, and his face inches closer to mine until his lips are a hairsbreadth away.

His hand whips away from my jaw at the same time his mouth descends on mine, covering it in what would be a soul-searing kiss if he wasn't trying to kill me. The hand that was holding my jaw pinches my nose, stealing my airways from me and sending me into a panic that has me attempting the one thing I shouldn't.

But it's all I can think.

Breathe.

I need air. Desperately. My body acts of its own volition even as I try to stop myself.

My mouth opens to his, and the poison pours in a second time. He holds me down as I struggle and whimper, pinning me in place until I can feel the burn in my lungs for the second time this evening.

What the man takes, he can give back. The fading edge of black seeps in at the edges of my vision, and I finally cede ground. If I don't give in, I'll die. If I drink, there's a chance I live to fight another day. Even if it's burned and battered. I've survived it before. I can do it again.

I swallow.

As soon as he sees the bob of my throat, his fingers release my nose. I take a deep breath, pulling as much air in as fast as humanly possible. The oxygen races through my lungs, and my vision returns, along with my thoughts. Finally able to focus on something other than the vice grip of death.

Something like the fact that his lips are still on mine. We're still locked in a lover's embrace. It's only been seconds, but it feels like an eternity. He starts to pull away, slowly, letting his lips glide over mine, his tongue teasing over them so gently.

I nip him in return, my teeth sinking into his full lower lip, and it draws blood. He pulls back, using his free hand to swipe at his chin, staring at the evidence of my violence on the pads of his fingers. Then he presses them to my lips, spreading the crimson stain over my mouth and staring at the mess he's made.

"You'll regret that," he warns. Somehow, I don't think I will. I have a feeling I'll wish I did more damage.

"I *hate* you."

"I know. Trust me, I know." There's a grin on his face, the kind you use to cover your emotions, filled with a distant kind of misery that's all too familiar. I almost feel a strange sort of sympathy to see it reflected back at me.

But I can't think about that now. Now it's about us surviving because worse than what he could do is what the drug can do. We both had more than our fair share tonight, and we could overdose with no one to find us until morning.

"It settles if you don't shake it up. You've probably had..." I try to warn him. "Too much..."

"Too much what? What is it? What did you give me?" He presses for answers.

"It's..." But my words are fading as fast as my memory, and I'm tired. So incredibly *tired*.

EIGHT

L^{evi}

I FEEL the slither of guilt up my spine as I slip the needle out of her arm, smoothing the Band-Aid over the pinprick-size wound. I need her out while I finish off what we started. She's given me no other choice.

I watch her breathing for a few moments, the rise and fall of her chest, before I finish gathering the bag of things I collected from around her room. A phone under the mattress, an old journal tucked in her desk, a smattering of paperwork, and personal items like her passport. I don't bother with her clothes or shoes.

I make her bed, and I straighten the room. I put out the coals in the metal container she lit to torture me with, disinfect the implement she used to burn me, and put everything back the way I remember it being on the desk. I tried to make mental notes of it while she worked, but the fog of whatever drug she used on me still hangs heavy. I need them to think she's around here somewhere for as long as possible. The more time we have, the more likely it is that we get away.

I check her again, holding my hand in front of her lips when I don't immediately see her chest move. She's still breathing. It's shallow and slow. The injection I gave her will do that. I just hope it doesn't interact with whatever else she's had. The search of her room didn't turn up any more of it.

I run my knuckles down her cheek, and her lashes flutter in response, like she might open them. I doubt I'll ever see the blues of her eyes light up when she smiles at me or hear her melodic laugh again. It's a shame. I'd grown fond of both. But I don't have time to ponder the things that might have been, only time to act on the now. And right now, I have an ever-narrowing window of time to get her to the airport.

IT'S a dreary night on the private tarmac just outside of Munich. The lights scatter across the small pools of water, and the rain has slowed to a mist as I pull up in front of the industrial garage and put the car in park. I hop out, grateful to see that Rowan's already here and waiting as he leans against the doorframe. The faster we get out of here, the better.

"Well fuck," Rowan mutters as he approaches the car.

"Fuck indeed," I grouch back as I round the front to open her door. She's still out cold, but she's started to move more, and the faster we get her on the plane, the better. This whole plan has gone to hell.

"You need help?" Rowan's brow furrows as he looks down at the redheaded bundle in the back of the car.

"I've got her." I lean down and pull her out, careful to

guard her head as I navigate the car door. I don't want anyone else holding her right now, not when she's this vulnerable. I've frightened her enough tonight. I don't need her waking up in a stranger's arms. Though she might prefer it once she remembers what I've done.

"She out cold?" He surveys her as she hangs limply in my arms, her head lulling against my chest with each step.

"Yeah."

"What did you use on her?" The furrow in his forehead deepens.

"Midazolam. But she has something else in her system too."

"What?" He's very interested in all the details. Rowan likes to be in full control of a situation like this. I've put him on edge with my sudden need for a late-night extraction when he was already on a job for Charlotte.

"No idea. Whatever she used on me. Left me a little groggy but functional. She put it in a drink she gave me," I explain as he motions for us to walk toward the front of the building. I can see the wings of his, or rather Hudson's, private jet sticking out past the walls in the distance and feel a keen sense of relief. I was sure I was going to see the inside of a German police station tonight.

"She used it on you?" His interest is piqued, and I hear the thread of amusement.

"She drugged me so she could question me. It didn't go well for her, considering she gave me exactly what I needed to get her out of there," I explain in a clipped tone. I'm embarrassed for myself, but there's a part of me that's proud of her. The way she figured me out and tried to take control back instead of just running scared to the abbess or her father was impressive.

"Well, at least she was good for something." His biting humor cuts through the wee hour.

"She's surprisingly resourceful." My eyes linger on her face for too long before I meet Rowan's again, and I see a flash of disapproval.

"Father's daughter, I imagine." Rowan's eyes flick over her in a quick assessment and dismissal, and then he nods for me to climb the stairs first.

I pull her closer to me, making sure she doesn't get inadvertently bumped or bruised on the way up the narrow staircase. I glance up as a plane thunders overhead when it takes its ascent. It'll be us soon. A few more steps and we're inside—safely ensconced from the weather and from the questioning of the German police. The relief lets the adrenaline surging through my body slow to a dull roar. The flight attendant doesn't say a word about the fact that I'm carrying an unconscious woman who's bound in the same macramé-style cords she used on me. I deposit her in one of the plush private seats and buckle her in.

"How quickly can we take off?" I look between Rowan and the flight attendant, hoping for a positive answer. I forget her name, even though we've been introduced before. She was pleasant enough but all business, just like Charlotte. I imagine she was handpicked for that purpose.

"Now?" Rowan gives her a questioning look, and she nods.

"I'll let the pilot know you're ready. If you'll be seated, please." She motions to both of us.

"Thank you." I look at Rowan as we buckle in. "I know you had other plans for the evening."

"Nothing as important as this."

"I hope Charlotte's not furious."

Speaking of the devil, I'd rather not be on her bad side. Upsetting any of her business plans or one of her men is the fastest way to get there. He smirks and glances out the window as the pilot turns our overhead lights low.

"She can be fun when she's angry." It's the only answer I

get. At least one of us is excited about it. I'd have her and my brother to deal with when I get back.

"Well, maybe she can have a talk with our new friend. Because she takes the fun a little too far when she's pissed," I grumble as the seatbelt brushes over the burn.

"She get you?" He looks at me with concern.

"Burned me." I move the seatbelt aside and lift my shirt to expose the fresh wound. "With one of those things they sprinkle holy water with."

Rowan inspects it, tilting his head and pressing his lips together like he's impressed by her handiwork. If he told me he's done the same once, I wouldn't be surprised.

"Nice pattern at least. Might scar well."

I level him with a deadpan look, and he lets out a low chuckle.

"Just trying to find a silver lining." His brow lifts. "She get your lip too?" He motions to his own, and I mimic it, brushing the pads of my fingers over the spot where she sunk her teeth in. It's still tender.

"She bit me." Probably because I was kissing her right after I poisoned her, but I can leave that tidbit of information out of our discussion. I still don't know why the fuck I did it.

"Burning and biting? Quite the vicious little thing, isn't she?" Rowan's wildly amused now.

"Something like that." My mind's drifting to the way she looked at me when she told me she hated me. I knew it was coming, and it still cut deeper than expected.

"There's a first aid kit in the back. Once we're at altitude, you can use it to get cleaned up. There's a shower too if you need it." He looks me over thoughtfully, scrutinizing my appearance and my mood. I have to be careful around him. He reads everything, every movement, every inflection.

"As long as I can get these wounds treated, it'll be fine," I mumble, tucking my shirt gently back into place. Hopefully, I can avoid an infection.

"She useful, you think?" He looks at the redhead sitting behind me.

"She definitely has information. I grabbed her burner phone on the way out." I pull it out from my pocket and hold it up for his review.

"Not the regular one?" He frowns.

"No. It's at the bottom of the lake. Right along with mine. That's why I contacted you on the other line I had." I sigh and shove it back into my pocket. I can't win tonight, and I'm too tired to defend myself.

"I see. Any particular reason for that?" Rowan's face is a mix of emotions he's trying to suppress.

"She fell in. I jumped after her."

"Do I want to ask?" Rowan shifts in his seat and loses his battle with the growing smirk. At least he's momentarily distracted from his suspicion.

"It's a long fucking story. The whole night is—which is why we're here." I make it clear I don't feel like getting into the details. I'm too tired and groggy to weave the white lies right now, and even though he's an excellent partner in things like this, I don't want him having my full hand.

"Hudson and Grant are unlikely to be happy that we aborted your undercover gig." He states the obvious, frustrated by my unwillingness to cooperate with his interrogation.

"They'll be happy enough when they see her." Grant will understand, and Hudson's reasonable enough. If I lay out the facts for them, they'll see I didn't have a choice. But Rowan's right that it complicates everything.

"Maybe. But now they'll be up against it. They'll have to decide whether to kill her or keep her." Rowan looks over her like an accountant assessing a balance sheet. She's of no more value than what she gives us to him. It's likely to be the same for Grant and Hudson, and it's a sobering thought.

"We're keeping her," I snap without thinking, and Rowan's brow climbs as his eyes rake downward over me in evaluation.

"Don't tell me you've developed a soft spot for her. They'll like that even less."

"Far from it. But she's my problem, and I'll decide how it gets resolved." It's a lie. I know it for certain as soon as I deny her.

"Well..." He shrugs one shoulder, and we both glance out the window as the plane accelerates. "I'll let you fight that one out for yourself."

NINE

Z ephyrine

I BLINK, opening one eye and trying to take in the vast amount of light that's assaulting my eyeballs. I squeeze my eyes shut to block it out and groan as I try to shift in my seat. I'm held in place by something strapped over my hips. It's not letting me move like I want. I swat at it. Then I try to pull, using my hands to reach forward to free me, but they come to an abrupt stop. My hands are bound as well. My wrists rub against each other. Reality seeps in through my groggy state. Flashes of what came before start glimmering through my memories, and it sends a wave of panic through me.

I blink my eyes open, still pained from the light and trying to avoid it. But I realize it isn't actually all that bright in here. It just feels that way because I've been asleep for an eternity. Asleep or unconscious. The more the memories come flooding back, the more I come to the conclusion it wasn't voluntary. I need to get my head straight, try to figure out where I am. That's the first order of business. Pain or no pain.

The room I'm in is dimmed. A small overhead light above me is the only thing giving me any real illumination, and it feels like a full midday sun because of how much my head hurts. I've either been hit with something over the head or I'm hungover.

I've been unconscious for an undetermined amount of time. A frightening thought, since it means I have no idea what's happened to me in this state. Unconscious and tied up, I realize, as I look down at the way my hands are bound together. My heart takes off in a sprint as adrenaline starts to bleed into my consciousness.

I'm being kidnapped.

I'm desperately trying to replay my last memories. The lake. A shower. Father Levi. Father Levi, who isn't Father Levi after all. Instead, he's bad. I don't remember how or why he's bad, but he is. Sort of anyway. We certainly left things in a complicated state. I remember that much at least.

I'm cold—freezing cold if the goose bumps are any indication—and the vent next to the light that feels like the brightness of ten suns is also putting out frigidly ice-cold Antarctic winds that are only fueling my discomfort and panic. It makes it hard to concentrate. This is what they do to kidnapping and torture victims, right? They do their best to disorient them. I shift again, trying to get myself out of the direct path but only managing to remind myself that I'm belted down.

Right. I keep forgetting the smallest details. It must be part of the hangover. I finally focus enough to look down at my state and realize I'm wearing a seatbelt. My hands are tied with macramé rope—the same rope from the robes I'd been ironing earlier in the day. The ones I used to tie up Father Levi back at the convent.

Back at the convent.

Those words sink in hard because I am decidedly not at the convent now. And that would be the death of me.

I'm seat belted into a vehicle. One that's taking me away from the convent. I blink one more time, and my vision finally clears at the same time my brain decides to fire on all cylinders. It's as if a veil has been lifted.

I'm in an airplane. A small one. It's a private jet of some sort, and there are only a couple of other people I can see seated nearby. One is Father Levi, or rather Fraud-ther Levi, and the other is a man I don't recognize. They're both in street clothes though. Levi has dropped the pretense of being a priest and is instead embracing his real calling. Kidnapper.

My heart is in full breakaway dash now, like I'm racing toward a finish line. My life had only one crucial, formidable, unbreakable rule—never under any circumstances leave the abbey grounds.

"No!" I shout. "Tell the pilot to go back. We have to go back!"

I work to undo my seatbelt despite my bound hands. Tears start to collect in the corners of my eyes. For years, I've done exactly as I was told, but he'll never forgive me for this. It won't matter that it wasn't my choice. It'll only matter that I broke the rule. And for that, we'll all suffer as he scorches the earth in his wake.

Levi is asleep, head canted back and eyes closed, but when he hears my shouting, I see him shift. Finally. The flight attendant peers her head around the corner from where she's preparing something, and I try to motion to her. She quickly ducks it back, though, recognizing that I'm not the one in charge, and she owes me nothing. It's been a long time since I've flown, but I can already say I like the flight attendants in commercial better.

"Levi! Please!" I hope that's his real name, even if he isn't a priest. I need him to understand the seriousness of what he's doing, what it will mean for him. For his friend. For all of us.

I see his head bob for a moment, and then he sits up, rubbing a hand over his face to try to clear the fog of sleep.

Yes. Please. Wake the fuck up so you can put us back where we belong.

I bite the inside of my cheek. The carefully managed tone and mask I worked so hard to cultivate while I was in the convent is already slipping. It's replaced by dread as I try to get his attention. Every minute feels like an eternity. I'll swear a million times more and a thousand times louder if it means I get his attention. I can't afford carefully managed now.

"Levi!" I shout again, and this time he's up and aware that I'm awake. A frown mars his otherwise perfect face, and he pushes his glasses up as his brow descends in irritation.

I can see the look of agitation on his face when I finally get my seatbelt to snap free, and I jump up from my seat.

"Sit down," he growls when he's close enough.

"Listen to me. We have to go back. I have to get back to the convent." I sound as anxious as I feel, but I lower my voice to sound more rational.

"Yeah, we're not doing that." He's calm. Too calm.

"We have to do that. You don't understand. This will end badly," I insist.

"Are you threatening me?"

"I'm warning you," I snipe back.

I know I pissed him off thoroughly at the convent, but I'm still hoping some part of the Levi I thought I knew is real. I just need him to be sensible. Listen to me. Is that too much to ask?

"I think you'd better think twice about who's warning who in this situation." He grabs me by the rope around my wrist as a reminder of where I stand.

"I'm trying to help you by warning you. We've got to get back to the convent."

He shakes his head, unimpressed with my pleas. "We're thirty thousand feet in the air. You can sit down and finish your nap."

"You're not listening to me! We have to get back!" I lose my patience and start to rush past him, hoping the flight attendant will see more reason than he does right now. My attempt is futile. He extends one massive hand, catching me around the waist and wrapping me up. He pulls me tight to his chest. His lips pressed against my temple when he speaks.

"You need to sit down." He enunciates each word.

"No. You need to listen." I try to pull away from him but only manage to get enough separation to meet his eyes. "If he finds out I left, we're both dead."

"Who finds out?" I hear the confusion in his tone.

"My husband."

"Your *what?*" His brow furrows deeper, and his eyes narrow behind his glasses.

"My husband will kill us. You have to tell the pilot to turn the plane around."

"How are you married if you're a nun?"

"I'm in training. I haven't taken my final vows yet. You'd know that if you were a real priest."

"So you've been pretending to be a nun to hide from your husband?"

"He knows where I am. Or knew where I was, and now I guarantee he knows I'm missing. He always knows." I talk faster because I know every moment we're on this plane we're putting more miles between us and the convent.

"I don't give a fuck what he knows. He can't touch us on this plane." He scowls at the way I'm still struggling against him. I just want someone who will listen to the words I'm saying and take them seriously.

"But he will when we land."

"He can try."

He's snide. Self-assured. Not the least bit concerned. Just like he was when I was ready to burn him. I'm starting to think the man doesn't have a self-preserving bone in his body.

"Your arrogance—" I start and then realize it's a failing venture. "Ma'am? You. Hello! You, in the galley! Can you tell the pilot to—"

"Is there an issue?" The other man on the plane stands up and turns his attention to us, blocking my view of the flight attendant.

He's heavily tattooed, and his hair is carefully styled. The suit he's wearing is perfectly tailored, barely a wrinkle despite hours on this plane. He looks expensive. Lethal. Sinister steel-gray eyes stare at me from across the plane, and I can tell he's irritated with my very existence. I'm a gnat to him—one he'll gladly swat away if needed. A chill runs down my spine, and I look back at Levi.

"Ignore her." Levi dismisses the man, but he slaps a hand over my mouth and drags me toward the back of the plane. We're through a door, and I'm tossed onto a bed before I know what's happening.

"What are you doing?" I look around at what appears to be a private bedroom, styled and decorated in the same detail-oriented manner as the man who wants me dead.

"Giving us the opportunity to talk this out in private. You won't have a chance to worry about your husband killing you if you continue pissing off everyone else in your wake." A muscle in Levi's jaw ticks in frustration. It seems like he's almost as worried about his companion's temper as I am.

"Do you work with him?"

"He's a colleague. Yes." He's impatient with my questioning.

"He looks like a murderer."

"Good guess."

I glare at him. "I can't believe I ever thought you were a priest."

"And you had me believing you were a nun. Now we're even."

"I'm working toward it. I live like I am one. You clearly don't." My eyes drift over him, trying to reconcile the two versions in my mind. The affection that had been slowly growing for him is tainted by this series of discoveries.

"That's what you're upset about right now?" He pulls his glasses off and cleans a smudge on the corner of his shirt before he returns them to his skeptical face.

"It's on the list."

"Let's focus on the top priorities. You have a husband who will allegedly kill you for leaving the convent?"

"He'll kill you. Me? I don't know, but he'll certainly make me wish I were dead." I feel sick if I ruminate on the thought too long.

"Why?"

"Because our agreement was that I live out my life as a nun on the island, and in exchange, he'd leave me alone."

His eyes flick over me in curiosity. Like he's seeing me in a new light.

"You don't like him then?" It's rhetorical.

"What gave it away?" I meet his sarcasm. If we're going masks off, we might as well stop pretending altogether.

"And what about your father? Couldn't he get you out of it?" he asks. I guess that answers one question. Part of me had worried he was working for one of them. But one mystery solved only creates a dozen more in its wake.

"Is that who you're after?" I frown.

"He's certainly high on the list."

"If you think I can help you get to him, I can assure you, you're absolutely mistaken."

"Oh, I think he'd be interested to know I've got his daughter."

"Interested, maybe, but not invested. You think a father who cares about his daughter marries her off to a monster?"

He flinches. It's there and gone in a flash, but I don't miss it, and I log that information for later.

"I haven't thought about it at all. Ten minutes ago, I thought you were a chaste little nun. So embarrassed she couldn't stop having dirty dreams that she confessed it to a stranger."

"The confessional is supposed to be a sacramental sanctuary." I'm offended by how callously he brings it up.

"And if I had been a real priest, it might have been." He lobs my words back at me.

"So what then? You'll use it against me? Assuming your friend out there isn't going to kill me? Do you want my father's money? A say in his politics? He won't budge. Not for me." I wish he understood how little I was worth to that man. Maybe then he'd let me go.

"What about being on a private plane makes you think we need money?"

"The fuel bill?" I snark right back at him.

"You have a smart mouth."

"So we've established. Are we done talking in circles yet? I'd really like to get back to the convent. There will still be damage to manage, but it might be doable. We land somewhere else..." I shake my head. "Hopeless."

"We're not changing plans."

"Where are you taking me anyway?"

"Colorado."

I feel a wave of nausea. He's leading us right to the slaughter. We'll be sitting ducks. Ripe for the taking the second we're wheels down in my father's state and so close to my husband's home.

"Are you mad? Have you done any of your research?"

"Research is all I've been doing for weeks." There's a sly smile teasing at the corner of his mouth.

I realize now that every conversation I thought I had with him was a practiced trap. One he was luring me into. Everything I thought I'd felt or seen in him was manufactured. Carefully crafted in order to get my attention and prey on my weaknesses. I hate him for it.

"Not enough. Clearly." His pride over his intelligence is a weakness I'm willing to press on.

"You're here, aren't you?"

"Your friend doesn't seem happy about it. I imagine this wasn't the original plan."

"Not exactly. I didn't expect you to be lying about being a nun."

"I didn't expect you to lie to me about *everything*." There's a hint of anger in my tone, and I'm trying to control it. It won't help me, not if he's anything like my husband. He'll just punish me more for making him feel guilty.

"Why did you have drugs in your room anyway?" He's uninterested in my accusation.

"A backup plan in case things ever went badly." I meant it for my husband if he ever returned to take me, but this man made me waste it. Now I have to find more.

"You should have practiced tying your knots a little tighter as part of that plan."

"I'll be sure to make notes for the next time. Trust me."

There's a flash of amusement over his face before the well-practiced mask returns.

"I'll make sure we have extra security. Do you want to tell me your husband's name, or should I just keep going through this phone?" He holds up the secondary phone I kept hidden under my mattress.

I rarely use it. Only for my required check-ins. It's the only connection to my husband I still have left besides the inconvenient piece of paper that keeps me bound to him. I'd burn it if I could. The man tortured me with the offer of an annulment whenever he needed my compliance. But it's been eerily quiet lately, like maybe he finally started to let me go.

My disappearance would certainly be the end of that silence though. Any disobedience of his rules was an attack on his ego. He'll be back with a vengeance unless I figure out a way to stop it. I jump up and grab for my phone, but he yanks it back out of my reach.

I'm tall, five eleven to be exact, but this man still has close to a half dozen inches on me. He can dangle it high enough to keep it just out of my grasp.

"If I can text him, maybe I can explain." I try to reason with him.

"Explain what?" He looks at me like the thought is ridiculous.

"That there was a misunderstanding. I don't know. I haven't thought that far ahead."

"Why do you have two phones? Why not just talk to him on the other one?"

"This was my old life. That one is my new one." I feel my heart sink when I realize the phone has too, straight to the bottom of the lake. I'll never get those pictures back or the memories I've saved in it.

"There's no misunderstanding to explain. If he wants you,

he can come and get you. Or die trying." His voice is flat, but I don't miss the glimmer in his eyes.

"You're cocky," I observe.

"I'm not worried about a man who makes his wife run off to a convent. He sounds like a cunt."

"A cunt who has the full force of my father's money and political power behind him. He's ruthless. Untouchable. You don't get it," I counter because I really don't think he understands the seriousness of the situation.

"It almost sounds like you've got a schoolgirl crush on him. I thought you swore off those."

I try ignoring his jab, but my cheeks pink anyway. "I'm just trying to get you to understand the reality."

"Let me worry about that. You just focus on behaving yourself on this flight and not disrupting the crew."

"Or what? You'll have your friend take care of me?"

"I don't need anyone's help to take care of you." The threat sends a chill down my spine, reminding me that, however much I might have thought I knew this man—as a selfless priest who wandered the archives and gardens with me, only too happy to discuss literature and art and music—I had no idea who the wolf really was behind the sheep's clothing. His brow raises at my silence, and he asks again, "His name?"

"Corey Craig," I say his name quietly. Judging by the way Levi's face falls, he knows exactly who my husband is.

TEN

L^{evi}

"SHE'S NOT JUST Abbott Schaefer's daughter. She's Corey Craig's wife," I explain to my brother as I drop into the chair across from him in his office.

"Wife? You told me she was a fucking nun!" Grant's brow arches skyward as he sits up straighter, his palms flat on the desk.

"She hated him that much, I guess. She said they have a deal that she can live out the rest of her days at the convent. But if she left, he'd kill her and anyone who helped her leave." I speak about it as if it's a third-party business rather than a woman I know involved. I'm still reeling from the information.

"Live at the convent? Why not just divorce her?" Grant sits back in the chair across from me. He takes a sip of whisky to dull his irritation.

"Ego? Power? The connection to her father, I assume." I haven't gotten to the bottom of it yet, but I will. I just need some time to adjust to the changing roles Zephyrine and I have found ourselves in. Not to mention the fact I haven't slept in way too goddamn long.

"If he'd sell her off to a man like that..." Grant's face darkens.

Corey Craig is the used car salesman of the underground world, wrapped in dangerously thin skin. He fancies himself old money while barely having enough of the new kind to fake it. He's poached a few clients of ours. The kind that are too impatient to do all the layers of paperwork and deal with the standard wait time to keep their money squeaky clean in the laundry.

Corey should be dead for the way he does business, but he's got an unhealthy love of bombs, a deranged attachment to brutal violence, and enough connections higher in the food chain that he manages to survive year after year like a cockroach. Imagining Zephyrine as his wife makes the sandwich I had on the plane threaten to resurface. It's revolting that her father ever considered him an option, let alone forced her into it. The convent makes perfect sense now.

"It explains her disappearance. Why she never comes home." I'm rambling because my mind is imagining the feisty little nun in the hands of a man like him. I want to break every finger he's touched her with slowly and methodically. Take each nail and—Grant's voice interrupts my daydreams.

"If Abbott and he are working together, we have a bigger problem than we imagined. Who knows how many people he's in bed with or what we're up against when we start turning rocks over."

"All the more reason we have to put an end to it sooner rather than later." I'd like to put an end to him. I don't need her to tell me what he's done. I can guess. The thought of him being alone with her is more than enough for me to sign his death warrant.

"I suppose it makes her all the more valuable." Grant mulls the thought.

"She's valuable. She knows Abbott's business. Corey's. She might know things she doesn't even realize are valuable. Rowan thought you and Hudson would want to kill her." I scoff at the idea in retrospect.

"Kill her? No. Not unless we have to. Ransom might be an option though. We might be able to get the relics back for her." Grant takes another draw off his glass.

"She doesn't seem to think ransom's an option. She warned me as much." I think back to the way she swore up and down that she had no control over her father.

"What do you think?" Grant pins me with a serious look.

"I think I don't know enough yet. I need more time with her. She trusted me at the convent, but now, well..." I shrug my shoulder and tilt my head to the side. "Now it's a little more complicated."

"Understandable." He takes the last swallow of whisky and sits up in his chair. He studies me before he asks the last thing I expect. "You fuck her yet?"

"No," I snipe at the question.

"Why not?" His brows knit together as though it's confusing to him. "She's not Dakota—no one is. But she's not hideous. It wouldn't be a hardship for you."

"It seemed unnecessary." I grit the words through my teeth. I don't like the idea of Grant assessing her like that, even though I know damn well he doesn't have eyes for anyone besides his fiancée, Dakota.

"Have you been this grumpy with her? She might like you

better if you kept your mouth busy with other things." He smirks.

"Noted," I reply tersely.

I'm trying not to imagine the picture he's painting. It might make her like me more. Worse, it seems it'd be likely to make me want her more than I already do if I hear her saying anything in praise of my real name instead of Father Levi's. Best not to tempt fate.

"The more attached she is to you, the better. And now with the husband? The more compromised, the better." He's matter-of-fact.

My brother puts business first in everything, and normally, I'd be the first to agree. But in this case, it feels callous and cruel to use her. She's been a pawn for two men already.

"Do you hear yourself? How would you feel if someone talked about Dakota like that?" I push back.

He levels me with a dark look before he speaks again. He doesn't have to answer that question. He'd murder any person who even so much as thought something vaguely of the sort. His fiancée is the center of his universe and has been for longer than he'd like to admit.

"This was Dakota and Charlotte's idea, remember?" he presses.

"Yeah, well..." I shift in my seat.

"Well, what?"

"I'm not cut out for the undercover agent shit. You want me to hack a system for information or kill someone, I'm your guy. I'm a blunt instrument. I'm not a fucking Romeo." The unease of the idea creeps up my throat.

"That out of touch in the romance department?" Grant laughs, and it takes some of the tension out of my shoulders. "Why don't you ask Dakota or Charlotte for help then? You're the only one Zephyrine knows well enough that she might spill something. You said you were making progress. It seemed like you knew her well enough after all that surveillance you were doing. I assumed—" He stops short, and his eyes shift. "You're not in love with her or something, are you?"

"Don't be ridiculous. Just because you've lost your edge doesn't mean I have." I'm not in love with her. She's a con artist and a liar, but the more I learn about her past, the more I see reason in the choices she's made. The more she makes sense to me. The more I feel for everything she's gone through, and I don't want to be another painful memory for her. "Of course I want answers from her. We all do, but I don't plan to manipulate her to get them. There's no reason to. She'll cooperate if she understands it's the right thing to do. I just need time to show her."

"Rowan said you were cagey on the flight. He thought there was something going on under the surface there." Grant's watching me closely. Rowan certainly doesn't play favorites. I'll remember it on the next job.

"I was cagey on the flight because we had to abruptly shift course and drag her back to Colorado. After I pulled her out of a lake in the middle of the night. After she tried to poison me, and then I had to subdue her. Then search her room and carry her out of the convent. Drive all the way to Munich like a bat out of hell and then explain to his fucking highness Rowan that everything was fucked to shit. I was exhausted, and nothing was going to plan. I was restrained given the circumstances." I summarize the twenty-four hours that led us here, and even my head spins recalling it.

"Poison you?" He drops his interest in anything else, and concern mars his face.

I left that part out of our earlier discussion when I was on the flight. No sense in letting her know she'd gotten a very rare upper hand on me.

"She drugged me. Tied me up. Crawled on top of me. She's a wicked little thing when she's committed to it. Bit me too. It was not a fun evening, and one I'd rather fucking forget, all right?" I'm irritable all over again just thinking about it.

My brother's face transforms from worry to amusement.

"You sure? Sounds like your kind of fun." He leans forward on the table, grinning and swirling the last drop of melting ice at the bottom of his glass.

"Don't fucking start," I warn him with a sideways glance for all the good it does.

"Were you not giving her what she wanted, and she decided to try to take it?" He clears his throat to stop a laugh.

"She realized I wasn't a priest and was worried I was one of her husband's or father's men. She was trying to torture it out of me."

"How did she do that?" He frowns.

I let out a frustrated grumble and then raise my shirt to expose the bandage underneath.

"Burned me with one of those things they sprinkle holy water with. Heated it up in the incense burner. It'd be clever if I wasn't on the receiving end of it."

A laugh tumbles out of my brother's chest as he tries to suppress it, pressing his fist to his lips. He clears his throat again, but the look on his face betrays his amusement with all of it.

"Now she really sounds like your type," he remarks, studying the bandage for a moment before he looks up at me, his eyes glittering with the accusation.

"Fuck me. I regret telling you any of this. I don't have a type."

"Well, if you did, it seems married runaway nuns with a penchant for torture would be up there on the list." He gives me a pointed look. "You sure you can manage her?"

"I'll manage her just fine. My way. I just need some time. A little sleep."

"You've got days. Maybe hours. If what she says is true…" His brows raise, and he tilts his head. "Corey and the governor will be a handful."

"We'll need more men on the ranch. At the casino. Did you contract any of the men I suggested while I was gone?" I'd rather discuss the practicalities of security. That's what I'm good at, where I shine. I could keep the ranch and casino safe if we focused on maintaining awareness and security levels.

"The MC is on board. I'm in talks with the merc group out of Colorado Springs you recommended before you left."

"Good. We'll need all hands on deck. What about the extra digital security?"

"I hired the security team you asked for. They've installed cameras, and they're working on getting your little drone army together. This new shit makes me nervous. Especially knowing what you've been able to do in the past with it," he remarks, recalling the time I hacked into a rival's system.

"Well, let me handle it. I'll meet with them and get things online as quickly as possible." I'm antsy to do something more than babysit. Distance from Zephyrine would probably help with all of my newfound proclivities. If Grant knew the depth of some of them, he'd probably insist I take a break. Or fuck her to get her out of my system.

"The nun first. The rest is secondary to her when you're the only one who has a chance in hell. Put your priest uniform back on if you have to, and confess her. Whatever it takes." Grant's tone brooks no disagreement.

"Sure thing," I grumble. I want to argue, but the strategy is pragmatic.

"Where are you keeping her?" He's suddenly interested in the minutiae of my plan.

"The honeymoon cabin. I'm not breaking that news to Ramsey and Hazel. Figured you could do that for me." I smirk, thinking about him having to get his ass reamed for our takeover of our little brother's wife's guesthouse. At least one thing I don't want to do will be off my plate. At least I could celebrate small victories.

"Hazel'll hate it," Grant laments.

The honeymoon cabin is a new extension of my sister-in-law's bed and breakfast. I gave her my old hunting cabin, and she fixed it up, making it the perfect remote retreat for a newlywed couple who wanted to get away from everything. In my world, it was the perfect isolated interrogation spot. It's high on the mountain where we can keep a solid perimeter and prevent an easy escape.

Hopefully, I can get everything I need out of her before we take our next step. I need to know what we're dealing with. I doubt Hazel wants her property used as a prison, but I'm not sure what other options we have. So just like the rest of us, she'll have to come along for the ride.

"If Zephyrine's right about her husband, it'll buy us some time if he tries to come find us. The casino and the inn are too public. Her father will at least put out an APB once he finds out. One wrong turn where she bumps into a tourist who recognizes her from TV or a helpful local..." I explain.

"It's smart. What would be smarter is if you get as much out of her as quickly as you can, and we don't have to worry about these kinds of details. Something we can use to go on the offensive instead of continually walling ourselves in down here." Grant's like a caged lion, pacing back and forth, eyeing the options around him. He's usually more levelheaded than I am, but he wants blood for what happened to Dakota.

"I agree. I'll deliver on it. You know me well enough to know that." This is the part I'm good at; I can do this much.

"Good. Another whisky before you go?" Grant nods to my empty glass, but I don't have a chance to answer when my phone rings loudly, bursting the otherwise calm, stately atmosphere of my brother's broad executive suite.

I glance down, and it's one of our guys. Specifically, it's the one I left in charge of Zephyrine.

"Yes?" I ask impatiently, standing up to pace. I can't imagine this is good news.

"She's made a run for it," he admits. "Obviously, there's nowhere she can go, but she could hurt herself. We're on her trail. I knew you'd want to know as soon as possible." Jack's voice is patterned by his heavy breathing and the sounds of his boots pounding the ground as he follows her through the woods.

"Fucking hell. I'll be there as soon as I can. Keep an eye on her." I'm glad I tagged her while she was asleep. It will make this part easier at least.

"Will do."

I stuff the phone back into my pocket and glare out the window for half a moment before I turn around. This won't help my case. But I'm surprised when I see an amused grin instead of anger on my brother's face.

"Trouble with your ward?" My brother's terrible at hiding his humor.

"I've got it handled."

"Try to avoid getting tortured this time," Grant calls after me.

I shake my head and slam his door behind me like I did when we were kids.

ELEVEN

Z ephyrine

I DON'T KNOW what I was thinking. I suppose I hadn't been thinking at all. That's not true either. Run. That was my thought. Just knowing that I need to get back to the convent. I don't want to wait for whatever fate I'm going to be left to here.

Levi clearly doesn't care about me, or he wouldn't have disappeared no sooner than we arrived. He left me with two burly guards who looked at me like I was some kind of sideshow attraction and treated me like I was a child who couldn't be left alone for even one minute.

At least not until I informed them I needed to use the restroom, and I wanted privacy since I was on my period. That lie had sent them skittering away and gave me time alone in the bathroom. A bathroom that thankfully had a window just large enough for me to sneak through. By the time they realize I'm gone, I'll be deep into the woods and well out of their reach.

Or so I'd hoped. Instead, I'm stumbling along, trying to stay close to the trail and not lose the only direction I have by following it. At least I hope this leads to civilization.

The farther I walk and the darker it gets, the more I feel like I've made a mistake. I have no food, no shelter, and only the clothes on my back. I had a good, long drink of water from the faucet before I left on this adventure, but it isn't going to hold me over forever. I try to walk faster, but my shoes are already giving me blisters. They're not made for hiking trails in the mountains.

I'm hoping I can find a hiker or a camper out here with phone service to call the abbey and find a way to get out of Colorado and back home. I still have some friends up in Denver who might take me to the airport. It'll be a complicated story to explain how I got here, but I can cross that bridge when I come to it. It'll only work if this trail leads somewhere, anywhere other than deeper into the woods. With my luck, it'll probably just lead straight to his front door.

MY MORALE IS EVEN LOWER a half hour later when the sky opens up and drenches me. I dodge out of the open meadow I've stumbled past and hide under a tree, resting against the trunk, where it at least shields me from the worst of the downpour. But the rainstorm has sapped all of the warmth from me, and I'm left cold and soaked for the second time this week. It's becoming a terrible habit of mine.

I still have a little bit of hope and enough determination left that I start walking again once the downpour turns to a gentle rain. The mud makes it more difficult to walk, and I catch myself from slipping down the mountainside twice in just a few minutes. I pause to look around, hoping to see a glimpse of light somewhere in the distance. But there's nothing. Just rain and trees as far as I can see. I feel like I've been walking for miles with no change in scenery.

Just the Colorado wilderness and—I lose my train of thought when I hear a twig snap. One and then another, and a series of them until I hear the pounding of footsteps down the trail. I glance back over my shoulder, and in the fading twilight, I see the outline of a man. One who's following my muddy footprints and determined to track me down. The darkness of the forest in the storm makes it impossible to make out which of the guards is after me, but I'm not sure it matters at this point. Either one will drag me back to the cabin and back to Levi. I haven't seen him truly angry yet, but I imagine I will.

I pick up my pace, breaking into a full run, or at least as much of one as I can manage when my feet are already sore and blistered. The mud sucks the soles in and nearly makes me trip as it pulls the shoe from my heel. I slip it back in, glancing back to see the shadow lumbering behind me.

I steel my nerves as I start to jog downhill again. I just have to pay more attention. One foot in front of the other. I could make it out of here. I'm one person in this massive forest. It's getting late. If I could make it until sunset, I would have a real chance of escape.

Up ahead, the path forks. One heads down and another up. I'm racking my brain to try to decide which is the better choice. Down seems more logical, but what if I'm wrong? I can't afford to double back. I don't have the time, and I'd certainly get caught if I have to backtrack. Each step closer has my anxiety ratcheting up.

A split second later, and my choices evaporate when I catch

my toe on a rock. The contact sends me flailing. My bad ankle screams with the pain, and I land knees first, skidding across the dirt and debris on the forest floor. There's searing pain as it tears a layer of flesh from my legs and the dull ache from where my bone collides with another rock as I come to a rest ten feet further down the hill.

The tears come right along with it, slipping down my cheeks with the rain as I try to get up again, and my shoe is trapped in the mud. I try to dig it out, but even as I scrape away the mud with my fingernails and pull as hard as I can the shoe refuses to budge. I momentarily consider abandoning it. One step forward without it tells me it's a ridiculous idea. The broken sticks on the forest floor stabbing into the ball of my foot. I'll never make it out of here with one shoe.

My mind is racing with fear. I hear the footsteps drawing closer. I hesitate too long.

"Freeze," the unsympathetic voice demands. I do the opposite. Desperately bending over and digging through the mud to free my shoe and slip it back on. It works. I stand just in time to feel the cold metal of a gun pressed between my shoulder blades.

"Okay. Okay!" I yelp as I put my hands up.

"Get down." He nudges the gun until I hit my knees. "All the way!" he yells, using the barrel to force me face down in the dirt.

"I'm down!"

"Don't fucking move, or I'll pull the trigger," he orders, his voice monotone and unfeeling, nothing at all like Levi. He'd be angry, mocking, taunting me from his position of authority. This man is so apathetic about my existence that I think he might go through with it. I need someone reasonable before he does.

"Call Levi. I want to talk to Levi!" I plead.

The beep of a walkie-talkie precedes the buzz of static before he speaks.

"Got her. Little worse for wear but otherwise good," he calls across the line.

There's mumbling on the other end that I can't distinguish through his earbuds. I assume it's Levi. I hope it is.

"Roger that. I'll bring her there. She's asking for you." He laughs. There's another beep, another round of mumbled conversation, and he reaches down to grab me by the shoulder. His fingers dig into me as he tightens his grip, and he hauls me to my feet. "Time to march, nun."

WHEN WE REACH the end of the interminable walk back to the cabin, one I make on a hobbled ankle, caked in mud, and as bedraggled as one could possibly manage after something like thirty-six hours of kidnapping and traveling, I see Levi sitting in a chair. He's perched in an old wooden Adirondack, leaning back as he stares into an already roaring fire. The orange flames are a stark contrast against the dark night sky as he tosses another log in, fueling their dance toward the stars. The bonfire is surrounded by a neat circle of stacked rocks and sits just in front of the lake, where the ripples at the surface mirror the undulation of the flames. Up the hill is a quaint little cabin, reached by a gravel path that's been neatly maintained. A small porch with rocking chairs, a towering stone chimney, and windows that are neatly trimmed make it look like something out of a fairytale.

It would be one of the most gorgeous places I've ever seen, if it weren't for the fact that it's also likely to be the place I die. My latest captor, Mr. Man of Very Few Words, nudges me forward and onto my knees in front of con artist priest. Levi doesn't even spare me a glance. His eyes are glued to the way the embers break from the flame to float away on the smoke.

"You're good. Go." Levi nods to him, and there's a silent exchange before the guard disappears back to his post.

"Making s'mores?" I ask sarcastically when I see a long metal stick resting inside the fire.

He raises a brow and then grabs the end of it. "With this?"

When he pulls the metal out of the fire, I see the red-hot end of a branding iron. One that has the same bull with horns that he has on his chest. He stands slowly with it, forcing me back as far as I can go on my heels, brandishing the blistering metal until I slump over backward to avoid it. He looms over me, his cowboy boot resting on my inner thigh.

"Nah. Just thinking about where I might use this on you. You got any tattoos we could ruin? Maybe one of those cute little ones on your lower back you got when you turned eighteen? One of those sweet things you girls like. A butterfly maybe? Or do you prefer flowers? I bet you like flowers." He raises a brow, and there's a flicker of a smile on his face, but his tone is unlike any other he's ever used with me. He's furious.

He steps over my legs and hooks his boot under my rib cage, surprisingly gentle when he rolls me over onto my stomach. I'm face down in the dirt, buying a precious inch with my palms spread under my cheek as he bends over to pull up my shirt and reveal my back. Goose bumps break out over my skin with the cold air, and a bone-chilling sense of fear runs up my spine.

I hear the short exhale of air as he finds the tattoo I actually have there. One my husband forced me to get on our short-lived honeymoon. One of the best parts of the convent was that I didn't have a mirror long enough in the bathroom to see it reflected back to me. It was tattooed to look like a label with stitching all around the edges. Corey laughed when he saw the final piece on my back and slapped my ass. I cried when I read the words "Property of Corey Craig." That's all I ever was to him.

"He did this to you?"

I nod silently. I don't want to speak. I don't want to give him the satisfaction of hearing my voice waver.

"Why?"

"I refused to sign the paperwork to change my name to his." It was my one small act of defiance, the only thing I had control over at the time when I was forced to hand everything else over to him. I figured it was bad enough I was a Schaefer. I wouldn't be a Craig too.

"He thought this would change your mind?"

"He just wanted to shame me. Told me if I thought any other man would ever want me, he'd make sure they knew. Joke's on him, though, since I just wanted to be a nun," I explain, trying not to squirm under his touch as I feel his fingers run over the line of the tattoo.

"All because you wouldn't change your name?"

"The last straw, anyway. There was a lot he didn't like."

"Even bigger cunt than I thought."

I hear the clatter of the brand hitting the stone at the edge of the fire pit as he tosses it back into the flames. He wipes his hands on his jeans and mutters something under his breath. I'm still trying to make sense of it when he wraps his hands around my middle and drags me back up to my knees as he crouches down to meet me. His eyes search mine for a long moment. In the dark of the night, with the flames dancing over his glasses, I can't tell if it's pity or sympathy behind them.

"If you take me back to the convent, I can avoid worse. *You* can avoid worse." I try to warn Levi one last time, pleading with his better angels.

"I'm not taking you back to the convent. By now, he knows, and he's pissed off. But I'm not afraid of your husband, sweetheart. I want him to come find me. I have a growing list of reasons I can't wait to see his face."

The tears return, and I'm embarrassed that they do, born out of frustration as much as fear. I shake my head and close my eyes, wishing there were some way I could get through to him. It feels like the night before my wedding all over again. Me begging a man I thought cared about me to help get me out of harm's way, only to be rebuffed and promised that they had it all in hand, and I just needed to do what I was told. I imagine Levi will use me the same way my father did, as a bargaining chip to get whatever he wants.

"I know you're scared. Fuck... With men like that in your life, no wonder you ran to put yourself in confinement."

"And you think you're better? Lying, manipulating, kidnapping, threatening torture." I start listing off his sins. I can nearly match his fury by the time I reach the end.

"I'd say we're pretty even on that front." His eyes flick over me and settle in a frank assessment, like I'm not seeing the facts for what they are.

"Agree to disagree." I have my faults. I might have approached this the wrong way with him. But this is different. "I didn't deceive you for weeks on end, pretending to be a friend who was kind and caring. When in reality you just wanted to use me to get to my father."

"I'll give you that. You don't have many reasons to trust me. So far, I haven't shown you anything you haven't seen before. But you give me time, I'll give you reasons. And the good news is, we don't have to lie to each other anymore. I can be honest with you, and you can be honest with me."

"What does honesty get me? I'm being honest about how badly I want to go back to the convent, and you won't listen."

"You work with me, and I'll take you back to the convent."

"Work with you how?"

"For now, you don't have to do anything."

"Then why keep me here in captivity?"

"Bait." He admits it plainly, and I'll give him credit for the honesty he promised, as vulgar as the reality is. "The first thing I want is to meet your husband."

I let out a frustrated sigh. "You're playing a dangerous game, and you're arrogant if you think you'll win."

"Lucky for us, it's one I'm good at." He gives me a soft smile, a genuine one that reaches his eyes. It's the most vulnerable I've seen him since we were on the plane. "Now let's get you up and back to the house. You're a fuckin' mess."

"Thanks," I gripe at his astute assessment, glaring at him as he holds out his hand for me to take.

"You want honesty, you're getting it," he explains as he hauls me up to my feet in one swift motion.

"Ow," I whimper as I feel a sharp pain in my injured foot, hobbling, trying not to bear weight on the ankle. The awkward way I've been holding it to stay in the kneeling position has only further agitated it. His brow furrows with concern as his eyes travel down my leg and find the swelling that's started to form around the joint.

"Fucking hell. Did you trip again?" He sounds irritated with me.

"It was an accident."

"Of course it was." Without asking, he scoops me up in his arms again. "Starting to think you're doing all this on purpose to get a free ride," he grumbles at me, but the soft, sympathetic smile I remember flashes over his face again, and my heart twinges in its wake.

I wrap my arms around his neck to steady myself as he climbs up the small hill to the cabin. I stare at the horseshoe tattoo on his neck that had set this whole series of events in motion, but I don't argue with him.

Just this small act of mercy is more than I'd ever gotten from my own father. As I tuck my head against his shoulder, the painful memory of the sprained ankle I had as a child rolls like an old picture show.

It was a gorgeous summer day; the sky was brilliant, and the butterflies were dancing around the wildflowers that were growing in the meadow where my father kept his horses. I was attempting my first ride on a horse after my brothers had teased me relentlessly about my "training wheels" pony. But she was skittish even as the barn hand helped me into the saddle. It was like she felt my nervous energy and fed off of it.

I'd persisted, though, determined to win my brothers' approval and have my father see me as their equal. I'd tried to hurry out of the corral and catch up with them on the trail. Only to be thrown like a sack of potatoes a few moments later when a prairie dog darted out in front of us, startling the horse and sending me to the ground. I'd landed hard on my side, but only after my foot briefly caught in the stirrup and wrenched my ankle. The tears had come fast and heavy then as I gripped my burning joint.

I yelled for my father, and he circled back with his horse, frustration and disappointment written across his face. He didn't care that I tried. He didn't care that I was hurt. He was just annoyed I was slowing him down.

"Get up," he ordered.

"I can't." I sobbed. "I can't. It hurts so much!"

"Don't act like such a crybaby. Dust yourself off, and let's go."

"I tried, and I can't."

"You can."

"It hurts, Daddy. The horse threw me off. I think it's broken," I cried. I thought he just couldn't understand I was

really hurt. That he thought I was aiming for his attention when I really needed him.

"You've got to learn to push through pain. You can't fall down every single time it gets hard. Get yourself up and back to the house." He didn't wait for my response this time; he clicked his tongue and urged his horse on, trotting a few steps before cantering off to meet my brothers.

"Daddy, please!" I screamed after him, but he didn't heed my cries. I let out a wretched little croak of a sound and curled up in the dirt, begging for him while he rode off into the distance. It was nearly an hour later when I hobbled myself back to a point on the trail where one of the barn hands could see me and hurried over to find out what had happened. But even then, they'd been more worried about the horse that had run off than my ankle. As a child, it had broken my already wounded heart, but as an adult, I realized it was because they were terrified of losing their jobs, thinking of their own children going hungry with no money to put food on the table.

The barn manager, a surly bearded man who had barely ever spoken to me, finally scooped me up and carried me back to the house. There was no coddling or telling me I was brave. He eyed my tears like they were an inconvenience, and he was gruff as he ordered me to sit on the chair and put my leg up. But he'd gotten me a bag of ice and a juice box before he told me to sit tight while he got someone who knew what to do with kids. And in that moment, it felt like he was my hero. The small mercy of a rescue and a bit of care for my injury made him seem like he had super-powers my father didn't possess, and from that day on, I painted a picture for him every time we visited the mountain home.

I grin at the memory of him folding them up and tucking them into his back pocket. He told me he'd put them on his fridge, and for all I know, he was lying. But he didn't throw them out, and once he even smiled at the portrait I'd done of him and his favorite horse. He was probably the closest I'd ever come to having a friend at that house.

Levi reminds me of him. He makes me want to earn the soft smiles he doles out in moments like this. They're rare little sketches of hope I want in my back pocket.

If I'm honest, I don't hate him. Not really. This would all be easier if I did.

TWELVE

L^{evi}

"THIS IS ALL the ice we have right now. Until the ice maker gives us some more," I explain as I place the small bundle against her ankle. She smiles as she takes it from me, seemingly distracted by her own thoughts.

"Thanks." Her eyes dodge mine, and her smile fades as soon as she realizes I've seen it.

Her ankle's swollen up quite a bit more since I got her situated with a blanket underneath her to keep the mud off of Hazel's couch. I probably need to call in a nurse to take a look at it if it's not down by the morning. I'm hoping it's just a light sprain she got the night of the lake incident, which has been aggravated by walking on it too much.

"But I'm not sure this is necessary," she complains, holding up the wrist I chained her to the side table with.

"Can't trust you not to run, even with the ankle."

"I'm not going anywhere." She looks up at me from under thick lashes.

"Good. If you do enough of that, then maybe we can work our way back to being able to trust each other." I pat her leg gently and stand.

I need to prep dinner and get it in the oven if we're going to eat. She can ice her ankle while I work, and then we both need a shower. We've been to hell and back with all the travel and her adventure through the woods. If there were a delivery service up here, I'd be tempted to use it, but I'm not about to ask one of the guys to run for food after the chase she put them on.

"Do you think that's possible? The trust, I mean." Her tone softens from irritated defiance to something more reflective.

"I don't know. We got along well enough when we were a nun and priest, didn't we?" I ask as I start to pull out groceries from the fridge that I had delivered earlier today.

I'm making one of her favorites. A pot pie recipe that I found in her phone. There's a photo of a notecard recipe that she got from her mom, and I'm hoping the gesture of goodwill will help us bury some of the animosity.

"Didn't that get old? Pretending to be someone you're not?" She asks as I was my hands.

"I hated it, honestly. But I didn't have much of a choice."

"You could have come to me and said who you were, what you wanted."

"And you would have believed me? It wouldn't have alerted whoever your husband has watching the island?" I glance at her as I start to chop vegetables.

"I don't know, but I think it would have felt better than this does. I liked you, you know. I thought you were so sweet. Realizing you were lying to me felt like a gut punch. I didn't know what else to do but try to get to the bottom of it." She tries to explain.

"Guilt over drugging and burning me then? I agree, it wasn't very sisterly of you to do that." I try to make a joke to ease her worries.

"Very funny. I only did what I had to do."

"Is that what we're calling it?" I smirk.

"Isn't that what you'd call kidnapping me?" she volleys back.

"Fair enough, I suppose," I answer as I start to toss them into the heated cast-iron skillet. I need to make the filling, but Kit, the inn's chef, was gracious enough to give me a premade pie crust to make my life easier. Right now, I'll take any cheat code I can get to make it through this because I'm exhausted. "I was honestly kind of proud of you for taking the initiative."

"You didn't look proud. You looked pissed."

"It was a pretty even mix."

Her lips start to move like she's about to say something else, but she stops abruptly and stares down at her ankle instead. Whatever she's thinking, she's not ready to discuss it yet. I imagine she has a lot on her mind, between being held hostage and worrying that her rescue team will be worse than her captor.

I wasn't lying when I said I'm ready and willing to deal with her husband. When he shows up, I'll be more than prepared to rip his fucking head clean off his body for what he's done to her. I don't need any other excuses. Whatever her faults, she didn't deserve that fate. But I'm sure she doesn't trust me to hold true to that promise. I wouldn't if I were in her position.

I figured at some point she'd test her limits, but I didn't expect it quite so soon. So she isn't getting the full welcome dinner I had planned. The one I was going to try to use to attempt to smooth things over per Charlotte's hastily typed-out text suggestions. I want to win her over, but I want to do it honestly. I feel like I owe her that much.

"You ready for dinner?" I ask, feeling like I need to make small talk as I work.

"Starving. What's for dinner?"

I glance up and take in the sight of her. She definitely needs the shower. Mud is caked on her cheek and legs, a smear of it down her neck and over her arm. She still looks beautiful, even like this, with her bright-blue eyes staring at me and the disheveled halo of red hair that's come loose from her braid and curled in the humidity from the afternoon rain shower. I realize then she's looking at me expectantly because she asked a question. I turn my focus back to the veggies I'm chopping.

"Chicken pot pie." I risk a glance up at her, trying not to let my eyes hold too long on the spot where her chest is still rising and falling slightly faster than it should, as she's still coming down from her own exertion and fear. I feel half guilty for pushing her, and half tempted by the fantasy of doing it again under better circumstances.

"I love chicken pot pie. Assuming it's not poisoned." She gives me a teasing look.

"Sweetheart, poison is your thing. If I want someone dead, a gun or a knife is good enough for me."

"Should I be worried then about the proliferation of both in this cabin?" She's determined to be a smart-ass, and my lip twitches as I try not to smile.

"If I wanted you dead, you'd be dead," I state plainly. She should know that by now.

She rolls her eyes and turns her attention to the window.

"Such a tough guy," she mutters.

"Not tough. Practical. I could have killed you in the abbey. On the plane. When I first brought you out here with Rowan's help. Left you in the woods to die. Let Jack and the others track you down like prey. There are plenty of options where I would have had help to dispose of your body. Bringing you in here to kill you slowly with poison, and I've got to deal with body disposal on my own? Doesn't make much sense." I talk through the logic that should make her feel better, but when I glance up in the silence that follows, she has a horrified look on her face.

"You're kind of terrifying. Is this the trust building you had in mind?"

"I thought you wanted honesty?" I counter.

She tilts her head back and forth, mumbling something under her breath, but she doesn't argue again while I finish prepping dinner. Her surreptitious glances don't go unnoticed, and I'm not sure if she's surprised I can cook or still suspicious I'm slipping rat poison into the mix.

Once I've put it in the oven, I clean up the table, set a timer, and walk over to undo the lock on her wrist. She's adjusting the melting ice pack on her ankle, and she's surprised when she sees me freeing her.

"I'm free already?"

"Temporarily. Getting you cleaned up. You're a bit of a mess." I pick her up again, not wanting to test her ankle walking, and carry her toward the outdoor shower on the back side of the cabin. She lets out a little gasp of indignation that I've pointed out the obvious but lets me carry her without much fight to the shower. I'm guessing she's also ready to be free of the grime of the last couple of days.

"You're not looking so hot yourself," she complains, and I don't doubt that for a second. I need a shower as much as she does.

"Yeah, well, let's hope there's enough hot water for two," I reply as I cuff her to the shower pipe before I check the small gas water tank.

I'd started it up while I waited for Jack to return her, hoping that'd give it enough time to make a solid tank of hot water for us both. It's still warm enough to shower out here, even though the temps are starting to drop at night, but I wouldn't want to do it without some piping hot water in the mix.

"How am I supposed to shower like this?" She points to the way she's chained to the pipe.

"Told you. Can't trust you not to run if I'm not watching, so I'm afraid you're gonna have to make it work." I close the distance between us across the shower.

I motion to the dowdy skirt and blouse she's still wearing, the one that's tattered and torn and smeared with mud and stains. I shouldn't offer to help. I should leave her to figure it out herself, but I'd be lying if I didn't admit I want another glimpse of what she looks like when she's not drowning in layers of fabric. "You want help getting this off?"

THIRTEEN

Zephyrine

THE WORDS "YES, PLEASE," nearly leave my lips before I can stop them. This man is temptation incarnate. As much as I don't trust him, he's hard not to like, and even harder not to find attractive. I feel a lot less guilty admitting that to myself now than I did when I thought he was a priest. It was bad enough that I was betraying my conscience, but it was worse if I made him betray his vows in the process.

Now that I know he's some sort of unhinged vigilante cowboy? The guilt is fading, and the curiosity I've been trying to quell is rising. I can't give in to my thoughts though. I might be thousands of miles away from the convent, but it doesn't change the fact that I plan to take my final vows as soon as I can find a way to obtain the annulment from my husband.

I want to be back at the abbey, safe with my friends and far out of sight for anyone who wants to use me as a means to their end. Even if some of them are funny and kind of sweet in an offbeat sort of way. I'll never be able to return home if I betray my promises to the nuns and myself. Running away from my marriage to hide was a thing the other sisters understood. This? Whatever this is with Levi, I'm pretty sure they wouldn't be so forgiving.

"I've got it," I insist, knowing full well I don't. But my hand goes to the buttons on my shirt anyway, trying to work down them one-handed.

He turns his back, giving me privacy without me having to ask for it. At least I'm allowed to have a little dignity in this cage. I could appreciate that.

"You can hand me your clothes when you've got them off." He holds his hand out behind his back, and I rush to go faster.

I don't want to keep him waiting, and I don't know what he'll do if I can't get them off on my own. I doubt he'll unlock me from the pipe, and I'm not sure I can take him cutting my clothes off in what's starting to become a humiliating ritual.

"This would go faster if I wasn't chained to the pipe," I mumble as I continue to struggle with the second button, bending over to try to make use of the chained hand.

"I can close my eyes, and you can take them off while chained to the pipe, or I can unchain you and watch you get undressed. I assumed you'd prefer the former, but we can make the latter happen if you want." He gives me my options matter-of-factly.

"No, thank you," I answer him primly.

The thought of him seeing me naked has the flush on my cheeks chasing its way down my neck and chest. I'm disgustingly filthy and sweaty just like he said. I feel like a gremlin. I wouldn't want a nurse to see me in this condition, let alone this man.

But what I want and what I'm capable of aren't aligning because, despite moving into contortionist-like positions, trying to get out of my clothes, I'm making very little progress. I let out a frustrated sigh, and he tilts his head to the side.

"Problem?"

"What if I promise not to run?" I plead for reason.

"There's no way I'd trust you after today. I don't have it in me to chase you again."

"Well, I don't have the energy to run either. Not on this ankle," I huff out in reply. It's true even if he doesn't want to believe me.

"Sorry. No deal." He turns around and surveys my still-dressed state. "What if I close my eyes and help you?"

"I'm supposed to trust you not to look?"

His brow quirks up for a moment, and then he runs his hands under his glasses, pinching the bridge of his nose with his forefingers before he takes them off and sets them on the ledge next to a couple of bottles of soap.

"There," he announces. "Now you're a blurry mess to begin with, so even if I look, there's not much I can see."

I'll have to take his word on that, but I watch as he closes his eyes slowly.

"I'm not going to do anything you don't want me to. I wouldn't hurt you on purpose. I meant what I said. I want us to be able to trust each other. Let me help?" His tone is soft.

"Yes."

He holds out his hand so I can guide it to my buttons, and he slowly feels his way around the first one, the pad of his finger rimming the edge of the button while the other hand feels for the edge of the fabric. He makes easy work of the first and even faster work of the second. I use the time to study him up close without fear of his seeing where my eyes pause or for how long.

He's gorgeous. Priest or no. Prominent cheekbones and a

chiseled jaw. A perfect nose. His lips were just as beautiful as the rest of his features, soft and full. The thought takes me back to the memory of them pressed against my own.

At least until I bit him. I smile to myself. I wonder how long he might have kissed me for if I hadn't ended it so abruptly. If his tongue would have teased over mine. If he would have taken the kiss deeper. It's been so long since I've been kissed by someone who wasn't using it as a punishment.

I slip the blouse off one shoulder and then let it hang off the second, sliding it down my arm until it reaches the pipe, where it hangs from the cuff. A shiver runs down my spine as the cool night air hits my skin, and I feel his palm make its way back up my shoulder to my bra strap. He follows it down my back and slows when he hits the band.

He's so close I can feel every breath on my neck and shoulders as he works, and still, he presses in closer, reaching his arm around the back of me to feel for the hooks. He pulls at them gently, loosening every hook from its eye and making the bra go slack around my ribs. His fingers trail back up the bra strap to my shoulder, hovering there for a moment like he's considering his options before he slips it off my shoulder, and I let it fall down my arm, chasing the blouse to its spot on the cuff.

Another shiver runs through me, this time more at the vulnerable state I'm in and his proximity than anything to do with the temperature. My nipples harden, and goose bumps break out across my skin. Every unholy thought I've ever had about him is racing through my mind.

He's already on to the next task, though, unaware of the way I'm reacting to him because he's keeping his promise to keep his eyes closed. Not even saying a word to taunt me or tease me about the situation. His hands brush over my waist and start to move down, taking my skirt with him in one swift motion. He tosses it in a pile. His hands are back at my waist before I realize we're on the last bit of clothing. One I could easily get off myself, one-handed, with a little effort and balance involved.

"I can get that." I can hear how unnerved he makes me in my own voice. He must, too, because he grins.

"Gonna let me do all the hard work and not get the reward?"

My stomach tumbles as his hands smooth over my hips and hook into my underwear. But he pauses there.

"You can't say stuff like that to me." I'm trying to be good.

"Why, because you're not a nun?" His lips curl with amusement even as his eyes stay closed.

"I will be, but I'm married now."

"I think you'd better remind yourself of that because..." He brushes his fingertips over my skin, just above the waistband of my panties on the inside of my hip. "I can feel your heartbeat. Your breathing too. They're giving you away."

"You're mistaking nerves for interest." I hit back quickly.

"Is that what it is?" His thumb strokes over my skin, and I close my eyes, letting myself enjoy the soft touch I've imagined a million times at night the last few weeks.

"Yes. I don't even... You know. Think like *that* anymore," I lie. If he knew the truth, more than the little I confessed, I'd be doomed.

Something flickers over his face, and then it fades into a smirk. It's the most wicked smile, even with his eyes closed, maybe more so for it. The hesitation he had is gone, and he pulls on my panties, dragging them down my thighs and over my calves, barely waiting for me to step out of them before he pulls them completely off. He tucks them into his back pocket instead of setting them with the rest of my clothes.

"What are you doing?"

"Taking them." He takes a step back just as I lunge for them.

"For what?"

"Payment for lying again." He leans in and turns the water higher, the press of his body closer to mine, forcing me to take a step back this time.

"What are you going to do with them?" I call after him as he walks away.

"I have a few ideas." He snatches his glasses off the ledge and puts them back on while still keeping his body and eyes turned away from me. "You better start showering. I need one too before that hot water runs out."

I pull my jaw off the floor and turn to look for soap, finding a small bar sitting near the handle of the faucet. He was right. I needed to hurry up. Focus on the task at hand. That would get my mind off the fact that I'm standing stark naked just a few feet away from him.

I glance around and notice that there's a small alcove with towels and bathrobes. I tilt my head as I start to soap up. It was odd, along with the tiny but high-end kitchen and the fancy bed and other furnishings inside. I know I've been out of Colorado for a long time, but I can't remember rustic cabins belonging to lone men like him being quite this well-equipped. Something is off.

"Why does this place have all this stuff? The robes and outdoor shower? I thought this was your cabin?" I ask as I lather up my hair. The soap smells fresh and crisp like apples, and I notice the words Purgatory Falls Inn are imprinted on the surface as I run it down over my body.

"It was my cabin. Then I moved back into town, and my sister-in-law asked if she could turn it into a remote honeymoon suite as part of her bed and breakfast. Told her to knock herself out," he explains. I try to imagine this man with an innkeeper for a sister-in-law. The wholesome vision of all of them gathering for holidays and celebrating family birthdays flashes through my mind, and I try to reconcile it with the man I know. The priest and then the outlaw. So far, I like all the versions of him against my better judgment.

"So you kidnapped me and brought me to a honeymoon suite?" I muse.

"Why? Worried it's going to ruin your reputation back at the convent?"

"Very funny." I rinse the soap out of my hair, and it splatters to the floor. "I just thought it all seemed a little much for a place out in the middle of the woods. I imagine it's expensive."

"Not everyone wants to be doing penance on stone floors and scratchy sheets." He mocks my tiny room in the convent. It might not be much, but it was home, and I'd been happy there. As happy as I'd been in my adult life anyway.

"You're right. Some would rather have luxury than a clear conscience." I'm thinking of my father and my husband, but the barb hits him as well.

"My conscience is clear. There's nothing I've done that I would take back. In fact, the only regrets I have are times when I wish I could have done more. Is your conscience clear?"

I nibble my lower lip out of nervous habit. I have to remember who I'm dealing with, however soft he might seem at times. He's the kind of man who has a brand on his chest, a team of men to help him hold someone hostage, and access to private jets and rich men with murderous intent. I have to assume he's every bit as dangerous as the men in my family. I turn away to finish soaping up the rest of my body before I start to rinse off as I catalog my own conscience.

I've made more than a few mistakes. Done a couple of things I wish I could take back. I have some that haunt me. Vices that I wish I could overcome and yet seem to be chained to no matter how hard I try. Things that make me question if I'm really cut out to be the selfless person I need to be to serve with my sisters if I somehow manage to get an annulment. Past wrongs that I don't know if I can ever atone for.

"Sounds like a no." He interrupts the inventory I'm taking.

I glance back over my shoulder, watching as he leans against the wall that surrounds the shower. The low light of the setting sun casts him in shadow, and I can't help but notice every lean line of his body. The way the T-shirt clings to him and how broad his shoulders are.

He feels like a test—he *is* a test—of my morals, my priorities, the very fiber of my being. Of just how low I'm willing to sink to turn the tables in my favor. I could give him more than I am right now. I could put the full weight of everything I know into his hands and maybe, if my husband doesn't kill us, have a chance at a new life. The thought of that future taunts me. But it would mean putting everything I've been working toward at risk. There's no telling what sort of retaliation Corey or my father might take.

Besides, nothing about revenge aligns with who I'm supposed to be now. The person I thought I'd become when I surrendered to the rules of the convent and vowed to become one of them. Chastity, poverty, obedience. I'm trying my best to repeat them like a mantra, to hold tight to what I know I should do.

But I didn't have this temptation standing right in front of me. A man who's offering me the chance to do more than hide out in the mountains on a distant continent. A real chance at justice. Or revenge. Depending on which side of the coin you looked at. I don't need the abbess standing here to know what she would say.

"If you don't say something soon, I'm gonna turn around to make sure you didn't disappear," he warns.

"I'm here. I'm just... praying."

"Praying?" He scoffs in surprise. "For what?"

"Clarity."

"Clarity about what?" He pries.

"What the right thing to do is. If I should help you. What keeps my conscience clean."

"That's a waste of your time. There's always something we could have done better. Less selfish. More thoughtful. Less greedy. Trying to keep your conscience clean is a fool's errand."

"Then I guess I'm a fool." It's all I lived for in the wake of my marriage, learning the truth about my father and his associates. All I wanted was some way to escape the rot.

"You're nothing like him. If that's what you're fighting so hard to avoid," he chimes in, like he can hear my thoughts.

"I know I'm not." It comes out sharper than I intended. "But I don't want to just not be like him. I want to make up for what he's done."

"That's not your burden to carry."

"But it's yours?" I counter. "This is the problem with men like you, you know. You all think you're white knights saving the kingdom from danger."

"I'm not a knight, white or otherwise. There's no mandate. No kingdom. I just want the simple pleasure of watching men pay for the wrongs they've done. I don't want to wait for your hell or wherever you believe men like him go. I don't want to hope and pray for justice someday. I want him to feel that same kind of pain here on earth. I want to be the one who doles it out and know that I made sure some measure of it was served." He speaks with the kind of confidence I wish I had.

"How do you plan to do that?"

"I think you know as well as I do how I plan to do that."

"And you're asking me to help you. To doom myself to the same fate as you."

"What kind of fate is it if you stand by and do nothing, knowing you could have stopped him? You're focused on one life you might help take, but what about the ones you could save? Aren't you responsible for their deaths if you don't intercede?" He argues his case in a calm tone. He might have been a lawyer or a philosopher if he hadn't grown up with this life. I see reason in it, but I still have my qualms.

"That's a Faustian bargain."

I can see the slight shake of his head and the frustrated way he shifts his weight in the shadow.

"One I'd take again and again."

There's a long beat of silence as I finish rinsing under the showerhead. I turn the water off and reach for a towel, managing to snatch it with the tips of my fingers without having to ask for his help. I run it over my hair and then wrap it around my body, using my elbows and my free hand to get it into a position to cover most everything vital.

"I wish I had your clarity," I admit at last.

"I'm happy to help you find it." He turns, satisfied by the sounds of my movements and the lack of water that I'm covered up again.

He rounds the edge of the shower and pulls off one of the fluffy white robes I couldn't reach from my chained spot. He unfolds it and opens it for me, resting it on my shoulders while he undoes the lock on my cuff. He lets me go bond-free for a moment, stretching my wrist before I slip my arm through the sleeve. I lean forward while pressing the towel to my chest with my free hand to keep the robe on and repeat the process again with the other arm until I can wrap the robe around my waist and tie it.

He pulls my clothes from the cuffs as he takes them off the pipe and tosses them into a pile on the floor.

"Hey!" I protest.

"You gonna put dirty clothes back on or you want me to wash them first?"

"I just want to make sure I have clothes."

"You have clothes." He nods to the robe. "I've got a shirt you can borrow inside."

"Underwear. Another dress. Real clothes," I argue.

"Beggars can't be choosers." He shrugs before he slaps one of the cuffs back on my wrist, gently pulling me to the wall, where he chains me to another railing.

"You really think I'm gonna run off barefoot in just a robe?"

"I think I wouldn't put anything past you," he answers bluntly.

He reaches back with one hand, grabs the collar of his shirt, and pulls it slowly over his head. The sound that escapes my lips comes too fast to stop, and I try to mask it with a cough, but he's clocked me. A knowing smile dances over his lips as he goes for his belt. My eyes are torn between watching his progress and studying the ink that covers his chest and arms. There's so much of it, and I didn't get a good look at it in the abbey. But then I'm shocked back into the present when I hear the click of the metal on his buckle.

"What are you doing?" I ask the obvious.

"Getting undressed so I can take a shower. We don't tend to take them with our clothes on around here." He makes quick work of the belt, pulling it one-handed and tossing it down to the pile at our feet.

"With me right here?"

"No one said you had to watch." He turns the handle for the hot water, and the steam billows out as the rain shower starts up again.

"You couldn't put me back inside first?"

"Wouldn't be fair if I didn't give you a chance to peek when I did, would it?"

"You peeked?" I practically squeak the words.

"Did I?" He flashes another devious look in my direction.

"You said you wouldn't."

"I thought you didn't trust me."

"I don't, but I thought you were trying to earn it. I at least thought you'd have enough respect for a nun's innocence."

"Innocence?" He scoffs, a laugh rumbling out of his chest as his hands hook into his unbuttoned jeans. "I think we both know that's a word that doesn't really fit you. You had the list going earlier. What was it again—lying, manipulating, kidnapping? We can add lust to that too."

"Lust?" I return the scoff in full measure. "Over you?"

"Was there another priest you were fantasizing about in the middle of the night? Father Mark, maybe?"

"I don't know what you're talking about." I huff because he knows as well as I do it wasn't one of the aging priests with dentures and gray nose hair.

His mouth twists in amusement, and he closes the distance between us.

"I have my own confession." His eyes study mine for a minute before they rake down my body, like he's remembering me naked. I don't know if I can trust that he didn't peek now.

"What's that?" My voice comes out shakier than I intend.

"Before the kidnapping, there was a little light stalking."

"Light stalking? What does that mean?"

He presses his lips together and tilts his head in faux remorse.

"Truth be told, there was nothing light about it. I watched every single thing you did. Listened to every word you spoke. Followed you everywhere you went."

"You weren't at the convent that long, and even when you were, it's not like you could go all the places I did." I frown.

Guests and men are banned from plenty of the rooms at the abbey.

He reaches into his pocket and pulls out a phone, tapping it lightly.

"I didn't have to be."

"How?" My heart is skipping beats in my chest as the trepidation wraps its tendrils around tighter and tighter with each passing moment. If he had access to my phone, he knows so much more than I could have imagined.

"Spyware. I installed it on your phone. Created a mirror copy on the one I had. I could watch everything you did. Every search you made. Every file you opened." His eyes lift behind his dark lashes and meet mine. "I could turn your camera and mic on too. Listen to those muffled little cries you'd try to stifle on those long, late nights when you were alone and thinking about your mystery priest. Sometimes I could even watch as your fingers curled around your pillow when you—"

"Stop," I plead, closing my eyes because I can't stand to hold his gaze anymore. He does as I ask, and the silence that lies between us feels heavy enough to crater through the ground. I wish I could follow it down. I knew there was something he was keeping from me, but I didn't expect it to be that.

"So I *know* you, little nun." His fingers brush under my chin. "You don't have to hide with me."

"I can't believe you—" His thumb runs over my lips to silence me, and my eyes open at the same time my brows fall in anger. But he presses his thumb down to keep me silent and shakes his head.

"Stones and glass houses, yeah? You've been keeping a lot of secrets from me. A whole husband for starters. That you're capable of drugging a man and tying him up. You're not as innocent as you want to be." He releases me, and I tear my chin from his grasp and take a step back.

"We're not the same."

"I think we're more alike than you want to admit," he calls back as he walks away.

His hands go back to his pants, and he pulls them down. I whip around, closing my eyes, but not before I get an eyeful of his perfect cowboy butt in the process. A sight I won't be forgetting anytime soon, even if the humiliation of the last few minutes makes me wish I could.

FOURTEEN

L^{evi}

THE NEXT MORNING, I make her a full breakfast. Toast, eggs, grits, and a bowl of fresh fruit. The drip coffee is nearly ready, and I put the cream and sugar on the table, peeking through the open door to the bedroom to see her stirring. I left it open so I could keep an eye on her, still too nervous about whether or not she'd run to give her any real privacy.

I slept on the couch, not that I ever got much sleep, and she fell asleep on the bed almost as soon as her head hit the pillow after dinner. It's been a long few days for her, and now I have to press her one last time. Hopefully, with a full night's rest, a shower, and a belly full of food, she'll see reason and be willing to open up a little more.

"Levi?" she calls out. I put slack in her chain last night so she could sleep comfortably, but not enough that she could leave the room.

"Coming!" I call back, making my way inside the small bedroom.

Her red hair is loose around her shoulders, a change from its usual braided or bun-tied state. It makes her look a little wilder and a little less prim to see the way it falls in curls around her neck and down her chest. She tugs the hem of my T-shirt lower around her thighs to keep it from riding up, but it doesn't change the fact that her long legs are on full display and her nipples shadow through the soft white cotton of my shirt. For a moment, she looks like mine.

"Can you let me out of here? I need to use the restroom." Her voice is still raspy from sleep, and my mind wanders with thoughts of what might be possible in a different universe.

"Yep." I clear my throat when I realize I'm still frozen in the doorway and set to work. "Your bra and panties are dry. I brought them in this morning and set them on the sink in the bathroom," I explain as I undo the locks to free her from the bed.

"Thank you." Her brow furrows with a question as she inhales the coffee and buttered-toast scent that's working its way into the bedroom. "Did you make breakfast?"

"Yes. I made us breakfast."

"It smells amazing." Her stomach grumbles, and she runs her palm over it in circles.

"Well, the bathroom's open, so you can get ready. I'll have it on the table when you're done. How's your ankle? You need help getting there."

"Better this morning. The ice helped. The rest of my body is sore though."

"Hopefully some rest today helps. No climbing out windows." I tease her, and she smiles back.

She gives me a small grin and then crosses to the bathroom. I finish up breakfast and get the table ready while I wait for her to come back, pouring myself a cup of coffee and scrolling through my phone for information from Grant and Charlotte. She didn't waste any time getting to work on the archival materials I brought back.

When Zephyrine emerges from the bathroom, she's slightly more buttoned-up than before. Her hair is braided again, and she's less sleepy-looking. I pour her a cup of coffee, adding cream and her requisite three scoops of sugar. Her brow lifts in curiosity, and she has to smother a small smile that threatens at the corner of her mouth. She takes a big gulp as she sits down and lets out a happy sigh.

"Who knew room service in captivity was so bougie?" She grins over the rim of her cup.

"Did you sleep okay?" I ask as I watch her snatch up the buttered toast from her plate and add a dollop of jam.

"Would have slept better if I wasn't chained to the bed, but otherwise, yes." She takes a big bite, and her eyes close for half a moment while she chews. I ordered in her favorite sour cherry jam. The same kind she ate every day at the convent.

Every morning, her routine was the same. Except Sundays, when she added an extra helping of eggs and bacon. She told Father Levi it was to help her get through the multiple Masses and tours of the crypts, and she always piled a couple of extra pieces of bacon on my plate for the same reason. Small indulgences she called them.

"Well, maybe if we can come to an agreement, we can do something about that."

"Maybe." Her eyelids flutter, and she lets out another soft sigh of appreciation as she chews her food. "This jam is delicious. Almost tastes like the one we have at the abbey. What kind is it?"

I set the jar in front of her, and she looks at me in surprise.

"You remembered that?"

I nod.

"This, the coffee, and the pot pie last night." She gives me a mock look of suspicion. "If you're not trying to poison me, then what is this? A last meal?"

"I'm trying to make you see this doesn't have to be painful if we don't want it to be."

"I see. So you're buying me off with treats then for my cooperation?"

"For your trust."

"By reminding me you stalked me for weeks?" She gives me a cynical look.

I laid the last big secret out for her last night, even admitted some of my own sins. I'd crossed the line by listening to her at night, but I also hadn't lied when I said I don't have regrets. I'd do it all again. Now, though, I have to accept the consequences of those choices, so I'm feeling her out this morning to make sure it didn't completely obliterate a chance for us to work together.

"I prefer to think of it as keenly observing details." I take a long draw off my coffee. She might have slept. But I didn't. Not as much as my body needed. So it'll be caffeine and crisp mountain air to keep me going today.

"A stalker would say that." Her tone is flat, but when I look up, she grins at me.

"Then I'm a stalker. But one who takes the time to make you the recipes you like and order your jam. That should count as a peace offering."

"What does peace look like to you?" she asks, taking a sip of her coffee-flavored cream as she waits for my answer.

"You tell me what you want, I tell you what I can do for you, and we come to a deal that makes us both happy."

"Since when does what I want factor into it?" She hikes her eyebrow as she takes another bite of toast, with an extra smear of jam on it, and then washes it down with coffee.

"Always, as far as I'm concerned," I answer without thinking. I want to give her whatever her little heart desires. I want to spoil her rotten and see her amused smiles. She deserves a reprieve from the hell she's endured and her contemplative austerity at the convent. I also happen to believe the path to my family getting the answers we need lies in the exact same direction.

"Doubtful." She gives me a look over the top of her toast that challenges me.

"So tell me, what do you want, Zephyrine Schaefer?" I lean back in my chair, assuming she'll ponder all the options.

"Freedom." She doesn't need time to think.

"Besides that," I grumble.

"No, I don't mean this." She looks down at the lock on her wrist. "Well, this too, but I mean free. Really free. From my father. From my husband. I want a divorce, or an annulment really. If I had that, I could take my final vows as a nun and put all of this to rest. Have a life I can call my own. Finally."

"You *want* to be a nun?" I'm surprised.

She never seemed very good at it, not with her vices or her spirit. The kind of spirit that remained untamed despite everything she's been through. If the abbess couldn't do it in the years she's already had, I can't imagine she'll ever be the picture-perfect angel they want. I assumed she was just hiding out there, that it was somewhere safe she could hide. Or at least somewhere her husband was willing to settle on.

"What's wrong with that? There are worse things." Her countenance turns stormy, and she flicks a glance in my direction before she finishes off her coffee.

"Yeah, a priest for one," I hedge.

She glares at me and bites off another piece of her toast with the kind of vigor that has me wondering if she's imagining it's my head.

"It's quiet. The convent is beautiful. I get to do work that helps people. Most of the nuns are friendly. I'm happy there."

"You're happy there? You sure? It didn't seem like you quite fit in." I don't believe it. Happy nuns don't share her taste in extracurriculars.

"Just because I'm not perfect..." A flash of hurt across her face makes me regret my question.

"That's not what I meant. I just assumed it was a place you were hiding, not a place you'd chosen. If you chose it, then I'm glad you were happy there." I'd try to be happy for her anyway.

"I chose to visit the abbey because my grandfather spent time there."

"Did he take you there when you were younger?"

"No. He kept a diary of where he was during the war and his travels afterward. When I ran off, trying to get some time away from my husband, I used the diary as a travel guide. I followed in his footsteps through some of the cities and towns. It led me to the convent. He talked about visiting old friends there. Visiting the archives. The food. The nuns. The time in reflection. I wanted to see what all the fuss was about because he loved it there. I could tell the way he wrote about it. He spent more time there than anywhere else." She looks lost in memories for a moment before she returns to me. "And I love it there too. Despite my shortcomings."

"But it could be a place you visit rather than a place you live under the watch of the abbess."

"I feel safe there. Or at least I did before." She gives me a pointed look.

"Seemed like a real drowning risk to me." I try to crack a joke. Not that I'm very good at them.

"Ha!" She mocks me with a fake laugh, but her eyes light in amusement. "I meant to thank you for that."

"You were a little too busy torturing me to thank me."

"Did you die though?" A little smirk plays at her pretty lips.

"Not for lack of trying."

"How's it looking?" she asks, grimacing a little as she remembers.

"Not great. Feels pretty rough too." I hover my hand over the bandaged spot on my abdomen. I don't dare touch it because it still hurts like hell. It's gonna be weeks before it really starts to heal.

"More or less painful than the one on your chest?" She sneaks in the question. The mention of it causes a raw flash of memories. I'm used to seeing it in my reflection in the mirror when I get ready. A reminder of my past. But I've grown used to it, and the mention of the day I got it brings an old wound to the surface. I clear my throat and take another bite of food instead of answering immediately. I don't want to talk about that. Not yet. Maybe never.

"Don't change the subject. You could have killed me drugging me like that, you know," I admonish her, but she merely shrugs one shoulder in response.

"You could have killed me too. Besides, we might be even soon. Given you've put both our lives in danger now." Her tone flattens.

"I've got extra security on alert. If he tries to get on this ranch, we'll know about it," I reassure her.

"It'll be too late if he's already here." She sounds sad, like another memory is passing through her mind.

"You're very certain of his capabilities."

"Yes, well... I've seen what he's capable of."

"How so?"

"Before him, I had an almost normal life. Friends. A boyfriend. I went to college for a while."

"I know."

"Of course you do, stalker." A smile comes and goes as fast as it appears.

"And then what? He took you away from all of that?" I ignore the attempted dig. It's true, after all.

"He and my father decided it was bad for me. That those people were bad for me. I'd be better off spending more time with Corey. He would look out for me and my interests. He could help me manage my money, and didn't I realize how much he cared for me? No man would ever care about me as much as he did or work as hard as he would to protect me. I needed protection, according to my father. Our family had so many enemies that it wasn't safe for me to be on the street or attending classes. Any of those people could try to steal from us, lie about my father, hurt me. Corey was the only one my father claimed I could trust, and so he put us together more and more."

"Because he wanted you to marry him."

She nods, a melancholy look overtaking her countenance and making me wish I could see what she was seeing in her memories. Whatever they wanted from her, I'm doubtful she deserved the life they forced on her.

"Was he really in love with you, or was it a business arrangement?"

"Both. Or so Corey claimed."

"But in reality?" I counter.

"In reality, my grandfather left me a large sum of money in his will. I was the only grandchild, and he did well in life. He was an antiques dealer with some one-of-a-kind auction finds. He worked all the way up until the day he died. Hence all the travel in Europe and beyond."

"He left it to you instead of your dad?"

"He was my mom's dad."

"Why not leave it to your mom then? Or your siblings?"

She frowns and then looks down at her plate, pushing a bit of scrambled egg around and then glancing up at me. Her lashes lower as she tilts her head.

"Oh. Not quite enough stalking then."

"How do you mean?" The accusation that I hadn't been thorough chafes at my ego.

"I'm not the First Lady of Colorado's daughter. I'm the mistress's."

I'm surprised, but I try not to let it show on my face. It would explain a lot. Why her father wasn't treating her like a princess, the way I'd expect a man like him to treat a daughter. Why she'd been virtually banished and sold off like cattle the second she was old enough to be a commodity to him. I'm angry with myself for not having figured it out earlier.

"I see. So he didn't want your father to have the money?"

"No. He was explicit that under no circumstances would my father have access to it. That I was only to have the money when I had moved out of his house and married."

"So why not give it to your mom for safekeeping?"

"She died when I was ten, and I didn't know her well. My father separated us as soon as he was able, claiming she was unfit. Moved me into his house, and my stepmother raised me. She hated me. She never said that, of course, but she always treated her real sons differently, and my father did too. I never understood what I did wrong, or why, if they hated me so much, they didn't just let me stay with my mother."

"Was your mother actually unfit like he claimed? She didn't fight for you?" I know I'm asking painful questions, but I worry there's more to this story than what's on the surface.

Zephyrine's nose wrinkles. "I don't know, honestly. I

suspect not. I have a feeling it was a convenient fiction that allowed him to have full custody and let him sweep her under the rug. She was admitted to a facility when I was very young, and she never walked out the front doors again. My grandfather came to visit me a couple of times, and I heard my father argue with him the last time I saw him."

"And then your father corralled you into a marriage that I assume gave him access to some of your grandfather's money?"

"All of the money. Well, they split it up. I'm not sure how, but I didn't see any of it. I assume my father took the lion's share."

"So he trapped you in a bad marriage so he could funnel money to his political ambitions?"

"And his projects. He has a few going. It's tough work to look wealthy too. All the glad-handing and golf outings and fancy suits. He liked to spend money."

"Yes, I'm familiar with at least one of his ventures. Do you know anything about his projects? Have you ever worked with him?"

She stops mid-bite and looks up at me, her brow furrowing slightly.

"I feel like I've given you enough free information so far. I think it's your turn to talk." She slips a bite of eggs past her lips and then looks at me expectantly.

"What do you want to know?" I ask. As much as I want to build a foundation here, I'm not keen on offering any unnecessary details. I'm not one to talk about myself, and I don't think there's much she'll like about my past anyway. She barely likes my present.

She shrugs and takes another bite, waiting for me to talk. When I let the silence stretch out, she gives me a mildly irritated look and puts her fork down.

"What should I want to know? How am I a pawn in this

game? What do you want from my father that you think I can help you get?" She skips over the niceties.

"Relics."

"Relics? My father doesn't know the first thing about anything religious."

"He does, at least in this one case."

"Then you know something about him I don't." She shakes her head and waits for my explanation.

"He's been collecting relics, illegally speaking. Black market finds. Stolen goods."

"My father doesn't exactly strike me as a cat burglar. Not that he has morals, but he doesn't like getting his hands dirty if he can find someone else to do it."

"He's been using intermediaries, but it's his money funding it. Your grandfather's maybe. We figured out he was behind it a few months ago. That discovery is what led us to you. When I found you at a convent famous for its reliquaries, I assumed you must be on assignment for him."

"Ah. That explains a lot. Well, the truth must have been a disappointment then."

"It complicated things."

"So he's stealing relics, and somehow you think I might be able to do what exactly to help you?"

"I think you might be able to help us get them back."

"How?"

"That part I'm still working out."

"You kidnapped me without a plan?" She's indignant at the idea.

"There was a plan. It wasn't fully formed quite yet."

"That sounds ill-conceived."

"Says the woman who started tying me up and torturing me without one."

"Touché. But I don't see any way I could help you get the

relics back. Wherever he has them, I don't know. And if you think I'll make a good trade, I can promise you his projects always interested him more than I did. He won't care what happens to me if the alternative means giving up something important to him like that."

"No. But your husband might."

"Doubtful."

"Isn't that his thing? He's known for making deals, right?"

"Deals that benefit him. And he won't cross my father. As awful as he is, Corey's terrified of him. I think it's likely the only reason he ceded ground and let me go stay at the convent," she explains.

That just raises more questions. Corey and the governor must have some other agreements going on behind the scenes. Zephyrine was traded for something. Her father might not care about her as a person, but he knew she was a bargaining chip. She's smart and gorgeous. He wouldn't have given her up easily. Corey must have given him something he wanted in return.

"Your father cares about appearances though, right? He'll want to make sure it at least appears like he's a good father when he finds out his daughter is missing. I doubt he'll want it getting out that she's being held for ransom. Least of all when the people holding her are people looking for revenge because he's a thief and a murderer."

"Murderer?"

I nod. "And still actively trying. Just this past summer, he tried to have my entire family killed. Right alongside our friends and innocent bystanders. At a wedding, no less."

Her face pales, and her eyes hit the plate in front of her as she drops her fork. "Ah. Now I see why you told me your friends might want me dead."

"You're beginning to see, yeah." I lean back in my chair,

wrapping my arm around the backrest. "But I won't let them do anything to hurt you. I just want to make sure he never hurts my family again. I'm not above using his daughter to do that, obviously. But given your situation, I figure maybe there's a way we both get something out of this we want."

"Like?"

"Like we get you your annulment and maybe your money back for starters."

"For starters? I don't know how you'd manage either of those. I tried. It was impossible." She gives me a doubtful look, and it's obvious I'm not winning her over easily.

"I'm good at the impossible." I press my hand to my chest and tilt my head. "I faked being a priest well enough that the abbess had me holding English confession. I hadn't been in a church since I was seven."

I earn a small smile for that one. "Well, that is impressive."

"So let me worry about the details of how we pull off the impossible. You just tell me what you want."

"I'd be happy with the annulment. The money back would be a bonus. But I won't sell my soul for them. They'll be worthless to me if I do."

"I don't want your soul, sweetheart. Your body will do just fine."

Her eyes dart up to mine, a tinge of curiosity in them until she sees the smirk on my face.

"Crude." She purses her lips in disappointment at my teasing.

"If you think that's crude, you should hear the things nuns admit to when they're on their knees in the confessional." I press my luck, and that earns me the toss of a scrambled egg directly at my head. "Hey now! I grew up with three siblings and a whole mess of ranch hands' kids. You won't win a food fight with me."

"I won't win anything when you don't fight fair." She motions to her captive state.

"Well... we got a deal yet? The annulment and the money for information and anything that'll help me put pressure on your father?"

"Your side of the deal is pretty vague, so I'm not sure what I'm agreeing to."

"I told you, I'm short on specifics right now. I'm meeting with my business partners today to discuss what the future holds. Once I know where everyone's heads are at, and I can reassure them you're willing to cooperate, then I'll know what my options are."

"But in the end, you deliver me back to the convent in one piece? And everyone there will be safe?"

"As long as I'm breathing. I'll take you back myself. Apologize to the abbess for the mess we left and explain everything so that you can go right back to where you left off."

"And if you're not breathing? Then I'm on my own." She looks at me thoughtfully. "As cavalier as you are with your life, I'm not sure that's a promise I can rely on."

"As long as you hold up your end of the bargain, one of my siblings will make sure my wishes are carried out even if something happens to me. When a Stockton gives their word on something, it's as good as done."

Her eyes drift away from me, out to the window and the view beyond it. I can tell she's mulling over her options and wondering what will happen if she doesn't agree. She doesn't have many choices. I can reason with Grant and Hudson to a point, but I can't give them nothing.

"If you say no..." I pause, and her eyes dart back to mine. "Then my guess is they'll want to ransom you. Hell, they might not trust you as well as I do and might want to do that anyway. But we've got a chance if I can convince them."

"It's we now, huh?" She gives me a once-over, like she's sizing up how valuable that is to her.

"I want us both to get what we want. I hate your family and everything they stand for. But I respect you. The choices you've made and the way you've tried to make the best of a bad situation. You're brave. That's all we really can do in this world—try to brave our way through the worst of it and hope that when the time comes, we can seize the opportunity that makes it all worth it. The sacrifices you've made should count for something, and I want to help make them count for you." I give her the best speech I've got in me, one Father Levi could have given more convincingly. It might not be enough.

"I think I feel the same about you. Minus the family hate. For all I know, they might be perfectly pleasant."

"Well, you're about to find out because you're coming with me today."

FIFTEEN

Zephyrine

I'M NOT ready for his brother's fiancée. She's stunning, effervescent, and so incredibly easy to like. Worst of all, I'm pretty sure it's all effortless for her. From her makeup and hair down to her clothes and teal cowboy boots, she looks like she just wakes up this way. I think I might already love her a little bit as she spreads out the clothes on the table in front of me. Apparently, she came prepared and determined to dress up the dowdy captive woman from the convent.

"He gave me your measurements, but I wasn't sure what your style was. Or if nuns even have a style. I got you some very simple things if that's what you'd prefer," Dakota explains. I note the comment about my measurements to discuss it with him later. I'd like to know what stalking he did that led to him getting that information.

"I'm sure whatever you've got is perfect. I'm just excited not to have to keep rewashing the same thing while I wear one of his T-shirts."

"His T-shirt, huh? That sounds a little scandalous for a nun," she teases me with a smile.

I smile back and shake my head. I don't know how to read Levi. One second, I think the attraction's mutual, and another, I think he's barely noticed that I'm a woman. I'm an asset first, and everything else is second in his world. Which at least meant he'll work to keep me safe. I just hope he can convince the rest of his family that I'm willing to work with them.

"He's very set on keeping everything aboveboard. So I think I'm safe there."

"Ah, that sounds like Levi. Very practical and rules oriented. Sometimes they're his own brand of rules, of course, but..." Dakota trails off as she pulls out bras and underwear from another bag. They run the range from plain cotton granny panties to fancy-looking lace. My eyes must go wide because she suddenly gives me a sheepish grimace in return.

"Again, I wasn't sure, and I wanted you to have options. I know that sometimes when you have strict religious require-ments for your clothing, you like to get a little experimental with the details. I went to Catholic school for a while." She adds the last bit in as if to reassure me I'm not a complete conundrum to her, despite our disparate circumstances.

"You did? Did you like it?"

"Yeah. It wasn't my favorite. I got in trouble in my teens. My older brother raised me and thought I was getting a little out of hand. Too wild and too much freedom, he said. He wanted to make sure that I didn't end up dropping out or getting pregnant. He thought the nuns would set me straight."

"Did they?" I'm curious because I can only imagine she was a handful then, if now is any indication.

"Well, no kids and a degree is tucked away in the safe. So I guess you could say they did enough to get me through it." She grins at me as she pulls a couple of shoeboxes out.

"Oh, I'm sorry it wasn't a better experience for you. And you really didn't have to do all this." I press my hand to my lips as she shows me the cutest pair of shoes I've ever seen. "But I appreciate it so much." I grin and then pull out a pair of ballerina flats. "The flats!"

"Us tall girls have to stick together." There's another soft smile from her. "I didn't think heels were very practical anyway, but if you want some, I know a woman who knows the best places to get them."

"I do love a good heel. Or I did at least, before the convent. They're not very practical now. Especially not where Levi has me."

"That's fair. Which brings me to the last, but certainly not least thing, a pair of boots." She holds up a gorgeous pair of black cowboy boots with pink details. "I know you're from Colorado originally. I didn't know if that meant downtown Denver socialite or if you were a cowgirl like the rest of us down here. I figured it couldn't hurt for you at least to have the option available if you wanted it."

"Thank you. That's so sweet of you. All of this was so sweet. I feel like I'm on a holiday rather than being held hostage." I laugh.

Dakota grimaces through a smile and looks over me. "I'm really sorry about all this. I wish there were another way. But when the guys get an idea in their minds, the rest of us are just along for the ride. But I'm here if you need someone besides Levi. I imagine he isn't the easiest company."

"I appreciate that." I'm sure she'll be reporting back everything I talked about or did, but it's still nice to feel like I've had someone who could at least find me some cute underwear or a nice functional set of boots in my corner. We work our way through the rest of the afternoon sorting through the clothes and making small talk about our favorite things.

"ARE NUNS ALLOWED TO DRINK? Recreationally, I mean? I know communion wine and all, obviously." Dakota looks at me from across the room as she pulls out some glasses and whiskey.

"We can. As long as we don't get too wild."

"Well, that's unfortunate. I was thinking it might be nice for you to get a little wild." She gives me a conspiratorial look that has me laughing.

"A little wild is fine, as long as it's not too wild," I reason.

"All right then. Favorite drink, or do you want a surprise?"

"Surprise me."

Those turn out to be famous last words because an hour later, after flipping through all the streaming services to find absolutely nothing we're interested in watching—apparently, I'm not missing much at the convent—we're doing a taste test of all of Dakota's favorite drinks to keep ourselves entertained while we wait for Grant and Levi's return.

"Oh, and this one." She grabs a bottle off the shelf. "This one is Levi's favorite. Just in case you ever need that information for any reason." She winks at me.

"And why would I need that?" My brows knit together.

"Birthday. Christmas. Anniversary date." She shrugs, and I burst into laughter.

"Yeah, I don't think we'll be celebrating any of those together. I'll be lucky if he lets me survive. I think he's halfway between wanting to strangle me and reminding himself that he needs me for his plan most days." I grimace as I take a sip of his favorite whisky. It's strong, peaty. Not my favorite, but I suppose if you had a refined palate for those sorts of things, you might enjoy it.

"That's just how Stockton men show their affection. They can't just say they like you, they have to act like you're the bane of their existence and torture themselves over whether or not to admit they might just have a little crush."

The idea of Levi having a crush has me lost to the giggles for several moments before I can return to rational conversation.

"A crush? I don't think that man knows the meaning of the word. Bane of his existence, maybe."

"Grant would definitely have described me that way before, and now we're engaged." She flashes her ring as she takes a long draw off her drink, and I reach for her hand, steadying it so I can stare at the ring.

"That's gorgeous!"

"It was his mother's. I loved her so much."

"Were you close?"

"Before she died. Yes. She took me in when I was a teenager after my brother died. Grant was my guardian, but he had his own demons at the time."

"Wait. Grant was your guardian?"

"Not for long, but technically yes. I didn't have any family, and he was my brother's best friend. He made him promise. I don't think he would have volunteered for the task. I've always been a pain in his ass."

My eyebrows make their way north.

"He didn't touch me for ten years after that, so don't do the judgy-eyebrow thing."

"It's not judgment, just curiosity."

"I get it." She takes the last of her drink and then looks at me. "Have you slept with Levi yet?"

"What?" I practically choke on my own drink. "No."

"That's too bad. He needs to get laid. I swear he's so uptight he's going to snap one day from the stress of it."

"I think he might need to find someone who isn't a nun."

"So you've never thought about it? I mean, Grant's taken, I know, so you'll have to settle for the lesser version. But still. He's pretty, right? With the glasses and the serious-stare thing he does when he's deep in thought? The girls at the bar always liked it."

"He's pretty. Yes." I could admit that much, couldn't I?

"So why not?"

"The part where I'm a nun, and he's uptight?"

"It's not like the other nuns are going to find out. Purgatory Falls can be your small-town Vegas. What happens here can stay here."

"Even if I were tempted..." I trail off, staring down into my glass. It's not an if, it's a when, and these days it's pretty much every hour of every day since we're stuck in each other's constant presence. The smell of his cologne. The way his brow furrows when he concentrates. The way he makes me coffee with extra cream and sugar in the morning.

"Even if?" Dakota looks at me with the question as my brain stalls out in a Levi-induced spiral.

"He wouldn't. I'm the enemy's daughter. I'm everything he hates. He doesn't even trust me to be alone." I point to the space between us. "He thinks I need a babysitter."

"He trusts me to look out for you when he's not around. That's because he cares. If he didn't, he'd have left you up in that cabin again. His guys wouldn't fuck that up twice." Dakota pours us another round of drinks along with two glasses of ice water. "And you being off-limits is part of the appeal. Men want what they can't have. They like being tortured like that. They just hate to admit it." Her lashes lift to reveal a devious smile. "So all you have to do is let him know it's safe for him to admit it."

I sigh. "I wish it were that simple. He already knows I have a thing for him, and he doesn't care. He's too focused on my father and everything else to care about something as silly as a crush. And he's probably right. I'm silly for having one. Who crushes on the person holding them captive?"

"Oh, honey, I don't think anyone is blaming you for crushing on him. There's a whole list of women in this town who would pay for him to hold them hostage," she muses.

My stomach flips at the thought of other women in this town. When he was a priest there was no opportunity for other women. But now... The creep of jealousy winds its way up my spine. I'm not in a position to be envious. But I hate the idea of him with someone else the second the images start to appear unbidden in my mind. So I am, whether I like it or not.

"How did you even begin to get over the intimidation factor with them?" I ask abruptly. "I mean, I suppose you're not intimidated by them. You're so..." I wave my hand in her direction. "Everything I wished I could be when I was growing up."

A laugh tumbles out of her, and she shakes her head.

"Having a nun tell me she wishes she could be more like me is probably the best compliment I've ever gotten in my life."

"Well, it's true."

"You just fake it until you've actually got it. Confidence takes time. Especially with them. They're like angry bulls, stomping around, snorting, and demanding things all the time. You just have to hold your own. Show them you're not scared of them."

"Show him I'm not scared. Noted. Easier said than done."

"And if you want him, you'll have to make the first move. He won't press his way over a line he thinks you've put in the sand, but if you give him permission..." She tilts her head like she's remembering something, and it must be a fond memory given the way her face warms.

"The first move," I repeat, and she nods, clinking her glass against mine in a mock toast.

"Just try it. I promise you won't regret it. And if you do, you can just blame me." She shrugs, grinning as she tops off my glass, and we take another long sip together.

SIXTEEN

Levi

"SO, DO WE HAVE A PLAN?" Grant asks, leaning back in his seat at the head of the table.

"Yes, how is our vicious little nun? Hopefully, no more accidents." Rowan's eyes search the meeting table and land on me with a wicked smile. He's worse than my brother is about this situation.

"No more accidents. I've been transparent with her. She wants the same things as we do, more or less."

"No love lost with her father?" Grant raises a brow in surprise.

"No. She's got a list of reasons she can't stand him, not least of which is that he forced her into a bad marriage and stole her inheritance."

"Inheritance? That didn't run through him?"

"She's the mistress's daughter. The inheritance was from the maternal grandfather. A large sum, it sounds like, and he was an antique dealer."

"A dealer? Do you have a name? Charlotte can start looking into it, and I can see if anyone I know worked with him when he was alive," Rowan chimes in.

"I'll have to ask her." I clear my throat, realizing how simple a detail that is. It's the kind of thing I'd never miss, and Rowan and Grant exchange glances. I've been too caught up in her story, feeling sympathy for the way she was treated rather than focusing on the job. It gnaws at me.

"As soon as you can, please." Grant gives me a look that forgoes the lecture I should be getting, but it hits just the same.

"Of course."

"And the husband?" Grant puts us back on track.

"The bait's here, and the trap is set. We're just waiting for him to make his move. All the extra security should help."

"You don't think he'll reach out and try to set up a meeting? Ask if he can offer a ransom?" Rowan asks.

"I doubt it. I thought we were past the ransom idea." I'm terser than I should be.

"Hudson wants it on the table. He thinks it could still be an avenue to returning the relics to us, slowing the governor down."

"She says he won't pay up."

"You talked to her about it?" Rowan sits up straighter.

"I want to remind you all that you put me in charge of her and told me to run it my way. That's what I've done."

"But if you're wrong about her, we're fucked. She'll feed all this to them."

"She has no one to feed it to and no way to communicate it. She was at the convent as a runaway to escape his abuse. *Their* abuse. She's not going to help them."

"So you say." Rowan is always the skeptic. "Unless she's faking it."

"I know her well enough. This isn't just from spending time with her. This is from all the legwork and all the time I spent watching her when she didn't know I was."

"I don't like it. We should be treating her like a prisoner, and you have her running around with his fiancée, getting clothes. You're having heart-to-hearts about her past. It's distracting and useless." Rowan's lip arches like it's poised for a sneer, his eyes darting between us.

"I don't think it's useless," Grant interjects on my behalf. "We asked him to make a connection with her, and that's what he's done. Dakota might be able to get information he can't."

"Charlotte told him to seduce her and get what we needed out of her. Not play house with her up in the woods. His head is clouded, and you can't see it because you're too close to him," Rowan warns.

"We're not playing house."

"She shouldn't be walking free. She could walk straight out the door. Fuck, there's no could about it. She did."

"I had her tagged like fucking cattle. She didn't get far, and I'll remind you we've got the sheriff in our pocket." I point out the obvious because we discovered my uncle, the sheriff, was a former coconspirator of her father's. He's since come around to seeing things our way after we applied a little well-meaning pressure.

"Who does the governor have in his pocket? I'd imagine if he were a smart man, more than just the sheriff. All it takes is one spy on your team, and it all falls apart," Rowan argues.

"All of our guys are thoroughly vetted." Grant holds the floor. "I don't like the insinuation they're not.

"Until they lose too much money in your casino or get their

dick wet with the wrong girl, and then they're compromised." Rowan shakes his head.

"Let us handle security here." Grant shoots me a look when I go to argue again. The mood's deteriorating quickly, and it won't help us make progress.

"If you lose that girl, and she runs home to Daddy, he'll welcome her with open arms just to get information about us. I hope you remember that during your pillow chats." Rowan gives me a pointed look.

"Noted." I bite my tongue.

"Let's not let our concerns about this operation going well get the better of us. All right?" Grant looks between us.

I don't actually dislike Rowan. He's smart, cunning, and I have a fuckton of respect for his ability to get a job done. But we have our own approaches to situations like this, and the more that's at stake, the more tensions rise. Grant and Hudson provide the cooler voices.

"I just want this finished. Quickly. Efficiently." Rowan shakes his head.

"That's what we all want." I give Rowan a look, and he rolls his eyes, but I know he sees reason when he's forced to.

"Get me the grandfather's name. Let's hope the husband takes the bait or reaches out sooner rather than later. If not, we need to come up with our own plan of attack." Rowan summarizes our next steps, and we nod along.

We wrap up the rest of our meeting, and then I go in search of Zephyrine. Grant suggested leaving her with Dakota while we discussed details and they figured out clothes and shoes for her. I'm hoping that an afternoon alone with my brother's fiancée hasn't left me with a completely corrupted former nun, but there's always a chance when Dakota's involved.

"LEVI? Can I talk to you before you leave?" Dakota calls after me.

"Sure." I walk back toward the door.

"I got her a little drunk. Sorry about that." She gives me a sheepish grin. My future sister-in-law and I didn't always see eye to eye, but she means well.

"She probably needs a little fun after being stuck with me for so long, but if she retches and I have to clean it up..." I look at Dakota sideways.

"Just make sure she gets plenty of water and something to eat. I don't want her getting a hangover."

"Got it." I start to turn away, thinking that's the warning she wanted to give me, but she grabs the edge of my shirt to stop me.

"It got her to talk a little more." She lowers her voice to just above a whisper. "Open up to me and tell me a little about where her head's at."

"What did she say?" I fold my arms over my chest, worried Dakota might have turned their fun little girls' night into an interrogation.

"Not a lot, or at least not nearly as much as I hoped she would. Just girl talk mostly, you know? She's very reserved."

"She's a nun."

"Or maybe she was worried I'd tell you things. And you know I hate being a spy. I'm not cut out for this. She seems so sweet. I can't believe she's related to that piece of shit. I hope you're not ruining her with all this captivity stuff. I'd be a wreck if I were in her shoes, but she seems so stoic about it all." Dakota rambles on, tipsy herself from entertaining Zephyrine.

"She's fine, Dakota. She has it as good as anyone can have it in this situation. Her own bed. Home-cooked food. You to get her clothes. Air-conditioning in the cabin."

"But she's had a rough life, no?" Dakota frowns.

Dakota's life wasn't easy either, and her sympathy for others in a tough spot runs deep. She lost her whole family by the time she was seventeen. Her bar and apartment were the only things she had left of her past. Then the governor's plans made sure those were destroyed too. So if anyone can relate to the pain of being on your own the way Zephyrine is, it's Dakota.

"She has."

"Aren't we assholes for this then? To use her? Grant would have murdered someone for doing this to me."

"Someone might murder us for it too. We nearly all died for this. For her father's whims. I don't feel like an asshole for wanting to get to the bottom of it and free us from her father's focus for good. I'm not doing anything to hurt her."

"I guess," she reluctantly agrees.

"You wanted me to go after her, remember?"

"That was before I knew her, and when I was fresh off being angry about the bar. I don't want to hurt more people just because I'm hurting. We have to be better than that."

"We are better than that. If this goes the way I intend for it to, we'll be giving her hope she hasn't had before." It's what I keep telling myself.

"If you say so." Dakota gives me a slightly skeptical look, but it fades as she sees the reality for what it is. We don't have a choice, and this is the best chance we have.

"All right. I'm off then." I turn again, and she stops me. I sigh and glance up at her under my glasses. She frowns at my impatience.

"One last thing." She looks out at the truck where Zephyrine's waiting for me.

"What's that?" I glance back at her, lowering my cowboy hat over my eyes as the sun starts to peek out from behind the clouds.

"She's soft on you. In a not-very-nunly sort of way. Are you aware of that?" Dakota gives me a stern once-over.

"Wasn't that what you and Charlotte wanted? I seem to distinctly remember you encouraging me to seduce her."

"Yes, but you'll be good to her, right? You're not going to rip her poor heart out, are you? She doesn't deserve that. She's been through enough."

"Her heart isn't involved. She doesn't trust me enough for that. She's just lonely, and her dependence on me right now is probably confusing her feelings. But no, I don't intend to hurt her. I'm not an asshole all the time, you know? Just when it's necessary," I grumble.

I'm not about to admit to Dakota that I have some semblance of feelings myself. I haven't even figured out what they are yet, or if they're even real, or some of my own confusion over being so close to her for so long. But Dakota would run to tell Grant, and he'd be sounding the alarm bells and wanting someone else to stay with her at the cabin.

In their view, wanting to fuck her is one thing. He and everyone else could get behind that. It was part of the plan. Actually wanting to see her smile is another thing entirely. The kind of thing that will make them question whether my head is in the right place.

I already know it is, and more importantly, I know Zephyrine needs someone who will look out for her in all of this. I'm the right person for that job, regardless of what the consequences might be for my sanity.

"Well, in that case, maybe do the girl a solid and make her feel a little wanted back? It won't kill you. She's beautiful and so sweet. I'm sure you could endure the hardship," Dakota lectures me. Days like today I see why she and Grant are so well matched.

She's right. It wouldn't be a hardship at all. It would be

letting my interest turn into an obsession, though, and that's an entirely different set of challenges. Especially in these circumstances.

"You sound like my brother now." I turn and head down the steps, determined to end this conversation before she starts giving me tips on how I might make her feel wanted.

"Might do you some good too, considering how uptight you are!" she calls after me as I head for my truck.

I'm sure it would. Too much good. I look up as I approach the car, seeing Zephyrine sitting there in a pretty little sundress Dakota must have gotten for her. We need to figure out where to get her more nun clothes. Wool skirts and high-collared blouses with those oversized cardigans she likes to wear. Not fucking sundresses that make me wonder how things might have gone if we'd met under different circumstances.

SEVENTEEN

Z ephyrine

THE ALCOHOL BUZZING through my veins and the kind gesture from Levi have me feeling brave as we make our way back into the cabin. Dakota's advice is running through my head, making me want to test her theory. Nothing risked, nothing gained after all.

"If I run off into the woods again, would you chase me or send one of your guys?" I tease him.

"If you run off into the woods, it'll be the last time."

"Is that a threat?"

"A promise because you've clearly had one too many drinks, and you'll end up snapping your ankle."

"You're a buzzkill."

"I'll work on it." He gives me a side-eye, but I see the way his lips twitch with amusement.

"You should. Dakota said that's how you are all the time. All work and no play. Is that true? It would explain how you could do the priest thing so well."

"I'm focused. Yes." His tone tells me he's wary of where this is headed.

"She said you don't play ever."

"Dakota doesn't know anything about my personal life."

"But you don't have a wife or a girlfriend?"

"Do you think I'd be out here playing house if I had a warm bed with a wife in it?" He raises a brow.

"I don't know. My husband did." I shrug as he ushers me into the cabin.

"Your husband is a piece of shit. If I ever had a wife, she'd be the type who would slit my throat over something like that." His hand goes to his abdomen on the way in. It's my turn to raise a brow, but then I could see him with a wife like that. One who has the same penchant for violence and zero tolerance for any lack of loyalty.

"Are you okay?" I ask, noticing the grimace he makes.

"The bandage is just pulling a bit. I've got new gauze pads inside. I'm fine."

"So if your wife would slit your throat, does that mean you like me? I can never tell if I irritate or amuse you. But I feel like that means you like me." I flash him a grin, one that's probably ill-advised and fueled by the alcohol.

"That's what you get out of that?" He flashes me a look as he pulls out the first aid kit and the fresh box of gauze. He spreads the pads and tape out on the table alongside each other and gets to work.

"I mean, if it makes your wife violently jealous for you to be with me." I grin even though I feel awkward when I see the look on his face. I'm terrible at this.

"Except, I don't have a wife. And I'm not with you. I'm

watching you so you don't run off into the woods and break a fucking ankle in the process." He cocks a brow at me as he washes his hands, something like wariness behind his eyes.

"Here, I can help with that." I nod to his first aid kit and put my hands under the water. He passes me the bar of soap, our bodies practically touching as we lean over the old farm sink. I can feel the heat of him and hear his breathing, the hesitant way he's watching me. The air around us feels like tinder, and I take a step closer to him as I set the soap back on his side of the sink.

"I think you've done enough," he grumbles.

"I really am sorry. I thought you were one of Corey's guys, you know?" I give him what I hope is a remorseful look, even through the fog of my buzz. Whatever Dakota gave me was strong. I'd almost say she went a little heavy-handed on purpose if I didn't know better. But then... Maybe I don't know better.

"I know." His eyes search mine for a moment, and then he abruptly separates himself from me, grabbing a towel and drying his hands as he walks back to the table.

"Are you ever going to forgive me?" I dry my own and shut the water off, trailing behind him to the table.

"Maybe when it heals." It sounds honest enough, but I hate that it's going to be a reminder to him.

He preps the new gauze and tape, cutting the strips and opening the edge of the gauze package so it's ready. I kneel down in front of him and pull up his shirt carefully, exposing the old gauze and running my fingertips over the edge of the tape.

"What are you doing?"

"Helping," I answer, like it should be obvious to him, as I start to pull on the tape. He winces and glares at me, his hand covering mine.

"Not like that you aren't."

"What?"

"Just rip it, in one quick motion. Taking it inch by inch like that... You trying to torture me again?"

"I mean... you seemed to like it the first time, given the way you—" I stop abruptly and risk a glance up at him as I grab the tape and get ready to pull. He watches me, a glint of caution in his eyes, but doesn't say a word. I take the silence as permission to press the issue. "Do you like that? Pain, I mean? Or was it being tied up?"

"What happened to helping me with this?" he deflects.

So I rip the tape in one fast, smooth motion that tears it from his skin. There's a sharp intake of breath, and his fingers tease the edge of the wound—back and forth—smoothing the spot where the tape ripped some of the fine body hair on his abdomen out by the root. I run my fingers along the other side, following a parallel path to try to soothe the tape burn.

"Tell me how I can help," I say softly, slowly lifting my lashes to meet his.

He looks guarded as his eyes trail over me. Like an injured animal that doesn't know whether to trust me or snap at me before I have a chance to hurt it again. I can't say as I blame him, but the raw vulnerability disappears just as quickly as it came.

He stands abruptly, nearly knocking me over, and puts the second round of gauze on. He tapes it efficiently, one strip after another, while I pull myself up from my spot on the floor. My head is spinning from how quickly he's moving.

"Levi," I say his name softly and let my fingers trail over his exposed stomach as his shirt starts to fall back into place. He ignores me, cleaning up the mess on the table and repacking the first aid kit into its container.

He acts indifferent most of the time, but then there are rare moments, like this one, where it feels like he cares. Like he might see something in me, and I just want them to last longer than a fleeting minute. I can feel the tension between us, like the crackle of thunder in the distance right before a storm rolls in. I just need to get him to break it, lean into it, and give me some semblance of emotion beyond his practiced demeanor.

"We need wood," he announces, tossing the first aid kit back into the cabinet and putting distance between us. "I'm going to go chop some down for the stove. Think you can refrain from running off if I don't chain you to something?" He doesn't even bother to look back at me.

"I won't run off but..." I trail off. But what? I don't have anything I can really say. He's rejecting me. He's just being kind enough not to say the words out loud. The embarrassment threatens to sear my skin with a deep blush, so I'm reaching for anything that covers up my misstep. "Do you want help? Chopping the wood, I mean. I just want to be useful around here. I don't do well just sitting around."

"I don't need help. You can tidy things up in here. Make sure we have everything for dinner," he calls over his shoulder as he heads out the door, letting it creak shut behind him.

I press my hand to my tumbling, nerve-riddled stomach as I look around for something to do. Anything to distract me from my mistake. I can't believe I even hinted in that direction. I have no idea how many blatantly obvious rejections from him it's going to take to get it through my head. But the problem is when I think of him, I don't replay the embarrassment of having confessed my dreams to him or the way he looks at me like I'm a flimsy piece of cardboard that might fall apart in the rain.

No, instead my brain replays the way he felt underneath me at the convent, the singe of his lips on mine, the way his hands felt when he undressed me before my shower, and the way he looks at me when he thinks I don't notice—like some part of me might be remarkable. But I have to realize that I'm blindly reaching for a connection to someone where there are only figments of my imagination in his place. I set to work on cleaning up the cabin, forcing myself into manual labor to forget the whole ill-advised attempt.

WHEN I WAKE UP, it's the middle of the night. The cabin is pitch-black as I tiptoe across the wood floors barefoot, hoping I don't wake Levi up. I need a glass of water and something for my head. I had one too many to drink tonight. As fun as it was, I don't want a hangover. I'm hoping I can find both in the kitchen, but it means not disturbing him on the couch in the living room, which isn't all that far away in this small cabin.

I curse silently as the doorknob creaks when I open it, and the hinges refuse to be quiet as I ease the door open. I pause for a long moment, waiting to see if it wakes him. I don't want him thinking I'm sneaking out. I've only just gotten my freedom to roam back, and I'd hate to make him think he can't trust me. When I don't hear him move or call my name, I slip out of the room.

I can see the outline of his body on the couch, his head back against a pile of pillows, and his feet resting on the arm on the other end, his cowboy boots tucked just in front of the coffee table between them. It doesn't look comfortable. Tomorrow, I might see if he wants to come to bed. We could make it work—a pillow fort or something that provides space between us.

Dakota would probably scold me for suggesting we need space. She was clear that she thought I should go for him if I want him. But my drunken attempt at feeling him out on the topic had gone so poorly I almost think we've gone backward.

He'd spent most of the evening in silence, barely speaking to me at dinner and only grunting out a goodnight when I went to bed.

I look back at him as I grab a glass out of the cabinet and the pitcher out of the fridge. He's too self-controlled to take those kinds of risks. Risking his life, yes. Sleeping with the enemy's daughter, not interested. I frankly wonder if the man ever does anything but work. It seemed like an exaggeration at first, but I'm not so sure now. His life seems devoid of all fun. Like having some might be a sin. Maybe he would have been a good priest after all.

I open the next cabinet and find what looks like a bottle of pain relievers. I check the date and kiss the top as I pour one out. I'm guessing Levi might have had them for the pain from his burn. I wince. Just another reason not to want me.

I toss the pill back and take a large gulp of water, refilling the glass from the pitcher before I put it away. I steal a piece of chocolate out of the dish on the counter and then tiptoe back to the bedroom again, careful to walk slowly and avoid the squeakiest floorboards.

I glance over at him as I move to sneak past and freeze when I realize he's not really asleep. He's got one hand slung over his eyes, the other palm down over his stomach, but now that I'm closer, I can see the white outline of an earbud in his ear. In the dead quiet of the night, I can also faintly hear what's playing. Something I can't quite discern until I hold my breath to listen. I bite my lower lip when I realize what the sound is floating across the room: a woman moaning.

I watch as the hand on his stomach moves further south, palming himself through his pants. I take another short couple of steps, trying for a better angle and praying the floor doesn't squeak underneath my feet. I freeze when it does, but he doesn't move. At least not in response to me. He's too focused on what he's listening to, and a low rumble rolls out of his chest as he shifts his hips. His hand ghosts over the waistband of his pants like he's trying to decide whether to give in or not.

I have to know what he's listening to. It must be porn of some sort. I'm curious to know what kind. I take another couple of steps closer, and I spot his phone on the coffee table. It's dimly lit, but he has a playlist pulled up. I can't quite see it, though, when it's this faded by the screen. I squint, leaning over, careful not to spill my water.

"What are you doing?" His deep voice shatters the silence like glass, and I nearly drop mine when I jump back.

"What are you doing?" I press my palm to my chest to try to coax my heart back to a normal rhythm as he sits up. He snatches his phone off the coffee table, and it lights up brighter when he does. Just enough that I can read the words "Z's Late-Night Playlist" before he turns it off and rips one of the earbuds.

"Don't answer a question with a question." There's irritation rife in his tone. "What are you doing?"

"I got up to get a glass of water. I was trying to be quiet as I was headed back to bed, and then I heard your playlist. What are *you* doing?" I ask in return.

"Trying to sleep. Go back to bed," he orders.

For a moment, I consider it. He seems grumpy, like someone who's just been woken from a deep sleep, but there's something about the way his body shifts as he talks to me. How fast he snatched his phone up from the table. Like he's hiding something and hoping I don't notice, which only confirms I didn't misread the situation.

"Sure. As soon as you tell me why you're listening to porn in the middle of the night." I cross my arms over my chest, still careful not to spill the water.

EIGHTEEN

L^{evi}

"TO HELP ME SLEEP," I answer her bluntly as I tuck my phone nervously into my shirt pocket.

She's caught me dead to fucking rights listening to some of my favorite late-night audio. I have no idea how long she was watching me or what she saw or heard, so unless I want to lose her trust again by lying, I have to give her at least half the truth.

"Porn helps you sleep?" I can hear the skepticism piled on thick in her question.

"I don't sleep well. Or much. Ever. Sometimes it helps."

"It didn't look like you were sleeping."

"I didn't know I was being watched." I respond to her faster and grumpier than I should. It's not helping my case.

"Well, now you know what it feels like." Her arms tighten the knot they're making over her chest at my irritability. If she knew what I was listening to—who I was listening to—she'd probably like it even less.

"Did I wake you up?" I try to change the subject.

"No. I needed water and some painkillers. Don't try to distract me." She frowns and then presses on. "What kind of porn are you listening to that helps you sleep?"

"Does it matter?"

"It must be interesting then if you don't want to tell me." A wry little smile grows on her lips.

"Just go back to bed, Zephyrine." I should have remembered she can wander around now. I'm the one who let her. I just wasn't adequately prepared for it personally, treating this space out here like it's my bedroom instead of a living space.

"If you're into something kinky, I'm not going to judge you. I mean, like you said, you saw everything I was looking up." She tries to reassure me.

The last thing I need is to think about her kinks.

"Bed."

"Let me listen."

"Bed," I repeat.

"I know it said Z's Playlist."

I scrub my hand over my face and grab my glasses off the table so I can get a better look at her in the dark.

"So?"

"So was it stuff you found from me? Or something else?"

"Something else."

"Then why does it say Z's Playlist?"

"Have you considered I know someone else named Z, or that there's an adult star I like named Z?"

"Is that the case?" she presses, and I'm stuck between a rock and a hard place like usual with her.

She doesn't let things go, and she's too much like me when it comes to wanting the cold, hard truth. I can't lie to her. If I do and she finds out, and let's be honest, women like her always find out, she'll never trust me again. We swore no more lies.

"No."

"So they're my videos from my phone? You still have them?"

"Do you want them? That can be arranged." I try to distract her again.

"So, yes, you're watching videos from my phone, or no?" She's relentless now.

"No, they're not videos from your phone."

"Do you want to keep playing twenty questions, or do you want to tell me?" Impatience seeps through her tone.

"They're you. Fuck! They're you, okay?" I finally cede ground and steel myself for whatever reaction she's about to have.

"Me?" She goes stark still.

"They're recordings of you. Ones I made when you were at the convent, and I was surveilling you."

"They sounded like porn."

"Some of them are, sort of."

"Why are you listening to recordings of me that sound like porn in the middle of the night?"

"I told you. To help me sleep. I have trouble sleeping, and I got used to it at the convent." It's mostly true. Tonight, I just really wanted to hear her. "It's a habit." A desperate one, an embarrassing one now that she knows about it.

"I want to hear it." She sits down next to me and holds out her hand. I stare at her open palm for a long beat, trying to decide whether there's a way out of this. "I'm serious. Where you left off too. Not some random point you pick." She pushes her palm closer to me.

I let out a ragged sigh and drop one of the earbuds into her hand. I keep the other one in my left ear, and I pull out my phone. I've done a hell of a lot of things in my life. Dodged a lot of interrogations and charges. This little nun is about to take me down with the most incriminating evidence I've ever been caught red-handed with. She pops the earbud in her ear and looks at me expectantly as I unlock my screen and stare at the play button. When I take too long, she presses it for me.

I close my eyes at the sound of skin on sheets and the soft moan she makes through the remaining earbud.

"Oh," she cries softly through the speaker. "Mmmm." I can hear the muted sound of her licking her lips. There's another rustle of fabric, like she's pulling her pillow closer. A muffled moan comes through, and Zephyrine, the corporeal version in the here and now, hits the pause button on my phone.

I open my eyes and do my best not to look like I've been caught with my fucking pants down. I'd at least managed to keep my dignity there.

"You send me to bed, and then you listen to me getting off?"

I give her half a nod and sit back against the cushions of the couch. I'm ready for whatever lecture I'm going to get about how inappropriate I am. How fucked up this is. How I've broken her trust by having these.

"When did you record this?"

"I don't know exactly. I'd have to look it up on the file. A couple of weeks in. Does it matter?"

"I was just trying to figure out if I'd been thinking about you or not."

I cough or choke. I don't know which exactly, but her bluntness catches me wholly off guard, and I have to stop to catch my breath.

"What? Wouldn't you like it better if I were?" She gives me a look of mock concern that's highlighted by the moonlight streaming in. I'd never considered the possibility it was anyone else—especially after her confession.

"In my head, you're always doing it for me, sweetheart. If I thought it was another man, I'd kill him and make sure it was. Hypothetically speaking."

She stares at me through the dim light for a long moment before she speaks again.

"How does this help you sleep?"

"It lets me get my mind off everything else. Relax a little. I don't always sleep. Not a deep sleep anyway, but that twilight phase that at least gets me feeling a little rested until I can down some black coffee in the morning."

"I had insomnia for a while too. It's awful."

"It is," I agree.

She hits play again, and the recording ends, turning over to a new one. There's another soft intake of breath, and a muffled moan echoes through my eardrum, but this one is different. It's one I forgot I made. An accident I should have deleted considering it's about to bite me in the ass.

"Fuck you sound so pretty when you moan," I groan through the recording.

If I were capable of blushing like her, I would be. I slam the pause button, and she scowls at me, hitting play again. I recoil when I hear my voice come through again.

"I love listening to you touch yourself late at night like this. It's the best part of the job. I can only imagine how wet you get. How desperate you are to be touched. The way it bleeds through in the sound of your breathing and the soft gasps you make." I sound fucking obsessed with her.

I hit the pause button again.

"I think we can skip this one. It's just me making voice notes to myself while I was working."

"Absolutely fucking not." She presses play.

"That's it, little nun. Keep going." I encourage the past version of her as I listen to her touch herself. The sound of a zipper being drawn down comes through the line. It's very clearly mine. "Oh fuck, I need this." I groan low and heavy into the mic. There's a long exhale and the obvious sound of me palming my cock in the background of my heavy breathing.

I slam the pause button one last time and snatch the phone up off the table. I'd completely forgotten that this one has my running commentary.

"Don't! Please?" Zephyrine's hand goes to my wrist as I shove the phone into my pocket.

"Why do you want to listen to that?" Maybe she has a thing for humiliating men. I don't know. I imagine you might develop a taste for it after being married to a man like Corey, but I can do without her experimenting on me.

"Because it's the hottest thing I've ever heard in my life."

I make a dismissive sound at the back of my throat, and she squeezes my wrist.

"I'm serious."

"I think it's time you go back to bed, Zephyrine."

"Don't do that."

"Do what?"

"Send me off."

"It's late, and you're probably still drunk."

"What if I do it for you now?" She whispers the question, and the temptation winds its way around my spine.

"Do what?" I feign ignorance, buying myself time to try to talk myself out of this. All the while, the baser parts of me cheer her on.

"Touch myself." She swallows and takes a breath, her fingertips brushing a half circle on the inside of my wrist. "Would you talk to me like that? I want to know what it's like for a man to talk to me like that. For *you* to talk to me like that."

Fucking hell.

"Zephyrine." I say her name like a warning. I have an iron fucking will, but this is too much even for me.

"It could help you sleep, couldn't it? It always helps me sleep." She presses on.

"You've still got alcohol in your system on top of all the other reasons we shouldn't." It's my last desperate plea to talk her back from this ledge before I jump with her.

"I won't touch you. You won't touch me. It's dark. It's not that different from listening to the recordings, right?" She offers a convincing argument.

"And in the morning, when you can't look at me?"

"In the morning, this was all just a dream. I'll say an extra rosary if you want me to."

Who could say no to this woman? I don't think I can. Not under these conditions. Not tonight anyway.

I scrub a hand over my mouth as I contemplate what kind of fate this will earn me. What's it going to cost me to corrupt a nun like this? A hundred? A thousand times as much? I'm already going to hell.

"Fuck it."

NINETEEN

Zephyrine

"IF YOU WANT to listen to me, you're going to actually listen to me. You'll do what I say, when I say. Understood?"

"Yes." I'd agree to just about anything right now, if I'm being honest. I just want to hear him talk to me like that again. Listening to Levi on audio felt like pure adrenaline running straight through my heart, making it beat again, making my stomach tumble with excitement and my cheeks warm, and that's before we get to the way it lit up every single nerve ending in my body. Ones I barely remember exist most of the time.

"Fuck." He lets the curse rip through the darkness, and he sits up straighter, leaning back in the corner of the couch until he's facing me. His eyes study me through the dark, and I can feel my skin heat under his gaze. He presses his glasses up his nose and clears his throat.

"Lie back against the cushions on the arm there and get comfortable. Swing your feet up here." He pats the spot in front of his lap. I do as he asks, tentatively letting my feet drop in front of his knees as I lean back, wiggling my butt to get comfortable.

"Good?" he asks once I settle in.

"Good." I nod.

"Spread your legs," he orders. Apparently, when he's in, he's all in.

It's so quiet, you could hear a pin drop. Every brush of my skin over the cushion fabric sounds like it's amplified through speakers, but I follow his instructions. I let my right leg fall back into the cushion of the couch and my left drop to the side until I'm spread in front of him.

His eyes fall over me slowly, my face and my body first, then my legs and my ankles and toes, before traveling back up again, but this time, his gaze falls heavy between my thighs.

"Are those fucking lace?" The shirt I'm wearing—his shirt—is riding up on my thighs and giving him a glimpse of what's underneath. He scowls at the underwear I have on.

"Dakota got them for me."

"Of course she did," he gripes.

I should defend her, but all I can think right now is how beautiful he is and how much I love the sound of his voice. He's already filling all my thoughts and senses every second of the day when we're trapped together in this little cabin, tempting me with every quirk of his lips and each sexy little frown. The smell of his cologne is everywhere I go, and the way he pushes his glasses up while he's reading distracts me every single time.

"Pull my shirt up. I want to see all of them." I clutch the hem of the shirt and pull it the rest of the way up, until it bunches around my waist. For all my complaints about being stuck wearing his clothes, I've grown attached to sleeping in them.

I glance down, and I see now why he wanted me in this position. The moonlight from the windowpane pours in, highlighting my pale skin and the black lace panties in a neat little square around my hips and upper thighs. I suck my lower lip in between my teeth when I realize how obvious it is that I'm already fantasizing about him.

"This wet already?"

"Hearing you talk like that... I can't help it," I admit softly.

"Touch yourself."

My nerves come front and center then. Doing this in front of him in complete silence feels awkward.

"Can you hit play again?" I've still got the earbud in my right ear. "It'll make me less self-conscious," I explain when he gives me a skeptical look.

He nods then, pulling his phone out and hitting the play button. His low groan rumbles through my eardrum, and I hear the sound of his hand working over his cock. My cheeks flood with heat as he stares back at me, both of us listening to him through the speakers.

"Touch yourself." The live version of him reminds me of my role in all this. I run my fingers back over the top of my waistband, teasing the skin there until goose bumps start to form in their wake, and then I slide them under, closing my eyes to focus on his voice. If he can get off listening to me, I can do the same. It's only fair.

I part my index and middle fingers as I move past my clit, brushing it just enough to feel the spark light. I gasp and bite my lower lip when I feel how drenched I am, letting out a soft moan as I start to slip the pads of my fingers back and forth through my wetness.

It's loud, the sound of it piercing the night, and his eyes are glued to where my hand moves under the material as I listen to him moan through the recording in my ear.

"Fucking hell, Zeph," the real one curses, palming his cock through his jeans.

I tease my clit softly. I'm so sensitive I don't dare keep the pressure up for more than a second at a time. It has to last. I need to come hard but I want it to be with him. I have to take a deep breath to try not to let myself fall apart too soon.

It's like the audio version of him knows because he starts talking again.

"This part here, where you let out these stuttered little breaths. I can tell you're working yourself up to the edge, barely able to fucking take it, and then you stop. That frustrated little sigh where you tease yourself and then hold it at bay. Do you like being edged, darlin'?" He groans again, and I hear him slow his pace down as well. It's some sort of unholy trinity, the three of us together like this—the recorded version of him and the real one, with me pinned down in between them.

"Do you?" Levi repeats his counterpart's question.

"Yes." The word comes out on half a moan as my fingertips brush over my clit again, and the recorded version of him moans in unison.

Listening to him sparks every last nerve in my body. I let my head fall back as I start to work myself closer to the edge. The recorded version of Levi takes over all my senses as I hear the sound of skin on skin as he works himself over. He breathes heavily, and I imagine he's on top of me, his breath at my throat. I can hear the distant sound of my own muted moans in the background of his. We sound filthy. I can't get enough.

"Oh fuck yes. Work that pretty little clit for me. You sound like a fucking angel when you come," the recorded Levi urges me on.

"Oh," I let out an audible gasp that echoes through the cabin.

"Stop," Levi, the one whose eyes are glued on me, demands sharply, and I pull my hand away, fisting it in the blanket he left discarded on this side of the couch. I take a deep breath and pinch my eyes closed for a moment as I try to block out the way my nerves are lighting up. The recording goes silent, and I look up at him in question.

"Fuck. Didn't think it was possible to be jealous of myself." He lets out a coarse laugh as he tosses his phone to the coffee table.

"I thought this was what you wanted," I whisper, unsure what I did wrong.

"I do," he reassures me. "But if I only get to experience this once, I want every last second to count."

"Oh," I murmur my understanding in the soft sound.

"Take your panties off and give them to me," he orders.

"Are you starting a collection or something?" I tease as I reach for the waistband.

"Something like that," he answers as he shoves his pants down off his hips.

I'm distracted from my own progress when his dick slips free from behind the fabric. He's big, and I can't help the grin that follows. It's exactly how I imagined him. I try biting down on my lip, but it's useless, and I turn my head down so he can't see. I can feel the heat bloom on my cheeks as he watches me. The silent thoughts I'm having, making me feel more vulnerable than anything else so far.

"What?" he asks, his tone genuinely curious and not at all cocky, which surprises me.

"Nothing."

"Oh no. We're not doing that," he warns me, his tone still warm despite it.

"You're just living up to the fantasy, is all," I confess, and I don't miss the sweet little grin that flashes over his face before it disappears. It makes my stomach flutter with a hint of hope.

"The panties." He holds his hand out, pretending he's unaffected.

I raise my hips and slide them down over my thighs and legs. He helps me when they reach my ankles, pulling them off gently past my toes as his fingers brush over my skin.

"Fuck," he curses as his fingers slip over the fabric. They're drenched, and I worry I should be embarrassed, but it's dismissed a moment later with a low groan as he wraps them around his dick. "Perfect. Goddamn. I've been dreaming about this," he mutters as his eyes fall closed. He slides them up and down, and I watch his skin start to glisten with my wetness.

"Oh, hell," I whisper out loud, and he cracks one eye open, sliding it over me.

"Put those fingers back to work. I want to hear you working yourself up again, Zephyrine." His eyes are heavy as he watches me. The way he says my name feels like kerosene on a fire, and I do as I'm told. I want him sated, happy. Completely so. Because maybe if he is, if I'm the source of it, maybe I can have more of this—more of him. Which is the only thing that I want right now.

His breathing gets heavier, and he ditches the panties for the palm of his hand, slicking it before he uses it to work himself from base to tip. I tease my clit, careful not to allow too much. I'm already swollen and sensitive from listening to the recording; the live version nearly does me in.

"Fucking hell," he curses.

TWENTY

L^{evi}

I'M GOING to hell for this. Watching this sweet little nun work herself to the edge, knowing I'm the voyeur, is going to be the death of me. She's perfect with my shirt around her hips, her cheeks flushed, and her pretty little pussy glistening as her fingers circle her clit. There's just enough darkness in the room to cover the worst of our sins and just enough quiet that I can hear every breath and moan she makes.

When she comes, it's going to kill me. I'll wake up at the gates of hell. I can feel it. It'll be worth it, though, for this, to finally have the real version in front of me so close to her own little death.

I've made her the center of every fucking fantasy I've had for weeks now. Every single time I wrap my hand around my cock, it's her in my head. Imagining grabbing that wool skirt and bunching it up around her thighs so I could fuck her with my fingers while she bent over my lap and sucked me dry in the church pew after her confession. Dragging her into the confessional so I could fuck her up against the wall. Tying her up and spreading her thighs on that dorm-style bed of hers at the convent until I've eaten my fill.

If I tried to count the ways I wanted to corrupt that perfect little body before I sent her to her knees for atonement, we'd be here for days. If she knew how depraved I am, she wouldn't be doing this for me.

I groan on the next pass. It rips out of my chest louder than I mean for it to, but it's been too fucking long since I let myself have something. I've been trying to stop since we came to the cabin, using the recordings as a kind of exposure therapy. Listening but not touching. I've been too focused on trying to walk a line with her, flirting but nothing more. Except the longer we're stuck together like this, the more I feel like there's an inevitable cliff we're both about to fall off.

I glance over at her, and her fingers are soaked as she slips them in and out, using the heel of her hand to gently tease her clit. Edging herself. She loves to draw things out, take her time. She'd watch one video and get so close to coming, she'd whimper like she was in pain when she stopped. She'd breathe deep, steadying breaths, and then she'd start again. Slower the next time if her muted little moans were any indication. I loved those nights. It felt like I got more time alone with her. Like she was drawing it out just for me.

"Talk to me," she whispers. "You're so quiet."

I swallow, my mouth dry and my tongue heavy as I imagine tasting her off her fingers like water in a desert.

"I'm just thinking about how long I've been wanting to watch you like this. You're so fucking sexy. I can't believe you're real." I worry telling her the truth will be too much for her, and I don't want to ruin this, but I wish there were a way for her to know how singularly perfect she is.

"Me too. I can't stop thinking about you. I wish I'd known you were thinking of me," she confesses, and it reminds me how much more of her I've had in comparison. I know so many of her secrets, her intricacies, and she's barely learning who I am outside of my lies. I owe her more than that.

"I've been thinking about you for weeks. I can't stop, not since that first night I was watching you through your phone. Listening to you when you climbed under the covers to touch yourself. The way you sound when you come—fuck!" I groan just thinking about it. My cock is so fucking swollen, leaking from the tip as I try to hold off the inevitable. I'm getting desperate. "Can you come for me, sweetheart? I want to hear you."

"Okay," she agrees easily. She lies back against the pillows again, spreading her legs a little wider for my benefit as her fingers slip through her wetness. The sound of it takes my fucking breath away, and I bite the inside of my cheek to keep myself quiet. I don't want to drown her out.

"It won't take much," she whispers. "I'm too close from listening to you."

"Damn straight." I flash her a prideful smile. Another sin for the pile because I'm practically gloating with the fact that this woman is going to come to the sound of me fucking my hand for her. I can only imagine how much harder she'd come riding me.

"Oh. Fuck. Oh." She lets out little stuttered curses as her fingers work a tighter and tighter circle around her swollen clit, teasing herself one last time. "Oh my fucking god! Oh my god." She cries out, gasping for breath, as she works the peak of her release right off the edge of the cliff.

I'm coming with her as I take a firmer grip on my cock,

working it faster and using my forefinger to give myself pressure underneath my head. I come hard, shattering on the edge of my orgasm and the sounds of her as she mutters soft little curses across from me. It feels so fucking perfect after so many nights of taking myself close without any release. Thinking of her without having her here.

I groan as I lean back against the arm of the couch, my eyes closed and my mind lost in a sea of infinite fucking perfection as the sounds of her start to fade softly, and her breathing begins to slow. I just want to pull her against me and kiss my way over her skin. Confess how much I want her even though I shouldn't, as if that isn't evident by the mess I've just made of myself. Of both of us, really.

"You're really fucking gorgeous, Zephyrine. I hope you know that. Everything about you. Not just your face or your body. Your mind. Your laugh. Your heart. Every little thing about you. You're literally what dreams are fucking made of." I say the words before I can stop myself. She deserves to hear them.

"I feel the same way about you," she answers. "I've never done things like this. Wanted someone so much like this."

Anyone else is a pale distant memory compared to the woman I have in front of me. The woman I don't deserve, no matter how much I might want her. The act is so tame in comparison to things I've done, but it's never felt this fucking raw and vulnerable. Never as honest as it is right now with her. I wonder if she really might be the death of me.

"I know," is all I manage to say. I take a deep breath and then I stand, righting my clothes and tucking myself back in. I'll clean up in a few minutes, but I want her neatly tucked in her bed before temptation can creep back in.

I lean over and scoop her up from the couch. She doesn't protest like I expect, wrapping her arms around my neck instead. I resist the thought that urges me to kiss her, reminding myself she's forbidden fruit in every possible fucking way I could imagine.

"Do you think you can sleep now?" she asks.

"I hope so." My body is exhausted, but my mind's already whirring with all the newfound implications of what we've done.

"Do you want to sleep in here, with me?" she asks as I lay her down on the rumpled sheets she abandoned a short while ago. What if she never got up tonight? We'd never know now.

"I can't." My voice is rough when I answer her.

"Sweet dreams." She doesn't argue, and I'm grateful for it.

"Sweet dreams," I agree. Ones so fucking sweet they've bled over into reality.

TWENTY-ONE

Zephyrine

"IF THERE WAS something I wanted to make, could I get some ingredients from somewhere?" I ask the next morning, as if nothing's different.

He lifts his eyes from his phone to meet mine, but not before they sweep over me in appreciation. We're pretending just like we promised one another. Last night was a dream and nothing more. It was a one-time thing to get it out of our systems. Breaking the tension in this cabin would cure us both. But every time he looks at me this morning, I can hear his voice again telling me what I do to him, the way I affect him, him saying how gorgeous I am.

"Not if arsenic is on the list," he teases me.

"Ha. Not arsenic, just strawberries and cream. Things like

that." I roll my eyes and shake my head at the accusation. "I thought we agreed we weren't killing each other."

"We agreed I wasn't killing you. You might still have something to gain from killing me. If you could make it out of the woods without breaking your ankle anyway."

"Well, I have no intention of poisoning you. Just normal ingredients. I promise."

"Yeah. Kit could probably manage it if we gave her some warning. There are some wild strawberries just outside in the woods. I picked a couple yesterday. But why do you want to make something?" He gives me a skeptical look. "I thought you'd at least enjoy the break from all the kitchen work at the convent."

I do enjoy the break, but I also want to do something nice for him. It feels like the least I can do. He's made me several meals, has my coffee ready every morning the way I like it, put up with my drunken antics, and then was nothing but kind to me last night. For being a disgruntled and reluctant kidnapper, the man has a thoughtful streak a mile wide.

"I just have a taste for something, and I thought I could make it for us." I shrug my shoulders, trying to act casual before he gets any more suspicious.

Saying the word "us" feels weird, like I'm implying there is an us after yesterday. Obviously, I know there isn't. There could never be. I'm going back to the convent once this is done, and he's going back to whatever it is he normally does.

Right now, though, I'm stuck here with him, and I'm tired of this thick, lingering fog between us that makes it hard to think straight. I want to shine light on it and sort it through. I thought yesterday would have killed whatever it was by getting it out of our systems, but today only feels like the tension is just under the surface again, slowly building little by little. Like one tiny spark of static electricity could set this whole cabin on fire.

"Well, I could use the air if you want to go hunt for some fresh strawberries. There's a colander in the cabinet." He nods to it before he takes the last swallow of his coffee. That makes two of us who need air.

"Are you sure? I didn't mean to interrupt." I feel a little awkward now as I'm dragging him away from whatever he was doing on his phone. But he shakes his head and tucks it into his pocket as the screen goes black.

"I'm sure." He puts the dishes in the sink as he answers and pulls the colander from the cabinet. He slides it across the counter to me and then nods for the door. "Lead the way, darlin'."

WE WANDER along a path in the woods together, and he points out different edible plants along the way until we reach a patch of wild strawberry plants he found yesterday.

"I have a feeling there's more back that way, but I didn't want to wander too far. I didn't have my gun with me, and you never know up here with the bears and mountain lions."

"Bears?" I stop short. It hadn't even crossed my mind, but now it seems so damn obvious.

"I haven't seen any, not even tracks. I'll keep an eye out. Don't worry. When I lived up here, there was a family of them that had a den not far from here. Mom got a little testy with the little ones around." He surveys the forest as I kneel down to get a closer look at the plants.

"Well, she's trying to protect them."

"I'm the one who needs protection. They were climbing on my porch and stealing my food out of the garden. Lawless little things." He shakes his head.

"You had a garden?" I grin at the idea of his garden being

raided by cubs and him having to shoo them out without tangling with an angry mama bear as I check the plant for any signs of a ripe berry.

"A small one. Just enough to keep some kitchen vegetables and a couple of herbs ready. I didn't have a green thumb or anything, so don't get excited."

"I'm not." I smile at him. "But it explains why you were willing to help in the gardens. We never had a priest volunteer like that. The older nuns used to grumble about how they didn't want to get their hands dirty. Now it makes more sense."

A grin flashes across his face, and he shakes his head at me.

"Here's another patch of them. Bring the colander over. How many do you need?" he asks as he crouches down to start picking and I take my turn watching for unwanted guests.

"A couple of pints would be ideal. But one would do in a pinch. I could make a half recipe. There'd still be plenty for two people."

"You're not going to offer the guys any? Their feelings will be hurt." Levi gives me a mock look of concern.

Two of his men have been camping out nearby in the woods, keeping a night watch when Levi sleeps. I'd be more worried for them and bear encounters except one of them had been my bear, hauling me back to Levi when he beckoned.

"Well, *mine* are still hurt from the way your one guy dragged me back to the cabin unceremoniously."

He laughs. "I suppose that's fair."

"Do these taste good? They're so small," I ask, holding one of the strawberries up to inspect it.

"Yeah. They're sweeter than the kind you get at the store. Smaller, but they pack a punch," he explains. "Here." He picks one and spits on it. "Just spit on it like that and wipe the dirt off. Then you can taste them."

I watch him with a raised brow, and his follows until he realizes where my mind is wandering to.

"You have a filthy mind for a nun."

"I blame you. I was perfectly fine until you came along."

"Your recipe folder would beg to differ." He side-eyes me, and my cheeks pink under his watch.

"Yes, well. I'm working on that vice."

"How are the rosaries coming along anyway? Do we need to add extra?" he teases me.

"After yesterday, you mean?" I decide to push my luck.

"About that..." His voice fades, and he shakes his head like he's trying to clear it and find the right words.

"I liked it." I pick another strawberry, trying to distract myself if he's going to give me a lecture for mentioning the unmentionable. "Obviously," I mumble before I spit on the little red berry and wipe the dirt away on the hem of my shirt, then I take a bite. The juice runs down over my lip, and I press my fingers to my lips to try to stop it. "Oh wow." He wasn't kidding about the sweetness. "These are amazing." I throw a hand up in the air and grin before I see his face. I realize then he still hasn't spoken, and I worry my lip between my teeth, licking the juice off it with the tip of my tongue.

His eyes land on my lips, heavy and focused like he's thinking about things other than strawberries. I stand nervously, and he follows, taking a step toward me, closing the distance between us. It feels like that night on the pier all over again. But this time, he reaches out for me, his hand slipping under my jaw and tilting my chin up. His thumb slides over my lower lip as he studies the stain of the strawberries on my skin.

"I liked it too." His voice has a low rasp to it that sends a wave of anticipation through my body.

He tilts his head, and his lips descend on mine, the softest brush of a kiss until I meet him with my own. He pulls me close then, one hand snaking around my waist and the other around the nape of my neck as he deepens it. It's still soft. He's still tasting me like he's deciding which part he wants more of before he takes. My hands go to his chest, bracing myself as warm ripples of want start to bleed through my senses. I don't know what we're doing. Breaking all our rules. But I want more of it. More of him.

He breaks the kiss. Giving us both a chance to catch our breath, and his blue-green eyes search mine—something I can't quite read in them. His lips part, words on the tip of his tongue.

Before he can speak, there's a shift in the air. Like our kiss broke the underpinnings of our blissful little adventure, and there's a low rumble of thunder in the distance. He glances up at the sky, and his face clouds.

"Do you hear that?" he asks abruptly, all the thick fog that's wound its way around us clearing the second I hear the sharpness in his tone.

"Yes. Thunder?" He'd warned me before about how fast the storms come in up here. But no sooner do I ask the question than I hear it more clearly. It's not thunder. It's a soft, distant, methodical hum. Like the beat of massive wings. Ones that are getting closer and closer.

He holds his hand out, urging me to stay where I am before he takes off on foot, moving to higher ground where he can see. There's enough of a break in the canopy at this angle for me to catch a glimpse. There, at the top of our mountain, is a helicopter. The door on one side is hanging open, and if my eyes aren't betraying me, I see guns and a half dozen men readying themselves to scale down the rope they've just thrown out the side.

My heart bottoms out into my stomach, and a surge of fear winds its way up my spine.

"Run." He says it softly at first when he makes his way back to me, still staring up over his shoulder at the black metal bird in the sky, but when he repeats himself as he turns to face me, it's a clear demand. "Run, Zephyrine!"

We both take off in a full sprint, running for the cabin. I manage to pace him despite my still-sore ankle. I'm terrified. I don't have to wait to find out who's inside the helicopter. I know. It'll mean the end of us both.

"Get to the cabin. There's a spot in the floor in the bedroom where the boards lift. You need to get under it." He yells the instructions as we both pace our way back up the mountainside. My lungs are straining for air. It's thinner up here, at least a mile and a half up, and going higher with every step we take. I adapted to it since we arrived, drinking lots of water and sleeping more than usual. But I wasn't prepared to have to run for my life.

"Where are you going?"

"I'm going to hold him off until my guys get here."

He pulls the walkie out from his belt loop and presses the button. I can't hear what he says over my own heavy breathing, but I know he's radioing his security team. I just have to hope the two of them are enough to help us.

I didn't count them, but the helicopter looked full, and my husband's too much of a coward to come alone. If we live through this, it'll be a miracle.

I'm not sure I believe in them anymore.

TWENTY-TWO

L evi

"HERE." I hand Zephyrine my walkie after I silence it. "Get under here and stay here. Be as silent as a church mouse. Don't come out for any reason. I don't care what you hear or think you hear. You don't come out until I tell you or there're hours of silence, you got it? If you need to call for someone, I've set it so those comms go to the entire security team. They're already on their way. Someone will come for you."

"Yes, okay. But what about you? There's room!" She looks absolutely petrified, and it only steels my nerves.

"No. I have to take care of this. I've got a plan. Don't worry." I do my best to reassure her. I trust my team. I trust the perimeter. I just have to go through with the plan we put in place. I kiss her forehead, but her worried look doesn't fade.

There's a loud warning shot in the distance, and then another round of open gunfire. It's enough to get me moving.

"Get down, and whatever you do, stay quiet," I urge her. I put the false floor back in place over the top of her, taking her in one last time while I work to keep her safe. Her blue eyes hold mine until the darkness covers them.

I kick the carpet back into place and grab my gun, tucking it into the back of my jeans. I skirt the perimeter of the cabin, looking out the windows to see where anyone might be, but all I see is the wide expanse of forest and the lakefront. I take a deep, steadying breath. I'm not a stranger to this kind of situation. I've lived it before. Planned for it now. But there's always this moment where I wonder if this is it. The last one I get.

I close my eyes and breathe in through my nose and out through my mouth as I hear an explosion in the distance. I armed all the trip wires and explosives remotely just as soon as we arrived here. They're doing their job as promised, and I sit down at the table to take a sip of my coffee and pull open the drone feed. They're swarming now, even as Corey's guys take shots at them. The drones follow their path through the woods, and I start counting. One, three, five. I count my way through them as they cross into the second zone. Two men are already down. One's limping, another clearly fallen behind as he tends to a wound.

I zoom in. Seven of them and her husband, I presume, pulling up the rear. He's not interested in being cannon fodder for my defensive bulwark. He's brought expendables with him for exactly that reason. Hoping that he can use them to get into this cabin. Unfortunately, it'll probably work. I didn't expect someone to come from the top of the mountain down. A helicopter is clever. I'll give him that much. Zephyrine warned me I'd underestimate him, and she was right.

I just hope Jack and the rest of the team are watching the

drone footage too, using it to make the best of their positions until backup arrives. We're deep in the woods, but their response time was near-perfect when Zephyrine made a run for it. I'm hoping they have the same timing today. We'll need it.

Another round of fire comes that sounds closer than before. An explosion follows. More gunfire. It echoes against the mountainside, and there's shouting in the distance as another man falls within the drone's frame.

More screams echo through the forest, and the din of male voices gets louder and louder as they move closer. My heart rate kicks up a notch when I hear the footsteps on the gravel path below the cabin.

I grab my coffee and take one last swig before I stand, walking my way toward the door and putting my hand on my gun. I close my eyes, trying to take in every sound around me. Another round of gunfire, the sound of a body hitting the ground, and I hold my position in front of the door. I'm her last line of defense, and I don't want to fail her.

Footsteps fly up the gravel and pound their way over the front porch of the cabin. There's someone breathing heavily at the door, out of breath and heart racing. Someone rattled. Panicked. I could use that to my advantage.

I aim my gun and fire a round through the wall.

"Fuck!" He cries out, and I hear him crumple outside the door. For a moment, I move forward, thinking this was all easier than I thought. But he stands again, and I watch the door handle rattle and turn. The attempt grows more erratic as he loses his patience. I keep the barrel aimed on the entry.

The door bursts open, and I see the man I've baited out here. I know his face too well from previous experience. Corey's bleeding from his left leg and slightly hobbled, but very, very fucking pissed off as we aim our guns at one another. Mountaineering's not his thing, I guess.

"Didn't enjoy the hike?" I smirk at the sweat dripping down his brow. His shaggy blond hair is mussed, and his ruddy cheeks, along with the scowl that frames them, make him look even more unkempt.

"I've got this cabin surrounded. Give me my wife," he demands, spittle flying loose from his lips.

"Afraid you've got the wrong cabin." I give him a pitying once over.

"Give her to me now, Stockton, or I'll blow your fucking skull off the back of your head." He takes another step forward, blood leaking down from his leg onto the floorboards.

"What you've got isn't a high enough caliber for that. You're just gonna do enough to piss me off."

"Piss your pants, more like. Thought I wouldn't find you, huh? All alone in the wilderness. Your family name won't protect you now."

I roll my eyes and shake my head, amused by his attempts to intimidate me.

"I have a whole army coming up this mountain, and last I checked, you have one helicopter full of men who are scattered in pieces out in the woods. I suppose math never was your strong suit. So believe me when I say the odds aren't in your favor. It's your last chance to run." I pause, knowing full well he won't budge. "But if you plan on staying, I'm going to have to ask you to put that gun down. I can't have you breaking any of my sister-in-law's porcelain."

He fires his gun and shatters my coffee cup on the table. Impulsive when he's pissed. One less bullet to go. His reaction time is slower than mine. All good information to have.

"Now see, that's not very polite when you come into someone's home."

"Give me my fucking wife."

"I'm surprised you have a wife with that attitude. She let you break shit in her house like that?"

"I do what I want in my fucking house." He sneers. "I know you have her. Wherever she is, give her to me, or I will fucking kill you."

"What does she look like?" I'm trying to buy time, give my guys precious minutes to get up here and clear the woods so we can take him alive. I don't want to kill him outright. I need information from him, and this is my best chance yet to get it from someone who's close to the governor. But I don't want to die trying and give Zephyrine up to him in the process.

"Stop being a smart-ass, Stockton. Believe me when I say you're a fucking dead man!" His patience is waning.

"I don't suppose you'll ever find her then." I glance out the window. If he had backup still alive, I would have seen or heard them by now. It's just us up here. That at least gives me some solace.

"What the fuck are you looking at? My guys will be in here any minute. Then I'll have them start cutting you into pieces until you tell me where she is. I suggest you start talking now if you want to die easy." Corey crosses the space between us and waves his gun dangerously close to me.

"Easy there," I warn him, my finger warming to my trigger. I'm fairly certain I could get a shot off before him, but if I don't shoot to kill, he'll definitely kill me. "I think we need to slow down with the threats."

He answers me by firing off a round that goes whizzing by my head and shatters something else behind me. I take a deep breath. I might have to make a choice I don't want to make. At least I think I will, until I see the floorboards start to rise in the corner of my vision. Zephyrine's crawling out from under them, her eyes fixed on her husband and fury written all over her face. My stomach bottoms out. If she's out here, I have a whole new set of math I have to do, and quickly.

I can't even yell at her to stop or subtly try to warn her off. She creeps across the floor, and I have to chant silently in my head for them not to squeak under her bare feet. Any motion I make will have him following my line of sight and reveal her. So instead, I keep my eyes trained on him, staring back into his dark-blue, beady abyss. If they ever need a poster child for dead eyes, he's a prime candidate. I imagine that's what happens after years and years of the vapid pursuit of wealth and power. Eventually, the corruption leaks out into the body. The governor has a matching vacant stare.

"I won't ask again." He gives me an ultimatum just as Zephyrine lines up behind him and raises the gun in her hands. I hope she knows how to fire it.

"Drop the gun, you fucking prick," Zephyrine demands as she places the gun to the back of his skull, and his eyes meet mine as he tries to process what's happening. The look on his face is priceless.

"I'd listen to her. That caliber at that range." I draw a breath through my teeth. "Will definitely shatter your skull."

"You fucking bitch." Her husband curses her, recognizing her voice.

Zephyrine's eyes narrow, and I see her finger massage the trigger. I need him whole, and I beg her to look at me, but she's too angry, too ready to end this man for everything he's ever done and said to her. But her eyes close for a moment and then reopen with newfound clarity.

"Drop the gun," she repeats calmly, the nun coming through before the ruthless man's daughter returns. "Or I will happily use you to test the theory."

Fuck, I like this woman.

He does as she asks, realizing that she'll kill him if he

continues. She kicks the gun to me, and I take it, kicking it far behind me and then moving to put Corey face down on the ground. I pin him with my body weight as he curses my existence and hers. Before I can speak to give her instructions, she's on the move. Zephyrine works like she's done this a million times, grabbing the handcuffs still sitting on the nightstand in her room and helping me cuff him.

We both hear the sound of feet on gravel, racing toward the cabin, and our attention moves to the door while I keep Corey on the ground with my knee between his shoulder blades. She walks backward slowly, lining up next to me as we each keep our gun on the door. The footsteps slow, moving cautiously, as they reach the porch and then turn into the cabin. All of us startling when they come into view.

"Fuck! Sorry!" Jack apologizes, lowering his weapon when he sees it's us.

"Took you long enough."

"I'm sorry. We ran as fast as we could once we cleared it, but his guys kept us in the woods longer than we thought they would." Jack's head dips with regret.

"They're all accounted for." Jack's second-in-command lets me know when he reaches the doorway.

"Minus this fuck." I nod to the man beneath me. "Let's get him out of here."

"Where do you want to take him?" Jack asks.

"The cellblock for now," I answer, and they both nod their understanding, hauling him up and out of the cabin as soon as I step back. "The rest of our guys are on their way. Make sure if you pass them out there, you get them sorted."

"What about the helicopter?" Zephyrine looks at me, worry dancing behind the blue.

"They're long gone. There's a drop-off point up there, but nowhere to use as an exfil. My best guess is that they have another vehicle waiting at the bottom of the mountain that my guys already destroyed." I try to assuage her concerns.

"You're sure?" I hear the adrenaline in her tone. She's still shaken, and I just want to comfort her.

"Positive. But I'll check in with them in a minute. First, I want to make sure you're okay." I look over Zephyrine as she watches her husband get dragged down the gravel path.

"I'm... It's been a long time since I've seen him." She blinks rapidly like she's holding back tears and then turns to look at me. "I thought he might kill you. I didn't trust him not to, and I saw an opportunity, so I took it. You're not mad, are you?"

"I'm not mad. No. It was brave. So fucking brave." I run my hand down her arm. "But dangerous too. You fucking scared me." I look up at her, studying the way her face contorts as she tries not to cry and manages to swallow it back.

"I couldn't let him take someone else. Not again." She leans into me, and I wrap my arms around her, sweeping her up in a tight hug.

"You did good. It's okay. You took care of him," I reassure her softly as I rub the backs of her arms. "Look at me. He's gone now, okay? You got him. He's never going to bother you or anyone else again. We'll make sure of it."

She nods, but the tears fall from the corners of her eyes silently. I pull her close to me again, letting her bury her face in my shoulder. A sob racks through her chest and vibrates through my own until it echoes like a conviction.

I'd take all the hell this man put her through and erase it for her if I could. I might not have the power to do that, no matter how much I wish I did. But I can certainly make him pay for it, slowly, painfully, while I work to get the information I need about her father. I'll make him regret the day he laid eyes on her with his last fucking breath.

TWENTY-THREE

L evi

"DO you want to be in the room when I deal with him?" I ask her as we sit in the truck outside the barn where I had my guys bring him tonight.

I let the fucker squirm in a holding cell in the basement of the casino. He was living like a cockroach in the dark, with no food and only a little water spilled as a puddle on the floor to keep him going while he wondered what we had in store for him next.

"I don't know, honestly. Part of me wants to never see him again. I'd forgotten how much I feel physically ill in his presence, how reviling he truly is. But another part of me wants to see him suffer. I want to see the fear in his eyes when he realizes that you aren't just going to let him run free after everything." She has rosary beads in her hand, and her fingers slip over them in contemplation.

"Whatever you want is what we'll do. But if you want to be part of it, let me know. We'll need to make you look like a hostage, keep up the ruse for appearances. But it gives me ideas."

"Ideas?" Her tone is curious. "Like what?"

"What would he have done to me if he'd gotten a hold of us like he'd wanted?" I ask.

Her face contorts with that thought, grimacing and shaking her head.

"I can't imagine," she says softly. She always gets quiet like this, used to making herself small for his benefit.

"You can. Your face tells me you can. So tell me what he would have done."

"Torture you. Beat you half to death. Slice you open. It's anyone's guess how he would have continued. Chopping you up or using electric shocks. He's inventive when he wants to be, at least with the things he would brag about to me when he was trying to scare me. He wouldn't stop until you were a bloody pile of nothing."

"And you?" I want to be sure he suffers a fate equal to whatever he might have tried.

"It depends on what he believes happened between us. If he thought you touched me, he'd make me pay for that. His jealousy would send him into a rage."

"How do you want him to pay for it?" I ask, and she takes a deep breath. Her eyes dart back and forth out the window, and I can tell even the thought of him makes her uneasy. She still fears him even when we have him locked down, and that sends a chill through my body.

"He'll never touch you again. I promise you that. And if it's too uncomfortable, you don't have to talk about it. I'm asking because whatever he would have done to us, that's his worst fear. And I want to make it come true for him. I want every second of this today to be pure fucking hell for him," I explain.

"What about getting information about my father?"

"If we get him to confess something we need about your father in the process, all the better. But my main focus is making him realize how badly he fucked up with you. Making him pay for anything and everything he ever did to you."

"I think you overestimate how much my husband cares about me. I doubt you'll get much that way. You'd be better off offering him cash or leverage. He'd probably betray my father easily for that. If you gave him a better deal, I mean. I'm surprised it hasn't happened yet. Corey never was very loyal." She shrugs.

"He cares. Trust me. The tattoo he put on you? The other women? That's all because he wants you, and you don't want him. That eats at him. It'd fucking kill me to have a wife like you and have you hate my guts. I'd probably fucking hang myself. Unfortunately, he didn't do the right thing and listen to that instinct. But we'll fix it."

"You're going to hang him?" She sounds surprised.

"In a manner of speaking." I can't help the morbid grin on my face. Torturing this man is going to be a simple pleasure.

I put him in the cell to fuck with him for a while, but I also wanted time to plot how I'm going to make him suffer. Any of the ways I could get him to talk for us and exact the most retribution possible for what he's done to her.

"Well..." She shifts in her seat.

"Well?"

"I do want to see him suffer. Of course some part of me does, but it feels wrong at the same time. Like I'm betraying the promises I made at the convent. It would make me feel like one of those peasants in the crowds of medieval movies. Cheering on his demise."

"You're not cheering on his demise. You're cheering on him getting a taste of his own medicine. The tiniest bit of justice for everything he did. You don't need to feel an ounce of guilt. I'm doing this because I want to. I'd do it regardless of whether or not you were here. I'm just happy to let you watch so you can know he'll never touch you again."

"Touch." She blurts before she takes a steadying breath. "Touch me in front of him."

"Touch you?" I repeat, making sure I heard her correctly.

"Touch me like you've already been with me. He doesn't know the truth. It'll kill him. He obsessed over the fact that I wasn't a virgin on our wedding night. He said that my former boyfriend had ruined me for him. Do that, and you'll get a reaction." She stares out the windshield, smoothing her thumb over her nail as she speaks.

"You're sure?" I ask.

"I'm sure. I trust you." She nods, turning to look at me.

I'm not sure she should trust me. Touching Zephyrine will be playing with fire. Doing it in the same room with him, I'll be tempted to make him understand how terrible he's fucked up. Like playing with gasoline next to a bonfire.

TWENTY-FOUR

Zephyrine

I WATCH, half mesmerized and half horrified, as Levi uses the pulley system to hoist the gambrel with Corey attached like an animal ready for slaughter. His arms are spread wide, and I watch the tendons strain as they take on the weight of his body dangling in the air. Levi stops just as the tips of his toes can almost still touch the hay-littered floor at his feet.

Levi winds the rope around the pole to hold it in place, tying a quick knot to secure it. He pulls it tight and then walks around to get a better look at his prey, tilting his cowboy hat out of the way for a clear view.

Corey grimaces, his jaw tightening as he strains against the position that Levi's put him in. His fingers are stretched, and a deep, pained grunt emanates from his chest. He sneers down at Levi.

"Comfortable?" Levi looks over him in amusement.

"Fuck you." The tone of his retort is less sure than his previous swagger.

Whatever they did to him while he was in that hole Levi put him in, he looks like death warmed over. His blond hair is greasy and stuck to his forehead, his clothes are dirty and rumpled—one pant leg still ragged and bloodstained from the bullet wound Levi gave him, and several days of stubble on his cheeks makes him look slightly gaunt and adds to his general disheveled state. His bleach-white veneers look out of place with the rest of his appearance, one of the many things he prided himself on. He's lost weight since I saw him last too. There used to be some muscle to him, but it all seems to have evaporated, and it makes me wonder what he's been up to.

"Good. Glad to hear it." Levi gives him several hard pats to the side of his cheek. "Just wanted to be sure you have a front row seat for the show."

Corey doesn't answer this time, only giving another groan as he tries and fails to pull himself up, using the leverage of one arm to try to dislodge the other from the gambrel. It makes a loud clanging as he moves, and I jolt a little at the sound.

"Don't wear yourself out. You'll need the energy," Levi chastises as he grabs a saddle stand and drags it to the center of the room. He pulls the saddle off it, handing it to one of his guys, and instructs them to move it out of the way.

Then Levi's eyes meet mine, the shimmer of deviant delight dances just behind the pale blue-green of his irises. I can feel the spark of anticipation run up my spine. He closes the gap between us and grabs my wrists by the rope he put on them before we walked in here. He leans forward so he can keep his voice soft enough that only I can hear when he speaks.

"Trust me."

It's a simple enough reminder of his promise that he'll keep me safe. The funny thing is, I do. I trust him in this moment like every other one in recent memory, even though I'm questioning my own sanity for it. He tugs me forward, and I shuffle along behind him. My booted feet are slow and meticulous with each step across the boards, still unexcited at the prospect of being brought closer to Corey.

I watch as Levi nods to the men waiting for his orders at the corners of the barn, giving them the signal that they can step outside. I'm sure they'll be within earshot, but it leaves only the three of us behind standing in the center of the space. The late-day sun casts long rays over Corey's body and onto the stand Levi's placed in front of him like a sort of makeshift altar.

"Your wife and I have been getting to know each other better over the last few weeks. She's been filling me in on some of the details of your arrangement. How you met. What kind of man you are. Fascinating, honestly," Levi mutters as he brings me in front of my husband.

"Stay away from my wife," Corey growls.

Levi just laughs in response, guiding me to the saddle stand.

"The way I hear it, you don't treat her like much of a wife. More like discarded property. It doesn't sound very romantic, and that's before we even make it to the problems in the bedroom."

"There are no fucking problems. In the bedroom or else-where." I can feel Corey's eyes on me, hear the silent accusations he's hurling in my direction.

"That's not what I heard." Another taunting laugh rumbles free from Levi's chest as he places his palm at the base of my spine and then smooths his hand upward over my back, applying pressure that nudges me forward over the saddle stand.

He grabs the rope that binds my wrists and pulls it forward, making my chest meet the worn wood in front of me as he secures it to a hook at the far side. It holds me in the bent position, vulnerable, like an offering laid out across it. He tucks the stray hairs in my face behind my ears and brushes some of the longer, wispier bangs to the side as he gives me a reassuring look. One that tells me this is for my husband's benefit and not his own, silently reminding me to trust in our plan.

"Get the fuck away from her." I hear the tremor in Corey's voice as Levi rounds the stand to the far side, moving behind me. Corey's eyes dart nervously back and forth between Levi and the stand, never quite making eye contact with me.

"I wouldn't be making demands up there if I were you." Levi mocks him.

"I'll do whatever the fuck I want. You think you're getting away with this? I'll have your fucking balls if you lay a single fucking finger on her."

"We'll see about that," Levi snaps back, but his focus returns to me. I feel his hand caress my hip and then cup my ass through the skirt I have on. "Go on. Stop me," he taunts Corey. I hear the rattle of the gambrel as Corey kicks his feet, gritting his teeth and trying to get momentum in his favor again.

It's folly to try. Even if he could somehow defy gravity to overcome the hooked ends, he'd likely fall face-first onto the floor.

"That's right. You can't stop me now. Just like you haven't been able to stop me for weeks. You know what the worst fucking part of it is for you? I don't have to force her. I don't have to plead with her. I don't have to parade other women in front of her. She comes to me in the middle of the night all on her own. She asks for me."

"You fucking piece of shit! I will fucking kill you." He grunts as he wiggles, making himself look even more pathetic when he fails to accomplish anything.

"Little late for that." Levi gives my ass cheek a soft squeeze, one that sends an unexpected bolt of awareness through my body.

"Don't you fucking touch her," he snarls uselessly.

"How does it feel anyway? Knowing your wife would rather never know the touch of someone again than let you touch her?" Levi asks. "Going to a *convent*. Fucking hell. That has to cut deep, right?"

His hand slips under my dress, and the tips of his fingers dance up the backs of my thighs. They light little fires in their wake, making my nerve endings come to life under his care, just before his palm smooths back over my skin and calms the storm. He repeats the attention as Corey growls back at him. I don't even hear the words. Only Levi's voice when he speaks again.

"You know she confessed to me once. On her knees. Told me when she goes to bed at night and slips her fingers between her legs, that it's me she imagines. Even though she thought I was a priest at the time." Levi's amusement is evident in his voice, and I hear the desperate sound of frustrated anger tear out of Corey. "Can you fucking believe that? She'd rather touch herself at night, fantasizing about a priest fucking her senseless, than have you anywhere near her. That's gotta fucking hurt. I don't think I could live with myself if that's how my wife felt about me. I told her I would've done the honorable thing and hung myself years ago."

Levi pulls my dress up, exposing the sheer underwear I have on underneath. It was one of the pairs Dakota got me, and it feels wildly appropriate for the moment.

"Fuck. Look at these." Levi runs his finger under the elastic band that wraps around my upper thigh, starting on the outside and moving slowly inward. "Do you think she wore them for me?"

"Fuck you."

"You're right. She probably wore them hoping she could fuck me." His fingers stop short of where I want them, and the realization that I'm enjoying it, that I want him even like this, hits me hard.

"Then she's a fucking whore."

Levi sucks in a breath and gives me a swift pat on the cheek, one that feels like a promise of more, before he turns his attention back to Corey.

"Call her that again, and I'll cut your fucking tongue out."

"You don't have the balls."

"No? You don't think so?" Levi threatens, staring him down, the muscle in his jaw ticking as his hand balls into a fist. Levi is terrifying when he wants to be, and it's enough that even Corey seems rattled. Not that it stops him.

"You put your dick anywhere near her, and I'll cut it off." He lobs another hollow threat in Levi's direction.

"Well fuck. What an inspiring thought!" Levi snaps back. "You know, I really thought I had today all planned out. But sometimes we have to improvise."

He hollers for one of his guys again, and they have a tête-à-tête. His guy returns a couple of minutes later with a kit. One Levi opens and sprawls across the table in front of Corey. I can't see the contents, but whatever it is has all the color draining from Corey's face.

"Zephyrine, could I borrow you a moment?" he calls after me, seemingly wanting to demonstrate that I'm not actually restrained. I pull the rope off the hook and stand, meeting Levi in front of Corey. It's another insult to injury for Corey to have to endure.

I watch as he processes the fact that his wife isn't a victim but a willing participant in his torture. His face contorts with the information and lands on a vicious sneer that'll be burned into my mind for the rest of time. But I keep calm and follow Levi's instructions.

"Could you undo his pants for me, sweetheart? Pull them and his underwear down to his ankles. He won't be needing them. In fact, I'd guess he's about to piss them, so you'd be helping him avoid the embarrassment," Levi explains.

Even as he speaks to me in a tone laced with sweetness, he looks up at Corey, their eyes meeting as Levi gives him the most diabolical look I've ever seen cross a man's face. I almost, *almost*, feel sorry for Corey. For all of nearly half a second before flashbacks of how he treated me in the past come flooding back. The punishing blows across my cheekbones for daring to ask to leave the house. The back of my head tearing through the stucco as he launched me across the hall for forgetting my place at a dinner with his men. The bloody lip and black eye from him ruthlessly backhanding me for telling him no when he tried to crawl into bed with me. Independence was a cardinal sin in his world. One that always deserved corporal punishment.

The memories keep my fingers working his button and zipper open even as he viciously orders me to stop, cursing the day he met me. They keep me going even as the orders turn to pleading, and he begs me to have mercy when I start to pull the fabric down. His dick springs free from his boxers out of the corner of my eye, and it garners another round of low chuckles from Levi. Corey's face blanches in the wake of it.

"Which part's got your dick at attention? The part where I fuck your wife or the part where she humiliates you in front of another man?" A low whistle comes next. "Or is it both? Fuck, I bet it's both."

"I will fucking kill you." Corey swings his weight forward, and his dick pokes me in the chest as his body contacts mine. I grab it, squeezing tight, letting my nails dig into his skin and draw blood.

"You won't touch him, you witless little dipstick," I snipe at him.

"You fucking bitch!" He lashes out at me, his eyes wide with horror at the idea I might actually be siding with this man. They go wider still when Levi presses a blade to the base of his dick.

"Say it again," Levi threatens. "Call her a name one more fucking time."

Corey's teeth grind together as he glares at Levi, but he stays silent. I have no doubt Levi will make good on the threat, and Corey must finally believe him too. After a long minute, Levi retracts the blade and looks at me, a softness returning to his face. His eyes search over me as if he's trying to make sure I'm visibly unscathed. I offer him the briefest half smile to reassure him, and he nods.

"Good girl," he praises before he offers up his next instruction. "Go back and wait for me at the stand."

And God help me because I do exactly as the man asks. The priestly version would probably tell me to add rosaries to the count if he knew my thoughts. Hell, I think I need to tell myself to add them, given the situation we're in. Even my darkest dreams didn't touch it.

"Now, I want you to tell me where the governor is keeping the other relics," Levi says casually as he runs his fingers over the implements in the kit that's sprawled out in front of him on the table. He looks like he does in the kitchen, sleeves rolled up, surveying the drawer for whatever tool he needs next.

"Do I look fucking stupid? I give you that, and he'll kill me." Corey's sardonic tone grates on Levi, and his eyes narrow as he looks him over.

"Well then, you're in a bit of sticky fucking situation

because if you don't tell me, I'll fuck your wife while you watch, and then once I've made her come a few times, and I've got my energy back, I'll start dismantling your limbs piece by piece until you start saying words I want to hear."

"You wouldn't fucking dare. You do that, and he'll have every head in your family."

"He tried that once. Didn't work out for him."

"You don't have the fucking men. The gear. The fucking guts to take him on." Corey shakes his head.

"Watch me."

"I'm not fucking telling you shit. Anything you could do, he would be worse. No fucking way." He spits at Levi's feet, nailing the tip of his cowboy boot. Levi looks down, grinning like it's the funniest thing he's seen all day, before his eyes meet Corey's again.

"Is that a challenge?" Levi looks up bright-eyed at him, like he's just gotten the little push he needed to set the ball in motion. Levi pulls out a device and holds it up for Corey to see. "You know what this is, or are you too much of a city boy for that?"

"No fucking idea," Corey sneers at him.

"Ah well. This is an elastrator. You put this band here..." Levi grabs something out of the kit in front of him and attaches it to the device in his hand, admiring his handiwork for a moment. "Then you just slide it under here." He moves the device underneath Corey's scrotum, working it back and forth until the band he attached snaps tight around the narrower stretch of skin at the top.

Corey howls at first, so high-pitched that I wonder if he's scared the bats out of the rafters when a spray of dust rains down. He bellows out in pain as Levi pulls the device away from him, leaving the band in place, and tosses it back into the kit. I watch as his face goes beet red and tears stream down his cheeks, fat ones that roll slowly and remind me of the kind he made me cry in the past. The ones he told me were obnoxious and beneath me, reminding him of a pathetic little child.

"And that right there lets you castrate a bull. Slowly but surely, if you leave it on like that, it starts to constrict the blood vessels until they wither and the whole fucking thing sloughs off. Keeps the weak bulls from breeding." Levi continues his explanation. "You'll know when it starts to work its magic. The pain will ease up, and everything will start to go numb down there from the lack of blood. Then again, if you take it off soon enough, everything can still be in functioning—if not a little painful—order. So the clock's on, Corey. You let me know when you're ready." Levi slaps the side of his leg hard enough that it jostles him and makes him whimper. "I've got better things to do while I wait."

Levi crosses the room after he tosses his gloves to the table, his boots hitting the floor one slow step at a time in my direction. It feels like slow motion, like all of this is a dream I've invented in my imagination. The other side of the coin from the priest I met at the convent. I have no idea what he really intends to do. He told me to trust him, and so far, I have no reason to stop.

He leans down when he reaches me, his cowboy hat shielding my face from the view of Corey.

"You good?" he asks, raising a brow that tells me he wants an honest answer.

"I'm good." I do my best to show him, without words, that I can handle this.

I might have spent the last handful of years sheltered away, but I can hold my own with men like him and Corey. I'm not a flower that's about to wilt.

"Good," he echoes.

His fingers trace down the back of my neck, following my

spine. It sends shivers through my whole body, highlighting the contrast of the way he exacts the worst kind of violence on my husband and then treats me like I'm priceless vintage glass. His hand follows the curve of my ass, and he gives the other cheek a soft squeeze and a swift pat like he's telling me I've done a good job so far. It's another jolt of awareness, a reminder of exactly how long it's been since a man has really touched me.

He lifts my dress again, pulling it up higher this time and running his palm in small circles. It's like he can read my mind. I glance up at Corey. He's writhing against the restraints, willing his toes to reach the ground to gain some sort of leverage and failing. His dick hangs limply, swinging left to right as he attempts to move.

He looks pathetic, but not enough for me to feel sorry for him. Not when I remember how hard I tried to make him happy despite everything, when I held out hope in the beginning. Wishing there was some way to make our marriage bearable and then crying myself to sleep night after night. I'm just hoping Levi doesn't cut the band and give him a chance to make another woman as miserable as he made me.

"You're doing good," Levi whispers more words of reassurance to me as he comes around and crouches down in front of me. I use the back of my knuckle to touch his as he reaches out. He wraps his middle finger around mine, giving me a squeeze of reassurance, and his eyes say everything he can't right now. That I'm strong and capable. That I'm brave. That he's proud of me. It's enough to steel my spine and remind me of my worth. I blink slowly in recognition, and he nods before he forges on with taunting Corey.

"Fucking hell." He paces slowly back, his fingers trailing over my spine and down my ass as he walks. "You should see how much this is turning her on. Soaked her panties all the way through already," Levi explains loudly for Corey's benefit as his hand slides back down my thigh.

Corey's eyes fall to me, the disgust at my disloyalty on his face apparent. It doesn't feel like betrayal though. It feels like justice—just like Levi promised it would. "You want to start talking about the relics, or you want me to see how much wetter I can get her with my dick?"

"F-f-fuckkk..." Corey only manages that much as he grits through the pain. I'm sure there was supposed to be a "you" at the end of it. Maybe even a "both of you."

"You want me to fuck her?" Levi pretends to misunderstand his meaning. "I mean, I guess it'll have to be me." Levi smirks at the sight of his balls. "You obviously won't be capable anymore." Levi's fingers trace over my panties, down over my ass, and to my upper thighs. He uses the toe of his boot to gently kick my legs wider, and his hand goes to his belt. "Maybe that's what you need to help with those blue balls. The sight of me dripping out of her as encouragement."

"Don't... you fucking da—" Corey's voice is back, it's hoarse and strained though. Weak. It falters before he can even finish. His face is red, and his cheeks are stained with tears.

"Then start talking."

"I fucking can't," he wails, gasping for another breath before he finishes. "He'll kill me."

"I think you need to see this for yourself." I hear the snap of a shutter and the flash of light that tells me Levi's used his camera. He's taken a photo of how soaked I am, and now he's marching it over to Corey. "You see that? She's desperate for it. Do you know how many years it's been since she's had a man touch her? Oh. Right." Levi clicks his tongue. "I guess you would. What with her running away from you and all."

Corey grinds his teeth, working his lips together as the last round of his tears drips off his cheeks. There's fury as much as pain in his eyes, and I hope that his restraints hold. If they don't, he won't stop until we're dead.

"If you don't want to watch me fuck that tight little cunt full, start talking. Tell me where he keeps the relics," Levi demands.

Corey takes a deep breath, closing his eyes and grinding his teeth before he opens them again. He's steadier when he speaks this time. It's low, just above a whisper, but he has full sentences now.

"Fuck her if you need to. Just take this off. You can have her. As many times as you want, just please." He spits as he bargains, and his eyes shift to me. I'm sure he's imagining the ways he'll hurt me if he ever gets free. I don't want to think about him though. Just Levi. As far as I'm concerned, he's the only one that matters.

Levi's even angrier now. The muscle in his jaw practically vibrates with rage, and I can see his fist ball up, his knuckles stark white as his thumb runs over them. He stretches his hand again, a tell I've noticed when he's trying to stem the tide of his anger and hold off his worst impulses. If I were Corey, I'd be terrified.

"You're a fucking worthless piece of shit. You never fucking deserved her. You know that? Tell me where the relics are, and I'll take it off. That's the only way you keep your balls. You tell me, and you tell me now. The offer expires in the next sixty fucking seconds. She and I will walk out of here and leave you to rot."

"Fucking hell," Corey whines. "Fine. Fine. His compound in the mountains. The house. She knows where it is. He has a vault. You'll never fucking get to it. It's fortified. Armed. A whole system. They'll mow you down before you even reach the gate."

"Where's the vault?" Levi presses.

"The basement of the house. Now take this fucking band off!" Corey bellows.

Levi nods and takes his time putting his gloves back on and then reaching into his kit again. He pulls out a bowie knife. He holds it over the small fire, heating the blade to snap the elastic band before approaching Corey again.

"Does he know you came here?" Levi asks one last question before freeing him from his torture. I'm almost sorry to see it end.

"I didn't tell him where I was going. Just that I was getting his daughter back." Corey sneers at me one last time.

"Good." I watch the flash of the blade as Levi goes to remove the band. But he doesn't cut the rubber; instead, he slices through the skin below the band, and there's a plopping sound that echoes through the room. I gasp. Corey's face drains of color, his mouth agape. Levi skewers the remnants with the tip of his knife and tosses them into the fire.

"Not a fan of Rocky Mountain oysters then?" He looks at Corey and smirks. "I suppose they are better battered and fried, but gotta make do with what we have." A dark chuckle emanates from Levi's chest, and Corey passes out, from shock or pain, I don't know.

Levi takes a bottle of water and uncaps it to splash Corey's face. His eyes open, but there's nothing but panic in them. He's deliriously looking around like he can't remember where he is—able to escape to the safer hallways of his mind for a few moments before he remembers the living hell he's currently experiencing.

"There we go. Back with us again. You awake now?" Levi asks.

Corey nods and looks down between his legs, letting out a horrified shriek when he sees the missing piece.

"Oh, right, I was supposed to cut the elastic." Levi hovers

the knife back over the fire before he moves back into place as Corey watches in terror.

"No! Fuck! No. No. No," Corey begs, but it's too late, the heat does its job, and the elastic snaps, blood pouring out from the wound. "What the fuck have you done?"

I'm out of position now, jolted up as I watch the gruesome sight unfold. Levi wipes his blade on Corey's shirt as the man screams for his life.

"A man who doesn't have the balls to protect his wife doesn't deserve to keep either." Levi shoves the blade through his throat, offering him a small final mercy. Blood spurts from the wound at first, and then it seeps down the edges of the knife, rivulets of blood forming over his neck and chest, soaking his clothes. I can't stop staring—mesmerized by the sight of it. A few moments later, his eyes shutter, and his head lolls to his chest.

Levi pulls the blade, a river of blood streaming out in its wake. He wipes it on a clean part of Corey's shirt and lays it down on the table with the rest of his implements of torture.

He glances back at me, to make sure I'm all right before he hollers for his men. I nod to let him know I'm fine, and he lets out a sharp whistle that summons them like obedient dogs. I'm not okay. Not really. But I will be now that Corey's dead.

"Pull his balls out of the fire and put them in a box. Send them to his father-in-law with a note that says his daughter is next unless he confesses to the murders of my parents and Kelly's grandparents at the Governor's Gala." One of his men nods his understanding while another moves to extinguish the flame and extract the gift from its fiery resting place.

They move quickly, rounding up everything they brought into the barn. Levi turns back to me, crossing the room and closing the distance between us before he speaks again.

"That's for his benefit and yours. Let him continue to think you're a victim and not working with me. It'll help him stay motivated to do the right thing." Levi searches every inch of me with methodical assessment as if he needs to make sure I'm still in one piece.

"Okay," I whisper my response.

"Are you okay?" he asks, knowing my answer isn't certain. "I know that was a lot to take in."

A lot is the understatement of the year. My hands are still gripping the saddle stand for dear life, and my heart hasn't come down from the adrenaline rush of watching it unfold.

"You're a sadist." I state the obvious so bluntly that he grins.

"Only when there's someone who deserves it. I enjoy meting out justice." He studies me for a moment, a sober look wiping away the vindictive smile. "Do you hate me now? I'd understand if you did."

"No. I don't hate you. I've just never met anyone with two sides quite so opposite. One so reasonable, and one so..."

"Reason never works with men like him. Not in his world. Certainly not in mine."

I couldn't argue with him there. I tried dozens of times to reason with Corey. It never worked. I tilt my head silently in understanding.

"It's not an annulment, but hopefully it still gets you what you need to make the abbess happy." There's a wry sort of humor in his tone.

"I don't think the abbess will ever let me become a nun if she finds out about this."

"Your secret's safe with me, and everyone else thinks you're my prisoner. She can't blame you for that, can she?"

"No. I suppose she can't."

"Then you're free to do what you want."

Free. I asked and he delivered, just like he promised.

TWENTY-FIVE

L evi

SHE WALKS down to meet me at the fire pit as I toss my clothes into the flames. We can't risk there being any evidence, and I already called my guys in to clean up the body and the barn. I don't know if it's better or worse that we do it so often, we have a near-flawless protocol in place. I take a long swig of my beer as I watch her hips sway on the walk down in some sort of thin nightie that Dakota must have purchased for her. It accents every curve she has, and it's the last thing I need to be seeing her in right now.

"Can you get this button? My arms are sore from being in that position on the saddle stand, and it's hard to reach." She turns her back to me, and I get a waft of the soap she showered in. It's turning into my favorite scent. I'll have to find out what the inn uses and keep it in my apartment once she's gone. The thought of her being gone echoes through my head, and I push it away. I don't have time for my own bullshit right now. I have to be here for her.

"Sure." I close the distance between us.

She sweeps her long red hair over her shoulder and to the side, exposing her pale skin under the low light. The long line of her neck and spine dips down to meet her shoulder blades, like delicate wings beating as she moves. My dirty hands contrast against the pastel fabric of the nightgown, a stark reminder of where we stand. She's barely free, and the last thing she needs is another man with a penchant for violence. Even if my causes are nobler.

I probably scared her half to death today, anyway, with how far I'm willing to take things when the situation calls for it. If she wasn't ready to run back to the convent before, I've sealed that fate now.

"It's a shame we have to burn it. It's pretty." She frowns at the sight of her dress being consumed by fire.

"I'll buy you another one. There are plenty more in the cabin. Fuck, even this nightgown is pretty. Dakota has good taste; I'll give her that." I offer up a smile, trying to let us both come down from all the adrenaline of the day.

"It felt nice to feel pretty in front of him for once," she admits quietly as she risks a glance up at me.

It grinds over my heart to hear it because the woman is gorgeous. Stunning in light like this. Even without her makeup or hair done. I still remember the first time I set eyes on her in person. The dull black of her uniform couldn't dim the way her hair shimmered in the light, or how soft her skin looked, and how bright her eyes shone as she smiled and laughed.

"You'd look pretty in a paper bag. You know that, right? Whatever he said or did to you, whatever doing time with the rest of the chastity cheerleaders has convinced you of. I hope you know that much, and if you don't, I'm happy to tell you as many times as you need to hear it."

"Careful. I'll pretend just to hear you say it again," she teases, turning to look at me with a small smile on her face as her nightgown slips off her shoulder with the movement. A grin breaks on my lips in return, and I turn back to the fire, nudging the pretty set of lace panties she wore today into the heat of the flame.

"Having to burn those is the real shame," I mutter without thinking it through.

"There are plenty more in the house." Her voice has that melodic quality to it that I love so much. "Minus the pair you stole, but I gather we're still not talking about that."

"Probably better that we don't."

"What if I want to?"

"Meaning what exactly?" I take a draw off my beer, annoyed with myself for letting curiosity get the better of me rather than shutting this down immediately.

She stands a little straighter and crosses her arms over her chest.

"I was thinking that I'm free now, and all the things that means. All the possibilities it finally opens up for me." She pauses and studies me.

"More once we get your money back from those accounts he hid it in."

She shakes her head. "That's going to be impossible."

"Nothing is impossible. Not if you want it bad enough."

"Well... I suppose you have a point there. I thought it was impossible to ever get out from under his thumb, and you managed that. But I still think some things are highly unlikely."

"Like?" I'm curious what else she's hoping we can take care of, but ready if I can take another worry off her plate. Especially now that I know just what kind of scum she was subjected to for years.

"You—sleeping in the bed tonight."

My hand tightens around the bottle for half an instant before I realize what she's saying. She's probably raw and vulnerable, processing a fuckton of emotions even if she did hate him. I doubt she wants to be alone. I'm not even sure if I would in her position.

"You know I don't sleep much, but I can lie with you and keep you company. Happy to if you need it," I offer.

"I'd like that. I just don't want to be alone tonight."

"You're never alone here. I'm always around, and I won't let anything happen to you." I know the last few days have been hard on her, even if the outcome is one she could be happy with eventually. I'm sure she's worried about what comes next. I'm sure news of Corey's demise will only antagonize her father and draw out his ire. I need to remind Grant to bolster security later tonight.

"I know you won't."

"All right. Go on back to bed. I'm cold just looking at you. I'll put this fire out and be right in," I promise her, and she leans forward and kisses my cheek.

It's a chaste kiss, but it leaves a brand on my skin all the same. Reminding me of the way I kissed her in the woods. The taste of strawberries on her lips. I'm lost in the thought when her voice breaks through again.

"Thank you. For everything. Truly." She offers a small smile and then takes off back up the hill.

I DRAG my feet a little longer than I should going back to bed. I'm hoping to find her passed out and sound asleep. I'll still lie on the bed for a while to make sure she knows someone's there, but then I plan to wander back out to the living room.

When you have the kind of insomnia I do, entertainment and distraction are your best friends. The last thing I want to do is stare up at the ceiling, listening to her cute little snores while I contemplate how to choke myself just enough that I pass out, but not enough to die, because I can't take the lack of sleep anymore. Working on casino business, checking the security cameras, plotting our next move. That's what I do in the middle of the night when I'm all alone with no interruptions. But I want to keep my promise to her, and if she needs someone next to her tonight, I'll do it.

I creak the door open slowly and see her sprawled on the bed, looking angelic with her eyes closed and curled up on her side. Reaching behind my head, I pull my shirt off, tossing it over the chair. I hesitate as my hands go for my belt buckle. Normally, I'd strip down every night if I were sleeping in my own bed, but with her here, I'm not about to. I don't need the temptation. So I slip the belt off slowly and the jeans and socks with it, but I leave my boxer briefs on when I slide under the covers. I keep my distance from her, curling up on my own side of the bed so she's still got plenty of room.

The sheets are soft, perfect really, thanks to my sister-in-law's taste in decor. I'll be in trouble for that mug Zephyrine's ex broke, but I can replace it with a new set that she'll hopefully like just as much. I could look for that online tomorrow at breakfast. I'm trying to think about anything right now that isn't the woman lying next to me as my head hits the pillow.

The vision of her wet for me and bent over the saddle stand won't stop replaying in my head, even though I know it's wrong. It was meant for his benefit. I wanted to prove to him that he was a fucking loser for not treating her better than he did. That she's perfect in every fucking way possible, and he never had the fucking vision to see her for what she was. What she *is*.

She was wasted on him, but that doesn't mean she's meant for me either. Even if every day I want her a little more. She wants the convent, and I promised her I'd give her what she wants. I have to rein myself in.

"Levi?" She hums my name softly and turns her head. "You came." I can hear the relief in her voice.

"I said I would."

"I wasn't sure."

I wasn't either. This feels like asking for trouble. Not to mention, I haven't slept in a bed with a woman for years. Breaking that streak with her seems as perfect as it is dangerous.

"Nah. I'm here. You can go back to sleep now, sweetheart."

Her lashes flutter, and her eyes are heavy with exhaustion, but she offers up a small smile in the darkness. I don't know how anyone could want to do anything but protect this woman.

"Would you..." The words fade on her lips, and she turns away from me again, like she wishes she hadn't started the request.

"Would I?" I repeat the question. Curiosity getting the better of me.

She risks another glance back at me before she stares down at her pillow.

"Would you hold me?" She asks the question so softly it's barely audible.

"Of course. Come here." I force myself to sound more confident than I am. I want to be here for her when she needs someone. Tonight of all nights.

She slides across the bed tentatively, and I reach over, wrapping one arm around her thigh and another under and around her waist, dragging her until her body is flush with mine. She curls up on her side, curving her body to meet mine. When I move to pull my arm away to give her space, she wraps hers around it, pressing it to her chest. My heart thuds low, and my chest swells at the fact she's seeking me out like this. She's an angel, and if she needs me to keep her safe, I'll do anything she wants.

"Thank you for this. For everything. It means a lot," she whispers.

Her words crack straight into my heart and momentarily steal my own from me. I don't want to say the wrong thing here, and I don't want to ruin this moment, so I squeeze her tighter in response, hoping it gives her what she needs, and she rests her head on the pillow next to me. We stay like that for a long time until her soft little snores lull me to sleep.

TWENTY-SIX

Z ephyrine

LEVI WAKES me up with his hand around my throat and one arm snaked around my middle as he takes me from behind. He's already slipped inside me while I slept, waking me by demanding that I say his name. I let out a soft moan when I realize how wet I am already. He's hitting me at the perfect angle, his grip on me tightening as he kisses his way down my throat. I'm completely lost in it now. Lost in him. The rhythm he keeps is perfect, and his hand drifts between my legs, softly brushing over my clit as he takes me closer to my orgasm. I knew it would be like this with him.

His voice is rough and throaty as he orders me to take him deeper and switches his position until I'm nearly coming with each successive thrust. I could cry for how good it is. Every touch I'd had from Corey had been selfish and neglectful, and on the worst days, baselessly cruel and often painful. He'd told me to shut up, to stay quiet so he could concentrate, while Levi begs to hear more from me again. So I give him everything he wants in return.

Just as I'm getting close, his hand moves to my hip, and he shakes me, rocking me back and forth and pulling away from me. I let out a whimper of disappointment. Instead of demanding his own name, he's calling out mine, more and more urgently with every shake of my body. I frown as the cabin walls around us start to meld into darkness, and I take in a sharp gasp of air.

I blink. It's pitch-black, with only a small patch of moonlight arcing in through the window of the cabin's bedroom. My skin is heated, and the low bloom of want is still here in my body. But he's not inside me. He's not even touching me besides where his hand rests on my hip.

"Zeph?" Levi sounds half awake and more than a little unsure, putting more distance between his body and mine. Nothing like the version that had just been so in sync with me. "You okay?"

I freeze.

"You were..." He pauses, and I realize he's searching for words. I hear him swallow hard before he continues. "I think you were having a dream."

"Oh, um. Yes. I was having a nightmare. I think. Did I wake you up? I'm sorry."

"Yeah." He's short, and I'm worried I've pissed him off somehow.

"I'm sorry. I didn't mean to." I shift in the bed to turn into a new position so I can see his face, and I misjudge how close we are. My hip grazes his dick as I move, and I can feel how hard he is.

He clears his throat. "Sorry," he apologizes. "Whatever was

happening in your dream. You were, uh, grinding back against me. I swear I woke up like this and woke you up as soon as I realized."

"You're fine." I shake my head. Still trying to process how this man and the one who spoke to Corey are one and the same.

"Your nightmare..." The words fade on his lips, and I hear him shift. "Whatever it was. I'm sorry. Especially if it was him. Feel free to let me kill him again in your dreams."

"No, it wasn't him. It was you."

"Me?" He sits up. "Fuck. I'm sorry. I thought today was probably too much for you, and I shouldn't have—"

"We were having sex." I interrupt him, and he goes silent. "In my sleep actually."

"In your sleep?"

"I woke up in my dream to you already inside me," I explain, feeling the creep of embarrassment up my spine. "I'm sorry. It's awkward, I know. I'm just telling you so you don't think it was anything bad. I'm not awake enough to come up with a white lie."

"You said it was a nightmare." He sounds concerned.

"Okay, well, that part was a lie. I guess I can lie, but not creatively." I laugh softly, trying to get him to relax, but I can feel the tension rolling off him.

"I can sleep on the couch," he offers after what feels like an eternity.

"No. Please don't. We're fine. We can go right back to the way we were. It was just a dream. I'll say a rosary for it." I try to make a joke to ease his worry. I turn and scoot back, trying to snuggle up to him again. His hand braces against my hip, preventing me from getting any closer.

"I'm trying to be a good guy right now, Zephyrine." His voice sounds strained. "I'm trying to do the right thing. Trying not to take advantage of you. But I..."

"But..." I finish turning over to look at him. I want to see his face when he talks. It's so expressive, and it's so rare that I get a glimpse of him without his glasses on. Not that I don't find them sexy as hell, but seeing him without them makes me feel like I get a little bit of him that not many people do. Just like that first night here in the shower. A touch more vulnerable than he normally is.

"But you're so fucking pretty when you moan, and listening to you is one of my favorite fucking sounds in the world. I almost didn't wake you up. Which I realize is fucking depraved given our situation. So I can sleep on the couch." I can hear the guilt eating him alive.

A long beat of silence passes between us while my mind whirs. Part of me wants to give him an out. Another part of me wants to seize this chance. But I'm scared of him rejecting me the same way he did before. But nothing risked, nothing gained. My heart pounds faster in my chest.

"Did you fall back asleep?" He breaks the silence.

"Do you want me to?" I reach across his chest and grab his arm, pulling it around me as I curl back up with my back to him again. I press his hand to my stomach, just underneath where my nightgown has bunched up around my waist. He splays his fingers, his palm brushing just above my navel. He absently lets the base of his thumb stroke over my bare skin. "I think I'd like being woken up like that."

"Like what?" His hand freezes in place.

"You—breathing against my neck. Your hand tight around my middle. Fucking me awake."

"Is that how I fucked you in your dreams when I was a priest?"

"Sometimes."

"There was more than once?" He pulls me tight against his body, and I feel his hard cock nestle just below my cheeks, my panties and his boxer briefs providing the two thinnest of barriers between us. Ones I want to curse right now as much as I want to appreciate them.

"It was almost every night."

"I didn't give you enough rosaries." I can feel him smirk against my shoulder.

"You just wanted to imagine me on my knees," I tease him back, the darkness and the closeness of his body making me braver than I should be.

"You're right. I did. *I* probably should have gone to confession."

"For the way you were recording me, definitely." I grin.

"I'd like to see anyone resist after they heard you for the first time."

"I tried to be quiet."

"And failed. Thank fuck." He places a kiss to the top of my shoulder. "How was I fucking you in your dream tonight? Tell me. Because the way you were moaning and grinding away, it seemed like you were loving it."

"You were already inside me as I woke up. You'd snuck into bed, crawled under the sheets, and pulled my panties down my thighs."

"Like this?" His fingers hook into the elastic waist of my underwear, and he pulls them down so slowly I feel every single inch as the cotton slides lower and lower over the curve of my ass and down under my cheeks.

"Just like that."

"Where were my hands?"

"One was just like this, wrapped around my middle." I run my fingers over the backs of his knuckles. "The other was wrapped around my throat."

He slips his other hand under the crook of my neck and leans forward to kiss the side of my throat.

"Like this?" he asks softly.

"Yes," I whisper back.

"What else was I doing?" He kisses me again, this time at the base of my neck, and I can't stop the small sigh of pleasure that comes out of me when he does it.

"The hand you had around my middle... You moved it lower." I still feel shy, unsure of exactly how to handle a man like him. He's so rough around the edges, terrifying really, but so intelligent and soft when he chooses to be. It's uncharted territory for me to have both in the same person. I've only ever known the extremes in my husband and my teenage boyfriend before him. Both of them pale in every possible comparison, which only makes my nerves grow.

His fingers trail over my abdomen, his thumb brushing soft circles in their wake until he meets the waistband of my panties, pinned low on my hips from the way he's pulled them down in the back. His fingers creep under and slowly slip between my legs, his middle finger parting me and brushing over my clit.

He groans against my skin when he finds how wet I am and kisses a trail back down my throat. He nips at my shoulder and grinds his hips upward until I can feel how hard he is. I spread my legs wider for him, and he takes the invitation to add his index finger to the gentle exploration. He's so careful, so gentle that it leaves me wanting more, and I cant my hips to meet his fingers, rocking against them for more friction.

"Fucking hell. You're soaked, sweetheart."

"The dream sex was good." I grin against my pillow, thankful he can't see my face.

"Well, I'm glad I'm meeting expectations up there."

"Exceeding them, honestly. The perfect rhythm, angle, and you say all the right things."

"What do I say?"

"I can't repeat it. It's too much, and I'll die of embarrassment." I plead with him.

"It can't be worse than the things I said on the recording you heard."

"Things like that."

"Like what?" he presses, his fingers circling my clit with more purpose. "You tell me, and I'll give you more of this as a reward."

"Please." I roll my hips to meet him.

"Keep talking." He bribes me.

"You tell me I'm gorgeous when I'm wet for you. You say you can't wait to be inside me, and how well my pretty little cunt is gonna take your cock."

"All true. So far, your dream version seems accurate." His fingers start to move gently over my clit again. "Seeing how wet you got for me today, bent over like that in front of him. Getting to show him how perfect you are. I loved every second of it."

"I loved it too," I confess. "Does that make me terrible?"

"No. That makes you human. Men like him deserve what they get." His lips brush my shoulder, and he picks up his rhythm again. "And you deserve so much more than he ever gave you."

"You're good at this," I whisper.

"We're good at this. It's your dream. I'm just playing the part." He drags his lips over my throat, and I rock back against him as his fingers circle tighter over my clit. "Tell me what else I say."

"You make me say your name. You make me beg for you."

"Is that what you want?" he asks, a touch of surprise in his tone.

"I want you to stop treating me like a nun. Just for a little while." I brave out the request.

"I've never had my hand between a nun's thighs begging

her to tell me her fantasies in the middle of the night. So I think we've got that wish covered."

"Well. There's that at least." My words end on a moan, and I grind back against him.

"Oh fuck. Listen to how perfect you are. Keep moaning like that. I want to hear you."

His fingers slip inside me, and I whimper at the intrusion. Another gasp follows when he grinds the heel of his hand against my clit. He slowly increases his pace, patiently waiting and listening to the sounds I make to direct him.

It's so damn good that I almost don't want to come. I don't want it to be over yet. Tonight I'm celebrating being liberated. Having my freedom back and not having to think about what tomorrow looks like, or what it means if I go back to the convent. Tonight, I get him to myself.

"That's it. Keep going, sweetheart." I'm brought back to the present when I hear how loud I'm breathing, practically panting for air, and whimpering as he brings me to the brink.

I press my face into the pillow, trying to stifle how loud I'm being when it feels like it's echoing off the walls, my lips pressed against the cotton sheet until he nips at the spot where my shoulder and neck meet.

"No. There's no one to hear you out here but me and the trees. So don't you dare silence yourself." He corrects me firmly, softly kissing the spot on my shoulder he just nipped.

He's right. With him, I don't have to worry. I don't have to be embarrassed. There's no judgment. I can just let myself go.

I give him what he wants, moaning loudly as his fingers glide in and out of me, and I use his rhythm to take me crashing into the best orgasm I've had in a long time. Maybe ever. All because it's him with his hands on me. His words coaxing me on with the heat of his body at my back. It's everything I could have asked for, the freedom I've desperately needed.

TWENTY-SEVEN

L^{evi}

SHE'S the prettiest mess I've ever seen in my life. Her hair tangled, and her nightgown bunched up and falling off one shoulder. Her breast on the verge of spilling out while she lets herself go for me. Her hips rock against my hand, and I'm doing my best to follow the rhythm she dictates when she comes. Her sweet little sounds make me harder than I think I've ever been.

"Wow..." she murmurs as she catches her breath.

"That good?" I can't stop myself from gloating a little bit.

"So good. I think I saw stars." Her melodic, amused voice fills me with fucking pride.

"Next time we'll have to try for galaxies." I kiss my way down her jaw, pausing when I realize what I've said. She turns her head, ever so slightly in my direction, and kisses me tentatively on the lips, her lashes lifting as she meets my eyes.

"Sorry." Her eyes go wide at the realization of what she's just done. "I didn't mean—"

I kiss her back, running my fingers up her neck and threading them through her hair as I tilt my head to take the kiss deeper. Her tongue teases mine, and she rolls to her side, her hand running over my shoulder and chest in exploration until we're both out of breath and have to part for oxygen.

"You don't have to be sorry with me."

"No?"

"No."

I see her brows knit together in thought and her lip worrying between her teeth. I'm just about to ask her what's on her mind when her hand wanders down over my waistband.

"You don't have to do that." I swallow past the desire that's burning in my throat. I want this to be about her. Her freedom and her wants. Not about something she thinks she needs to do.

"But if I want to?"

"I'm not about to say no to you touching me if that's what you're worried about."

"I'm out of practice. Obviously. It probably won't be good but—"

I cut her off by kissing her softly, and her hand glides lower as I rock my hips forward, my dick settling in her palm. She teases me with soft touches, stroking me through the cotton.

"It'll be good. Everything you do is."

"Are you sure?" I can hear the nervousness in her tone.

"I'm sure, sweetheart. Whatever you want, I'm good."

Her fingers tease along the waistband, delicately lifting it and pulling it lower. I help her along, raising my hips and using my thumb to drag them lower, giving her access to touch me however she wants.

She's just as tentative as she was before at first, her fingers dancing so lightly over my skin I have to bite my lip to keep from squirming. But after a couple of moments, she wraps her hand around me, taking one long stroke and letting out a soft sigh.

"I hope that's a good sigh and not a he's-disappointingly-small sigh." I grin through the night.

"That was a holy-hell-he's-perfect sigh," she replies. "I knew you would be though."

"You knew, huh?"

"Same size as Father Levi in my fantasies, and he was perfect, so..." She shrugs one shoulder as a laugh tumbles out of her, and I lean forward to kiss my way along her jawline.

"Never thought I'd like the sound of a woman laughing while she has my dick in her hand, but fuck if you don't turn everything upside down. Your laugh is so damn sexy," I whisper against her skin.

She grips me tighter, stroking me with a little more confidence, and I let my hand ghost over her hip and thigh.

"Is this okay? I told you I'm..."

I silence her doubts with a rough kiss. I want to give her back the confidence he stole from her.

"Everything you do is good. You want to make it even better, slip your hand between those pretty legs of yours, get your fingers nice and wet, and then use them on me. It won't take much; I'm on the edge already." It won't take much now if I'm honest. Having this girl touch me when it's the last thing I deserve is already driving me over the edge.

She follows my instructions, though, and I groan when I feel her wrap her hand around me again. Warm and wet with the feel of her. She works me a little faster now, focusing on the sounds I make for her and using them to her advantage. I feel young again. Like we're two college kids who've snuck away to the family cabin for the weekend, only to spend the whole time lost in bed with no way out.

"Fuck yes, just like that." I groan into her neck as she brings me closer to the edge. "See, I told you. You're perfect. Every gorgeous inch of you is."

"I love the way you talk." She kisses me lightly on my neck, and her lips feel like heaven as she works my cock like she owns it. She does if I'm honest. Has for weeks now because she's the only one I can conjure up in my fantasies.

"Christ. You have me so close." I groan. "I should get a towel or my shirt."

"I'm wearing your shirt. So come on me," she murmurs. "Father Levi used to in my dreams."

"Fuck..." I groan.

The confession sends me careening. I come hard, spilling into her hand and onto the shirt she's wearing, and more on her stomach and thighs while I try not to moan so loud I wake the whole forest. I make such a mess of her that I expect her to regret her decision, but instead her eyes light, and she sighs softly. Her fingertips drift up my chest as she studies me.

"You're so beautiful, sweetheart." I try to catch my breath.

"I needed this. Thank you," she mumbles, resting her head in the crook of my shoulder. I smooth her hair out of her face.

"Me too," I agree. "I can get you a warm washcloth. Clean you up."

"In a minute." Her fingers dance over my arm absently as we both let our breathing slow and stare into the darkness of the room.

"That was sexy as hell, by the way." I grin at the ceiling.

"What?"

"That bit at the end. I think you might be good at this whole talking thing, too, with a little practice."

"You'd like that, would you?" she muses.

"I told you. I like everything you do."

When she starts to drift to sleep, her breathing getting

slower and heavier, I sneak off to get her a washcloth. Cleaning her up while she lets me move her limb by limb as she fades into sleep, little grunts of approval as I kiss every part of her I touch. Then I climb in next to her, wrapping my arm around her waist and dragging her close to me, surprised when I can barely keep my eyes open.

TWENTY-EIGHT

Z ephyrine

IN THE MORNING, there's a spread of eggs and toast and bacon that he's fried up in the cast-iron skillet alongside fresh coffee and plenty of cream. He fills my mug with a fresh cup of coffee and drops two spoons of sugar and a heavy splash of cream in mine and one short one in his before pulling it up to his lips. I grin at the way he knows how I take it. I'm not saying stalkers are healthy, but I am saying it's nice to wake up to my coffee exactly the way I like it every morning.

"Morning." His eyes meet mine over the rim of his mug.

"Morning," I answer. "Quite the spread here."

"Yeah, I went a little overboard. It feels strange to be so well rested in the morning, and I wanted to get an early start on things."

"You have a plan in mind?" I nibble a bite of my toast.

"You still know where the ranch Corey was talking about is?"

"Yes. I know it well. Or I did. It's been a while, but we vacationed there in the summer when I was younger. It's a ranch in the mountains. There's an old western mining town at the center of it. He built a large house there. Said he needed a quiet retreat away from the city."

"Fortified?"

"Not back then, but I could see how he might be able to. Although it's huge. He'd only be able to protect the house and some of the outbuildings that are close. Not all of it. But if the vault is in the house, it makes sense that he would."

"So you haven't been there recently?"

"Not for a few years before I left the country. The security measures at the time were minimal. That was before he was governor."

"What about the house?"

"I know the house pretty well. Or again, I remember it well. If he changed things, it's possible it's different. He was still finishing it. There was always some new project going on there. He was always planning new things. He said he wanted to retire there someday. Make it his own personal resort."

"If I could get video of it, could you make it out still do you think? Help sketch a floor plan?"

"Maybe. But how would you get video?"

"Leave that part to me. I have a few ideas, but I need to try some things first. I just want to make sure whatever we get is useful."

"Are you planning to go up there?"

"Possibly. We need the relics out of that vault. Something as leverage."

"Since he doesn't care about me, you mean?"

"I mean, don't get me wrong, I'm still hoping he'll do the

right thing and confess to my parents' murder, then I can release you back to the real world early. You can start your life over without that useless piece of shit hovering in the background."

Except after last night, I'm not sure I'm as excited to be released as I thought I was. I might like it here a little too much. I might have my own plan beginning to form in my head. But first, I have to figure out how I can help. I owe him that much.

"Well, I hope that too, but I doubt it. Not after how he treated my mother. That's one of the things I'm hoping you can find in the vault. Any proof of what he did to her. Hospital records. Information on how he wrestled custody away from her. There has to be something somewhere."

My mother was my father's mistress when his sons were still young, long after he married his current wife. He considered them his real family and brought me into it after he had her sent away. I only saw her a handful of times when I was very little, and my grandfather a few more than that. Even though I was young, I saw enough arguments between them and my father to know something was wrong. I've always wanted to know more of the truth that he never gave me.

"If there is, and we get into that vault, I'll find it for you if I can," Levi promises. "Do you know what happened to her?"

"I suspect he drove her to her death. Emotionally, if not literally. My grandfather said she wanted to raise me, and my father wouldn't allow it. He didn't want her near me or his family. He was worried that having a mistress and a child—a whole other family—would ruin his chance in politics.

"So he used the power he had to push her to the brink of sanity. He had her committed after she tried to run away with me, and he nearly killed us both in a car accident. Had them treat her like a criminal, no visitors, hours and hours every day alone, refused to tell her where I was or even how I was doing." My heart hurts just remembering the little I learned about her from my grandfather and her records at the hospital. They were limited, painting a bleak picture of her life. But when I balanced them with what my grandfather had told me as a child, it was obvious that she was just another one of my father's victims.

"Fuck." He grimaces and shakes his head. "That's fucking awful. I'm sorry."

"Me too. She didn't deserve it."

"I just can't fucking believe the lengths some people will go to just to have things their way."

"Well, my father knows no bounds." I take a sip of my coffee, satisfied it's cooled enough not to scald my tongue. "You want the relics then? That's what you're looking for in the vault?"

"Yes. He has at least two of them in his possession. One, he paid my father to steal from a rich collector, and another, he presumably hired someone else to steal from Hudson Kelly's family. He murdered my parents rather than waiting for it to be delivered, and he burned the house down with Hudson's grandparents inside to cover the theft of the other. So we're alike because I want to use that history to tear his entire world asunder."

"Asunder." I can't help the smile that comes to my lips. "You have an interesting vocabulary for a cowboy. I like listening to you talk."

He returns the smile, his eyes drifting over me and the tank and shorts I have on, both emblazoned with "Seven Sins Saloon," before they come back to meet mine.

"It's mutual." The smile on his face curls up one side, and he takes another long drink of his coffee.

"You like listening to me talk?" I give him a curious look

because I don't think there's anything particularly interesting about the way I speak.

"Yes. I did a lot of it when I was stalking you. Feels like you're another voice in my head now."

"Is that a good or a bad thing?" I laugh.

"Time will tell."

"Should we talk about the elephant in the room then?"

His eyes shift from one side to the other and up to the ceiling, pretending to be looking for the creature.

"Which one is that? The pink one or the purple one? I'm partial to the pink one if you ask me." His eyes light with amusement.

"I didn't know there was more than one."

"Ah, well... Which one are you interested in discussing?"

I shift in my seat. I want to talk about this, need to. But I'm out of practice talking to men in general, let alone crushes. The last time I had one, I was a teenager. I have no idea how to navigate this with a man. Especially one a decade older than me.

"It feels like there's something here. An attraction..."

"You admitted as much in the confessional. How did you put it again? Acting on it alone."

My cheeks pink with the reminder of having admitted something so personal to him.

"Well, I didn't act on it alone last night."

"No, you didn't." He sets his coffee down. "And if that's bothering you this morning, you can tell me. I'm teasing you about the elephants, you know? I just know yesterday was heavy for you."

"It's not bothering me. The opposite actually. I wouldn't mind if it happened again." I risk a glance up at him, and his brow rises and falls almost as quickly, descending too much for my liking.

"I wouldn't either, but I don't know if it's wise."

"Why not?"

"You've been through a lot. You're going through even more right now. I don't want to make things any more complicated for you than they are. Or for me, for that matter. Especially with us working together. I don't want to lose focus, and nights like last night steal all of mine. We've got a lot on the line, other people counting on us too."

"When you put it like that, it sounds sensible." I can't argue with his logic.

"It is, and I know you know that. You're smart. Cunning even. I wish I had half your brains and self-control when I was your age."

"It gets dull always choosing self-control. I'm sure you were far more interesting." If this is what he's like now, I can only imagine what Levi in his twenties was like.

His smile fades as he remembers, and he shakes his head. "I made a lot more mistakes. If I can spare you one, I'm happy to do it."

I hate that his dismissal only makes me like him more. That's the thing about him. He's a rare blend, sadistic and methodical, but careful with his words and gentle in his execution of them. Cruel and kind, sometimes all in the same breath. I imagine he could talk a person into just about anything if he were given the inspiration to do it.

"You're right," I admit. It's a bad idea, and given that there's zero chance for a future between us, muddying the waters with attraction will only make a mess of our plans. "It's the cabin fever and the adrenaline. Hopefully, we got it out of our systems."

"Exactly," he agrees. "So, now that we've slayed the elephant. The plan?"

"Yes. The plan."

"We'll need to figure out how we can get to that vault. I

have a feeling it'll have a lot of useful material inside for both of us."

"If we can get past the mountains, the gate, and the guards. Then into the house, down to the vault, and break the lock, carry everything out with us—without being seen or heard. And then we'll have to get out again without being captured or killed while carrying the relics with us and somehow not damaging them in the process." I outline the impossible task in front of us.

"It's a tall order, but I was up early this morning thinking about it. I've got ideas. We'll still need some help and a couple solutions I don't have just yet. But I have the start of a plan. I need to run it past the rest of our team though. You up for heading down to the ranch house today?"

"Why wouldn't I be?"

"Yesterday was a lot."

"You did the majority of the work, and you're up all bright and raring to go. I'll be just fine."

"Well, drink your coffee, and then we'll head out. Jack already brought the truck over this morning. We should bring the ATV back. It can make it up the terrain out here, and then we won't have to hike it in if we don't feel like it."

"Sounds like a plan as long as you're the one driving."

"No horses. No ATVs. Next thing you'll say, no trucks."

"No trucks." I give him the ammunition he's seeking.

"You sure you grew up in Colorado?" He gives me an amused look.

"A very different version from you, apparently."

"Understatement of the year." He drinks the last of his coffee and then moves to pack his day bag. I do the same, gathering the few belongings I have and tucking them in the over-sized purse Dakota had been kind enough to get me.

"Do you think it's possible I can go to the store?" I'd love to just be able to pick out a few essential items, but given that I don't have money, know where a store is, or have the ability to get there, I'm at his mercy on the subject.

"I think it's possible but risky. Dakota or I can run for you. I'd be worried someone would recognize you otherwise. The governor has an APB out on you."

"You don't think he already assumes I'm here?"

"There's a difference between assuming and knowing. He might assume. But he might figure having you here would be too obvious. My uncle runs the sheriff's department, and he can turn a blind eye when he doesn't have any facts. If citizens start calling in reports, he won't have a choice but to investigate. He knows this ranch well. Your father won't believe he can't find you if we give him a reason to search it."

"All right. I'll put a list together then."

"We can make that happen. Let's just hurry up and get down there."

"You're awfully excited."

"This is the closest I've ever been to turning the tables on him. So yeah. Like a kid in a fucking candy shop."

TWENTY-NINE

L evi

WE'RE FINALLY all assembled around the dinner table that evening—Grant, Dakota, Zephyrine, and me, along with the requisite members of the Kelly family. Rowan and Hudson decided to fly out and back late tonight so we could have the meeting in person, but Charlotte was out of town doing research and Finn had other obligations. Ramsey's busy with his season and happy to keep the situation only on a need-to-know basis, and Hazel opted to stay out of the details of our plan but was happy to loan the ranch house for meetings, so long as we swept up afterward.

"How did things go?" Hudson looks between Grant and me.

"Successfully," I answer. "Along with some clues about where the governor's keeping the relics."

"He coughed them up?" Rowan gives me a surprised look. "Thought that fucker wouldn't talk."

"Levi gave a convincing speech," Zephyrine pipes in, a wicked smile and a knowing glance from across the table have me distracted for a moment.

"Did you now?" Grant looks at me with a raised brow.

"I applied pressure in the right places, and he squeaked a little. I'm not sure he knew much. I imagine Abbott knows better than to leak all his secrets to a man like him," I explain, hoping to spare Dakota the gruesome details. She's aware of exactly what kind of family we are, but I know Grant's still protective over whatever innocence she has left where we're concerned. At least when it comes to the torture and death part of the family business.

"He saw him as more of a convenient ally and less of a confidant," Zephyrine adds.

"Does he have a confidant we can pressure?" Hudson looks between the two of us.

"It's complicated. He has a few guys he relies on, but he always wanted my oldest brother to take over in his stead someday. But he's a fuckup. With only half the brains my father wishes he had," Zephyrine explains.

"And your other brother?" Grant asks.

"More brains, less impulse control. So it's a catch-22 for him." Zephyrine shrugs.

"So no one he trusts fully?" Rowan's brow furrows.

"No. He's paranoid and always worried about anyone outside the family too much. Corey only knew as much as he did because he became family through me. And even then, it was only what he felt was absolutely necessary," Zephyrine reveals. "At least as far as I understand. As you all know, I've spent quite a bit of time away from him."

"All right. So these clues, do we know where they're at?" Hudson turns back to me.

"A compound up in the mountains. Zephyrine knows where it is. I did a little research, looked it up, and tried to find anything I could online. There are no publicly available images, but I might be able to do some reconnaissance and get some private ones."

"Security?" Rowan asks. "I imagine he'll have something or someone keeping watch for drones."

"Lots of it, it sounds like. A private security firm is my best guess. Governor's team when he's in residence, so we'll need to avoid that. Armed presence. Gates on any exposed side."

"Exposed?" Grant seeks clarity.

"It's in a mountain valley. Steep climb in any direction around the main house besides the front entrance." Zephyrine taps the blurry map I have open. "He's always been paranoid."

"For good reason with the kind of extracurriculars he gets up to." Rowan tilts his head as he considers the landscape. "So how do we get in and out?"

"I need to do more reconnaissance to make a plan. There are a few blurry satellite images. Outdated but better than nothing. We'll get ones at street level of the entrance ourselves if nothing else. But I'm also going to see if I can hack the surveillance system. Someone as paranoid as he is has to have one, and we might be able to use that to our advantage to help us map the property, with Zephyrine's help, of course." I flash her a small smile.

"I've got a guy who's good with drones," Rowan offers.

"We just hired a few," Grant adds, glancing toward me as he leans back in his seat.

"I don't want to have them on any kind of alert. We'll need this to be a surprise. If he thinks we're gonna storm the castle, he'll lock it down. Fill the moats, pull up the gates. We don't want this to get any harder than it already is."

"What's the move then? Do you have one in mind?" Grant knows me too well. I was up early this morning—three large cups of black coffee deep by the time Zephyrine joined me for breakfast.

"Trojan horse." It's a simple enough plan, but one that would take precision to execute with any sort of success.

"How?" It's Hudson's turn to furrow his brow in my direction.

"Zephyrine drives a truck straight into the compound. It's closer to Purgatory Falls than the governor's mansion. She's been there plenty of times. If she really escaped captivity, it'd be the first place she'd run to." I zoom out the map and point to the distance between our ranch and his. "He knows we've got her, but he has no idea she's cooperating. I already sent a message threatening her life to Abbott. So he'll assume she's in a hostage situation, not a willing participant. Which helps us set up the Trojan horse."

Grant barely flinches, but I know his tells, and I see the slightest tick in his jaw that I made a move that big without telling him first. He's gotten conservative since Dakota nearly died, and I don't want that interfering with how we play this game. We'll hash it out privately later. Rowan's tilting his head side to side, lips flatlined, earnestly considering the plan, but Hudson still seems skeptical, a feeling he confirms when he speaks.

"So you get her past the gates. Presumably with one or two people hidden in the truck—"

"Three hidden. We'll need at least four to pull this off. Bare minimum. Everything we take has to be carried out on our backs."

"So you somehow pull off hiding three people in the truck,

and you get her in there and trained up in time to be both an actress and a gunslinger. You get past the guards, the security systems, and into whatever dungeon he's keeping the relics—"

"No guns for her. She'll have to go in unarmed, or they'll be suspicious. But yes, a vault housing the relics is in the main house. We're still determining the location of it."

"Then you somehow manage to crack the vault there. Extract the relics from whatever other collection he has inside. Then what? How do you get out undetected? You can't drive out. Any car you take will be called in, and every state trooper in Colorado will be looking for you. You can't walk out because you're in the middle of nowhere. His security presumably still at your back."

"We ride out."

"Ride out?" Hudson's furrow deepens. "How?"

"He's got horses on the ranch. Or he did. I'll need to confirm he still does, but we steal what we need from the tack room, grab the horses, and ride for the mountains."

"And what stops the guards from following you in a car?"

"Nothing. We'd have to outride them to a place where they'd have to follow on foot. Then we could put enough distance between us to buy time."

"Time for what?" Rowan's intrigued by this plan. He always loves a challenge, which is good because he's one of the three I'll need on this mission.

"An airlift," I answer. I planned to take a page for Corey's book.

"My pilot's a former combat pilot, not a magician. Even he can't get a plane down in a valley like that. Let alone being shot at." Hudson shakes his head.

"Not a plane. A helicopter." I point to the top of one of the mountains, where there's enough of a clearing it could land, or worst-case scenario, hover low enough for us to climb up a ladder.

"And we're getting that where exactly?" Grant raises a brow, but I can tell he's intrigued.

"I'm sure we can find one if we look hard enough." I offer up a wry smile, trying to reassure the doubts I can feel start to rise in the room.

"And a pilot?" Hudson gives me a questioning look.

"Yours won't want the job?" I joke because I imagine he's used to flying a private jet back and forth across the country these days and is less interested in a job that gets him shot at.

"I doubt it."

"Wouldn't you want someone with more recent experience?" Dakota chimes in.

"Yes, so if any of you have ideas, let me know. I have a long shot in mind." I look to Grant, and his brows slant southward for a moment before he tilts his head in recognition.

"Worth trying," he agrees when he understands my meaning.

"Want to share with the group?" Rowan looks between us.

"An old friend of mine. Heard a rumor he's not the ghost we thought. If it's true, he's the guy."

"A pilot?" Hudson wants clarification.

"No, but he would know one we can hire."

"And who's our fourth?" Rowan already assumes he's along for the ride, and he's right.

"Him if we're lucky."

"She know how to ride?" Hudson's eyes land on Zephyrine.

"No," she answers him. "But I'm willing to learn."

"Make that two of us. I've met your horses but never ridden one." Rowan frowns at the idea.

"We can get you a refresher, and Zephyrine can learn. It's

easier than it looks." I look between them, thankful when Zephyrine doesn't disagree with me.

"I can help too," Dakota offers. "Hazel might be home for a visit soon, and she's excellent with first-time riders." She gives Zephyrine a reassuring look because the doubt is showing on her face.

"How long do we have?" Rowan asks.

"Less than a month."

"A month? To find a fourth, a combat pilot, map the property, teach these two to ride, and come up with a plan that makes those odds work?" Hudson gives me a skeptical look.

"We've pulled off difficult plans before." Rowan turns to his friend.

"Difficult, yes. Impossible, no. We tried impossible once, if you remember," Hudson recalls, a flash of something crossing his face before he clears it.

"We all survived." Rowan shrugs dismissively.

"Barely." Hudson emphasizes his displeasure at the memory that the rest of us aren't privy to.

"It's possible, just requires good planning and timing. We've got three-fourths of the crew already," I insist.

"Half. You'll need a pilot and a backup in case something happens to him, especially if we've got the cavalry on our heels coming in hot. But half is still a good start. Especially since we have her. The rest we can manage; we'll just have to work our connections until we find something." Rowan's always up for chaos.

"What are you doing about the cameras?" Grant interjects. "If you're using the cameras to map the property, what stops him from just reporting the theft and putting you all in jail?"

"I'll patch in clean security footage when I hack it. But I also plan to take out the local electric grid when I do it."

Hudson makes a guttural sound of disbelief, and it echoes

in the silent room. The faces around the table stare at me with concern.

"How do you plan to take out the local grid?" He asks what everyone is clearly thinking.

"A small EMP device."

"Right. So what's the backup plan?" Hudson looks around the table skeptically, surveying to see if there's anyone who's on board with this.

"We don't have a backup plan," I reply honestly because I doubt the governor will make good on the directions I sent him. "But I'm open to suggestions."

The table's quiet then. However unhinged and nearly impossible my plan is, it's the only one we have.

"So we're moving forward on this one?" I look for a consensus.

"Sounds like we have no other choice." Hudson's still skeptical, but he's willing to acknowledge our limited options. "If everyone on the team is willing..."

"Tell me what I can do to help." Grant nods his approval.

"Just let me know when you want me back out here. I have a few trips I have to run for Charlotte, but I can make it work," Rowan agrees.

I look to Zephyrine last, waiting to hear what she has to say. She might not usually have a vote on this particular council, but she's an honorary member for the time being. The most important one, if we're honest.

"I'm in." She nods, but the way her eyes catch mine, I can read her underlying concern. She's willing but worried. I have my work cut out for me to get her to a place where she feels confident.

"If anyone can pull this off, it's you three. You've got this. I know you do." Dakota does her best to boost morale.

We'll need all the morale we can get. This particular plan

doesn't have an exit strategy. If we fail, we won't just lose out on the opportunity to bring the relics home. None of us will ever see this ranch again.

THIRTY

L^{evi}

"WHY DIDN'T you ever learn to ride? I figured if you lived in the city, it made sense, but your father has a ranch with horses. I can't imagine he didn't have the money to have someone come out and give you riding lessons."

"He never let anyone who wasn't a business partner or security on the property for one." She gives me a look like I should have guessed that much. "But I saw one of my brothers get bucked when we were young, and I just never wanted to ride after that. When he made me do it anyway, I fell off, and I swore I'd never get on one again after that."

"Why?" I press, and she gives me a wary look, like her explanation should be plenty. "I mean, we've all fallen off. You ride horses enough, it happens. Was it that bad, or it just stuck with you?"

"Both. My brother broke his arm and a few of his ribs. Our father was furious because the horse got hurt as well, and it was one he'd spent a lot of money on. When I fell, I didn't get hurt that badly, but I wasn't in good enough shape to get back on right away either. He just left me there to fend for myself."

"Left you? What the fuck?" I'm sick at the thought of a smaller version of her hurt and crying with no one to help. "Did someone help?"

"That's just how he was. I got help eventually." She shakes her head. "All that, and I just always thought horses were intimidating. Beautiful, majestic creatures and all that—don't get me wrong. I loved watching them run from a distance. But up close? Terrified," she explains as we make our way down the gravel path from the parking lot to the stable.

"Well, you don't need to be scared of these horses. A lot of them are trail horses Hazel has for the guests, so they're as patient and steady as they come."

"They're still huge," she remarks as we reach the door, and she sees a few of them.

"Nothing you can't handle. I promise. We're just here to give them some treats and let you see them up close."

"No riding today?"

"No riding. Just visiting. I'll let Dakota give you some lessons. She and Hazel are horse obsessed, and she'll walk you through everything better than I could." I reassure her.

"So she's a horse apologist, is what you're saying?" Zephyrine gives me the side-eye.

"I swear if you give them a chance, you might like them."

"Kind of like you?"

"Kind of like me." I smile at her.

Fuck, I wish I'd met this woman under different circumstances. When we were young and carefree. Before things had hardened us and made us so jaded. Just being around her now makes me feel like I can breathe again.

"All right. Let's do this then. Which one am I trying not to be scared of today?"

"I was thinking Teddy. He got that name cause he's a big old teddy bear."

"Teddy," she repeats the name like saying it will help her suss out his character. "Which one is he?"

"The brown Quarter Horse over there in stall three." I nudge her on, but when she drags her feet, I slide my palm down the inside of her forearm and press my fingers into her palm until she takes my hand. "Come on. You can stay out of his reach until you're comfortable."

"Okay..." She sounds doubtful.

"Kell, you got any carrots out here?"

"Yeah. I got a few in that bucket." He nods to one hanging off one of the hooks, and I snag a few on our way to stall three.

Teddy's eyes light when he sees people approach. He's friendly as all hell, and he's immediately curious about the redhead holding my right hand, but even more excited about the treat in my left.

"Hey, buddy. How are you doing today?" I step forward, still holding Zephyrine's hand while she stays rooted in place. Teddy greets me with a happy little sound and a nuzzle of the hand that holds the carrots. "You want a treat, buddy?" I hold one out for him, and he takes it.

"He's pretty." Zephyrine's face lights up, and if she's scared of him, you can't tell it by looking at her right now.

"You give it a try." I hand a carrot to her, and she takes it gingerly.

"He won't bite me, will he?" She eyes him carefully but the smile stays.

"No. Just keep your fingers down here." I adjust her grip. "There you go."

She lifts the carrot up as an offering of peace to Teddy, and he takes it, chewing it while he checks her out.

"Can I touch him?" She looks to me for permission.

"Yeah, go ahead. He likes a little pat and scratch right here," I explain, taking her hand and placing it on his neck. She's gentle as she runs her hand over him, tentatively checking in to make sure he's okay with it. He leans in her direction, making a happy little chuff of approval.

"Is that good?" she asks.

"Yeah. He likes you." I grin at her.

"I think I like him too." She looks over him. "He's just got a friendly vibe to him."

"That's Teddy. He picked the wrong ranch, I think, but we love him."

"You're a good boy, aren't you? Such a good boy." She praises him as she runs her hand over him in gentle strokes. I hand him another carrot, and he takes it, gobbling up all the treats and attention.

"You need more time with Teddy? I gotta prep them for a ride this afternoon, but I can wait." Kell checks in with me.

"Nah, it's okay. We just came down to say hi today," I explain to Kell.

"When Dakota and I go riding, can I go with him?" Zephyrine looks at me hopefully.

"I think we can arrange that, right, Kell?" I look to the manager of the barn.

"Of course." He nods.

She grins at me and then back at Teddy. "All right then. I guess I'll be seeing you soon."

"You want to meet anyone else today?" I nod back at the rest of the stables.

"No. I think Teddy was a success. I like to start small." She smiles as we start to head out. Her fingers brush against mine accidentally, and I reach for them with mine, letting them link with the tips of hers as we walk. She glances down at the gesture and back at me, a question in her eyes.

"Thank you for trusting me."

"When do you mean? With Teddy?"

"With Teddy. With Corey. With this plan of mine." I stop to look at her.

"Ours. It's my plan too. I want to help your family the same way you helped me." Her eyes meet mine, and she's firm when she speaks.

"You don't have to, if you don't want to. I know what I said. But turning on your father like that... That's a big ask." I shake my head.

"I owe it to my mother and my grandfather to get to the bottom of all of this. I need to know for myself what happened to her. Who he really is. This is my shot to do that. Besides, you've done more for me in a couple of months than he's done my whole life. If I owe anyone loyalty, it's you, Levi."

"You don't owe me anything. But I'm happy if I can help you get to the bottom of things about your mom. The odds of this, though, Zeph... I just want to be sure you understand them. I can take you back to the convent, and we can do this without you. We'd figure it out. Are you really sure?" I ask her one last time.

"I'm sure." She nods, her blue eyes holding mine. "I know the risks. Rowan made the odds pretty clear at that meeting. But we've come this far, and I want to see it through. So if we go out like Bonnie and Clyde..." She shrugs. "Then at least we can say we tried."

I imagine her as a little gangster, robbing banks, and wielding a tommy gun while we drive an old V8 Ford getaway car on some winding backroads. I suppose it isn't all that different from what we're planning.

"You don't miss your peaceful life in the garden of the convent?"

"It was pretty dull compared to this. At least until a handsome bespectacled priest showed up." I hear her soft giggle as we start to walk again.

"Bespectacled, eh?" I adjust my glasses out of habit at her mention of them. "That into glasses then?"

"They highlight your cheekbones and make you a bit scarier."

"Scarier?"

"Yes. Like you're deadly and smart. You could slit my throat while you read me poems and explain their meaning and pentameter. That kind of thing."

I pull her close and kiss her softly. I shouldn't. Not out here in the open where my family can see. Because the way I kiss her isn't like I'm trying to seduce her or keep her in line with little favors. I kiss her like I want to make her mine.

THIRTY-ONE

Zephyrine

LEVI and I have spent the last week riding every day after Dakota gave me a couple of days of introductory courses. I'm still struggling to get in and out of the saddle gracefully, but once I'm in, it's not half bad. Teddy and I have bonded over our week together. The one day I rode Lady Luck instead because he was out on the trail, he greeted me with an enthusiastic neigh and sniff at my pocket for treats when he saw me in the barn again. I guess this is why people love horses so much. If I had one like Teddy, I might too.

As we wait for the horses to be saddled by one of the ranch hands, a blonde woman, whose lack of makeup and mud-caked state take absolutely nothing away from how gorgeous she is, grins at Levi. He tells her something that makes her laugh and touch his arm as I hover near the entrance to the stables. It's obvious they know each other well, maybe even as well as we do, and my heart plummets in my chest as the two of them continue chattering on while she finishes her work. It's a glimpse at his life before I got here, and likely after too.

Levi grabs one of the reins, and she grabs the other, walking the horses in my direction. They look like the perfect couple, side by side, both raised out here with horses in the mountains. She probably doesn't look like a fool when she climbs into the saddle, and he's probably never had to rescue her from drowning in a lake because she's clumsy as hell.

"You should come out with us for drinks," I hear her tell him as she nudges his shoulder.

"When are you going?"

"Friday night, after we've got things all closed up for the day around here."

"I might be able to make it," he says as he tilts his head in consideration, and the nerves prick at my chest.

"You'd be my hero if you did."

"You've got my number?" he asks, and my heart sinks even lower.

"Yep."

"All right. Text me when you know the time." He smiles at her, and she positively beams back in return, the golden strands that have come loose from her braid under her hat framing her perfect heart-shaped face.

I think I might hate her. Which is ridiculous. She seems like a perfectly sweet person. She's been nothing but kind the last couple of days we've been down here. Even downright encouraging to me when we brought the horses back the other night after she saw me attempting to ride. I can't blame Levi for liking her. I probably would too in his shoes.

"Teddy's out on the trail. She saddled Lady Luck for you.

Said she's a good pick for novice riders." Levi's grin remains as he brings the horses to me.

"I'll bet," I say as I take the reins, and we walk them both out of the barn. I frown at Lady Luck. It's not her fault she's not Teddy. Just like it's not mine that I'm a nun with a complicated past and not a carefree ranch hand with normal Friday nights.

"You all right?" He frowns as he looks me over.

"Fine. Just nervous," I deflect.

I'm not about to admit I'm jealous over him. It would be the most ludicrous thing in the world to be jealous over a man I have zero claim to when I'm a nun in training who's planning to return to her convent just as soon as I fulfill my side of this bargain. He doesn't belong to me, even if that wasn't the case. He's been clear all along that he's not good for any sort of attachment, that his only loyalty is to his family.

I'm the daughter of the person he hates most in the world. The one he's using to get to that person, training her to ride because he needs her to know how when they use her to penetrate his defenses and steal from him. This isn't some great love affair. It's a distraction. One I wanted. Needed, really, in the wake of everything with Corey. But one I absolutely can't get caught up in. Being silly and believing it's some sort of fairytale. Seeing them makes me realize how much the cabin fever has gotten to me.

Especially since I'm a novice rider, in every sense of the word. I might not be a virgin, but I'm wildly out of practice, and I doubt eagerness makes up for a lack of skill. It's a good thing I didn't have to try to seduce my captor to get out of this hostage situation. I would have failed miserably.

My heart stops in my chest. Isn't that what he's been doing this whole time? Flirting with me, leading me on, making me think he wants me just to get under my skin. It certainly worked back at the abbey and continues to hold me captive while we've been here. I rub the heel of my palm over my sternum. What if everything he's done has been a lie to get me to do what he wants and I'm just too dense to realize it?

"You ready? I can boost you." Levi helps me up the small set of steps.

"I've got it." I put my foot in the stirrup and swing my leg over the saddle. There's nothing like a fear of looking ridiculous to push you out of your comfort zone in a hurry. Blessedly, I don't fall off the horse, and Lady Luck is as patient as promised. Maybe she's in on the conspiracy to make me feel comfortable here too. I blow out a frustrated sigh, annoyed with my own need to over analyze everything.

"You good?" He looks up at me, still holding Reaper's reins. His brow furrows under his cowboy hat, and his eyes narrow behind his glasses like he's trying to determine what has me so terse. I'm hoping this ride keeps me focused enough that I forget all of this.

"I'm good," I insist.

We ride out into the expanse of the ranch, following a shallow river off into prairie land and toward the forest. It's a gorgeous day, and the leaves turning on the aspens have bathed the forest in a golden halo. The air is that perfect crisp breeze that you wish you could breathe in forever, and the sun keeps you just warm enough that you never get cold. Lady Luck is every bit as sweet as a horse could be, and she almost makes me forget how scared I am. I doubt the horses at my father's ranch will have this kind of temperament, but I suppose wilder things can happen.

By the time we head back to the barn, I've almost forgotten the blonde woman exists. Except she's there waiting when we get back, and Levi stops to tell her something as she walks the horses back into the stable and toward their stalls on the far side. I wait patiently by the empty saddle stands, watching as he looks around as if he's trying to be sure no one overhears. Then he leans in to tell her something that has her smile spreading wide, and she looks up at him like he's the best thing she's ever seen in her life. That much at least, I can relate to. Which tells me I've spent far too much time on this ranch. She wraps her hand around his forearm and presses her other hand to her mouth before she animatedly answers him.

He's flirting with her. Again. Right in front of me.

I can't believe I ever let myself fall into this ridiculous fantasy with him. As if I'm anything but a means to an end in his world. This right here is his real life. Now that I'm finally seeing him with people outside of his inner circle, everything's under a different light. She'll be here long after I'm gone, and they'll be laughing and whispering to each other about the nun who thought she had feelings for him. Hell, they might be doing that right now.

The worst part of all of this is that I just have to stand here and wait. I can't leave. I can't run off. I just have to watch it all unfold and then go back to the cabin with him for dinner. And I have to do my best not to crumble from sheer embarrassment. It's moments like this I miss the convent, and my friends there. They'd tell me I was being awful at this whole nun thing and to focus on things I can control, like the dinner I was making or how far through the catalog I've made it in the archives. Without those distractions, I have far too much time on my hands. Abbess always said idleness was an invitation for temptation. As I wait here, it's also an invitation for doubt.

As Levi walks toward me, he smiles, as if nothing in the world is wrong. Still happy from our ride, like I should be.

"You ready to get some dinner?" he asks. "We could eat at the ranch house or see if we can sneak some leftovers from the kitchen at the inn for a change."

"You sure you don't want to have dinner with her?"

His beautiful face is temporarily marred by confusion, and then he looks back over his shoulder.

"With Millie?" He turns back to me, his eyes sweeping over me as if he's trying to puzzle me out. "Are you jealous of Millie?"

"I'm not jealous. I just thought maybe you two have a thing going on. Like we do or not like we do. Obviously, we don't have a thing; we just have an inconvenient cohabitating situation." I can't even find the right words to discuss this.

He stares at me for a long moment, and it feels like I'll melt under his gaze. If I didn't die of embarrassment before, I will now. I don't know why I opened my mouth. I don't want to know they're having a thing. Like us or otherwise. I would rather live in blissful ignorance of anything they've had.

"We don't have a thing," he says at last.

"Had. Have. Will have on Friday night. Whatever the case might be."

"There is no thing. Now or ever."

"Okay. I know I've been living under a rock, or on one, quite literally, but I also know what flirting looks like when I see it. She was obviously flirting with you, and you were eating it up. You don't have to lie to me. It makes me question other things."

"Like what?" I can tell the implication rankles him.

"I don't think it's worth talking about."

"If it has you this riled, it obviously is worth talking about."

"Fine. Have it your way." I shift on my feet, crossing my arms over my chest. "I know you were there to kidnap me. That it was business to you. We were both dishonest. But did you... Was any of it real? All the flirting and the touches and spending time with me at the convent? Some of those conversations we had... Did any part of you actually like me, or were you just trying to get under my skin to get my attention? Seducing me on purpose?" We'd just sort of moved on without any discussion and now I feel silly for never asking.

He clears his throat and stands a little straighter, looking out across the field beyond the stables before he answers, and the delay makes my weary heart sink even lower.

"On purpose. But it wasn't my idea."

"Whose idea was it?"

"Does it matter?"

"If you want me to believe it wasn't yours, yes."

"Dakota and Charlotte."

That knowledge pricks, particularly because I liked Dakota so much when I met her. She seemed so kind and genuine.

"I thought she was so nice."

"She is nice. Has one of the biggest hearts I've ever met. But your father blew up her bar and nearly killed her and Grant. Destroyed the only memories she had of her family. She assumed you were on assignment for him. Can you blame her?"

"No. I suppose not. But I can blame you." Dakota didn't know me then, but he did.

"I told you what your father did to my family." Then his face falters like he's just processed what I've said. "You can forgive her, but not me?"

"You knew me. You spent time with me. You honestly thought I'd work for a man like that?"

"I didn't know you. As evidenced by the fact I let my guard down just in time for you to drug and burn me."

"I apologized for that!"

"And I've forgiven you, but there's a big difference between then and now."

"Is there? Or are these just more of your mind games to lure me in? Take advantage of the confused nun who can't decide what she wants to make sure she stays in line with your plan.

Seeing you with her..." I trail off, waiting for him to give me an explanation.

"I don't have the energy for those kinds of games. I told Dakota and Charlotte as much when they suggested it. I'm terrible at it."

"Well, you certainly know how to muck it up, considering you're making plans to have sex with someone else right in front of me." I turn to get away from him because I can feel tears claw at the back of my throat, and I refuse to let him see me cry under these circumstances. I might not have much pride left at this point, but what little I do have, I plan to hold on to for dear life.

He sighs, frustrated with himself or with me, I'm not sure, but an apology follows all the same.

"No one's making plans. I'm sorry I did that to you at the convent, but I've been honest with you since. Even when it was painful."

"I shouldn't have said anything." I don't know if I can believe him, and this fight is pointless. I should have kept my thoughts to myself. He might be sincere, but he'd likely say the same thing if he were just trying to weasel out of this. Either way, I feel silly for reacting so strongly when he's being so calm.

"No, you should have. I want to know if that's where your head is at so I can make sure you know that, however things started, that's not the way it is now."

"Right." I have to suppress my tone. I want to believe him— so badly. But these are the same kind of lies I was fed before. He didn't mean it. It was an accident. That was then, and this is now.

I don't have the stomach for it with Levi though. I trusted him, wholeheartedly. Stupidly, it seems. I just want to be back at the cabin and feel silly in private.

"If you just want to drop me off at the cabin. I don't want to be an impediment."

"Zephyrine." He reaches out for me, but I pull back.

"Who does she think I am to you, anyway? I doubt you've told her you're holding me captive."

"I haven't." His brows knit together. "She doesn't ask questions. She knows better than that on this ranch."

"Right. I suppose I should learn that rule as well."

For all the time I've spent around men who play these games, I've never gotten good enough at them myself. I've gone along with my father's plans, however much I hated them, capitulating before I ever really put up a fight. Then I retreated to the convent, forfeiting my life, instead of trying to beat Corey at his game. Now I'll lose another to Levi and the Stocktons.

"Are you trying to piss me off for some reason? I thought we were being straight with each other these days." I see the muscle in his jaw tick, and his eyes narrow behind his glasses.

"Excuse me?"

"I told you there's nothing going on with Millie. I told you the truth about how things started. I apologized. Yet you still seem determined to have it out over this."

"Just because you apologize doesn't mean the other person has to accept your apology."

"And you don't?" His brow lifts.

"I don't. I also don't know that I believe you about Millie. I can't think of another reason the two of you would be giggling and leaning in to talk to one another." They looked like two sweethearts together from where I was standing, and I have a hard time finding another reason. Especially when he won't tell me plainly.

"Christ. We weren't giggling."

"She was."

"But *we* weren't."

"Semantics."

"You're being infuriating right now." I can hear the tone of his voice change from frustration to something else.

"You are infuriating!" I snap at him and turn to walk away for real this time. I have no idea where I'm headed, but I'm ready to go there as fast as possible. Run if I have to.

I don't get far though. His arm darts out, and he snatches me back to him, pulling my body close to his. I can hear the forced patience in his voice when he speaks again.

"No. You don't talk to me like that and just run off. It can't work like that."

"Then take me back to the cabin where I can read in peace while you go fuck your girl! I can't believe I thought I had feelings for you!" I rip free from his grip and turn on him before I storm off.

I'm so angry right now, I'm irrational. Frustrated. Hurt. Sore over the fact that he played me so easily at the convent. I was so naive that I walked straight into the trap. It's pathetic that I didn't figure it out before now, but that he didn't tell me in the time we've had since? That's what hurts the most right now.

"Oh, I think I'm going to fuck her right here." He closes the distance between us, and I take steps backward as quickly as I can until I hit the barn wall. Then he pins me against it. At first, I think he's coming for me, but then I see him reach for something else, checking over his shoulder to see where Millie's gone.

"You wouldn't dare," I challenge him. I might not have many chips to play, but I'm not going to just sit idly by either.

"Right over this saddle stand." It was a rope he was reaching for from the wall over my shoulder.

"Now you're just trying to get a rise out of me. I don't deserve this."

He slips a hand under my chin, forcing me to look at him while he studies my face. I can't read everything behind his eyes, but I wish I could. I don't know how I misread this so badly.

"You're right, sweetheart. You deserve so much better than that, but unfortunately, you're stuck with me." He starts to kiss me, and I nip his lower lip. A guttural sound rumbles from his chest, and he pins me up against the wall as he kisses his way down my throat. It's the perfect distraction while he snatches my wrists and ties them with the rope.

"What are you doing?" When I try to pull my wrists free, it only tightens the knot.

"Proving to you that I don't have any interest in Millie." He pulls the rope and my wrists with it. My feet are forced to move to keep me from falling forward. The rope acts as leverage so he can bend me over the saddle stand. Then he uses the small hook on the far side to secure my wrists, just like he did in front of Corey. It leaves me completely at his mercy. He bends over to bring his eyes level with mine, smirking when he sees the shocked look on my face.

"I will scream," I threaten. It's empty though. My heart is racing in my chest, and everything is pooling low and warm.

"And she'll hear it. Not just her either. I imagine Kell and Grace are still out here somewhere too." Then the man winks at me. Winks! Just before he rounds me and pulls my dress up my thighs and over my ass. "I like you in this color. Complements you so well when you blush. If you want me to stop, now's the time to tell me."

I regret not keeping my pants on for the ride. But I'd been thinking about impressing him, instead of being practical, so I put on this green sundress with a pink prairie flower print, hoping he'd like it. Now I'm sprawled out over a saddle stand in a barn, only partially obscured by a half wall where anyone could walk over and find us.

I could tell him to stop. He'd listen. I know I can trust that much about him from the way he'd protected me.

But I want it. I want him against all my better judgment. Even with the frustration still bubbling in my chest. The only way out for us seems to be through, even when we know how much more complicated it will make things.

"Anyone can see." I point out the obvious, as if he doesn't know that already.

"They could," he agrees easily. Goose bumps rise on my skin. I thought he was just proving his point. "Say it. Tell me to stop, sweetheart. Otherwise, I'm taking you right here."

"You're not serious?" It's half plea and half question.

"Deadly fucking serious, Z. I want to make sure we've satisfied all your doubts. Maybe a few of your appetites too. We already know you like being bent over this saddle stand with an audience. I figure we'll see if you like being tied down while I fuck you loud enough for everyone to hear too. Last chance."

I roll my lower lip between my teeth. I don't want to capitulate so easily, but I don't want to tell him to stop either. I can already feel myself getting wet from the anticipation—a thing he'll gloat about momentarily when he pulls my panties down.

"I wish you could see yourself like this. I should take a picture so you can have it as a keepsake in your drawer at the convent. Then the next priest you try to tie up and ride can be forewarned about how you like to play." He continues on, his fingers slowly tracing their way up the backs of my thighs before he reaches the waistband of my panties on either side of my hips and grabs hold.

"I was not trying to—" I can't even say the rest. The words fade on my lips.

"Oh, don't be shy now. You weren't shy then. You were

straddling me, undressing me, and running your hands over my bare chest when I woke up."

"You make it sound like I was doing something—I was just trying to ask questions." It was a small space and a narrow bed, in my defense.

"If that's what it looks like when you're just trying to ask questions, I'd hate to see your version of an interrogation." He tightens his grip on my underwear and pulls them down, exposing me to the cool breeze that's whipping through the barn. I can hear the moment he realizes how wet I am for him, a smug little sound of approval from his direction has me warming under his gaze.

"You weren't exactly innocent, given you were hard." I try to distract from my own situation as he palms my ass and squeezes my right cheek, surveying his handiwork.

"Yeah, sweetheart, because the idea of waking up to you using me like your own personal ride does something for me. It doesn't change the fact you were just as guilty as I was starting out."

"Whatever you have to believe to live with yourself," I snipe in return. Although he's right. I wasn't exactly innocent, not at the beginning.

"Oh, trust me... I'm living with myself just fine right now." I hear him unbuckle his belt.

"Levi—" I start to protest, but he stops me mid-sentence with a caress of his hand on my hip and over my thigh before I feel him lean down, bracing me wide for him with his hands.

He teases me with the tip of his tongue, giving me a taunting lick that makes me ache for him, and another that elicits a soft cry I can't suppress. He uses the gentlest pressure, the kind that makes the need for him coil inside of me. He repeats the measure twice more, letting me plead to the point of begging before he ends with a kiss that feels somewhere between a promise and torture. There's a soft groan mixed with approval and regret as he stands again.

"You taste so fucking sweet, darlin'. I could spend all afternoon here on my knees. But don't worry. I won't actually let anyone see you. Not really. Too jealous myself for that." I hear the snap of his belt as he pulls it free, anticipation welling up inside of me.

It sinks in that he's about to fuck me in broad daylight in a barn. While I'm tied down. My cheeks burn hotter, but it sets every sense in my body tingling with expectation. I'm not even thinking when I arch my back to give him a better angle.

"That's my girl," he murmurs like he's in awe before he grabs my hips and lines himself up, nudging my entrance. "You know exactly how you like it, don't you?" he mutters, just as he sinks himself inside me. I let out a muted curse and bite down on my lower lip. "Oh fuck. Practically strangling my cock. Is that your revenge, sweetheart? For me taking you like this? That's gonna backfire."

He starts to fuck me slowly at first, gently teasing me as he increases his pace. He's still careful with me, mindful of making sure I know this whole thing would be over if I wanted it to be. His words are less gentle, and he gives me a taste of what it must feel like to be someone untethered from the mores of the convent.

"Fuck. You think they hear that? How wet you are for me? Echoes off these walls so fucking loudly, and they're all gonna know how much you like taking my cock," he whispers conspiratorially.

He's right. It's painfully loud, and there's no mistaking the sound, especially not when he shifts his angle and it elicits a moan I can't stifle. I'm so fired up from our argument and the way he manhandled me into this position, it won't take much to make me come.

"Levi, please."

"Please what?"

"More. Just more." I practically beg him.

He does as I ask, lost in his own rhythm and thoughts. Focused and careful to keep it perfect for me. But I need his words.

"Talk to me," I plead.

"I don't know if I can talk when it's this fucking good, Zeph. You spread out like this, choking my cock with this tight fucking pussy. This pretty little sundress all bunched up your back. Fuck..." He groans.

He smooths his palm over my ass. His hands dig into my hips, and he lifts me just a couple of inches until I'm practically on my tiptoes. The new angle is perfect, and he slips a hand between my legs to massage my clit.

I need it so badly. I'm aching for him. So desperate to come that I rock my hips back and forth with what little slack I have from the rope to counter his movements.

"Such a wicked little thing. You're gonna have to get on your knees tonight. Can you imagine if the other nuns could see you right now?" I can hear the smile in his voice.

"They'd be too jealous to bother with judge..." I say, or at least I try. The last word fades into a whimper because I'm dreadfully close to coming as he takes me deeper, and his fingers circle tighter around my clit.

"That's right, come for me. I want to hear you," he demands. So I let myself brave it out, moaning and muttering a soft curse as I start to crash over the edge. Right as something clatters on the other side of the barn. It jolts me out of my thoughts, so incredibly close to coming that I could cry.

"Shit!" A soft female voice echoes off the barn wall. It's Millie I hear cursing.

Levi lets out a dark chuckle. "Got exactly what you wanted."

"What you wanted," I argue, glancing in the direction of the noise.

"We both wanted," he murmurs. "Focus. I want this little cunt quivering around my cock. I want her to hear the way you sound when you come like this, all spread out and desperate, begging for more. Exactly the way we like it." He repeats the *we* again with emphasis.

He wants me. Claims me. With more than just his body, and for anyone who needs to know—for their benefit and mine.

"Fuck!" He cries out. "I didn't think to ask. Tell me you're on something." His voice is pained, and he stops himself. We were both so eager we didn't think.

"Yes." I had an IUD placed without Corey's knowledge before I married him. Another act of defiance, and one that pays dividends even now.

"Thank fuck because I need to come inside you." He starts again, taking on an even better rhythm than before. "I want this tight little cunt fucked so full you can't forget."

His admission takes me over the brink, and I start to fall apart. I can only imagine how I must look as I use whatever leverage I can to let him take me faster and deeper until I forget my own name and can't stop murmuring his, over and over.

"So fucking gorgeous. I wish I could bottle the sound of you coming like this. Even better because I know it's on my cock." He gloats for half a moment before his own orgasm takes hold, and he loses his words.

I whisper his name like a prayer when I feel him coming hard inside of me, closing my eyes to listen to him. He groans as he slows his thrusts, taking his time finishing us both off. He pulls out of me slowly as his palms brace my hips, and his thumbs work slow circles over my skin. There's a low rumble of approval from his chest as he takes a step back to admire his work. I feel his fingers slip inside me and back out again as I hear his sharp intake of breath and a muttered curse.

"Zeph, you should see this. My cock is soaked. Your tight little cunt so full of me. You're dripping out onto the saddle. Making such a mess." He's still breathing heavy. The low raspy sound of his curses are the only thing I can hear in the barn. I'm half jealous anyone else gets to hear them and half proud they're all for me. I'm too dazed to even respond. His hands follow the curve of my hips as he puts my dress back into place and then fabric rustles along with a zipper as he puts himself back to rights. He walks around, unhooking me and holds out a hand to help me up.

He kisses me sweetly, like he didn't just say all those filthy things to me or bend me over and fuck me senseless. He takes his time undoing the rope around my wrists, using careful ministrations as he rubs his thumb over my skin and makes sure I'm okay. I feel silly for starting the fight that led us here. I should have known better. Trusted him more. But I feel like we've torn down another wall that was keeping us apart in the process.

"Just so you know... She has a crush on one of the guys who works here, and she knows we're friends. She was hoping I could get him out to the bar one night, and I asked her why she didn't just ask him directly. Too nervous, I guess. Just between us, I'm fairly certain he's been in love with her since the day he laid eyes on her," he explains as he wipes down the saddle stand.

"You believe in love at first sight?" I'm surprised. "I didn't take you for that much of a romantic."

"I didn't, but a man can change his mind, right?" The intensity of his gaze as he looks at me makes my heart flutter in my chest.

"Right," I agree.

"So I was just offering to help her out. You read that all wrong, darlin'."

"I'm sorry. I just thought... I shouldn't have jumped to conclusions like that. I should have asked instead. This is so different from what I've known before." I wrap my arms around him, hoping that he understands I'm still navigating what having someone who's so honest with me means.

"I know." He kisses my forehead. "You don't have to apologize. Besides, if that's how we work through it, I don't think I mind a fight now and then."

THIRTY-TWO

L evi

"HAVE YOU EVER BEEN IN LOVE?" she asks as her fingers trace over the rocks at the edge of the spring, and her lashes lift to let her eyes meet mine. I brought her up here to the hot springs to give her muscles a much-needed break. Between riding horses and riding me the last week, the woman deserves it.

But I hate the question she's just asked. I don't want to talk about people from our past. We have so little time left together, and the last thing I want to do is taint it with the presence of ghosts. But if she's asking, I'm giving. I'm sure she has her reasons.

"Once. Maybe twice if you count high school first loves. But I don't think those really count much."

"Really? I feel like mine counts. He was the only one I

really had though." She glances into the distance, not meeting my eyes as I feel the pang of sympathy deep in my chest.

"How old were you when your father forced you to get married?"

"Nineteen." Her voice grows quiet.

"Did you ever think you might love him, or was he horrible from the beginning?"

"Both. I hoped I would love him or grow to. He wasn't my type, physically or intellectually. But he had moments where he could be kind or at least fake it for a while. He was funny on occasion. I thought maybe if I got more of those moments, it could at least be tolerable," she explains.

"Fuck. That must have been terrible. I'm sorry you had to deal with that. Especially at such a young age." I wish I'd known her then. I might have been able to help her escape sooner.

She shrugs. "When you don't think there's any way out, you can convince yourself of almost anything. You just want a moment where it doesn't feel like your whole world's dreary and sad. You know? So I tried to make the best of what I had."

"I get it." I nod along. "So this high school boyfriend, he still around? Should I be jealous?" I mean for it to be a tease, something to take the pall off this conversation, but her eyes go distant, and her face falls with the mention of him. I feel like I'm in a minefield, but I want to understand her more. "Did I say something wrong?"

"No. No. You didn't. It's just he's gone. They, um..." She takes a deep breath. "They set him up. Corey did anyway, after he and my father hatched this scheme to get me married off to him. That's how he died." I can hear the quiver of sadness in her voice, and I reach out to run my hand over hers.

"Holy fuck." I don't know what I expected, but it wasn't that. I knew Corey was depraved, and her father seemingly had no limits to what he'd do to consolidate and reinforce his power. But to kill an innocent man whose only crime was loving her? If I had regrets, I wouldn't now.

"I know. Especially after I just told you I tried to make the best of the marriage. Right? I must sound like a horrible person. I am a horrible person. It's part of why I went to the convent. I thought maybe if I did enough good in the world, enough charity work and giving back, maybe somehow I could make up for it." Tears form at the corners of her eyes, and one rolls down her cheek into the spring water.

"Did you know they were going to do that?"

"No. I didn't know. I didn't find out until after. I honestly still don't know for sure. I don't have the proof anyway. I wish I did. When I accused him, he told me I was crazy. That I'd lost my mind completely, and I was just reaching for some way to make him a villain. But I can't shake the feeling."

"What makes you think they set him up?"

"We were so young. So naïve. Chase, my boyfriend, was so happy for us to be together, but my dad hated me dating him. Chase thought he could change his mind. He wanted to prove himself to my dad. At first it seemed like my dad was open to the idea. He gave him an internship that summer and set him up with a nice stipend. My dad really made me believe that he was buying into our relationship. Told me if I was gonna be stubborn and pick someone for myself that he'd at least try to make a man out of him," she explains, her thumb absently swiping over the top of her knee.

"Fuck. Your father's such a prick. I mean, I knew that, but each new thing I learn makes me even more certain."

"You're not wrong." She looks distant as she swirls her fingertip over the surface of the water, breaking the tension and sending ripples out from the center. "Then one night, he gave him an assignment. It was just a courier job. Taking some paperwork and some cash to someone, one of my dad's business associates. Chase called to tell me he was going to be late for our date night. But it was at a bar known to be rough. A fight broke out, and he was caught in the crossfire. Allegedly. I wasn't there, and the cops didn't spend a lot of time on the case. So if it was premeditated or if he was set up, I'll never really know. Regardless, I felt responsible. My dad, his business. Plus, Chase was doing it all for me because he wanted my dad to accept him, you know?" She sniffs back another round of tears, glancing up at the sky to hold them back.

"Families like ours aren't safe for good people. The undertow of all the fucked-up shit ends up dragging them down too or rotting the relationship from the inside out." I stare up at the sky, thinking of the people who could have died at the wedding.

"You sound like you have personal experience," she notes, and I can feel her eyes on me.

"I did. It was a long time ago now though." I shrug. A memory of my ex flashes in front of me, the two of us in college, studying for our sociology finals at a local diner. Her with a giant milkshake and me with the biggest fucking mug of rot-gut coffee I could find.

"She died?" Zephyrine looks horrified for me, and I'm snapped back into the present.

"No. She left. She was smart enough to see me and all of this for what it was. A life of misery at best and a death sentence at worst. She wanted me to leave with her, and when I wouldn't, she got out. Packed her shit in her little truck and drove off into the sunset.

"I was hurt at first, angry for a while after the hurt dulled. Now... Honestly, I'm proud of her. She chose herself. She chose a future. One far better than I could have ever given her, especially with everything that's happened since."

"Is she still around?"

"I don't think so, but I don't know. We stopped talking. We tried for a little while. She checked in on me when my parents died, came to the funeral. But we just grew apart, you know? If she had died, I don't know how I would have coped. So I'm sorry, truly, for what happened to Chase. I can imagine how that must have ripped your world apart." I look at Zephyrine, and she gives me a sympathetic smile.

I don't think I've ever talked about this before with anyone. Not even Grant. Not honestly anyway. They all knew I was broken up over Cora, but not the depth of it. Ramsey might have understood, but then I was fairly certain Ramsey never really gave up on Hazel.

I knew Cora and I were over for good from the moment she walked. I wasn't going to fight her when I knew it was the best thing for her, and it didn't take her long to find someone else who could do better than me. But I at least knew she was out there, living her life, happy and free. A husband and kids. If I had to live with her being six feet under because of my own family, I have no idea how I'd have gotten through it back then. A monastery might have seemed like the only option besides putting a bullet in my head.

"I'm so sorry you've had to live with that." I run my knuckles down the side of her cheek, sweeping away the tears and wishing I could take the pain with them.

"Thank you," Zephyrine says softly, looking back at me glassy-eyed. I coast my finger under her chin and lean forward, kissing the corners, the left and then the right.

"Is he why you want to go back to the convent?"

She nods. "Part of it. It feels like I owe him that. You know? He never got the life he should have had because of me. It feels wrong to just go back out into the world after all this. Not to mention, my husband's family will probably want me dead once they realize I was involved in his death."

"Your husband's family will never know you were involved. All they'll ever know is that you were a hostage. Same as him. They can assume I just let you live because you had a fucking good side. That man didn't have a single redeeming bone in his body."

"His mother loved him. A lot. Too much, maybe. I think that's where his ego came from, the way she doted on him like he was God's gift to the world. She hated me too. Didn't think I was good enough for him." Zephyrine's face falls at the memory.

"Yeah, well. Mothers are blind to flaws like that, I think. They have to be, I guess. I know mine was. She talked about us all like we were perfect angels when we were anything but."

"I bet you drove her mad when you were younger. I can only imagine you and Grant." A smile threatens to return to her lips.

"We gave her a lot of hell, yeah. I think she couldn't wait for high school to be over so she could ship us off to college just to get a break."

She grins at me. "I believe it."

"Speaking of... Do you want to finish college? You dropped out, I assume because of the wedding." I wonder about the woman she could have become if they hadn't derailed her—the one she might still be once the last of them is out of her way.

"I'd like to. The convent funds a few students each year. I was taking some art history courses and archival ones that I could find online. But now that Corey is out of the way, and I can leave the grounds, I could probably take something more rigorous. Maybe enter university at a smaller college or take a course in Munich, if the abbess approves."

"They let you take classes?"

"Yes. As long as it's not too expensive and it helps us with our role in the convent. They want to make sure the money eventually leads back to charity work or something that benefits the convent, you know?" She looks up at me, and the sun lights up the halo of red around her face.

"What if you have your own money? I'm still working on the bank situation for you, by the way. Don't think I've forgotten." I just want her to have full freedom to do what she wants, not to bend to the will of another mistress like the abbey that'll demand that every moment of her day serve them.

"I don't know. I suppose they might allow it, but we give all that up when we take our vows. It goes to family or charity. Charity in my case since there is no family. None I'd give it to anyway," she explains.

"Fair enough. What if a benefactor pays for it then?" I counter with another idea. I'd gladly pay for whatever classes she wanted.

"Are you offering to be my sugar daddy from beyond the convent walls?" The corners of her mouth turn up, and her blue eyes flash with a coy amusement.

"Just a thought." I shrug.

"I'm sure they'd allow it under normal circumstances, but given ours, I doubt it."

"Ours?" I press just because I want to hear her description of us.

"A former lover. I think they'd frown at that. Worry it could be corrupting my mind."

"Do you plan to tell them about us?"

"I'll probably have to confess it. I should. Obviously, the confessional is a private sanctuary—or it is when the priest is real." She pauses to flash me a look of admonishment. "But the priest would know then, and it'd be up to him if I should stay or not. I don't think he'd tell the abbess, but he could recommend that I not continue on."

"And what if that was the case? What would you do then?" I ask because I'm worried it's a real possibility, and I'd hate to be the cause of her losing the work she wants to do.

"I'm not sure. Probably see what other aid or charity work I could do. Something actually useful and not just idle busy-work, you know? I want to feel like I'm actually atoning for the past. Changing the future in some way. I don't want all of this to be for nothing. Chase's life to have been for nothing." She takes a deep breath, slowly clearing the tears.

"I understand that. More than you know. It's all I've wanted since my parents died," I admit. "If we manage to take your father out, I'll have to figure out what's next."

She reaches across to me and takes my hand, the pad of her thumb massaging my knuckles.

"Will taking out my father give you relief, do you think?" There's no judgment in her eyes, just empathy for what we've both gone through.

"No." I don't even have to think about the answer. It's a question I've asked myself a million times since finding out he was the one behind all of this. "The people he hired to kill my parents. They're dead, and I felt nothing. A temporary wave of excitement that we'd made it a step closer to the truth, but it was just followed by a flood of grief. Killing them didn't change the fact that my parents are dead. It didn't let me go back in time and stop it, or be there at the house to call for help when they needed it. Which is what I really want, and obviously that's not possible." I tried therapy for a while after their death, and it gave me clarity about why I was so angry, but it did nothing to assuage the guilt or stop the slow pull of the void where there had once been a whole family to support me.

"Right." She nods her understanding.

"Your father is about revenge. Absolutely. I won't lie and say he isn't someone I want to see suffer. But what's more important is that we stop him before he does worse. I don't trust him not to hurt someone I care about again. My family. You. If I don't take him out, he'll be out there roaming the streets. All that power. All that leverage to hurt people. Whatever the fuck he has planned with these relics."

"You want to keep everyone safe. I can see that about you. Your brother too." She tilts her head in thought. "But is it worth all the risks? The potential price?"

"I can't sleep at night knowing he's out there."

"You slept last night." She tries to tease me gently, and I give her a small smile in return.

"Because you're next to me." Her brow wrinkles, and I continue on. "When I slept with you, it was the first time in a long time I made it through a whole night."

"Oh, well, I'm glad to hear that." She gives me a sweet smile. Her lashes lower before she looks up at me again, something more wicked in them. "I'm surprised, given how I've woken you up before."

"I mean, it might be better for it. The reward of maybe waking up that way again probably helps me sleep. Just a thought." I raise a brow and run my fingers over her knee.

"Noted." She grins, but I can see her thoughts whirring over everything we've discussed. I don't want her to dwell anymore on anything sad, so I figure it's time for a change of scenery.

"Ready for a picnic then? It's Kit's favorite thing, so I'm sure we have something delicious packed." I stand and climb out of the spring, turning around to hold my hand out for her.

"You don't know what it is?" she asks as she puts her hand in mine.

"Nah. I just let her surprise us. That's part of the fun." I pull her up next to me and kiss her cheek. "Kind of like you."

THIRTY-THREE

Zephyrine

DAKOTA HAS me on a horse and riding a trail that's so beautiful I almost forget I should be afraid. It helps that Teddy is absolutely living up to his name, greeting me like I'm one of his favorite people—probably because of all the treats I feed him, if we're being honest—and being incredibly patient while Dakota tries to build on the basics I've already learned.

Levi went off to work on some elements of his plan. Meeting a guy he thinks could help us get onto my father's ranch and spending the day with Grant while his fiancée tries to make a horsewoman out of me. I don't think I'll be entering any riding competitions anytime soon, but Teddy has definitely made me feel like I might get used to this whole trail-riding thing. And maybe even like it a little bit.

We make our way around another bend, and suddenly the

creek we're riding along opens wide, and I can hear the sound of gushing water in the distance. Dakota looks back at me and grins.

"Thought I'd show you the falls today!" she calls out as we continue around.

My heart nearly stops when I see the full force of the waterfall, the spray creating a colorful arched bow in the midday sun, and the rush of the water into a sizable pool at the bottom.

"They're gorgeous!" I call back as Teddy brings me around to get a better look.

"Right?" She hops down and ties off her horse before coming to help me.

I've gotten the hang of it, but I appreciate that she's there to spot me when I climb down. We tie Teddy up next to her horse and walk to the edge of the water. The mist blows toward us with the soft breeze, and she pulls out a flask from her jacket, offering it to me.

"I don't know. I got myself into trouble the last time." I look at the ornate little container cautiously.

"Good trouble, I hope?" She glances over at me.

"I think so. You'll have to ask Levi his opinion."

"I don't think I need to ask. It's pretty clear to anyone who pays attention that he's obsessed with you. I was waiting for him to throw his coat on the ground the other night so you didn't step in any puddles on the way back to the ranch house." She flashes me a knowing look because Grant grabbed her and threw her over his shoulder on our walk back.

"He's so sweet." I shake my head, taking the flask against my better judgment. I take a long swig before I hand it back to her, letting the flavor sit on my tongue for a moment before it burns its way down my throat.

"See that right there; you're the only person on earth who describes Levi Stockton as sweet."

"I mean, not always. Obviously."

"No, definitely not always."

"You two don't get along?" I ask.

"We do. We just both sit on Grant's shoulders and sometimes pull him in different directions. But I'm learning to love him. Those Stockton boys." She shakes her head. "Ramsey's nearly back in my good graces. Hazel's a lot more forgiving than I am."

"What about Aspen? Have you met her?" I'm so curious about the absent sister.

"Oh, I've met her. She's terrifying."

"Is she? Levi said she's a professor. I thought maybe she was a little less Stockton-like than the rest."

"She basically threatened to cut my heart out with a spoon the first time she saw me with Grant, if that sounds less Stockton-like to you."

I let out a low whistle. "Okay, maybe I don't want to meet her."

"Nah. She'd like you. You're smart, and she'd probably love that her brother's fallen for a nun."

"Oh, I don't think he's fallen for me. Fond of me, protective—yes. But he doesn't strike me as the settling-down sort."

"Who says you have to settle down? One of Grant's best qualities is that he likes supporting whatever wild ideas I have, just as long as he can be the safety net when I jump."

"You two are adorable together. You're such a good match for him. I can see why he'd pick someone like you."

"Someone like me?" Her brow arches skyward.

"Strong, independent, outgoing, goal-oriented. You're everything I wanted to be when I grew up."

"Well, I hate to be the one to tell you, but you're all grown up."

"I'm not remotely extroverted," I argue.

"I mean, I don't think I'll see you throwing any wild parties, but you do all right. You're friendly, thoughtful, approachable. I wish I did a better job of that. We all wish we were a little bit of something else, you know? Grass is always greener."

"True," I agree. "But I just know the way he sees me, like I'm a lost little nun he has to protect. Someone who he needs to watch after. And sure, that's been nice, but after a while, he'll get bored with that. I see him more with someone like you."

"Strong, brave, able to overlook all his vices and violence to see who he really is?"

I nod at her assessment of herself. "Exactly."

"Agreed. He'd need someone who can take her hurt and turn it into something productive. Teach him how to do the same. Someone who can sit in the silence with him long enough that he's willing to talk. Someone who knows enough about loss that she can give him the empathy he needs. Sound like anyone you know?"

I glance over at her, and her brow lifts again.

"I'm just saying..." She takes a sip from the flask. "Actually, it's not just me. Grant's pretty convinced of it too. Worried, I think, that you might dull Levi's edges a little bit. I think it'll be good for him. All of the Stockton men could use a woman who knows how to hold the reins when they need it, you know?"

"I think I have a big learning curve there, literally and figuratively." I laugh.

"You just have to remember who you are." She gives me a once-over and nudges me with her hip. "From what I hear, you're quite dangerous when you want to be. I don't think you grow up with a father like him, survive a man like Corey, and come out the other side powerless. The opposite, really. You get to take what they wasted and make something new. Let yourself hold that power. Wield it for what you want."

We stand in silence for a long minute then, staring out at the beauty of the forest, listening to the roar of the waterfall.

"I'm trying to help with this plan Levi has."

"You're not trying. You're doing." She asserts it for me. "When Grant went through something similar, I didn't get a chance to help him. Levi has you front and center in this plan because he believes in you."

"You weren't helping with the plan when you told him to seduce me?" I risk a glance at her, and she bows her head, shaking it as she kicks a small rock into the water.

"To be fair, I didn't know you then, and I was pretty fresh off a concussion. I'd have to have been to think he could seduce anyone with that attitude. Although the glasses help, right? Grant's just started using readers at night before bed, and they're like kryptonite. It should be studied." She goes down a rabbit hole but reels herself back in and looks at me. "I won't apologize for wanting to protect this family and my friends, but I am sorry it hurt you. I hate that it did."

"It's okay. I would have done the same in your position. I just want to clear the air. When I go back to the convent, I don't want to spend weeks in confession."

"You're going back?" I can hear the disappointment in her tone.

"I think so. I have things in my past that I wish I'd done differently, and the convent makes me feel like I'm doing something about them instead of just moving on like it's nothing. I just wish I didn't have to give up Levi in the process."

"There's nothing else you could do? It's convent or bust?"

"I..." The words fade. I've considered what I'd do if the convent didn't want me anymore, but I haven't thought about what it would mean if I didn't want the convent. If I don't have to run from Corey or my father, there might be other ways of achieving the same goal.

"Because Levi aside, just woman to woman, I think you're wasted there. I know I'm biased. I'd probably catch on fire if I tried to put on one of those habits you all wear. So maybe don't listen to me. But I don't think you could do even half the good you're capable of locked away on that island, living by their rules. I mean... Is it what you really want, or was it what you chose out of the options the men in your life made you feel like you were limited to?" She hands the whisky flask back to me, and I stare at it as I think about her question.

"I'm not sure, I guess. I hadn't thought about it like that."

"Maybe you should."

"Maybe," I agree.

"All right, back to learning to hold the reins then?" She nods to the horses, who are patiently waiting for us to ride back.

"Sounds good." We both start walking toward them, and stretching our legs one last time before we get back on the trail.

"And if you need any tips on the other set, let me know." She grins as she gets back on her horse. I follow suit, and we take off back to the ranch house.

THIRTY-FOUR

Z ephyrine

"WE'VE GOTTA TEACH you to tie a proper knot." Levi watches me tie his horse off as I walk with out with him to fix once of the fences. The other ranch hands were busy and he wanted to show me this part of his childhood home.

"This is a proper knot." I frown as I look at the perfectly serviceable knot that I've used to tie the rope off.

"Square knots don't hold, sweetheart. They're fine if you're tying your shoes or a present, but not much else." He takes the rope from me and redoes the knot before grabbing the picnic and blanket off his horse. I brought a book and some water in my bag so I could keep him company while he works.

"Well, it's the only knot I know. It's been perfectly good until now." I follow him down the bank a little way and luckily there's a nice spot near the fence that's in need of mending with a view of the mountains.

"The fact that you're standing here says otherwise. If you would've put me in something stronger, I might still be on that bed back at the convent." He winks at me as he lays the blanket down in the grass.

"I still think you worked some sort of magic to get out of those." I flash him a suspicious look.

"Nah. Square knots just have a loose hold with rope like that. Here, I'll show you." He grabs a set of extra ropes off the saddle and walks back.

The sun illuminates him from behind like he's an angel—one with lots of tattoos, a cute butt, and a cowboy hat and boots, but honestly, that's my kind of angel anyway. He grins when he sees me staring as he gets back to me.

"What's that look for?"

"Just admiring the view." I shrug as he holds out his hand to help me back to my feet.

"It's a good one, isn't it?" He glances back over his shoulder at the mountains.

"Perfect." I grin, not bothering to correct him.

"All right, well, come here. I'll show you how to tie one that'll hold real quick. You never know when you might need something like this."

"I thought we were having a picnic before we started work. That was the bribe wasn't it?"

"We are. But you're on a ranch now, cowgirl. You have to earn your supper." He flashes a boyish grin, and it makes my stomach flutter.

"Yes, sir." I roll my eyes and laugh, but I follow him to the fence. I'm more interested in getting to watch him work than I am in learning knots, but if it makes him happy, I'll try.

"Did you all work out here when you were younger? Or did

you just have it as more of a playground as kids?" I ask, peering out at the vast sprawling acres of land that seem to go in every direction.

"We worked it. We still had some cattle here when I was a kid, before we sold them off. Grant and I got put through the wringer, but he made Aspen learn too. Ramsey got off a little easier than the rest. My dad wanted us all to learn to run the ranch though. He used to say we couldn't hold anyone else accountable for the work if we couldn't do it ourselves." Levi follows my line of sight and stares out at the field as a small group of mule deer takes their supper a couple of hundred yards away.

"Do you miss it? Or do you like the casino better?"

"Casino is definitely less hard labor. But I miss the ranch too. Ramsey and Hazel are gone quite a bit now with him playing back in Ohio, so I'm here plenty to keep things going. It's been nice to get back a little more than I was when they were separated."

"They're the ones whose wedding was attacked when they were getting remarried?" I ask. I haven't had a chance to meet them yet, but I'm curious about all the Stockton siblings.

"Almost, yeah."

"Did they get to finish the wedding?"

"No. Not yet. Everyone was a little too worried about your father making a second go of it."

"But they will? I hate that he ruins so much." I wish I could fix everything he's broken.

"They will. They're just trying to plan it, and now that Grant and Dakota are engaged, I'm not sure what they've got going. Dakota and Hazel are real close, and they were talking about having a double wedding." He squints in the sun while he looks at me. "You'd have to ask Dakota. I don't keep up with all that. I just take my marching orders when they tell me to get things done." He grins.

"Does that make you the last one then? That isn't married or about to be, I mean."

"Yeah, I guess it does. I hadn't thought of it that way. But last I heard, Aspen might be calling it quits, so maybe not."

"Do you think you'll ever get married?" I realize what an awkward thing it is to ask after the words leave my lips. We aren't exactly together, but our complicated mess of a situation certainly isn't headed down any aisles. "I don't mean—I'm just curious, to be clear." I laugh nervously, and he smiles sympathetically in return.

"So this isn't a proposal?" He grabs his heart, massaging it like I might have broken it.

"Very funny. But it was a halfway serious question. You seem very lone-man-on-the-mountain, at least what I've known of you. I suppose I haven't seen you under normal circumstances," I ramble out loud, realizing I might not even know the real version of him. I haven't seen the everyday version of Levi. The one who goes to work each morning and heads up security at the Avarice, a guy who probably grabs his coffee out of a break room and validates time cards during the week.

"It's not something I've thought a lot about." He shrugs. "Grant and I have always been so focused on the business side of things. The normal side is a lot more paperwork and time in front of the computer, and a lot less time in the cabin or outdoors. It's been nice to have the break."

"Do you wear a suit normally?" I look at the jeans and pearl snap he has on now, rolled up at the sleeves from the work he was doing earlier in the stables.

"Often. I don't know about normally. Why?"

"I'm just curious about what you'd look like on a normal day. Or at a wedding, all dressed up."

"Not a fan of Wranglers and cowboy boots?" He shifts his hat on his head and gives me a mock forlorn look.

"Oh no. They're my favorite so far. I just feel like I need the full range of experiences." I grin at him.

"All right, well..." He gives me half a smile like I'm making him nervous. "Speaking of tying the knot..." He holds up the rope.

"Right, back to the lesson at hand." I nod, putting on my serious face and trying not to laugh when he raises his brow at me.

"I'm gonna tie you up if you keep being so damn sassy." He pretends to come at me.

"Sounds like fun." I tease him in return.

He shakes his head, but I see a flash of appreciation in his eyes.

"Gimme your wrist." He holds his hand out. I eye him warily, but I offer mine left one up and allow him to take it.

"You wanna tie a solid knot, it's easy as hell. You take it like this. Make a tree like so, and a little rabbit hole at the bottom. Then you take this side. The rabbit comes up through the hole, runs around the tree, and goes back down the rabbit hole again." He explains it to me like I'm five years old, and I giggle until I feel him tighten the rope. He pulls me closer to the fence and wraps the other side around the rail. "See, you've got the tree here. Rabbit hole here. What does the rabbit do?" He looks at me.

"Comes up through the hole, runs around the tree, and then goes down the hole again." I repeat his instructions back to him, and he follows them nimbly with his fingers, tightening the rope when he's done.

"There. Now try to get away." He leans back against the fence, crossing his arms as I try to pull away and find myself stuck. He grins. "See how you can't just slip out?"

"Point taken. Now let me go." I raise a brow in his direction as I watch him take in the sight. I can tell he likes it a little too much.

"Ask me nicely, and I'll think about it."

"Let me go, please."

"Hmm..." He hums in contemplation, watching me squirm again. "I'll think about it if you give me a kiss."

"Now you're changing the terms. You said you'd let me go if I asked nicely."

"No, I said I'd think about it, sweetheart. And I did think on it, like I promised. I decided I want something in exchange for your freedom." He rounds me, bringing his body close to mine as his eyes rake over me.

"This is becoming a real habit of yours." My eyes lift to meet his, and he grins like he's got an ace up his sleeve. I feel my heart do its favorite little flutter-and-flip routine in my chest. The one it can't seem to stop doing in his presence.

"It keeps working out so well for me. Why would I stop?" He tilts his head, leaning down slowly until his lips are an inch away, and I can feel the heat of his body pressing close to mine.

I close the gap between us, kissing him like it's our first time, and deepening it as his mouth explores mine. I reach forward while he's distracted, snatching the other rope off his arm and looping it around his wrist. He looks down when he parts from our kiss, a questioning look on his face.

"My turn to try it. Practice makes perfect, right?"

"Right." His eyes scan mine, heavy with desire, but he steps back. He adjusts his hat and unties my wrist from the fence, letting me stretch it and handing me the second rope.

I make quick work of the first knot on his wrist and the second on the fence. He clicks his tongue with a sound of approval and nods as I move to the next one.

"How did you say it went again? I'm trying to memorize it

so I don't forget." I feign the need for his help, and he repeats the story about the rabbit for me as I follow the instructions.

"All right. First, I make the tree and put a hole in the side?" I look to him for clarification.

"At the bottom." He nods, so focused on the way I'm tying the knot that he doesn't see where I'm tying it.

"Oh right. At the bottom. Then the rabbit comes up through the hole, around the tree, and back in?" I race the rabbit through her last steps and pull her tight before he has time to question it. Grinning at my handiwork when I see the final product.

"Just like that." He nods his approval and then moves to show me something when he's stopped by the rope. I've tied him to either side of the fence rail, and I watch the moment his eyes light on the realization.

He's my prisoner now.

THIRTY-FIVE

L evi

SHE SNATCHES the cowboy hat off my head, placing it on her own. Her lashes lift, and the shadow of the brim falls over her face. Her sapphire-blue eyes have lost their angelic quality; there's something devious behind them as her lips curl into a wicked little smile.

My heart skips a beat in my chest. A small whisper of apprehension that I've read her wrong. Wondering if she's played the long game with me to get me into this position because she's definitely pleased with herself.

"Zephyrine." I use her name like a warning as I tug on one of the binds. She was paying attention because they're done perfectly. Enough slack that I can move around, but not enough to have any hope of getting out of them without assistance. I'm at her mercy.

"Looks like I did a better job this time," she muses as she sees me try the other wrist, and it's equally snug.

"You're a fast learner."

"I am. It's the key to surviving." She closes the distance between us. "Or getting what you want."

"Meaning?" I ask.

"Meaning I pay attention. I remember. Then I use it to my advantage when the time is right." Her palm presses to my chest and drifts down.

"That's what you're doing now?" I have no idea what the fuck is happening right now, and I don't know which of a half-dozen emotions coursing through me to embrace.

"I mean, I do have you all tied up. Just like at the convent. I don't think you'll get loose this time though. No one can hear you yell either. Not all the way out here." She grins at me and then peers back at the ranch in the distance.

The late light of the day hits all the angles of her cheek-bones and lips, the light bouncing through her irises illuminates the blue, making it even brighter than usual. Fuck, she's gorgeous even when she's threatening my life.

"What's your plan then?" I ask, careful to keep my tone level.

"Oh, I have a few ideas." She brings her body up against mine. "More than a few really. I spent a lot of time thinking about what I'd do if I ever got you into this position again." Her palm slips under my shirt and drifts up over my skin, and she leans closer to me. The scent of her shampoo envelopes me, and I wonder if this is the last time it ever will.

"If you're going to run, you'd better make sure Rowan never finds you. He'll kill you if he does," I warn her. Her palms freeze, and she pulls back to look at me. She gives me an admonishing look.

"I'm not going to run, cowboy. But you might wish I had when I'm done with you."

I frown at her, trying to make sense of her meaning, and her wry smile spreads as she sees my confusion.

"In fact, I think I'll go even harder on you for thinking there's a chance I would run," she says softly, her eyes studying me.

"Harder on me, how?" I ask, still grasping at straws for what her plan is.

She grins brightly, rolling her lower lip between her teeth as her eyes meet mine.

"How did you put it that one time? 'It does something for you.' I think that's what you said when we were talking about you all tied up and me spread over your lap."

Oh.

"Well fuck..." I can't help the smile that breaks on my face, and it's reflected back to me in hers. I dip my head low as I laugh at myself, and I fucking feel heat curl up my spine and back down my neck. I'd never have guessed this of her in a million fucking years. She's been so soft-spoken about everything so far, so sweet.

"So my memory is right then?" She pulls close to me again, her voice a low whisper, and I can feel her warm breath at my neck. "You like the idea of your enemy's daughter tying you up and stripping you down? Using you to get what she needs? Or would you rather have the undersexed nun who can't stop thinking about how much she wants you?"

"I like them both," I admit.

"Hmm. Well, I suppose they'll both have to get a turn then." She kisses my throat, her lips moving over my skin in soft strokes as her hands drift lower.

"What happened to my shy, sweet girl?"

"You'll get her back when I'm done." She palms me

through my jeans, and I bite back a groan. I'm already going hard for her, and she grins against my skin. "I don't know if there'll be anything left of you for her though."

"Oh yeah?" I choke on the taunting words when she runs her palm back up the length of me, just enough pressure to make my cock twitch.

"Yeah. I have every intention of using every last drop up."

"Fucking hell, Zeph." I breathe her name like a prayer because I don't know if I'm prepared for this version of her.

"Ah, ah," she tuts. "You don't get to say my name. Not until you earn it back." She kisses my neck one last time, and then her hands fall to my belt, working the buckle to undo it.

"How do I do that?"

"Following instructions. Doing what I say, when I say it. I don't want to have to punish you for not listening, you know?" Her eyes lift to meet mine as she tosses my belt to the ground, and her fingers nimbly work their way over the button on my jeans.

"Got it." I nod. I don't think I've ever been this fucking hard in my life. No woman has ever been brave enough to try this on me.

"Yes, ma'am." She pauses as she drags my zipper down, looking me dead in the eye when she says it.

"Yes, ma'am." I repeat it back to her, and her lips quiver with amusement.

"That's good." She finishes her work on the zipper, and her hands go to the waistband of my jeans and boxer briefs. She tugs them down, sliding them off my hips and down my thighs. "And this is even better," she murmurs softly, her lip rolling between her teeth again as she reaches for me. She wraps her hand around me, and the softness of her palm drags down the length of my cock. It feels like fucking heaven, given how tight she's got me wound up already. So good I let out a soft whimper before I can stop myself. Her eyes light up at the sound.

"Oh, you're going to be so good for me, aren't you?" She strokes me again, and I try to cover the next one, but she draws it out of me anyway. Her smile spreads as my hips jolt forward of their own accord. "I need you ready for me. I won't last very long. Not with how big you are. How wet you make me. But you know that, don't you?"

"Fuck." I take in a sharp breath when her other hand cups my balls, and she strokes her thumb up and down, squeezing gently while she keeps up a slow, steady pace on my cock.

"Don't worry. I won't let anyone know the big bad wolf likes to be put on a leash sometimes." She drags her lips up my throat, from the base of my neck all the way up to my ear. "It'll be our little secret."

"Fuck me," I curse, closing my eyes. Apparently, that's all I've got right now. A series of curses and whimpers. She's already got me so focused on listening to her. I can't even think straight.

"You're right. We should get the first one out of the way. Take the edge off for you." She lets me go momentarily, studying me as if she's deciding if I'm worthy of her. The loss of her touch nearly kills me. I lean my head back and look up at the faded blue of the sky, closing my eyes as she gives me one last stroke to make sure I'm ready before she takes what she wants.

"Sit down." She breaks the silence, and my eyes snap open to see the serious look on her face as she orders me into place. I have to move carefully, twist my wrists a little, and grip the rope as I move to a seated position. "Lean back against the fence." Another order from her follows, and I do as she says.

She grins down at me once I'm in position, my hands still wrapped around the rope and my arms spread wide. I can feel the rough, dry grass against my ass and upper thighs, and my mind drifts for a moment before I see her reach under her skirt. She pulls her panties down her long legs, taking her time like she wants to make me suffer. She lets them pool in the grass and steps out of them one leg at a time. It feels like I'm watching her in slow motion, like none of this can be real.

She walks over the top of me, one boot on either side of my thighs until she hits her knees and tucks her feet under, lifting her skirt and dropping it neatly around me. She hovers over my dick, a sincere look in her eyes as she searches my face.

"Should we have a safe word?"

"I won't need one." This woman could ride my cock raw if she wanted, and I'd just beg for more from her.

"You might. You don't know what I'm capable of." There's a sly little grin teasing at the corner of her mouth, and her eyes flash with amusement.

"I don't, but I'm a fast learner," I counter.

"Just in case. We should. Do you have one you like?"

I shake my head. "Never needed one."

"Hmm." She presses her lips together, and her eyes wander skyward as she thinks. A smile breaks across her beautiful face, and she looks at me in amusement. "How about confess?"

I shake my head with a smile, remembering that vulnerable, sweet voice behind the wall of the confessional. Wondering if it's this very scenario she was conjuring up at night. I wouldn't hate it if it were.

"You're a wicked little thing, you know that, sweetheart?"

"Is that a yes?" She refuses to be deterred.

"Confess it is," I agree.

She doesn't waste time after that. Guiding herself down onto my cock. I groan, leaning my head back against the rail of the fence once she's fully seated. She's so fucking warm and wet and perfect. I don't deserve her, but I think I might love being at her mercy.

She braces her hands on my shoulders, and she rocks herself up and over my cock. Once. Twice. It's too fucking good. I could die like this. She could kill me once she's done with me, and I'd thank her for it.

"God, I love the way you feel. You're so perfect." She praises me softly as she works her tight cunt up and down on my cock.

"Are you always this nice to your captives? I think I could get used to this. You feel like an angel of fucking mercy." I manage the words in between stuttered breaths as I watch her.

She's fucking stunning, her dress splayed out around our laps, fluttering as she works up and down. Her chest and her neck flushed from the effort, and her cheeks bright with color. My cowboy hat slips back on her head as her lashes lift.

"I'm just going easy on you this first time. Letting you get warmed up for me. Don't get used to it," she taunts me, her lips twitching as she suppresses a smile.

"You better use your fingers on that pretty little clit of yours since I can't, sweetheart. I won't last if you keep up like this. You'll be disappointed," I warn her because I can feel the wave of my orgasm building already.

"Oh, I'm counting on being disappointed and having you apologize with that mouth of yours for a good ten minutes before I come," she snaps back, not missing a beat, and fuck does it do something for me to hear her talk like that. She can see it on my face because she grins in response.

"I have bad news if you think that's going to punish me."

"I have bad news if you think that's the worst of it." She kisses her way up my jaw and lets out a soft moan against my ear as she switches her angle slightly. I lean forward and groan into her shoulder. Her tight little cunt squeezes me for everything I'm worth as she breathes curses against my cheek and down my neck. She fucks me until I'm so close I can feel the edge of my orgasm. I can tell she's working herself close too, almost there, when she wrenches herself away.

She climbs off me and takes a long, deep breath, pinching her eyes shut like she does when she's trying to concentrate. I think she's going to climb back on, work me over from a different angle, but instead she deprives us both.

"What the fuck?" I stare up at her, confused and aching for her to finish me off.

"You don't get to come that easy." She shakes her head, unmoved by how wickedly cruel she's being right now. But I can see her struggle to concentrate, turning her head toward the mountains to take a breath and steady her own impulses.

Her attention returns to me as she works to clean me up gently. The touches taunt me, her sweet ministrations only a hint of what she's capable of as she handles me like I'm glass instead of the reality. A cock so fucking hard it might as well be granite, the head swollen and dripping as she wipes me clean with the hem of her dress—every inch as desperate as I am to be back inside of her.

I want her. Fuck, if we're honest, I need her. Especially now. But she won't let me get off easy. She'll torture me, I can see it in her eyes.

"Fine. Come here." I nod to her soaking wet little cunt. "Let me taste what I did earn." My voice is rough, but she doesn't miss the arrogance in my tone.

"You didn't earn it." She looks to me, her brow rising in admonishment for being smart.

"No? You're that wet for someone else?"

"I did all the work."

"On my perfect cock." My smirk spreads wider, and her eyes narrow in response.

"Get on your knees," she demands, standing up along with me. It takes me a minute with the way she's got my jeans twisted, and she smiles at me struggling. "Do you need help?"

I grumble under my breath, and she grabs the waistband that's trapped around my legs. I assume she's going to help me pull them back up, but instead, she yanks them to the ground.

"What the hell?" I ask, looking up at her.

"You didn't ask nicely. Besides. I don't want them in my way next time." She studies my face as I lift a brow. "Don't worry. I have faith in you. I'm sure Father Levi can work a miracle even if the cowboy in here can't." She pats my chest gently, taunting me with a wry little smirk.

It gets the rise she's hoping for because now I'm determined to get her off as many times as it takes to satisfy her little game. I kick off my jeans and boots with her help and kneel down in the grass, looking up at her. She nibbles her lower lip like she does when she's nervous, and I run my tongue along my teeth and shake my head.

"No time for being shy now, darlin'. You wanted the fucking wolf, so get up here so he can fucking eat you."

Amusement and desire flicker over her face in rapid order, and she takes two tentative steps forward. If she let me out of these fucking ropes, I'd have her in the grass by now, face down, ass up while I ate her until she screamed. But as it stands, it'll be more of a challenge. I can coax her through it with my tongue though.

"Spread wider and stand over me. If we're doing this, we're doing it right." I look up at her, holding her gaze while she brings herself within an inch of my mouth. "Lift the skirt."

She pulls it up slowly, inch by inch, until I have a full view of her. My mouth waters with the thought of how she tastes. If she thought she'd win this game, she picked the wrong man.

"Grab the fence post," I order. "You'll need it."

THIRTY-SIX

Z ephyrine

HE TAKES ONE LONG, careful lick of me, and already I have to tighten my grip on the wood, reaching for a better purchase when his tongue laves over me again. I was too close when I stopped. It'll take next to nothing to get me off. I let out a soft moan as his tongue starts to circle my clit, and he pulls back.

"I want a good fucking taste of you first." He's determined to taunt me.

"Levi, please." I beg him to do his worst. I want to edge myself, give my body a few more minutes on the brink before I fall apart. I have no idea if he'll ever let me do this again, and I want to savor it while I can.

"Fuck, I need this. The taste of you soaked into my tongue

like this. Spread wider." His tone is rough and demanding, and I do as he asks.

I grip the bunched-up hem of my skirt tighter on his next pass. He lights up every fiber of my body with each stroke of his tongue over my skin. This is what I get for getting him so riled— pure torment. But I don't regret it. The only thing I'm regretting right now is the fact that we're out here, where I have to try to maintain my balance, instead of in a bed where I could just let him shatter my focus into a thousand pieces.

His tongue teases at my swollen clit again, and I nearly topple over from the sensation. The fence post barely keeps me upright. I roll my skirt under, tucking it under the waist of the dress to free my hand. I reach down for him, and the backs of my knuckles brush over his cheek softly. I try to coax him down from this punishing pace, but he won't relent, sucking my clit instead until I start to whimper.

My fingers slip through his damp brown curls, finding purchase at the crown and rocking my hips up to meet his tongue when he lets go again. He's determined to fucking devour me. He only pauses intermittently to lap up the wetness that falls like tears down my inner thigh.

"Oh please. Please." I plead with him when he brings me close again, and he lets me go, the cool air whipping around my heated skin as we stare at each other.

"Don't beg." He drags his tongue over his lower lip, a cocky grin forming as he sees the state he's put me in. "Order."

Oh.

My eyebrows lift in surprise at just how much he likes this. I'm going to have to get Dakota a gift basket. Or a lifetime supply of her favorite whisky. He waits patiently as I take a deep breath and pull myself back together again. At least enough to finish this. I let it back out slowly.

"If you want any hope of getting out of these knots tonight, you'd better make me come. Hard and fast," I challenge him.

A flicker of something flashes behind his eyes, and he follows the order as his mouth descends on me again. His tongue and lips working overtime to bring me close again.

"That's it. Finish me off. Just like that. Such a good cowboy." I tighten my grip on his hair and rock my hips against his face as he starts to suck on my clit once more.

I whimper when the wave finally hits me, crying out as my vision fades, and he keeps up his end of the bargain. This must be the galaxy he promised—stars, supernovas, and a lack of gravity that leaves me spinning. I'm moaning as my breathing stutters, slowing, tapering as I try to catch my breath. My knee starts to slip back down his chest as he laps me up, trying to get every last drop until I take a step back and drop to my knees in the grass.

"Tired?" He taunts me, and I look up at him. A self-satisfied smirk grows on his face as he looks me over. "Or you think you can ride me again?"

I glance down, and he's still hard. Still in need of relief that only I can give him.

"Again?" I ask in between deep breaths, unraveling my skirt from where I'd bunched it around my waist. I grin as I let my eyes wander over him. The sun is setting, and the dip of the sun behind the mountains casts harsh shadows that highlight his broad shoulders and every rise and fall of the muscles in his arms. I fall back onto my elbows and throw my head back to look up at the way the moon is starting to fade into the deepening blue of the sky.

"I'm not sure you're up for it," I say softly, looking at him with one eye half open, hesitant to taunt him further. His brow arches in response. "I think we might be starting to push your limits, and I worry about what happens when you finally slip out of those." I nod at the binds on his wrists. They've held better than I could have hoped.

"Oh, when that happens, you're a dead woman. So you'd better make sure you've thoroughly enjoyed yourself." He grins as I crawl over to him through the grass. I run my hands over his shoulders as I stare up at him.

"Have you?" I ask softly.

"Yes," he whispers back, his eyes studying mine and then dropping to my lips. "I enjoy everything with you."

"Me too." I admit the truth.

I kiss him tentatively, testing the waters to make sure he'll kiss me back. His lips press against mine in answer and then part to let my tongue brush over his. My fingers explore his traps and slide down his back as I get lost in the feel of him. He takes the kiss deeper, giving me more even as I withhold the one thing he wants most. Levi Stockton is everything I dreamed Father Levi was and more. Better in every way possible. We break the kiss for air, our foreheads touching as he takes in a steadying breath.

"It's getting late. We should get you home. Get some food before the next round," he whispers.

"Okay." I nod, rolling my lower lip between my teeth and shuffling to the right to loosen the knot.

No sooner do I create some slack in it, he slips his left wrist free. His fingers go to the spot where the rope has left its mark, running his thumb over them before his eyes turn on me. He pulls a knife from his back pocket, flicking the blade with one smooth motion. He doesn't have to say a word for me to realize I've made a grave mistake. His eyes say everything.

Run.

It's all I can think. My heart's already pounding in my ears, and my adrenaline surges through my body. I scramble to try to get to my feet, but I'm exhausted. I slip when I try. My ankle's still not one hundred percent. Before I can even crawl away, his hand catches my good ankle, and he drags me back into his arms.

"Levi, please," I beg him as I try to squirm out of his grasp. "I was just teasing you. It was all in fun. Please." I try to reason with him as he tightens his grip.

"Now you're scared?" A sinister-sounding laugh rumbles from his chest. It makes the goose bumps rise on my skin. I try to pull away, but he pulls me back, and my body slams into his, my back against his front. I can feel how hard he is at the base of my spine and his warm breath dancing down my neck. I know he won't really hurt me, but my body can't tell the difference. "You didn't act scared before, but you should be. You've seen what I'm capable of."

"Yes." I nod and close my eyes, remembering the way he slit Corey's throat after he tortured him. He's right. It should scare me, but it doesn't. It makes me feel safe knowing he'd kill for me. It makes me want him even more than I already did, even when I'm nervous he's about to punish me for turning the tables on him.

"And you still tied me up like that?"

"I'd do it again."

"Of course you would." He huffs, a tinge of amused pride belying his vengeful tone. "That version you built up in your head the first time you tied me up, you remember him?"

"Yes." I forget how well this man knows me sometimes. How much he's seen inside my head.

"You're about to meet him." He curses under his breath as I squirm to free myself, and his cock slips between my thighs, teasing both of us. He presses his lips against my ear again, taking a deep breath. "You'll have an extra minute while I cut myself loose. Another two while I put my jeans and boots back on. I'd use every single one of them if I were you. Wear me out on the run. Because you're getting every last drop I have in me when I get my hands on you free and clear."

THIRTY-SEVEN

Z ephyrine

MY LUNGS BURN as I climb the next hill, the running and the lack of oxygen at this altitude tearing into my chest as I try to catch my next breath. But I move as fast as my feet will take me, up the hill and through the long prairie grass. One after another until the top of this ridge is nearly close enough for me to reach out and touch. I'm so close and yet so far.

I glance back over my shoulder. He's not far now. Gaining with every long step of his stride. One that far surpasses mine and leaves me desperate for another escape. I'll lose the race in minutes, and he'll be on me, his hands wrapped around me as he drags me down to the ground. All reason gone. Replaced instead by the man who's determined to get his revenge on me for my trick.

My heart flutters in my chest when I crest the next hill and see a small, slightly dilapidated church at the bottom of it. It looks abandoned—the stones are thick with ivy, and there are wildly overgrown bushes at the entrance. But if I can get inside and lock the doors behind me, it could buy me precious time. I'd wait for his adrenaline to recede, and then I'd apologize for taking things too far. It could work.

I race toward it, my feet carrying me as fast as they'll go. It's one last burst of energy on my part. But I make it, quickly wiping the sweat from my brow as I take one last trudge of ascension up the steps to the door.

My hands are on the door handle, my palms slippery until I wipe them on my dress and try again. It cedes to my pressure easily, swinging open and allowing me into a small vestibule. It's cooler inside than outside, the stones working as an insulator from the sun. A sigh of relief ripples through me as I see him on the top of the hill, glaring at me as he watches me disappear inside. I slam the door shut, my fingers fumbling for a lock but failing to find one. I search for something to bar the door with, but there's nothing. My heart speeds its rhythm, panic setting in as I see him through a window, halfway down the hill and gaining on me rapidly.

How could this not have a lock? It has to have one somewhere. My fingers swipe over the inside of the heavy wooden door, trying and failing to find a locking mechanism to bar it shut.

I can hear him now. His feet across the gravel in front of the church. I have minutes, seconds even, before he's on top of me.

I abandon the oak door, falling back to the other side of the vestibule and slipping beyond the wrought iron gates that lead to the sanctuary of the church. My eyes float to them, rapidly assessing to see if they'll close and discovering they're on a track that runs along the wall on either side of the arched entryway. I wrap my palms around one of the wrought iron spindles and pull, heaving as hard as I can to bring it to the center.

But again, I fail. The iron is heavy, and the tracks are worn, gathering dust and debris from all the years of disuse.

I heave again, harder, throwing all of my body weight into it. This time, it creaks, threatening to move at first and then finally complies with a loud squeal of protest as I reach for the other one, hoping it goes easier than the first. If I can bring the second one to the center, I can find something to wedge them shut together. It shouldn't take long. If I can just—

I hear the sound of his boots on the stairs. The echo of them hitting the stones of the entryway, and the thud as he crosses it. I can feel him before I see him.

I look up slowly, his chest rising and falling with the effort of every breath. He's tired. That's my only saving grace. Because his eyes are filled with fury, and his face is as stormy as I've ever seen it when he's been alone with me.

"Sanctuary." I claim it even though it's been centuries since anyone respected it.

He lets out a sardonic laugh in response, his dark lashes lifting as he looks around the room. The blue-green of his irises lighting as a ray streams through the stained glass, catching on them. He almost looks angelic in this light. Almost.

"It will be," he mutters.

"Levi." I say his name like a prayer. His eyes shift from studying our surroundings to taking me in.

He steps forward and slams the wrought iron gate behind him; the clang resonates against the stone walls and through my body. He grabs the rope I used on him off of his hip, tying the two sides of the gate together, sealing me in with him. There's a soft staticky hum in my ears that grows along with the echo of his boots closing the space between us, one methodical step at a time. I feel the oxygen slipping from my lungs with every inch he draws closer.

He pins me against the wrought iron, the cold touch of the metal against my skin making me arch forward unwillingly. I hold up my hands, pushing against his chest in a way that buys me exactly zero leeway. He snatches my wrist, pinning it up behind my head. The second follows the first. His lips curling in a devilish sneer before he leans forward, his tongue darting out to lick the sweat that drips down my neck.

I close my eyes until I hear the distinct rip of fabric. His knife tears into the left strap of my sundress and then the right. It slips from my shoulders and exposes my breasts. He stares, blatantly, a blush blooming over my chest, and my nipples bead under his watch.

"Disrespectful to try to lock me out when I'm generous enough to give you a head start." The short puffs of his breath are cool against my heated skin, and I squirm underneath his watch.

"You're being disrespectful. This is a sacred place. You didn't even bless yourself when you came in," I rasp. I'm reaching for any excuse to slow him down, even though my body is lighting up under his touch. I need some semblance of the reasonable version of him I know. I'm not even sure he exists in this room right now, but a girl can try.

"Oh." He pulls back, his eyes searching mine, and then he holds my gaze so intently I fear I might melt under the weight of it. "We're back to propriety now that it's your turn?"

"Yes," I answer him.

"As you wish." He nods, the sneer of irritation thawing into what I could almost describe as amusement. And for a brief, fleeting moment, I feel like I might finally be free of his retribution.

He reaches over to the water stoup, dipping his index and

middle finger inside to draw on the holy water, and predictably finds it empty after years of neglect. He frowns with disappointment.

"Well, that's unfortunate. I suppose I'll have to make do with what I have available." His grip on my wrists tightens, holding me with one hand, and slipping under my skirt and between my thighs with the other. I'm drowning in the anticipation of his plans, and he groans against my throat when he finds me wet for him again. "Look how good you are to me. Giving me exactly what I need. A fucking angel if there ever was one." He teases me, slipping just the tips of his fingers in and out, painstakingly slowly, before he pulls them free. He holds them up, studying them as they glisten in the low light before he uses them to wet his thumb.

He can't be doing what I think he is.

He can't.

He wouldn't.

"How does it go again?" He looks at me in question before he brings his thumb to his forehead, making a small mark. "In my mind." He brings his thumb up to his lips. "On my lips." He smears his thumb over his lower lip and then uses his tongue to swipe up my wetness from the soft dent at the center. He drops his hand to his heart and repeats the gesture. "In my heart."

He smirks as he watches my reaction; my lips parted, and my brows frozen in shock. Reaching out, he grabs my jaw and swipes the remnants over my lower lip before he leans in and sucks it into his mouth, kissing and nipping at the lush bit of flesh before he pulls away again.

"That better? Or you think we have more to make up for?" He drops my wrists from above my head but holds onto them, looking to me for permission.

"More," I murmur, the creep of excitement and anxiety

blending together to develop another wave of desire that pools low inside me.

"I think so too."

He takes my wrists and turns me around, bringing us to the back of the church where ascending rows of half-melted candles sit in wait for the churchgoers who will never return. He kicks a prie-dieu forward from its place in front of the votive stands with his boot and drags me down, making my knees hit the tufted kneeler.

"Hands here." He manipulates my wrists gently to place both of my hands on the prayer rail. "Palms down." I follow his instructions. "That's my girl." I hear him murmur as I'm eyeing the iron gate and wondering if I could untie the rope as fast as I'd tied it earlier. I don't have much time to think, though, because he releases his hold on me and rounds the other side, climbing the small riser there.

The sound of his zipper lowering echoes in the quiet of the chapel. Bouncing off the walls and reverberating around us. The chapel has been deconsecrated, the crucifixes and the tabernacle removed, but it still feels wrong.

"Levi, please." My eyes lift to meet his. "This is—we shouldn't. I shouldn't. I know you're not religious but..."

My protests are meaningless though. He palms himself under his boxer briefs and then frees his dick, hard and swollen, a bead of precum already swelling to its full potential at the tip.

"You're wrong about that, sweetheart." His knuckles drag down my jaw, and then his hand cups my chin. "I'm very fucking religious when it comes to you. Listening to your confessions. Worshipping this sinful little body back to life night after night. Forgiving your transgressions—like using me as your own personal fucking sex toy while I'm tied to a fence." He lets out a low whistle. "That last one though. That might be a cardinal sin. A few of them, I think. So I'm going to need more than a simple apology."

"I'll say another rosary tonight."

"No, sweetheart. That's not enough this time. Not with your immortal soul on the line."

He swipes the precum with his thumb and drags it over my forehead, and then down, pausing to swipe over my lips before he makes a final mark over my bare chest.

"You need to meditate on what you've done wrong. Dedicate yourself to it body and soul. What did the abbess call them?" He snaps his fingers, and his eyes light. "Devotionals. That's what you need to practice. Thank fuck I'm here to help you."

His palm cups my jaw, and he presses his thumb down on my lower lip, slipping his cock in between them while they're parted.

"Give me those pretty blues," he demands, and I do as I'm asked, letting my tongue swirl over his tip while he stares back into my eyes. "Now pray."

THIRTY-EIGHT

L evi

I RUN my fingers through her hair and curl them around a fistful of it, anchoring myself as I start to fuck her pretty little mouth. I'm slow at first, gentle even, as she hums her apology around my cock. She's so warm and wet, her tongue as eager to please as the rest of her.

She lifts her hand from the rail to touch me, and I snatch her wrist, halting her and shaking my head as I place her palm back on the wood. I want full control of this—some measure of revenge for the way she used me so fucking dirty out in the field. Even if I did love every second of it.

I won't take her freedom from her, stealing it away like her ex would have. I want her submission, freely given and greedily fucking taken. I want her on her knees for me, staring up at me like she is right now. Reminding her I'm the one who's given her salvation. That I'm the one who will do anything and everything she needs. She might be reciting devotionals, but I'm the devoted one, drowning in my obsession with her.

It doesn't take long before I feel the first tingle of awareness, the slow build of my orgasm against her tongue. It's too soon. I'm overstimulated from hunting her down and cornering her in her little sanctuary. Taken too close to the edge by watching her eyes stare up into mine with unfiltered desire as she sucks my cock like she's been dedicating her life to the task for years behind the convent walls.

I pull back, shallowing the thrusts of my hips into her pretty little mouth. Making her work for every lick and swirl of her tongue around my tip. Her fingers curl around the rail and grip it as she works herself up in the process, the kaleidoscope of light from the stained glass falling over her breasts and making her look like a work of art. One I want to add my mark to. But not yet.

"Stop," I demand as I pull my dick back from her lips. She whimpers at the loss, and it almost tempts me to finish off right here and now on her tongue. My eyes land heavy on her hard nipples, beading up from the cool air that wafts through the stone chapel.

"Please," she begs.

"Please what?"

"I need something. Anything. It's torture." Her eyes are wide and imploring as she stares up at me.

"Come here." I tuck myself back in before I take her hand and bring her to the benches, placing her in front of me as I sit down. "Hands on the rail again," I instruct.

She looks back over her shoulder doubtfully, but she follows my lead, gripping the wooden rail. I use my boot to kick her feet wide and slide myself to the edge of the bench.

"Bend over." My demand resonates against the rows of wood pews.

She eases over slowly, and I lift her skirt, resting it on her lower back.

"Lower." I urge her down farther and farther until her ass and pussy are on full display, so wet and swollen for me, I can hardly stand it. My cock strains against my pants as I palm her cheeks, rubbing small circles over them and then squeezing a handful.

"So fucking beautiful and wet for me. I think you like it best when you feel like it's wrong, sweetheart."

"Please, Levi." She whispers my name like I'm her last line of defense against torture.

So I put her out of her misery, taking a long, slow lick up her core, tonguing her cunt, and using the pads of my fingers to rub circles around her clit. She lets out a soft moan of approval and spreads wider for me. I wrap my hands around her thighs, laving my tongue over her, and following her cues until I have her so worked up that she rocks back against my face with each touch of my tongue.

I let out a dark chuckle, gently nipping the inside of her thigh, expecting her to squeak and curse my name.

"Fuck, do that again," she mutters.

"This?" I nip the inside of her other thigh, letting my teeth barely scrape her, while I tighten the circle around her clit with the pads of my fingers.

"Oh god, that feels good. So good." She climbs to her tiptoes and rocks back against the next pass of my tongue. I move lower then, nipping the back of her thigh, just under her cheek. Another soft pleading curse follows.

"You like a little pain?"

"A little. It makes it easier to stay on the edge, and the longer on the edge the harder I come," she confesses.

"Good." I run my tongue over her again and then squeeze one of her cheeks. I'll be keeping that bit of knowledge in the arsenal I've built up for her benefit.

I let my fingers wander, dipping them inside her and softly working over her sweet little cunt until she drips. Then I brush the pad of my thumb over her second, tighter entrance, letting it glisten in the low light.

"Have you ever let someone take you here?"

"No." She shakes her head and glances back at me. "Never wanted to."

"Would you let me?" I meet her eyes, and she nods.

"If you were gentle, I'd try for you," she answers quietly. "Is that my punishment?"

"Fuck no. I'd make that a reward. For both of us." My dick and my heart swell at the idea of having something of her for myself. Something she'd always remember as being mine.

She smiles back at me, one so soft and sweet that it erodes whatever was left of my need for revenge. Now I just want her sated. Staring up at me in appreciation like I've given her all the things no other man can.

"Come up here on this bench." I stand to make room for her. "On your elbows and knees."

She moves into position, her skirt bunched around her hips and her ass up in the air, taunting me like a pretty little peach. I wish I could take her there, sacrifice her on that altar while she says my name like a prayer. But I can't. I'd need more patience than I have left to take her slow and easy, working her up to take all of me. I want her to love it—love me—so fucking much she can't forget. So much that she begs me for it the next time. We'll save it for a day we both need her to remember how good I can be to her.

I make quick work of my clothes and slide into her with a

low groan. She clenches down around me, and my fingers bite into her hips as I start to move.

"Oh fuck," she cries out and splays her hands, trying to find purchase on the pew as I take her deeper.

I don't waste time fucking her slow or sweet. I take her like she belongs to me. We've both spent far too much time on the edge today. The room fills with the sounds of us, moans and muttered curses, skin on skin, and her slick little cunt working me to crest the next wave. I wish I'd thought to record her here like this.

"That's it, sweetheart. Look how well you take me like this." The praise has her cunt practically choking my cock in agreement.

"I'm so close," she murmurs as she shifts her hips up to take more of me.

"Fuck me. Sometimes I think you're so tight I won't make it." I curse, pausing to turn her over to her back, lifting her leg to my shoulder and nipping the inside of her ankle.

Her fingers slip down her neck and over her sternum. Her breasts glitter with sweat and the light of a thousand different refractions of blues and greens and golds from the stained glass. She uses the pads of her fingertips to tease her nipples, and they peak under her touch, her skin rippling with a fresh round of goose bumps as I take her closer. She's always beautiful, but like this? She's art, and I get a private showing of the rarest kind. Something no museum or reliquary could ever dream of having.

"Oh god." She bites down on her lower lip and arches her back, rocking her hips against every stroke of my cock as she moans my name. "I'm close, but I—" I switch the angle I'm at, leaning down to tease her nipple before I scrape my teeth over the tip and suck hard. "Oh god. Yes, like that. Oh my..." Her words fade into moans; her sweet little cunt shivers around my cock as she comes hard.

I use my thumb, circling her clit to take her through a second wave as I pull out, using my right hand to finish myself off with heavy-handed strokes until thick streams scatter over her chest and stomach. Her eyes follow my addition to the artwork, and she runs her fingertips through the pearlescent splatters, dragging them through a rainbow of color. She streaks it over her left nipple as she throws her head back and arches into the last crashing wave of her orgasm, calling out my name as I bend to run my tongue over the pink tip of her breast.

I make easy work of the cleanup as her breathing slows, lapping up the mess I've made—the taste of us melding together on my tongue. Her fingers run absently through my hair, brushing it off my forehead and curling the ends around her knuckles while she watches me.

"Am I forgiven for the rope?" she whispers.

"Until the next time you do it." I kiss my way up her chest.

"I'm not sure I'll risk a next time." She grins down at me, and I lift my head to meet her eyes. She rolls her lower lip between her teeth. "Seems dangerous to taunt a wolf like that."

"Let's hope you do, little red." I smirk, placing one last kiss in the center of her chest.

THIRTY-NINE

L^{evi}

"ALL RIGHT. WE'RE IN." I glance over the screens in front of me as they light up with the cameras I've hacked into in the governor's home.

Zephyrine, Bishop—my latest acquisition to our team—and I are all in the basement of the Avarice, the casino and resort that Grant and I own. I keep all of my latest equipment here in one of the subbasements because it's the closest thing we have to a fortress, and usually the most convenient. It's not at the moment, but I can't exactly do this work out in the middle of the woods.

But doing the work here means I had to bring Zephyrine to the Avarice with me, as she's the most likely to be able to identify rooms and help me create a floor plan we can use to navigate the governor's mountain home. She's sitting next to me, her fingers playing with the gold cross on her necklace as she slides it back and forth and takes in the scenes in front of her. The home looks dead at the moment, with only one or two people walking the grounds, but I'm sure it brings back memories seeing a place she hasn't been in such a long time.

"He's not there, is he?" she asks as her eyes scan the displays.

"Shouldn't be. The copy of his schedule we have says he's in Denver all this week." Bishop scans his phone again as he takes a bite out of an apple, his foot propped up on a chair at the back of the room.

Bishop's an old high school friend of mine who lived with us and worked for my father when we were younger. His family and mine never quite saw eye to eye, and our fathers had a tense relationship that went back decades. His family owned another ranch outside Purgatory Falls, one that had failed years before we sold our cattle off. When his dad turned to other sources of income to make ends meet, it sent him on a collision course with the Horsemen. But it didn't stop my father from taking Bishop in when his father kicked him out, as long as I was willing to vouch for him.

He joined the military when I went to college. I tried to reach out a few times, but he disappeared like a ghost, and rumors of his death circulated a few years after that. When we looked for him when my parents died, he was declared missing and presumed dead. So when I heard his name mentioned when I was looking for mercenary help earlier this year, I made a mental note to find out if it was really him. He came well recommended but completely off book. So I spent last week tracking him down in earnest through an elaborate game of cloak-and-dagger and was relieved as fuck when it really was my old friend who met me in the back of a dark biker bar up in the Springs.

He all but jumped at the chance to run this job with me, shrugging off how god awful the odds were and completely unbothered at how little of a plan we have to go on. Like it's fate, he has connections for a pilot and a medic who are up for the challenge too. So now the three of us are in the casino's bunker, working through the hand-drawn map that Zephyrine created from her memories and matching it with the view from the security cameras I managed to hack on the property. We'll need to use it to plan our heist and memorize it well if we have any hope of getting out in one piece.

"This is the main living room," Zephyrine speaks up again after she's had some time to study the screens. "This hallway over here is this one. It leads into the kitchen. There's a butler's pantry behind it that has a stairwell to the basement."

"Is there another stairwell?" Bishop asks.

"Yes. Three of them. One at the back of the house. One in the butler's pantry, and another is at the main stairwell in the side entry near the garage. It leads up to the second floor and down to the basement," she explains.

"Perfect. The more entries and exits, the more likely we are to get out of there alive." Bishop furiously scribbles notes on the tablet in front of him.

"This is the hallway to the bedrooms. That door on the left was the master, and the ones on the right were my brothers'." She points them out on the screens, tapping the stylus on the map in front of her.

"Which one was yours?" I ask. We don't need it for operational security. I doubt there's anything useful left in there now, but I like the opportunity to see a window into her past.

"Um." She hums under her breath and scans the screens again. "If you turn left when you get up these stairs, there's a room on this side. I don't see it anywhere on the screens. It's a shorter hallway. Just a closet and a laundry room and then my room."

"Any of those rooms with large windows we could breach or exit if needed?" Bishop pipes in.

"The laundry room's window would be too small. My old room, yes, you could. But it's high up. You could break an ankle jumping from it." The way she explains it, I can tell she thought about doing that very thing once or twice.

"Better a broken ankle than a bullet to the head." Bishop's scribbling away behind us.

She tilts her head back and forth as her lips press together, acknowledging the fairness of the statement.

"This is the hallway to the garage. I'm hoping they'll let us pull in there with the truck. Then you'll have easier access to the house. You'll just have to get through this door." Zephyrine taps the screen with her fingertip. "It should be easier than any of the others."

I sit back in my chair as she continues, recommending the best path she can think of in her head as she closes her eyes and describes the surroundings we can't see on the cameras. If I didn't already have a massive fucking weak spot for this woman, I'd be developing a crush right now. For an apprenticing nun with no background in operations like this, she's a natural. Asking thoughtful questions and answering Bishop's like a pro. I'm just thankful as fuck she's on my side because I think her father picked the wrong child to be the heir to his legacy. I'm fairly certain, given the right resources, she could have made an empire out of his tiny fiefdom.

FORTY

Z ephyrine

"SO," I say softly as I crawl into bed next to him. His eyes are glued to the tablet he's holding, his brow furrowed as he rapidly scans the screen. I see the reflection of vault schematics in his glasses. He's been reviewing everything they've prepared for the tenth time today, even though I'm fairly certain he could recite the information backward in his sleep.

"Hmm." He hums, his fingers running absently down my bare thigh as he continues reading. He doesn't even notice the fact that I'm naked except for a pair of panties.

"I think you should ravage your enemy's daughter the night before you storm the castle for good luck," I whisper before I kiss him just underneath his jaw, my hand wandering over his abs as I try to distract him from what he's reading.

"What?" he asks, clearly not listening as he digitally flips the page of the document.

"I said I think you should fuck your enemy's daughter for good luck for tomorrow." I'm blunter and louder this time. It gets his attention, his eyes lifting and going wide when he sees me—dropping the tablet in his lap and adjusting his glasses to get a better view.

"Christ. Have you been like that the whole time?" He sets the device on the nightstand, forgetting what he was doing, to wrap his hands around my waist and drag me into his lap.

"Yes. You've been too busy to notice." I roll my lip in a mock pout, and he reaches up to kiss me.

"I'm sorry. I'm here now." His eyes run down my neck and chest in appreciation, and he reaches out to cup my breast, his thumb brushing over my nipple as I spread my legs a little wider and settle over his lap. "What was that about my enemy's daughter now?"

"You have her all to yourself, in your bed, nearly naked. You can do whatever you want with her," I say softly, my finger-tips exploring the peaks and valleys of his chest and stomach as we talk. I pause when I notice the bandage is off his burn, and it's healing nicely.

"Does that mean my feisty little nun is gone?" He runs his palm up the center of my body, over my sternum, and takes the delicate gold cross on my necklace between his fingers. His eyes lift to study mine in expectation.

"No, but I thought you'd prefer the other tonight. Take out some of the anxiety and aggression while you wait."

"Oh, hmm..." His brows knit together in contemplation of my offer.

"You don't fantasize about that version?" I'm surprised.

"Oh, fuck yes, I do. But that's not my favorite version."

"What's your favorite?" I ask, surprised. "The nun?"

"When you're just you." He lets the necklace go, and his hands ghost over my sides as he talks, studying every line and curve. "I fantasize about meeting you before you went to the convent. Before you got married. Before I became this fucked-up version I am now. Your ex and mine don't exist in this version either. None of the baggage or the jaded pasts." He sighs. "Just us. We meet somewhere randomly when we're out, and I ask you out on a date. I take you somewhere you'd love. An old church. A museum. We walk around the city, just trying to make it last, and then we go to a café. We talk for hours before I walk you home. You ask me upstairs, and I'm nervous as fuck because you're the most beautiful woman I've ever seen in my fucking life..." He trails off, and I've gotten so engrossed in his story that I'm in the fantasy with him, waiting for the ending. He's staring into the distance, lost in his thoughts.

"And then?" I prod him to continue. I need to know how it ends—how we end in this otherworldly version.

"I somehow manage not to fuck it up completely, and you take me up to your room. You kiss me and tell me you want me. So I ravage this perfect little body like my life depends on it. Because it does. I already know, even though we've just met. Every second I'm with you I know that it's exactly where I'm supposed to be. I just need it to last another hour, another day. So I take my time. All night until the sun comes up. I bring you coffee in bed and spend the morning with my tongue between your thighs. But you have to go to classes, so I walk you there too. I want you safe, so I plan to register at the same university you attend. I start visiting the same bakery where you get your breakfast. Haunting the café we visited. Following you home from work to make sure you make it okay."

"You're still a stalker in this version?" I'm amused at his consistency even in a fantasy world.

"Of course. That's the only way I have a snowball's chance in hell of winning you over." He beams at me.

"What do I do about this relentless stalker?"

"Well, one day, when you've had a really long day, you're so exhausted and frustrated with everything, you decide to just let yourself have an escape. I'm right there, a couple of tables over at the café, and you remember how fucking good I am with my tongue." He pauses to study me, a wry grin on his lips, when I giggle with delight at the details of his story. "So, despite all your misgivings, you agree to go out with me again. You sit through dinner and all my rambling just so you can get me back to bed. And it keeps happening again and again on your bad days. And sometimes the good ones too. You have an addiction, if we're being honest. You can't stop ending up in bed with me.

"Until I'm there so fucking often you can't imagine me not there. You realize you need me across from you at your little balcony table the next morning, where you drink your morning coffee with preposterous amounts of sugar and cream. After I finish the morning ritual of worshipping your clit with my tongue, I stare at you, just soaking it all in. How beautiful you are. How smart. How sweet. Then, just before I'm about to leave, you finally tell me that you don't think you can live without me. And I admit that I'm madly in—"

I press my fingers to his lips to stop him from saying the words I so desperately want to hear. My eyes are watering at how perfect his story is. How much I want it and wish it could be us, even if it's only for a little while. His forehead wrinkles, and his face falls when he sees the tears in my eyes.

"Zeph," he mumbles against my fingers.

"I'm sorry. I love the story. That version sounds so beautiful. I want it so badly. So very much, but I... Don't say the words. Not yet. I don't want to jinx tomorrow." The tears fall, and I press close to him, the fear and vulnerability getting the better of me. I want to be strong for him tonight. The sexy version that keeps his mind off tomorrow. But I'm failing already.

"How will it jinx tomorrow to tell you the truth?" He pulls back so he can look into my eyes.

"Because it's too good to be true, and there's so much we don't know yet." Whether we'll live or die. Whether he can get the evidence we need. Whether he'll look at me the same when he's faced with the reality that I'm that man's flesh and blood—the same one who took the people he loved away from him.

"I know that much."

"Then save it, and tell me when we're back here. Safe and sound tomorrow night."

There's a small jerk of his chin in acknowledgment of my wish. A long minute of silence passes with him just pulling me close and holding me tight before I speak again. I just want to pretend for a little while that tomorrow is just another day, the two of us locked in this perfect bubble together.

"So, since we can't quite manage the walk through the cobblestone streets or the café, what do you want to do instead?" I ask, tracing my way over the brand on his chest. "And while we're at it, am I allowed to know who did this to you?"

"Does it matter?" The melancholy has seeped into his tone, and I hope I haven't ruined the night by pointing out the uncertainties of our future. He might have stated them bluntly the other day, but I should have known better than to draw attention to them tonight. The only thing I want in the world right now is to offer him the same kind of unflinching support he's given me.

"I mean, I just want a brief word with them. Practice some of those knots you taught me. That kind of thing, you know?"

"I'm afraid we're all out of thuribles at the moment, and I'm not thrilled about a matching set of burns." His lip curls finally.

"You did it? Why?"

"I wanted the reminder with me. Always. I was afraid I might lose focus someday and forget how much it hurt with my parents. Enough time passes, and it dulls the pain, you know? I wanted to make the reminder permanent."

I nod my understanding. I can imagine the kind of pain he was in, losing two parents who loved him. Just losing one I barely knew had torn my little heart in two. I lean down and place a kiss to the center of the brand, tracing it one last time before my hand falls to his thigh.

"I'm not sure there's anyone quite like you." Everything I can conjure up to say feels like a feeble attempt. I adore this man so much more than I have words for.

"I guess we're an odd set then." He grins and kisses me softly, his lashes low and his eyes heavy when he pulls back to look at me again. "Do you want to be ravaged? Because I think I'd much rather take my time with you tonight." His palm splays across my back and presses me close as he kisses down my chest and over my sternum. "I want to watch you fall apart for me slowly. Hear you make those quiet little prayers of devotion when I get you close."

He leans forward and takes my nipple into his mouth, circling it softly with his tongue, and I can feel the echoing sensation building lower. Feel it rising and ebbing as he takes the other nipple between his thumb and forefinger, pinching it until I let out a soft cry, and he gently sucks the pain away.

"I bet your body will confess the words you can't say. What do you think?" He nips the swollen tip when I don't answer him.

"I think I want you," I say softly, rolling my hips, desperate for friction to sate the need he's building inside me as I grind over his lap.

"How badly?" he asks, and I lean forward, bracing myself on his shoulders as I rock my hips back and forth, trying to get a better angle.

"Desperately."

His hands slip down to my ass, and he cups my cheeks, his fingers digging into my flesh. His tongue darts out, curling under the gold cross and sucking it into his mouth as he shifts his hips lower. The position gives me better access to him. I use the leverage to my advantage, working my clit over the ridge of his cock through the cotton until I'm practically panting. It brings me so close, but it's not enough to give me what I need.

"Take the panties off." He nods at them.

I stand and drag them down my legs, letting them fall to the floorboards. I watch him run his hands under the waistband of his boxer briefs as I climb back onto the bed next to him. He lays me down, settling himself between my legs and kisses down and up my throat. He lifts his lashes to look me in the eyes as he slips inside me, taking me slow and sweet like we have all the years we could possibly want ahead of us.

He takes his time, kissing me softly and running his hands over every inch of my body. He torments me, dragging me to the edge and back again until I finally beg him for mercy. And so he delivers, taking us both crashing over until we're both a perfect mess.

He presses his lips to my heart with one last featherlight kiss. We lay there together in the quiet for a long while, while our hearts settle and our breathing slows. His voice has a raspy, sentimental edge that I haven't heard before when he speaks again.

"Sometimes good things are going to be true, even if the

past tries to trick us into believing they're impossible. You taught me that."

FORTY-ONE

Zephyrine

MY HEART IS BEATING out of my chest as I pull up to the gates at my father's ranch. It's been so many years since I've been anywhere near it that I do a double take at the sign to be sure I'm in the right place. I let all the emotions flood my senses. I think about the times my father ignored me growing up, the day he forced me down the aisle with his arm wrapped around mine, and the night I begged for his help to get away from Corey. It does the job, the tears start to form in the corner of my eyes, and my hands shake as I roll down the window and press the call box. There's a video link, so I need to play the part of the emotional damsel in distress who's fled captivity for the freedom only her father can provide.

"This is private property."

"This is..." My words fade on my lips, and I take in a deep

breath before I continue, doing my best to sound a little hysterical. Much like the night I begged him to keep me safe. "This is Zephyrine Schaefer. This is my family's home. I've just—I drove as fast as I could. Please. I need help! Please!"

"Zephyrine?" the man repeats.

"Yes. It's Zephyrine. Please help." My voice is shaky from nerves and I hope it serves its purpose.

"Just a moment."

He kills the intercom, and everything falls silent, save for a few birds in the distance and the low rumble of the engine. It feels like an eternity before he comes back. But then I hear a beep and a new voice booms over the sound system.

"Come down the drive and straight to the main house. We'll meet you there," the voice instructs. This one sounds older, more authoritative. I don't recognize it. I used to know all of my father's old staff, but now, so many years later, with his paranoia having grown, it's likely I won't know a single person here. Which is probably for the better. If I have to fight someone to get out of here, use force if necessary, I'd rather not be thinking of their family at home when I do it.

"The main house?" I confirm.

"Yes."

The truck rolls over the gravel at a slower pace than I'd taken the paved roads to get here. As I travel down the long path, I start running through all the scenarios we practiced. Thinking of all the ways I'll need to think fast once I'm inside the garage of the main house to make decisions that will keep the guys stowed away and safe until it's their moment.

When I get to the house, the garage door opens, and I can see two of my dad's security guards standing at the door to the house, watching as I pull the truck in. My stomach tumbles, and I feel nauseous. I hate how stressed I am. I wish I could be calm. But then, it will look more convincing if I'm anxious and frazzled. I'm supposed to have escaped the Stocktons' clutches, stolen a set of keys to a truck, and run screaming home to my father for help. So nerves and stress should make sense to them.

My window is still rolled down, and I plan to keep it that way. Just in case they take my keys. My thoughts go to the guys. Levi under the seats in the back, and Rowan and Bishop who are neatly tucked in the false compartment in the bed.

One of the security guards rounds the truck, checking for anything unusual, and opens the lid to the bed, peering inside to find it appears empty. The guys are silent as church mice when the first security guard opens my door and ushers me out. I take a breath, saying a silent prayer. The tears are still fresh on my cheeks as I step out but security has little interest in my wellbeing. They're too busy following protocol.

"Let's go." He motions for me.

"Is my dad here? I need to talk to him," I say immediately as I step down out of the truck. He shouldn't be. He's at a meeting in DC according to his schedule.

"We'll get to that part." The second guard gives me a once-over and then starts to pat me down.

So far, it's going just like the guys predicted it would. This was my home. My family's home growing up. I came here a million times, and now I'm being treated like an enemy combatant. I feel violated. Searched and watched suspiciously when I'm telling them I escaped captivity. They offer little in the way of consolation, and I'm shuffled toward the door and barked at without any remorse.

Genuine tears start to form in my eyes as I think about how we got here. How I used to play here as a little girl, happy and careless and free. It was so different from the reality I faced as I got older. When I stopped being a cute kid and he started looking at me like a product to be bartered instead. An advantage on the campaign trail, an asset to raise money, and a pawn to deepen his connection to people he felt could keep him safe. To him it might as well be the Middle Ages, and I was nothing more than another commodity to buy and sell in his empire.

"You escaped, but you could grab your purse?" The one guard gives me a doubtful look. I was grateful for the belt buckle and the lipstick case tucked in my pocket that Dakota gave me as security guard one snatches my purse and rifles through it.

"I had my purse with me when I escaped." I give him a nasty look and return his once-over with one of my own. Two can play this game. He wants to treat me like trash that's beneath him? I can do the same. In fact, I was raised to think exactly that way. Something that never settled well on my conscience.

"I see." The second guard waits for the first to finish searching my belongings.

"Can I see my father? Please? I just want to see him. I was kidnapped by these awful men. Tortured. They kept me caged, and I just want to see my father. I want to tell him what happened," I plead, doing my best to sound hysterical.

Satisfied that they've checked me for weapons and electronics, they usher me in the door. Down a hall I played in thousands of times—racing my half brothers and sliding in my socks while I sang into my toy microphone. The memories won't stop flooding back. We turn another corner, and I see the dining room. I assume that's where they'll take me. Hopefully, I'll be able to talk to my father via video chat. It'll be the first conversation in a very long time, but it might convince him to have his guards calm down with their armed interrogation.

But we don't stop in the dining room. They march me all the way to my father's office, and when they open the door, my heart stops. Seated behind the table, grayer around the temples than I remember him, is the man in the flesh. This part I wasn't prepared for, and the sight of him knocks me off kilter.

"Zephyrine," he acknowledges me, and his eyes drift over my countenance. We purposely dirtied my clothes, even ripped them in a few places—a thing I was very grateful for in this moment when I was likely about to give the greatest performance of my life.

"Dad!" The tears flood my eyes and fall down my cheeks as I race around the desk and throw my arms around him. One of his security guards moves to stop me, but in a rare turn of paternal tenderness, he holds his hand out to stop them and lets me wrap my arms around his shoulder. The last time we hugged was almost certainly when I was still a child, seventeen years old, and getting ready to start college. He gave me one last hug as a send-off to adulthood. Right before he lectured me about being on my own without the help of someone holding my hand. I think I did all right without him.

"How did you get here?" he asks, briefly hugging me before he pulls back to search my face.

"I stole a truck. It was the first place I could think of to come from where I was."

"Is Corey with you?"

"No. Just me."

"Did you see him?"

We hadn't discussed this part. I didn't have a plan for my answer, so I lie because I'm too afraid of the questions that will come if I tell the truth.

"No. I don't know where he is. He's not at home?" I force a worried look on my face.

"He went looking for you when he found out you left the convent."

"I didn't leave. I was kidnapped. You have to tell him that. I don't want him hurting me again." It's what I would have said if

I thought he was still after me, what I pleaded with Levi to let me do in the first place.

"Kidnapped by who?"

"The Stocktons. They claim that you stole things from them. Killed their parents. I told them it's not true. It's not true, is it?" I know he won't admit it but I hope if he has any conscience at all left, he feels shame at the reminder.

Something flickers across his face. A look I learned as a child was a premonition of him telling a white lie or a fib. It appeared when he talked about where he was or why he couldn't make a dance recital or a soccer game just as often as it appeared when he talked about Santa or the Easter Bunny.

"Of course not. I doubt I even know who they are. You know how people are with us. Making up stories for attention. The way they always do."

"Why would they think that? They were so insistent that you killed their parents. They were threatening to kill me as retribution, but I begged them to let me go. I told them I was just a nun. That we didn't even talk anymore. But they were furious." A sob racks out of my chest as I explain. I'm still thinking of Levi. How much it must have hurt him to get the call.

It feeds the lie I'm trying to tell my father, buying the guys time, but the tears are for Levi's parents. Because I know for certain what he said was true. Somehow, someway, my father was behind it. Regardless of whether or not he pulled the trigger.

"I have no idea." He shakes his head, and then he studies me again, looking at me like he might find evidence of something on my skin. "Did they touch you? Rape you?"

"No."

"Good. Corey would be even more furious if he found out.

I don't need him starting a war right now. I'm up for reelection soon."

"I don't think his opinion or the election matters right now." For a million reasons, including the fact that he's six feet under rotting away without his balls at the moment. A thing I have to assume my father knows and is pretending not to for my benefit. Whether it's to catch me in a lie or keep me from going hysterical, I'm not sure. "These men, dad. They're serious. I could have died."

His countenance changes then, at the anger I'm having and at the fact that I've accused him of being responsible for the danger by implication.

"I told you that convent was a bad idea. That you should have stayed close to your husband. He would have never let this happen." He turns away from me, back to the work on his desk and his phone. "I think you should see a doctor."

"I will tomorrow. Tonight, I just wanted to see you and sleep in a familiar bed. Is my room still here?" I didn't care about the bed. But I do care about the bedroom's proximity to the staircase that leads to the basement. The one where I need to meet Levi, Bishop, and Rowan so we can steal whatever we can find in the vault.

But my father being here complicates things because now we can't be sure it's just a few members of his private security on the property. Now we have to worry that it's a small army. That part I'm not prepared for—none of us are.

"There's still a bedroom, yes, but Caroline put your stuff away a long time ago."

"Is Caroline here?" I ask about my stepmother because I hope she's not. The older I got the less she liked me. I always assumed it was because I looked like my mother.

"No. She's at a fundraiser in DC," he answers, looking at me carefully like he's trying to see if he can figure out more than I'm telling him. "Do you need to talk to a woman about things?"

"No. I was just hoping to see family. It's been days and days of being away from anyone I know with not very much food or water."

"Well, we'll get the cops here soon enough, and you can make a report." He eschews my basic needs for protocol. I knew he'd want to call them, but I was hoping I could buy some time first. I should have known my father's number one priority never wavers.

"Can't I do that tomorrow? I just don't want to be interrogated tonight. I just want to be here with you and sleep in a real bed. Maybe have some food." I try to think as fast as I can.

He blows out a breath. "They won't like that. Especially since you came here. They'll worry about my safety as much as anything. The governor's house, even if it isn't the governor's mansion, you know."

Of course I knew. I always knew.

"I don't think anyone followed me here. I'm sure they would have caught up to me by now. And even if they did, you have a small army here. Please, Dad. I just want a night of peace. Then I'll talk to whoever you want, and we can call Corey to come up here. I just want one night of peace first." I plead with him, hoping it won't fall on heedless ears.

"I suppose it won't hurt. If they follow you here, my guys will take care of it. I can't believe they thought they could touch my daughter and get away with it." He makes a disgusted noise at the back of his throat as he complains.

"Is there a phone I can use? I want to call the convent. Let my friends know I'm okay."

"That can wait until tomorrow with everything else. You should go to your room and get some sleep. Take a shower. I'll see if we can scare up an extra set of clothes for you somewhere in the house. Some food too."

"That would be amazing. Hot water and sleep sound like a dream." I offer up a small smile through my drying tears, forcing it for his benefit because the fact that he won't let me do something as simple as let people know I'm okay says everything.

"Okay. I'll send someone to help you shortly. I'm glad you're okay, Zephyrine. But now that I know you are, I'm on a tight schedule. I'll be sure to see you in the morning, though, when we call the authorities and start getting to the bottom of this," he explains brusquely.

If this were real, if I had really been kidnapped and escaped when I was younger and more naïve, this would have crushed me. Broken my heart into a million pieces. I'm a minor inconvenience. One that's to be scheduled alongside other more important matters.

"Of course. I understand," I lie, and I give him a quick squeeze before I head to my old bedroom.

FORTY-TWO

L evi

"SHE SHOULD HAVE BEEN HERE by now." I look around nervously, like maybe she'll suddenly appear from the corner or the stairs. We've already blown the local grid, taken the vault, with some difficulty, and packed our bags with the relics and any of the paperwork that looks relevant. Rowan is finishing up one last assessment of the shelves inside the vault to make sure there's nothing else that's imperative. The delay has cost us time and ammunition as several of his security team have made their way down the staircase Bishop's been holding.

The same staircase she should have come down five minutes ago. My stomach turns, and the bile rises in the back of my throat. I hate myself for letting her go in there alone, for using her like this. I should have called off the plan the second I learned how cruel he'd been to her over the years. There's no telling what he'll do to punish her if he thinks she's a willing participant in this.

"She might be somewhere she can't leave yet. She'll be here." Bishop tries to reassure me.

"We can't wait. We'll lose all of this and get killed in the process," Rowan states plainly. Ever the pragmatist.

"I can't leave her behind." I let my tone make it crystal clear I'm not leaving without her.

"The fuck you can't. This is a job. It's his daughter. This is her home. They're not going to kill her. She'll be fine." Rowan's dismissal of her safety presses on a raw nerve.

"His daughter, who betrayed him to help us," I snap back. "His daughter, who he sold off to the highest bidder in order to get more political leverage. He might not kill her, but he'll destroy her."

"That's not our problem. It's hers." Rowan looks at me like I've lost my mind for even broaching this argument. "We're fucking leaving. Like it or not. You don't blow a whole fucking plan." He shoves my bag into my arms.

"No fucking way. I'm not leaving her." I stand firm. "You wouldn't fucking leave Charlotte like this."

"Charlotte would have been down here five minutes ago."

"Fuck you." I close the space between us, seeing red.

I stretch my fingers, trying to think of a reason not to slam my fist into Rowan's face. I know it's the adrenaline and her life on the line setting me on edge, but I've had enough of his carelessness when it comes to her. I'd never encourage him to leave Charlotte behind.

"Do it. Do it and see what fucking happens." Rowan's steel-gray eyes scan mine.

"Hey, hey. Let's think with cooler heads. We can give it another minute or two. She'd do it for us." Bishop tries to be the calm voice in the chaos.

Rowan blows out a breath and rolls his eyes, shaking his head and giving me a wary look that manages the slightest hint of empathy. One that lets me take a step back.

"We need to get out. If his security has her somewhere, there's no telling where. We don't have time to search a house this big. We don't have enough men or enough ammunition to clear it. Your guy knows that; he just doesn't want to tell you." Rowan looks between Bishop and me.

I turn to Bishop, who glances back at me. It's my plan, but he's the head of the operation now that we're on the ground. He knows the odds better than I do. I need his assessment.

"He's right. I hate it, but he's right. If your priority is getting out of here with any of this, we're out of time. Too many things have to go perfectly for us to get out of here, and the more we go off schedule, the less likely it is." Bishop's tone is strained.

"This was mission fucking impossible from the beginning." Rowan starts moving toward the window of the basement that we plan to use as egress. "So let's fucking go. Now."

"You two go. I'm going after her." I shake my head and move for the stairs so Bishop can fall back. I toss him my bag as we pass each other.

There's no way. Absolutely no way I can leave her here alone. I wouldn't want to live with myself if I did. I couldn't. Even if I thought he wouldn't hurt her, the leaving alone would break her into a thousand tiny pieces. I can't do that to her. I won't.

"Are you sure?" Bishop's eyes search mine, telling me without saying a word that I've absolutely lost my shit to think this is a good idea.

"I'm sure. Just get the horses ready for us. Hopefully, we'll meet you in time; if not, we'll catch up."

Rowan turns back to look at me one last time, frustration in his tone and worry etched on his face. The man has a heart after all.

"You should leave with us. She knows where to find us. She knows the grounds better than anyone." Rowan tries one last time to convince me.

"You know you wouldn't leave Charlotte. I can't leave Zeph. Now go." I urge them on, and I head up the stairs.

"Wait!" Bishop calls after me, and I look back as he tosses me an extra clip of ammunition. "You'll need it up there."

I nod my thanks, and an unspoken goodbye passes between us. I know as well as he does that my odds are absolutely fucking abysmal. We were going to be lucky to get out at all, and this will seal my fate. But at least she'll know someone came back for her. She'll know that for once in her life, someone put her first—loved her enough not to leave her behind. I need her to know I'm that person for her. Always.

Besides, nothing's impossible if you want it badly enough.

I jog up the stairs, reminding myself of that fact over and over until I get to the main hallway. It's hard to see in the dark, even with the night-vision Bishop supplied us with. It's pitch fucking black, but down the hall I see a flicker of light. There's a kerosene lamp on in the far room. It has to be her.

I race toward it, as quickly and as quietly as I can. Hoping and praying that nothing's happened to her in all this chaos. I'll say a million fucking rosaries a day, join a monastery, whatever I have to do, just as long as it means I can get her out of here unscathed.

I lean against the wall, taking a deep breath before I breach the door and see the last thing I'm expecting—the governor with a gun to Zephyrine's head.

FORTY-THREE

Ten minutes earlier...

Z ephyrine

WHEN THE LIGHTS GO OUT, I know it's my time to run. The guys had a plan to kill the local power grid. It would give us darkness to escape in, and it would make it easier for them to hack the vault. The clock's ticking now for all of us to get out of here, and I have to make it to the basement.

I jump up and head for the door, pausing when I hear the sounds of my father's security team in the hallway. They're yelling to each other about the breakers and making sure to secure the doors. My hand hovers on the doorknob, and I feel my heart pounding in my chest as they walk by.

I close my eyes and count backward from ten. I can do this. All I have to do is make it to the basement. Out the door, around the corner, and quickly down the back steps. It'll be over before I know it.

Gunfire rings out. It's distant but distinct. Coming from the floors below me. I don't have time to wait and see. I don't want to have his army between me and my only way out of here. I have to hurry. I yank the door open, and my face pales when I look up to see my father staring back at me.

"Where are you going?" He's livid already.

"I was coming to see what all the noise was. The lights went out."

"Security is on it. You should stay in here. Wait until they tell you it's clear."

"I don't want to be alone in here," I argue. It's the best I can come up with, but it's the wrong thing to stay.

"Then I'll stay with you." He shoves his way inside my door, and I take several steps back.

"No, I—"

His brow raises.

"No, you what?" He echoes my words back to me.

"I don't need you. I'm sure you have more important things to do. Won't security be looking for you?"

"Is that what you were counting on?" He sneers.

"What?" My heart sinks like a rock in my chest.

"Did they ruin your hearing? I asked if that's what you were counting on. You know, when you came here with them. I assume you're the distraction."

"I don't know what you're talking about."

"Of course you do. You think I believe you just ran away from the Stocktons? That they just let you slip right through their fingers? They don't lose one little woman out in the woods. They're not like your incompetent husband,

Zephyrine." My father tut-tuts at me, his brown eyes dark with fury.

"I told you. They didn't see me. They probably don't even know I'm gone yet."

"So you're in on it then? Cooperating with them?"

"I'm not doing anything but trying to get free. I just want to go back to the convent!" The tears start to form in frustration as I hear another round of gunfire. The panic wells inside my gut.

I'll never make it to them in time.

"Of course you do. So fucking useless. Just like your husband. I told him to find you and bring you back before everything got worse. Couldn't even manage that." He shakes his head. "You always were a fucking brat. Always focused on yourself. Never focused on what was good for your family."

"What did I ever do to you?" I snap at him. "All I ever did was try to make you happy."

"This isn't about you. This is about things far more important than you. But you never understood that."

"Then maybe you should explain it to me."

"You wouldn't understand."

"Because you're a murderer? A man with no conscience." My hands shake even as I accuse him. Holding his furious gaze without flinching like I might have when I was younger is one of the simplest but most difficult things I've ever done.

"You believe their lies? Of course you would." He shakes his head.

"You didn't kill their parents?" I counter him.

He laughs, long and hard. But it's insincere. An act on his part. One he's gotten good at from always being in the public eye.

"Is that what they told you? You think I had time to go down there and shoot two random, meaningless people? That

I'd risk going to jail for that? I have more important concerns, Zephyrine. You're ridiculous."

"So you didn't try to blow up a wedding either?"

There's more gunfire and shouting in the distance, and my stomach tumbles with the panic building its way up my spine. I need a plan. Some way to get out of this situation. But I can't think straight. The sounds of the gunfire and shouting drowning out reason. Even after all these years, I still fear him too. No matter how much I try to forget it.

I can't forget it. But I can fight it. I have to try.

He's as distracted by the sounds in the hall as I am, trying to listen to hear what the commotion is. I try to use it to my advantage, reaching for the doorknob, but he snatches my hair and drags me back down onto the bed next to him while I scream out in pain.

"Shut up! You're not going anywhere. You're staying right here with me. I don't need you running off to give them more information."

"I don't have any information to give. You don't care about me. Just let me go! You always kept me in the dark. I told them as much. You don't need me." I bargain with him.

"Because you would have never understood."

"What? What was I supposed to understand? Stop talking in circles."

"You sound like your mother now." He looks at me in disgust. "I always hated that you had her eyes."

There's a gut-wrenching bellow from the hallway, and the sound of someone screaming for help. It tears his attention away. For all his bluster, I can see the fear in his eyes.

"We should get out of here." I try to stand again, but he holds my arm tightly.

"We'll wait. They'll come up here eventually."

"I don't want to die." I hate the way my voice breaks in frustration.

"Neither do I. But you brought them into my fucking house. You let them come here and disrespect me like this, didn't you? For what?"

"I want to know what you did to my mom. I want to know why Grandad hated you. Why you'd kill their parents. All for what? A treasure hunt? Some relics?" I press him. I know it's dangerous, but it's the only way I can imagine I'll get answers.

"Your mom was in an institution. You know this. Your grandad blamed me. He was always trying to blame someone else for his faults."

"Was it your fault? Did you drive her there?"

"Your mother just couldn't accept the terms I offered her. She thought she could tell me what to do. Just like you now. I should have given you up for adoption. It would have spared me so much trouble over the years."

I won't let him see me cry again. I refuse.

"What do these relics have to do with anything?" I change the subject. Maybe I can at least get some information out of him. An answer or two would be better than nothing at all.

I hear my father's comms crackle with voices. They're counting the bodies. Someone's asking for more rounds of ammunition. Another is screaming that he's bleeding out on the stairs.

My father's face blanches. He's doing the math, and it must be in Levi's favor.

"Why are you collecting relics? Why did you have the Stocktons steal them? I want to understand."

"They belonged to your grandfather, and I wanted them back. They should be in this family where they belong. I was just trying to hit two birds with one stone. But no one in this business is fucking reliable. If they'd just done what they were told, this would have been over a long fucking time ago."

"What do you mean?"

He doesn't get to answer, though, because the door bursts open, and it's a familiar face that's aiming the gun in our direction.

Levi. He's alive, and he's here. My heart riots in celebration for all of half a second until I feel the gun against my temple.

"I'll kill her." My father warns him. "Do anything stupid, and I'll kill her."

FORTY-FOUR

L evi

"LET HER GO. She's your own daughter, you sick fuck," I demand, but I can hear footfalls down the hallway. My words are an empty threat. We'll be dead in a matter of moments. Or at least I will be, and I'll have left her to whatever fate he's divined for her. If Corey was his first choice, I can't imagine what he'll do to her now. My stomach churns with the thought.

"No daughter of mine would debase herself like she has. Working with scum like you against her own family. It's disgusting." He spits on her cheek, and my finger twitches on the trigger.

"Let her go."

"Shoot me, and see what happens. You'll both be in a thousand bloody pieces," the governor threatens, and I feel the blunt end of a barrel bump the back of my head. "Drop the gun."

"No."

"Drop the fucking gun, Stockton." The governor's face is bright red and he spits as he yells, his mouth twisted with the effort and his normally perfectly styled hair shaken loose from the confines of his pomade.

"No."

"You won't like the alternative," he seethes, pressing his gun to her head as the guy behind me nudges me forward a step with pressure from the barrel.

"Neither will you." I aim my gun at his head.

"Fine. We'll do this your way." He tilts his head to the side, a quick gesture of hand and I see black.

There's a loud bang. Deafening in my right ear, in fact. Followed by a searing pain in my shoulder. My finger twitches, and my gun goes off as it falls from my hand. I can't hold the grip any longer. It all happens in a fraction of a second, and suddenly I drop to my knees. My fingers go to the wound in my shoulder, blood pouring out through the hole there and down onto my shirt, between my fingers. It races down my wrist and my forearm. I'm in shock for a moment, trying to process what's happening until her screaming pulls me out of it.

It's Zephyrine. Tears are surging down her cheeks, and she lets out a blood-curdling scream as she looks between me and her father. She rips the belt buckle from her waist and flips the hidden switchblade out, jamming it into her father's thigh.

He drops his gun, disbelieving, and I reach for mine with my left hand, trying and failing at first for all the blood but eventually getting my grip on it. I knock the guy behind me onto his knees and disarm him before I look up to see Zephyrine reaching for the blade, ready to rip it out, while the governor screams for help.

"Stop!" I shout, and she does. Her terrified blue eyes meet

mine. "You pull that out, and he'll bleed to death in seconds. That's his femoral artery."

I can hear the sound of footsteps down the hall. We have seconds to act, and my mind is whirring for us to find a way out of this. A way we survive. A way she doesn't go to prison for life for armed robbery, parenticide, and assassination of a sitting governor. I take a deep breath, and I see the only way forward.

"What do we do?" I hear her ask over the sounds of her father's wailing. I manage to pull myself up from the floor. The searing pain makes the room spin, and I have to fight to keep my grip on the gun even with my good hand. The governor reaches for the blade himself, and I swat his hand away with the barrel of the long gun just in time.

"You'll fucking die if you take that out," I mutter, the room swaying as I try to stand straight.

"I'll fucking kill you both first." His eyes widen as two men enter the room behind me. I put the gun to his head.

"You try anything..." I look between his two security team members. "I'll shoot him. He'll be dead before I hit the ground."

They look to the governor and then at each other in rapid order.

"Do something, you fuckwits," the governor yells at them, but I can tell from their disoriented state, they have no idea what to do. No plan. Their orders come from the man I disarmed and knocked unconscious on the ground in front of them, and he won't be talking anytime soon.

"Put your fucking guns down, or I will kill him," I shout.

They stare blankly. Their eyes dart between the governor and me.

"Do what he says! Or I'll tell everyone you got the governor killed," Zephyrine shouts. We have the upper hand since these two don't know what side she's on. They follow her order, dropping the guns to the ground and holding their hands up.

"Now kick the guns to me," I instruct, and they follow. We might have a snowball's chance in hell of getting out of here if they continue to cooperate.

"You fucking whore." The governor lashes out at Zephyrine, and I slam the barrel of my gun into his head. He falls backward, unconscious, and blessedly fucking silent. Zephyrine's eyes snap up to mine, waves of worry and panic crashing in the sea of blue. I give her an unspoken word of reassurance before I turn my attention back to his guards.

"Pick him up. Carry him down to the panic room. Whatever you do, don't drop him. Don't jostle him. That blade comes out of his leg, and you'll have killed him," I order the two men.

We descend the steps. Slower than I'd like for us to get to the horses. I'm much slower than I need if I'm going to handle the wound in my shoulder. I'm trying to apply pressure as we move, and Zephyrine shoots me a worried look as she eyes the blood soaked into my shirt. We cross the basement, the security guys nearly dropping the governor, but only once, and make our way to the panic room.

"Get inside," I demand. They exchange looks of worry, and I press my gun to one of their shoulder blades. "Now."

They follow orders reluctantly, probably ultimately deciding that this is less of a death sentence than what they'll face if they continue to stand there looking like deer in headlights. I'm sure the governor will be rethinking his entire staffing if he survives this.

I slip inside behind them for half a second, pressing the panic button and engaging the lockdown protocol, and then I slide back out through the automated closing door, keeping my gun trained on the security guards. The governor is as much a guarantee of my safety as anything; he's a ticking time bomb, and their wrestling with me over my gun or trying to stop me will only lead to the knife being dislodged from his leg. They stand glaring and hopeless over his unconscious body as the doors slide shut.

"Whatever you do, do not pull that knife out or let him do it," I remind them before I grab Zephyrine's hand. We start racing to the window egress that Bishop and Rowan left through what feels like an eternity ago. I'm running on pure adrenaline at this point, hoping it's enough to get her back to them.

"What stops them from just coming right out after us?"

"That model will only open on his retina scan. So we have at least until he wakes up or they decide to risk prying his eyes open."

"How do you know this? And how the hell is that working when everything else electronic is down?" Zephyrine risks a glance back over her shoulder as she climbs out the window.

"We almost bought one ourselves. It's a Faraday cage," I explain before we take off running for the barn.

"Can you ride like that?" She frowns at the tender way I hold my shoulder.

"I will." I don't have another answer.

I have to be able to ride, or we don't get out of here alive. But in reality, I know I've lost a lot of blood. I'll be lucky to get on the horse and make it halfway to where we need to go. I'm just hoping by some miracle I get her far enough away that she'll continue on without me. Somehow, by then, I'll have the words to convince her to leave me behind and meet the helicopter.

Right now, I just need to take one thing at a time, and for the moment, I'm thankful Bishop and Rowan saddled the horses and have them waiting for us when we get inside the barn.

"Where are they?" Zephyrine looks at me, confused.

"They went ahead. Wanted to make sure we got the stuff out of the vault."

"They left you alone?" I see the fury on her face.

"Not the time." I urge her up onto her horse, boosting her with my good hand as she struggles to mount him in her panic. Then I climb onto mine, groaning at the way it forces me to extend and rotate my shoulder. The pain radiates through my chest and I nearly black out. I'm having a harder and harder time getting my breath, but I don't dare tell her that.

"We should put something on that." She looks across at me as her horse shakes his head impatiently, pawing at the ground, ready to go.

"We don't have time. We need to ride as fast as we can. They'll wait a few minutes, but any longer, and they'll leave," I warn her. I grab the reins with my good hand and click my tongue. "Let's go." I urge my horse on. Zephyrine looks at me, fear and recognition for what I've done for her laid bare behind her blue eyes, but she follows me out into the night.

FORTY-FIVE

Z ephyrine

WE'RE RACING across the field to the base of the mountains, and it's taking everything I have just to hold on to my horse as it breaks into an all-out gallop. I'd been too afraid to practice this speed more than once or twice with the horses at the ranch, and they all felt much smaller and safer than this one. The wind whips through my hair and I swear I'll be thrown from the saddle with one wrong move.

But I don't have time to think about my own fate. I'm too worried about Levi as I see his head bobbing from side to side and the way he tries to hold the reins and apply pressure to his wound at the same time. This was an ill-fated plan from the start. My father only making it worse.

I glance back over my shoulder toward the house and don't see anyone following us. My guess is that even if he did wake up, their first instinct would be to make sure he received medical attention. But it won't be long after that before he has the entire resources of the state hunting us down.

I have no idea how we can escape that. Our plan relied on going in and out relatively unnoticed. Shutting down and rewriting all the camera footage. Leaving no prints or evidence behind. A small security presence. We never had a plan for me stabbing my own father, or Levi knocking him unconscious and having his guards force him into a panic room.

For now, though, all we can do is keep riding. Hoping that we make it to the mountain and up it in time to meet the helicopter. I sneak another wary glance in Levi's direction. I have no idea how he'll make the climb. It feels impossible. I'll never forgive myself if he dies from trying to save me. I should have planned for my father. I should have known what to do. These things were my responsibility to handle, given that it's my family we're dealing with. Rowan, Bishop, and Levi handled every other aspect, planned it down to the minute, and I couldn't even manage my small part in this well enough to keep him safe.

I don't have time to keep berating myself, though, because I see Levi start to slump out of the corner of my eye. He's slipping to one side and clearly struggling to stay seated and maintain his grip on the reins. I see the horse start to slow, and I pull back and turn to meet him, thankful when my horse complies readily.

"Levi!" I scream his name as he starts to nod off. "Levi!!" This time, he hears me and sits up straighter. He blinks and shakes his head.

"I'm fine." He's barely audible when he speaks; I read his lips more than hear the words.

"Give me the reins." I reach out as I sidle up next to him.

"Hold the pommel so you don't fall off, and give me the reins. I can pony your horse."

He starts to refuse, but I can see how pale he is, how exhausted. He's lost too much blood.

"You have to listen to me right now. It's the only way. It's an order not an ask," I insist, and he finally yields. He hands me his glasses too, and that's how I know for sure how dire it really is. He feels his way to another rope, reaching for it and wrapping it around his middle as he winces in pain. He ties a knot to the saddle, giving himself an extra measure of safety.

"Go," he says, his voice so weak it hurts to hear it.

I tuck the glasses in my shirt before I resituate us both, taking his reins in my left hand and holding mine in my right before I click my tongue to get the horses going again. He holds on to the horn and lets himself settle forward enough that if he nods in and out, he won't completely fall off. We have a few thousand more yards to go before we reach the tree line, and then I'll have an entirely different set of problems on my hands.

"ZEPHYRINE!" I hear my name called from just beyond the trees and look up to see Bishop standing there as I try to help Levi down from his horse.

"Bishop!" I shout back, never more relieved to see someone in my life.

"What the fuck happened?"

"He got shot in the upper chest. Through the Kevlar. It's bad. He's been close to losing consciousness. He needs a doctor. I have no idea how he'll make it up the mountain to the helicopter," I explain, and Bishop steps in to help Levi down.

Levi tries to speak and fails, pale as a ghost and barely able to hold his head up. Bishop lays him out on the ground and pulls off his shirt and bulletproof vest. He wipes the blood away to reveal an ugly wound.

"Fucking hell. It's a sucking chest wound. We have to get this patched. His lung is collapsed, and he can't breathe." Bishop roots through a pocket in his vest and extracts a foil packet. He rips the corner with his teeth and pulls the patch free.

"Will he be okay?" My heart drops to my stomach. I knew it was bad, but a collapsed lung sounds dire. Like he's about to die, and I cannot lose him. Not now. Not ever.

"He's gonna be good. We're gonna get him patched up." He peels the protective layer off and smooths the patch over his chest, his eyes meeting his friend's. "I can't believe you got this far like this. You're fucking tough as nails. You keep that shit up, okay?" Bishop tells Levi.

But Levi's lips are turning blue, and his head lolls to the side.

"Tell me the truth." I look at Bishop.

"The truth is, we need to move fast. There's a medic on the heli. The faster we get him there, the better this will go."

"He can't walk." I point out the obvious and feel ridiculous the second the words leave my mouth.

"I've got you, brother." Bishop reassures Levi as he lowers himself and hoists Levi over his shoulder in a fireman's carry.

"Are you sure?" I ask Bishop, worrying my lip between my teeth as I see him stagger for a minute before he readjusts the weight of Levi's body. I can only imagine what it must feel like to have that kind of weight on your shoulder and walk over a flat road. I can't begin to fathom climbing the boulder riddled mountain this way.

"I've got him," Bishop reassures me. "This way. As fast as you can."

I follow behind, in awe of what Bishop is accomplishing,

keeping my eye on Levi as I scramble to keep pace. Bishop grabs his walkie and opens comms.

"We're headed up the mountain now. We need the medic ready. Will be a minute or two longer."

"We don't have two extra minutes. One tops. Move!" Rowan's voice orders through the static.

"What do we need ready?" the medic calls back down.

"It's a tension pneumothorax." His voice is labored from his heavy breathing as we weave through rocks and brush up the mountain, branches scraping over my arms and forcing me to dip and dodge as we hurry. Allegedly, there's a cleared spot of jutting rock at the top where the helicopter was able to land, but this terrain makes it hard to believe.

"Roger that," the voice calls back.

"Fast as you can." Bishop glances back at me one last time, and I nod, not wanting to waste precious breath on speaking. The altitude and exertion are taking all I have.

Bishop picks up his pace, making it hard for me to even keep up. I suppose he's had to run hundreds of drills like this over the years, maybe even carried a man just like this. But watching him has me disbelieving as my lungs burn in my chest, and I struggle to keep up.

Somehow, by a complete miracle, we make it in time. The helicopter blades whir over our heads as we duck low and are pulled on board by the medic and Rowan, who are already waiting along with the pilot. I barely have time to strap in before the pilot's taking off from the mountain. I watch the tree-tops disappear from below our feet, and my head swirls with vertigo.

My father's house in the distance still lies dark, but I see the tiny looking car headlights that are moving outside it. He called for backup, and he got it—quickly. So quickly, in fact, I see why Rowan told us we didn't have time, as three more men surface on the mountain at the exact spot we just took off from.

Rowan and I exchange looks, and he shakes his head. There's nothing he can say that I haven't already thought of myself.

"You're lucky. He's a better man than most," Rowan mutters, his eyes returning to the chaos at our feet.

My heart twists in my chest as I look at Levi. I'm dying for the chance to tell him how much it means to me that he came back for me, and I hate myself for not telling him last night. I feel my stomach tumble as they struggle to get his body in a position where they can start to assess the damage, a red medic's bag perched next to him as Bishop and his friend work to save his life.

"Is there something I can do?" I offer, desperate to be helpful in some way. I feel like all I've done is act like extra baggage—a burden the rest of the team wishes they could get rid of. Besides my initial role in getting them into the compound, I don't know that I've been any help at all.

"No. Just stay clear." Bishop shakes his head as he assists the medic. They work in sync like they've done this a million times before, probably because they have.

"I feel useless," I mumble.

"You got us inside. That was your job, and you did it well," Bishop reassures me. I don't have the heart to tell him I might have doomed us all by killing my father. I can't think about him right now. His life seems inconsequential compared to the man lying on the floor of this helicopter.

I watch as the medic pulls out a giant needle and moves the tip to Levi's chest. I turn away just as he slides it in.

"Is he going to live?" I force the question past my lips. I'm not sure I want the answer, but I have to ask it.

"He'll live." The medic answers instead of Bishop this time.

The shock of it seems to be finally setting in as Bishop slumps back against the closed door of the helicopter.

"Thank fuck." Rowan shakes his head. "I wasn't going to be the one to tell Grant we let his stubborn ass get himself killed."

I think, despite his unbending pragmatism, deep down the man sees Levi as a brother. Someone who irritates and confounds, but he loves underneath it all. Not that he'd ever admit it. He and Levi are both stubborn that way.

"I just hope his stubbornness saves him," I say softly, and Bishop looks up at me, patting my knee and giving me a reassuring look. One I need. Because I want the chance to tell Levi how much he means to me and thank him for coming back for me. I want to tell him how grateful I am for all the time we've had together and how he's made me believe that good things are possible again. Most importantly, I need to tell him how madly in love with him I really am.

FORTY-SIX

L^{evi}

"HOW ARE YOU FEELING?" my sister, Aspen, asks when she busts into my room without asking. I've been convalescing for the last twenty-four hours in the main ranch house. Grant's old room was converted to a guest room with its own en suite and a massive TV that means I haven't had to leave. Zephyrine and Aspen have been holding twenty-four-hour court in my room, watching over me and deciding who is and isn't allowed in to see me. Nothing stressful, per the private doctor's orders.

A nurse has been assigned to come in at semi-regular intervals to check on all my bandaging and administer any medicine, and between the medical professionals and my family, I never seem to be alone. So I've barely had a moment to process what happened to us.

"I'm fine." I'd shrug, but my shoulder still hurts like hell, the pain radiating out from the wound in my upper chest and down to my elbow. I can't wait to be healed and back to normal again. I'd skip days if I could. Especially since Zephyrine has been near silent in the wake of everything. Not that I blame her.

"You're not fine. Not physically. Not mentally. You can talk to me, you know. I'm your sister. I take secrets to my grave. You can't tell me anything I don't already suspect."

"What are you getting at?"

"You having an affair with a nun." She raises her brow.

"She wanted to have an affair with me." I hold my hands up defensively. Aspen gives me a doubtful look, and I give her a defiant one in response. "It was her idea. Ask her if you don't believe me."

"I don't even know how I'd go about that. 'Hi, ma'am. I know you took a vow of chastity, but you didn't by chance betray that vow to sleep with my brother, did you?'" Aspen's lips flatten, and she shakes her head. "There's no way I'm asking that."

"Well, you could just believe me." I grump at her.

"I'm trying." She gives me a skeptical look.

"Shhh." I hold up my hand and unmute the news when I see the governor's face appear on the screen.

"What?" she asks, irritation at being shushed rife in her voice until she sees what I'm looking at.

"Tonight, we have breaking news that Colorado's governor, Abbott Schaefer, is in serious condition in a Denver hospital after being attacked by a radical in his mountain home. Sources say that the attacker has been taken into custody and will be questioned this evening," the news anchor announces on the television.

I let out a long sigh of relief. I've been waiting to know if he lived or died and how his team was planning to quell speculation. I can't imagine that if he lives, he'd want to point the finger at Zephyrine; dragging her into court would allow too much discovery and public airing of laundry. But I'm not willing to trust the man for anything. This will probably be the only time in my life that I can say I'm happy that the man is still alive.

"Well, that's good, right?" Aspen looks at me with hope in her eyes.

"Yes, very good. Is Zephyrine around? Has she seen it?"

"I've seen it. It's good news." Zephyrine comes around the corner and sits next to me on the bed, patting my hand. All the previous affection she had for me seems to have evaporated and been replaced with nurse-like concern.

"Good? It's better than fucking good." I'm irritated by the soft, careful way she approaches everything with me.

"Well, just don't get too excited. The doctor said—"

"Fuck what the doctor said," I grumble.

"Lev." My sister's brows descend into an admonishing scowl. "She's right. You need rest."

"Fucking hell. I know I need rest, but I'm not comatose. I'm allowed to be happy that Z's not going to jail, and we've got a few more days of him in the hospital to figure out a plan. I'm allowed to celebrate that, aren't I?"

"Of course you are," Aspen answers more calmly than I appreciate. It's like they're all playing a game of who can be more irritating in their lack of emotional display.

"Well, thank fuck I have your permission."

"You could have died." Zephyrine rubs her palm over the back of my hand like I'm too excitable.

"But I didn't."

"All right. I'm going to leave you two to it, but be on your best behavior, or I'll be back." Aspen eyes me from across the room as she closes the door behind her.

"I don't need to be mothered. I'm fine."

"She means well. When she heard you were shot, she came racing here as fast as she could. Grant said he was worried she was going to crash on the way from Denver."

"And what's your excuse?"

"I watched it happen." She levels me with a look that tells me I've walked into dangerous territory.

"Is this what it is now? You treat me like some patient you've never met or some guest at the convent who you treat like a ward? Because I'd rather skip it if it's all the same to you."

"I just feel responsible, Levi. If you'd just gone with Rowan and Bishop, you would have never been shot. It never would have been this scary with you so close to death. You should have gone."

"I don't leave people behind. Least of all you. I had no idea what he would do to you if he were left to his own devices."

"Yes, but I wasn't critical to you all getting out of there. Rowan and Bishop might not ever trust you again."

"Rowan can go fuck himself, and Bishop will understand. Don't worry about them. They've both done far more questionable things. Besides... At some point, you do what your gut tells you is right, and that's what I did. We would have never gotten as far as we did without you. We're alive, and we're here, so you can let the guilt go."

"I guess," she answers softly and then sits up a little straighter. "What can I get you? Do you want dinner yet? Some more ice water?"

"*You* to come sit next to me and watch television with me." It's the truth. All I want in the world right now is time with her. It feels like the most precious resource I have, and I don't have any way to buy more of it.

FORTY-SEVEN

Z ephyrine

OUR WHOLE GROUP is assembled for Charlotte and Dakota's presentation on the relics. I helped them, spending time in the makeshift office we created out of the spare penthouse suite in the casino. Charlotte brought what felt like half a library's worth of resources from her home, and Grant and Dakota supplied anything else she needed to work.

It allowed the three of us to grind out long hours in a safe place where I could still be close to Levi during his recovery, and Grant could oversee progress, while their mutual teams maintained security over the relics. Charlotte was too nervous to transport them out of state to her normal office while we waited for the governor's next move.

I glance over at Levi, checking to make sure he's comfortable. He insisted on being here today, and I'm worried that he's pushing himself too hard, too fast in an effort to seem unbothered by his near-death experience. I get a look of reassurance from him when he sees me checking, and I run my hand over his knee under the table when I see it anxiously tapping out a rhythm as Charlotte explains how she drew her conclusions.

"Three relics were found in the vault along with several other antiquities I'm still researching. But for our focus today, it's these three." Charlotte brings a picture of the relics up on the screen at the far end of the table. "This relic here belonged to Jameson Kelly, Hudson's grandfather. This relic was taken from the private collection of Edgar Markdale in a heist six years ago. And this last one belonged to Charles O'Leary, Zephyrine's maternal grandfather."

"There was paperwork in the vault alongside the O'Leary relic that leads us to believe it was kept in a safety deposit box as part of a collection willed to Zephyrine on her wedding day. At which point, we believe her former husband, working on behalf of her father, extracted it and delivered it to the governor," Dakota adds as she passes around a copy of the paperwork, and my heart breaks to see my grandfather's signature again.

"Zephyrine?" Charlotte looks at me.

"My grandfather was an antiques dealer, but according to his journal, he obtained this piece when he was deployed during WWII, when he won it in a card game. According to his notes, he and a couple of other men in his unit were playing. He couldn't recall the names of the other men, except for one man, who he knew from back home, Abbott Schaefer Sr. My fraternal grandfather. The same man who lost the game and paid off Charles O'Leary with the relic."

Rowan lets out a low whistle, and I see Grant's eyebrow arch skyward.

"Schaefer Sr. continued playing cards that night after

O'Leary turned into his bed after his win, and he believed that Schaefer Sr. may have lost additional relics in those games," I explain.

"And my grandfather served around the same period, so you believe he was in the unit?" Hudson asks, turning his attention back to Charlotte.

"Yes. We can't say for sure yet. There was a massive fire in the seventies at the National Personnel Records Center, and many of the enlisted men's records from that time were lost. So we're piecing it together with the help of some archives back East, but with what we know so far, yes. We think that's how Jameson Kelly ended up with one," Charlotte explains.

"Markdale's family doesn't appear to have anyone connected to WWII service, though, so we think that it may have been a private purchase long after the war." Dakota looks at Levi, and I glance between both of them. I'm unaware of anything new he might have, so I'm as curious as everyone else.

"And while I was searching bank records on another matter, I was able to find a seven-figure deposit that ran through an offshore bank account into Abbott Schaefer Jr.'s account. The same one he used to purchase the relic we put up for auction earlier this year." Levi grins at my surprise.

"What a fucking coincidence," Rowan muses.

"So Schaefer loses two relics in a card game, brings a third home, and gives it to his son. He sells it off in order to bail himself out financially?" Grant asks.

"Yes. It happens right around the time Schaefer Jr. got involved in politics, and it was not long after that he became involved with Zephyrine's mother," Dakota explains.

"Another coincidence?" Rowan asks.

"Unlikely. Given my family's personal history and what I was able to glean from my maternal grandfather's journal, I think my father pursued her in order to seek out the third relic," I explain.

"Kelly's and Markdale's would have been inaccessible to him. He was a nobody at the time, politically and financially," Charlotte interjects.

"But according to the journal, my grandfather said he was obsessed with it. He would ask questions about it whenever he saw it in his display cabinet and asked more than once what he planned to do with it and whether he'd ever considered selling it," I add in.

"Why?" Grant's brow furrows. "If he sold the other off. Why did he want another? The money?"

"Not long after my fraternal grandfather gave my dad the relic to sell, he became sick. It was a degenerative genetic disease, one with no cure. My dad believed that selling the relic was linked somehow, that selling it had put a curse on him. At least, that's what he told my mom. He told her that if he wasn't able to get them back, he feared that he'd die of the same disease, and his children would too," I explain. "When my mother, who was his mistress at the time, became scared of his obsession and tried to warn my grandfather and the authorities, he had her committed."

There's another low whistle from Rowan, and this time Levi presses his hand to my knee, gently stroking me with the pad of his thumb as I try not to get emotional.

"She died there, and I remember my grandfather and my father argued loudly at the funeral. My father used her death to solidify his custody, and I only saw my grandfather a few times after that."

"I'm so sorry, Zephyrine." Grant gives me a sympathetic look across the table. I give a small nod before I continue.

"When I turned eighteen, a lawyer visited me and gave me the terms of my inheritance from my grandfather. I'd get the entire fortune he'd amassed as an antiques dealer and several of his personal collections, but only when I moved out of my father's house and was married."

"Which we assume was because her grandfather was trying to keep Abbott from having access to the relic," Dakota explains as Grant's brow furrows.

"And when I married Corey, they had access to everything. Including the safety deposit box that held the relic." I finish the sad story of how I not only fell for my father's trap but also betrayed my grandfather's wishes in doing so.

Levi squeezes my knee again the table, and I place my hand over his, linking our fingers. I only wish I could watch Corey suffer all over again for his part in this.

"Which would have been just before Schaefer contacted our father to steal the Markdale relic." Levi makes the connection clear for everyone at the table.

"And was just before they burned my grandfather's house down to cover the theft of the Kelly relic." Hudson pushes another piece of the puzzle together.

"There's a gap here because we don't know for sure why he killed Mom and Dad. But we can assume he incorrectly thought they had the relic in hand already and wanted to cover up the fact that he was the one to pay them to steal it. Using the money he stole from Zephyrine's post-marriage inheritance." Levi looks at Grant, and they exchange unspoken words.

"Fuck me. What a bastard." Rowan shakes his head in disbelief.

"So then, after last summer, when we auctioned off the relic we had... He has all three. Why not leave us alone?" Grant asks out loud.

"Covering his tracks? I assume he knew we wouldn't let Mom and Dad's death go." Levi offers his best theory.

"But why not Hudson, too, then?" Grant's brow furrows.

"One giant problem at a time, I guess. We were an easier target given that we were in state, and he had Uncle Jay in his pocket to help him with his dirty work," Levi posits.

"Fucking hell..." Grant scrubs a hand over his face. "So what now?"

"We wait to see what he does." Rowan's back up as part of our security council. "We see how he covers up our robbery. *If* he covers up or if he retaliates."

"But we might have some hope there too," Dakota pipes in.

"How so?" Grant asks.

"Some of the documents we've found look like off book transactions. I'm having an accountant friend go through them with Rowan." Charlotte's lips curl into a devilish grin. "Because if they are, we might have everything we need to destroy him."

"Let me know whatever you need to speed that along." Grant returns her optimism.

"Will do." She nods.

"And the relics?" Hudson asks. "What do we do with them?"

"I'd like to take them back to where they belong. If we all agree," I suggest.

"Which is where?" Hudson's brows knit in confusion.

"Oh, we forgot to tell him the best part." Charlotte looks at me with a smile.

"My grandfather spent a bunch of time traveling through Europe. Trying to figure out where they belonged because he suspected Schaefer stole them opportunistically at some point during the war. My grandfather went to the abbey several times to do research in the reliquary archives there, and between his research and Levi's, we think he was on the right path. I think the nuns there and the archive might get us the answers to return them to where they belong," I explain, looking around the table to get their reactions.

"You have my support," Hudson agrees easily.

"Mine too." Grant nods.

"And you know you already have ours." Charlotte gives me a look of encouragement.

I turn to Levi, and he gives me a conflicted smile. One I completely understand.

"You know I support you. I'll take you myself as soon as the doctor clears me." His eyes meet mine, and I nod because I don't trust myself to speak.

"Perfect. Then let's get this black book accounting sorted and end this mess for good," Grant announces.

FORTY-EIGHT

L evi

"THANKS FOR BRINGING THIS OVER." I greet Bishop when he walks in the back door of the ranch house with some paperwork Grant needs me to look over.

Bishop decided to stay on with us temporarily while I'm recovering and we're sorting through the aftermath. I'm grateful for it because he's one of the few people outside of the Kellys I feel like we can trust to do this kind of work, but doubly so because he's such an old friend.

I spent the years since my parents died so focused on making things right that I lost a lot of the guys I was close with. If they weren't family or they didn't work with me at the casino, the friendships all but vanished. Not that I blamed them, grief changes people, and for me, it wasn't for the better.

"Not a problem. Was heading this way anyway and

thought it would save you a trip. How are you feeling?" Bishop looks me over.

"A lot better. Up and moving around. Not that I'm allowed to do much around here."

"Zephyrine keeping an eye on you?" He grins at my distress.

"I'd call it more of a prison watch than an eye, but yeah. Between her and Aspen, I'm on lockdown." I laugh.

"Your sister's around? I didn't think she lived out here anymore. Thought she was back East with the husband."

"Trouble in paradise, I guess. She's back in Colorado right now. Looking at a job up in Denver. She came down when she heard I got hurt. Never misses the chance to tell me I have to stop doing dangerous shit," I explain.

"Ah, well, I'm sorry to hear that. But glad she's keeping an eye out for you."

"Yeah, they're having a girls' night tonight, I think. Zephyrine, my brother's fiancée, Dakota, Aspen, and her daughter. So if you want to stay and have a beer, I'm short a couple of wardens for the next few hours. We've got a couple of pizzas coming." I'm excited about the prospect of being treated like something other than a patient, and Grant is busy with work this evening.

"Yeah, actually, that sounds good. I wouldn't mind sticking around if I'm not in the way."

"Not at all. Fuck, you'll be giving me some entertainment. What kind of beer do you want?" I open up the fridge.

"Whatever you got's good. I'm not picky, and you all always had the good shit anyway." He flashes another grin in my direction, and I toss him a longneck and a bottle opener.

I hear footfalls down the steps, and I turn to see Aspen coming down them already dressed in short cotton shorts and an oversized Highland State T-shirt, her hair up in a bun, and blowing on her freshly manicured nails. She sees me first and grins.

"You're up! Feeling okay?" Her eyes run over me in survey to make sure I'm not doing anything I shouldn't be.

"I'm great. You need something?"

"Just gotta get some snacks for the girls," she explains, and I grin at how well Zephyrine's already fitting into the family that she's already considered one of the girls.

When I close the fridge to let Aspen pass, she stops short. She's frozen as her face goes deathly pale, and I'm just about to ask her what's wrong when she speaks.

"I thought you were dead." She's staring at Bishop like he's a ghost.

"Well, whoever told you that exaggerated." His signature swagger is still thick in his tone, but the way he's staring back at her has my attention.

"Apparently."

"Heard you're back in Colorado."

"Sort of. I needed a change of scenery."

I'm so distracted watching this bizarre game of verbal tennis that I don't hear the second set of footsteps coming down the steps until they hit the last one.

"Hi, Uncle Levi." My niece, Fallon, greets me.

"Hey, kid. You pick out a movie?" I smile down at her. She's fifteen already and talks like she's going on twenty-one half the time, but to me, she's still a kid.

"Still deciding. Mom won't let us watch anything rated R, so it's narrowed the options." She huffs as she rounds the corner, but just like her mom, she misses the interloper in the room until she almost runs into him. She gives Bishop a once-over and finds him wanting as he stands next to her mother. It's unclear whether it's the distance between them or his general existence that puts her off. "Who are you?"

"Manners!" Aspen chides, immediately straightening her spine and standing a little taller as she shifts on her feet. "He's a..." Aspen looks at me to fill in the gap, like she doesn't remember all the time he spent on this ranch.

"Family friend," I fill in, raising my brow at her like it's me who needs to be concerned about *her* health. Nothing is a challenge for that woman, and right now, she seems to be struggling just to have a normal conversation.

"Sorry. I didn't expect a stranger in the kitchen." Fallon side-eyes her mother and Bishop before she steps around them.

"He's not a stranger. He's working with us," I chime in when Aspen doesn't correct her. My sister and I exchange frowns. I'm still trying to suss out the reason the room's managed to drop to twenty below, and I'm somehow expected to read her mind in the process.

Bishop holds out his hand in Fallon's direction. "My friends call me—"

"Bishop. His name is Bishop." Aspen cuts him off, and Bishop looks at her with an arched brow.

"Well, you have a good name at least." Fallon follows up, not noticing or not caring that her mother's behaving oddly.

"Thanks." Bishop chuckles. "What's your name?"

"Fallon." My niece carries on like nothing is amiss.

Bishop's eyes drift back to Aspen, but hers stay glued to the candy drawer in front of her like it's the most interesting thing she's ever seen.

"So you're Uncle Levi's friend?" Fallon asks, glancing between us.

Bishop shifts his focus back to her and clears his throat.

"Yep, and I used to work for your grandad on the ranch."

"Were you a cowboy or a horseman?" She asks the pointed question, and Aspen's eyes slowly close in embarrassment, the only sign she's still listening and not reading every label in the drawer.

"A bit of both." Bishop winks at her.

"I bet Grandad loved you then."

"Your grandad was a good man." Bishop sobers a little.

"I miss him. He used to take me riding when I was little. He had good jokes that made Mom mad and made the best chocolate shakes too." Fallon's mood shifts with the memories, and then she looks at her mom. "Oh! Mom. That sounds good. Can we make some? Aunt Hazel still has the milkshake glasses."

"Let's stick to ice cream bars and not make a mess of the kitchen right now."

"Chips?" Fallon pouts.

"That's fine," she answers, and I see her eyes drift to Bishop again now that he's not looking at her.

"Can you bring up the dip?" Fallon asks as she grabs a bag from the counter and then bounces to the fridge to grab a pop before turning on her mom again. "Mom?"

Aspen snaps out of her thoughts and nods, coughing before she speaks again.

"I'll bring it with me. Take these Sour Patch Kids to Zeph, and tell Dakota I've got our drinks coming right up."

"Got it!" Fallon calls back. "Night, Uncle Levi! Night, Bishop!" Her voice fades as she climbs higher.

"Sorry," Aspen apologizes, head down like she's just trying to sneak past us. "I just need to get snacks for movie night."

Bishop's eyes are locked on her like he's in a trance while she pulls things out of the fridge, and color me fucking fascinated.

"Can we join, or is it a girls' night?" I ask because now I'm dying to watch this play out. Bishop looks at me, his brow raised in curiosity.

"I think it's just us girls tonight. You guys have fun. The pizza should be here soon. Just call for me, and I'll come get it. Don't hurt yourself trying to do it all!" She shakes her head and walks past me without looking at Bishop again, the sound of her retreating footsteps echoing on the stairs.

"I can get the pizza," Bishop says, taking a swig of his beer like nothing at all odd just happened.

"You're not going to tell me what that was?" I ask, but before Bishop can answer, the doorbell rings with our pizza.

FORTY-NINE

L evi

"YOU CAN REALLY STOP FUSSING. I'm fine." I give Zephyrine a doubtful look. She's been at my bedside in the ranch house every day during my recovery from my collapsed lung. Fluffing my pillows, feeding me, and trying to make sure I have everything I could possibly want to read and watch while I was on bed rest.

I loved the first few days of it. Having her care for me in the wake of everything, knowing she was alive and well and safe from her father. It kept my mind at ease. But now, I'm ready for the end of the nursemaid-nun routine, and eager to have some semblance of what we had from before—to have my girl back.

My girl.

For now. Not for much longer though. With Charlotte and Zephyrine's research into the relics, it's obvious we need to return them. They belong back in the hands of the nuns at the convent, where they can stay safe until they're returned to their rightful place. The same is true of Zephyrine. She'll go back to being Sister Mary Anthony, and I'll lose her forever.

But first, we have to make a final decision on the information we have about her father. How to best get it out to the public, and I want Zephyrine in on the decision process. So tonight, we've got one final meeting with my family and the Kellys to see what options we have in front of us.

***

"SO TO SUMMARIZE..." Grant glances around the table, sitting back in his chair as he surveys the whole group of us— Zephyrine, me, Charlotte, Hudson, Finn, Ramsey, Hazel, Dakota, Aspen, and Rowan. "There's a series of black books that were pulled from the Schaefer vault. A forensic accountant we hired confirmed it has all the telltale signs of off-book accounting— embezzlement of public funds, bribery of public and private officials, and some piss-poor money-laundering scams that seem to have lost him money."

"That's what he gets for going to someone other than the Stocktons," Hudson muses.

Grant tilts his head, a small smirk forming in acknowledgment.

"We need to decide what we want to do with it. How to wield it in the most politically damaging way. If we can find a journalist who we might trust to break the story," I explain.

"How do we prove that the papers are authentic without getting you arrested?" Dakota asks thoughtfully.

"That's part of the problem we have to solve," I answer.

"This is fucked." Ramsey stares at the stack of paperwork on the table.

I made physical copies just in case something ever happened to the digitals, but I also made backup drives of the backup drives, so it's unlikely. Still, I like to be thorough.

"I mean, it's unsurprising. It seems like he caught Dad up in one of his bad deals, and that's how he got dragged into all this relic business in the first place. They were trying to recoup losses. The governor wanted Dad to help with his little side project, and he roped him into it by telling him it'd be the way to make himself whole again with money," I continue.

"Knowing full fucking well it was never going to pay off because he was never going to sell them." Grant's pissed.

"Which is probably another reason why he killed them. They can't ask for their money back or turn him into the cops for reneging if they aren't alive to do it." Ramsey comes to the same conclusion the rest of us have.

"And why he wanted us dead. It's the only way to bury this for good," I add.

"But why go after the ranch? That's the part that doesn't make sense to me. He sent Curtis on a mission to marry me in hopes of what?" Hazel asks.

She thought she was divorced from my youngest brother, Ramsey, when this mystery started to come to light. She was engaged to a man who was working at our casino, and he was involved with her almost from the day he appeared in town. Thankfully, Ramsey had come home from jail just in time to intervene and help us unravel his plan and win his wife back.

"Well, he knew we never handed over the relic. His guys jumped the gun and killed our parents before we had a chance to come home. So I imagine Curtis was here to find it on the property."

"It seems like a reach, but then it seems like the governor was making a lot of unforced errors." Hazel shakes her head, and half the table nods along.

"Thankfully. I'd hate to see what someone fully competent in his position could do," Rowan comments.

"But he's always had a problem with money. Never enough of it, right?" Hudson looks between Grant, who's summarizing the findings, and Charlotte, who uncovered them.

"Correct," they agree in unison.

"He's drowning in debts, and they've made him vulnerable to a lot of bad actors. He's chosen to get in bed with a number of them. This information"—Charlotte taps the stack of paperwork as she speaks—"could take down his whole career and half the people in the state of Colorado."

"Including us?" Ramsey asks.

"Our parents. But they're already buried," I answer.

"But what about your role in the robbery?"

"Tougher, but we've hired a lawyer who says it would be an easy deal for immunity if we had the right people on our side. But we need to find some people in high places if we want to get that immunity deal." I explain our biggest dilemma.

"Someone who wants the same things we want." Hudson points out the politically advantageous nature of the documents. Any opponent of the governor would be eager to have it. We just need to know we can trust them to use it wisely. I don't want the governor weaseling out of career-ending headline stories because he's still in recovery or because he finds some way to spin this.

"I have an idea," Hazel chimes in, looking at Ramsey, who nods supportively.

"Share with the class." Finn smiles at the two of them and then looks back at Charlotte. The four of them are good friends.

"Our friend Bea in Cincinnati. Ramsey saved her life a while back. It's what landed him in jail," Hazel explains for Zephyrine's benefit. "Her father is a senator. In Washington, but still... He's likely got connections to the senators in Colorado. I wonder if he could set up a meeting?"

"That's genius." Dakota smiles at her friend.

Charlotte and Hudson nod along and look at Grant.

"Can we trust her? There are a lot of secrets to keep. A lot of family baggage."

"She knows family baggage," Ramsey chimes in. "And she knows secrets. She works in the PR business. If anything, she might be able to help us find the right journalist to spin it, or knows someone who can."

"Then let's reach out to her. See what she thinks and if she's willing. Agreed?" Grant looks around for a consensus from the table, and the plan meets with everyone's approval.

Zephyrine squeezes my hand under the table, and I give her a reassuring squeeze back.

FIFTY

Zephyrine

"I'M ANNOUNCING today that I'll be stepping down from my office as Governor of Colorado, and my Lieutenant Governor, Robert Davis, will be taking over, effective immediately. It has been the honor of my life to serve the people of Colorado, and I'm grateful that I was able to accomplish so much in my term here. I know Robert will continue my legacy into the future, and I look forward to the next chapter." My father announces his resignation on live TV, and it feels like a movie in slow motion.

I never thought this day would come, not in a million years. Even when we talked to Bea's father, the senator from Washington. Even when we met with the senators from Colorado and members of the statehouse. I didn't believe it. When the journalist came under the darkness of night to take copies of all the evidence we had of embezzlement and fraud, it felt like one of my daydreams. A thing I imagined to help make reality more tolerable. I hadn't even dared to hope it would have any real effect.

But then we got word through back channels that the FBI and the CBI were opening investigations into my father. They were already working on the case and had frozen his assets. They started pursuing leads from the paperwork we gave them. It wasn't a conviction of anything—far from it—but it was a start. Enough of one that it cast the kind of dark cloud of relentless questioning over his office that he felt compelled to step down. I've never known a bureaucracy that could move with this kind of efficiency against corruption. Then again, no one has made as many enemies over the years as my father has.

Once we started making noise, they came pouring out of the woodwork to offer their assistance on the case. People who were willing to turn state's evidence. Others were willing to give us access to recordings that could help solidify the case. Apparently, everyone was just waiting for someone to be brave enough to do the right thing.

"You all right?" Levi asks, reaching over and threading his fingers through mine.

"I'm just in shock. This is real?" I look at him for confirmation that I'm not just imagining it.

"It's real. Unbelievable but real." He holds my hand and brushes his other palm over the back of it.

Tears are falling down my cheeks before I realize what's happening, and my body starts to shake with how hard I'm crying. I feel like I'm floating, watching this all happen like an out of body experience. Seeing some semblance of the justice I always wanted but never thought I'd get.

"Hey. Hey. Come here." Levi speaks to me softly, and I curl up against him. He wraps his arm around me and kisses my forehead. "I know it's a lot to process. I feel the same, honestly."

"It's not prison. I hope someday it's prison time, but at least this means he has fewer resources at his disposal. Fewer means to retaliate against us, right?"

"Right." Levi nods. "He's still wounded though. His ego as much as anything. We'll still have to be careful. He might be angrier than ever, but if the firestorm of press continues like it has the last few days, he'll have trouble leaving his house without an entourage of paparazzi."

That's our main protection now. The press has been slowly leaking all the details of his wrongdoings. The politicians we met with to help get the word out have been steadily taking action against him, moving pieces across the board to try to corner him until he has nowhere to run. I thought he'd hunker down in the governor's office, maybe even start trying to find a way to punish us, but someone must have finally convinced him to throw in the towel and walk away.

"Well, hopefully they continue to hound him. Could he flee the country?" I don't think he could, but then I don't know for sure.

"No. A judge mandated that he stay in Colorado unless he gets permission, and he's required to check in regularly. I'm guessing that helped the case for him stepping down. It's hard for him to do his job if he can't travel and is being watched everywhere he goes. Thankfully for us, that's going to keep him from his after-hours job as well." Levi lets out a sigh of relief.

"Thankfully. Not that it'll stop him from trying to get someone else to do it for him. He has other men like Corey. My brothers too. But they'll be too nervous to want to deal with the firestorm, and without his assets they'll have a lot less money too. But yes, you're right. We'll still have to be careful." I agree with Levi's assessment, and then I remember I won't have to worry about my father because I'll be out of the country after tomorrow.

We've been so glued to all the news reporting and all the leaks that were coming out around my father's scandal that we've barely had time to think, let alone talk about the fact that we're heading back to the convent tomorrow. We're returning the relics, but I'm also planning to go back with them.

I don't know how long I'll stay, but after talking to the abbess over the phone to let her know our plan for the relics, it was obvious I have amends to make. Corey's men ransacked the place after I was kidnapped. Two nuns were hurt. Thousands of dollars in damage done. Tourists were frightened enough to leave, and the loss of revenue hasn't helped pay those bills. Likewise, someone needs to make sure the relics are returned to where they belong, and it was my family that made a mess of everything. It's the least I can do to try to atone for their sins.

I look over, and Levi must be having the same thoughts because sadness washes over his face despite the small smile he's forcing. I feel it echo in my own heart.

"Are you packed for tomorrow?" he asks. It's his way of asking if I'm ready to leave. I'm not. I'm not sure I'll ever be ready to leave him.

"I love you." I blurt the words out, and his eyes widen for a moment before a real smile, one that's pained and full of conflicting emotions, but still very real, forms on his lips.

"I love you too." He says the words back easily, like he's said them a million times before now.

"I know I said we shouldn't say it the night before anything big, but lately all the days and nights are big, and I don't want to keep waiting to tell you how I feel. I need you to know that no matter where I am, or how far apart we are, I love you."

"You're taking my big speech away from me. I was saving it

for tomorrow." He chuckles and smooths my hair out of my face before he leans over to kiss me softly.

"Well, fuck tomorrow." I grin when he pulls away to look at me.

"In that case, I love you, Zephyrine. I think you know by now that I'd do anything for you, but if I need to say it, then know I've said it. If you ever need me, all you have to do is say the words. I'm always here. No matter what happens. No matter how much time passes. I will always be here for you. Okay?" His blue-green eyes are glassy as they search mine.

"Me too," I agree, because I can't say more. Not with the way it feels like my heart is going to shatter.

"I know you need to do this. For yourself. Because of the past. To make it up to the nuns who helped you when you didn't have me yet. I don't blame you one bit for this. It still hurts to let you go though."

"I hate leaving you. I don't know how I'll manage without being able to talk to you every day. Being able to see you laugh and making dinner together. And Teddy." I sigh. "I'll miss Teddy, and he doesn't even understand I'm leaving."

"He'll miss you. But maybe someday you can take some vacation time and come visit him. Visit all of us."

"You'll come see me at the convent sometime?"

"If the abbess ever forgives me and doesn't have me killed on sight, absolutely. Otherwise, you'll just have to sneak off the island and meet me in town." He grins.

"I'm sure she'll forgive you. We'll apologize for everything. Once she sees we've brought the relics back, she'll have to forgive us on some level. I hope. I'm sure it'll take a while for her to let it go." I groan. "I can't wait to find out how many toilets I'm going to have to clean."

"There's still time to run away with me."

"Don't tempt me. It's a much better offer. But a wise man

once told me we can't give in to every single temptation that comes our way."

"He sounds wise. You should listen to him more often." Levi winks at me, and I descend into giggles, my tears and my sadness forgotten as I kiss him a dozen times, and he wraps his arms around me.

"Speaking of temptation, I have something for you." Levi lets me slide into the spot next to him as he releases me and walks over to the cabinet next to the mantle, pulling out a gift box.

"What's this?" I ask as he places it in my hands.

"Open it and see." He nods, dropping back to the couch next to me.

I carefully undo the gold ribbon, and the dark navy-blue wrapping paper follows to reveal a thick rectangular box. My brow arches upward in curiosity, and he grins as I open the lid.

"It's a phone." I pull it out.

"Your phone. Or a copy of it, anyway. The real one's still at the bottom of the lake keeping mine company. But I backed all of our data up every night before then," he explains.

"All my photos and messages?" My eyes go wide at the prospect of having all of my memories back.

"All of them. Your videos and recordings too," he muses. "Restored just the way you had everything. Well, I might have added a few things."

"Like?"

"The recording of me you liked so much. Another I made for you. I know you're trying to be good. To make up for everything with the abbess. But just in case you get too lonely at night. There's something for you to listen to." A grin teases at his lips, and I can feel my cheeks heat.

"Can I listen to it now? I don't think I can wait for the

convent to hear the new one." I give him my best pout, and he shakes his head.

"I suppose, if it means I get to watch your reaction." His eyes rake over me.

"Deal!" I pop up and hold my hand out for him. He barely uses it for leverage now that he's almost fully healed, but I want him to have the help if he needs it. "My headphones are in the bedroom. Now I see why you got me the new ones." I look back at him with a conspiratorial grin.

"I might have been thinking ahead a little," he admits.

We move to the bedroom, and I climb into his lap, my dress spread out around us as I turn the phone on and put my headphones over my ears. He settles under me, his hands on my hips as he studies me. I thumb my way down to the playlist and find one called "Z's Late-Night Playlist" and hold it up to show him. He nods, and I click to open it. There's a series of tracks he's put together. Some songs I recognize, some I don't. Then tracks that are labeled with our names or his. I click one and it starts to play.

The sounds of my moaning in the background start, and soon I hear him in the foreground. A low rumble of a groan. The sound of a zip and the rustle of fabric. I can hear the creak of a chair like he's leaning back.

"Fuck, you sound so sweet like this. I bet that pretty little pussy could use a tongue like mine. I'd make you moan for hours."

My eyes meet his, and the blush that was just beginning to bloom earlier floods my cheeks. But it's not embarrassment anymore. Now it's just pure anticipation. I nibble my lower lip as I wait to hear what happens next.

He groans through the speakers, and I hear the sound of his hand on his dick, slowly at first, just barely brushing over his skin. Then a little faster, a low moan, and the sound of him spitting into his palm before he resumes working himself over. The slick sound of the movement sets me on edge and makes me shift in Levi's lap.

"Wish this was you, sweetheart. Your mouth on me. Those pretty blue eyes staring up into mine. Just the thought of it... Fuck."

I bite my lip, and I feel Levi's hands dig into my hips, his face tightening into a half scowl as he looks at me like I'm torturing him. I push one of the earphones back from my ear and look at him in question.

"What?" I ask.

He grabs my hips and pulls me forward, centering me on his lap, and I feel how hard he is.

"You're grinding away on my thigh while you listen there, sweetheart."

"Oh. Sorry!" I give him a sheepish look, but then I jump up, setting my headphones to the side. "I have an idea!"

"What's that?" he asks, clearly confused by my sudden abandonment.

"I want to make one for you." I walk to the door, making sure it's locked. Aspen and her daughter are out for the day, and Grant and Dakota are likely busy having their own listening session wherever they are. But I don't want to risk any family trauma.

"Right now?"

"When else will I be able to suck you off without company in earshot?" I ask, and his face crumples with amusement. "We have to be a little loud, right? To make sure the mic catches it?"

"A little, but it picks up a lot. I really didn't mean to make the original recording you heard. I just forgot it was still on from when I was making notes earlier."

"All right. So can you do it again? Set it to listen while we do this?"

"Are we doing this?" He looks at me thoughtfully. "Because we don't have to. I appreciate the thought, but—"

"You don't want a recording of me?"

"Of course I fucking do." He looks at me like I've lost my mind if I think he'd say anything else.

"Then take your pants off and hit record."

FIFTY-ONE

L evi

I HIT THE RECORD BUTTON, and she hits her knees in front of me, patting the edge of the bed until she finds the phone to bring it closer as she situates herself on the floor. I drop my pants slowly, and her hands slip up my thighs, her nails teasing the backs of them, her lashes low as she watches me.

She's in the prettiest white dress, little pink flowers all over it, and in the dimly lit room, against her pale skin, she looks like she might be an angel. Too sweet to be on her knees for me like this.

"Is this dress one of your favorites?" I ask.

"No, I—" I don't give her a chance to say anything else. I lean forward and rip the front down to her waist. She lets out a surprised gasp as her breasts spill out. Her eyes lift to meet mine, and I expect her to chastise me, but instead she just looks up at me like I'm her own personal god.

"I don't want you looking like an angel tonight. I want you looking like you belong to me." The same way she did in that church.

"Because I do," she answers, not missing a beat.

I reach down, running my thumb over her lips. They're so soft, so perfect.

"I'm so addicted to this pretty little mouth. Everything little word. Every little smile. I want to see what it looks like wrapped around me. Can you do that for me, gorgeous?"

Addicted doesn't cover it. I've been in a full-blown obsession for weeks. One I know I'll never recover from, and like a desperate man about to lose it all, I'm giving her everything she wants. I tell myself it's because we're saying goodbye, but deep down, it's because I'm hoping she'll remember the way I'll do anything for her, and maybe, just maybe, come back to me someday.

I don't have time for any more melancholy thoughts, though, because her mouth slips over the tip of my dick, and all of my focus is consumed with the sensation. She's tentative at first, and her eyes seek mine, looking for the validation that she's doing it the way that I want. The sight of her so eager and submissive like this makes my dick twitch with want. I might not last long enough to enjoy it.

"That's right. Get me nice and wet. Get it dripping just like that sweet little pussy does," I encourage her. "Lick me up and down."

I brush her hair back from her face, my fingers sinking into her red hair at the crown. I massage her scalp, and she moans over my cock, taking me a little deeper to let my hand slip lower.

"Oh fuck, you like that, don't you? My greedy girl." I

tighten my grip as she starts to suck on me, rocking my hips to get a better angle, and she moans again. "You're so pretty when you moan. Even better when it's on my cock like this, and I can feel how much you like it."

Her hands run up my thighs slowly, lighting the nerve endings in their wake. She wraps one hand around the base of my cock and slips the other between my thighs, massaging my balls as she starts to stroke me. This woman is going to take me down in a matter of seconds if I let her keep it up like this. I tighten my grip on her hair and pull her mouth back, the cool air contrasting with the loss of her warmth.

"Spit on it. I want it soaked," I order her. She does as I ask, spitting on my cock, and I watch as it drips down. She catches it mid-fall, using her palm to wrap it around me, and spreads the warmth of her over me. "Good girl, now take me again. As slowly as you can. I want to feel every inch slip in between these pretty pink lips."

She does exactly as I ask, carefully and perfectly, moaning when I bump the back of her throat. I ease back out of her, letting every second of my dick sliding over her tongue count. I need these memories when I'm alone without her. I need to remember what she feels like if I'm going to get through it.

She eases the tip of my dick back into her mouth as soon as she catches her breath, and her tongue swirls around the tip, massaging it and sucking like she's never wanted anything more in her life. I can feel the wave of my orgasm start to build, threatening as a few drops of precum spill out onto her tongue and lips.

"You look so pretty like this. Blushing like you're too inno-cent to confess how you like to imagine me fucking you in the middle of the night. Until I put you on your knees behind the confessional walls and make you do penance." She hums her agreement over my cock, and it nearly doubles me over.

I sink my fingers into her hair again, trying to stop myself from taking her too deep or too fast, but she starts to urge me on. Her mouth bobbing over my cock while one hand works me over, and the other slips from my balls to just behind. Her fingertips dance over the sensitive patch of skin there, circling and then massaging until I've been holding my breath from how good it is for so long that I'm nearly ready to black out.

I let out a loud groan and take a deep breath, trying to steady myself again. It's useless though. I'm gone for her. The sounds of her mouth on my cock, the feel of her hand wrapped around me. I'm hers. She owns me.

"Sweetheart..." I try to warn her. "Fuck." I moan from how close I am. "Your pretty mouth is doing me in. I'm gonna come on that sweet little tongue if you don't let me go." I look down, and her blue eyes are determined, lost in the task of making sure I know I belong to her.

I come hard, fucking her perfect mouth and spilling over her tongue. Rivulets of me are dripping out over her lush lips and streaming down onto her bare breasts as she tries to swallow me down. Staining her with the evidence of my obsession. I drop to my knees to lick it up, my tongue making its way around her nipples as they peak under my touch.

Her hands run through my hair and down the back of my neck as I try to clean up the mess I've made of her, and she whimpers as I suck one of her nipples into my mouth.

"Levi, please," she whimpers, and I reach under her skirt, sneaking my fingers into her drenched panties to tend to her swollen clit.

"That better? You need fucked, don't you?"

She whimpers her agreement, and I slip my fingers inside her, letting her rock her hips to the rhythm she needs as she tucks her head into my shoulder.

"Oh god. Yes. Like that." She breathes against my throat as

I press my thumb to her clit. "Levi." She moans my name one last time before she starts to come, murmuring curses until she finally breaks the last wave, a stuttered breath before she says the thing that I'll replay on this recording on a loop. "I love you. So much. So so much." She stays wrapped around me as I slip my fingers out from under her skirt and kiss my way up her jaw.

"You own me, sweetheart. I love you more than life itself." I whisper against her temple. "I hope you remember that when you're over there." She lifts her head, her eyes watering, and kisses me gently.

"I hope you know it's mutual. I've never loved anyone the way I love you."

I kiss her one last time and then scoop her up off the floor.

"Your shoulder!" she warns me, but I'm mostly healed now. My body at least. The rest of me may never recover.

"I'm fine. Let's get you cleaned up and into bed. We have an early flight."

FIFTY-TWO

Zephyrine

I'M as nervous as I've ever been sitting in the abbess's office, even with Levi by my side. Honestly, maybe even more so because of him. I'm so in love with him I feel like it's written all over my face every time I look at him.

I stare up at the cross on the wall and wonder if I've made a mess of everything. Because I thought once I walked through the gate, behind these walls, and in through the door of my old home, everything would feel right again. I'd feel peace. I could breathe easy knowing I'd dealt with all the things that held me back before now.

I'm sure widowhood won't solve every concern the abbess has. I'm almost positive she'll have me doing penance for weeks, if not months, before I'm anywhere close to being back in her good graces. But I'll have my friends, my garden, my room back.

I'll have my freedom back to live life as I want within the convent. Walks along the lake and quiet time reading and reflecting in the archives will be at the center of my world again.

Levi won't be here though.

I won't run into him in the garden or see him smile when I serve dinner. He won't appear in the archives asking for help looking for a document. He certainly won't be the surprise voice on the other side of the confessional telling me to say three rosaries a day. I'm not sure this place will ever be the same for me without him.

Worse yet, he won't be the one holding my hand while I feed my first horse or tease me while I learn to tie a proper knot. He won't kiss me goodnight or cook the perfect breakfast for me in the morning. I might still get the occasional letter from him. He promised a rare visit or two to check in on me and make sure I'm getting along okay. But his life will move on.

Putting the relics back to rights and taking my father out has been his life's mission. It derailed everything he thought he wanted. But now, with all of that behind him, he can start a new chapter.

A real girlfriend could slip into the spot I'm leaving open in his bed. One who isn't plotting a return to nunhood. One who could give him the life he wants—holidays on the family ranch, children in the future, and a home they could call their own. Nothing would be holding him back.

I'm so lost in my thoughts about it, I don't even notice the abbess enter the room or hear her getting my attention until Levi squeezes my hand.

"Schwester Mary Anthony?" Abbess looks quite surprised to see me and annoyed that she has to repeat herself.

"Grüß Gott, Abbess." I bow my head, and she gives me an impatient, questioning look. So I dive right in and explain why

I'm here in my best broken German. It certainly hasn't improved in my absence. Levi's head bobs back and forth, doing his best to keep up with the conversation using context and inflection, but I can tell he's losing the thread.

"The relics? Can you bring them out?" I nod to his bag on the floor.

"Got it." He pulls each carefully packed box out and sets it on the abbess's desk. I unbox each of them and show them to her. Her eyes widen, and she calls out the door for her assistant.

Her assistant appears, and they speak in fast, quiet whispers of Bavarian before her subordinate disappears out of the room again as fast as she can. Abbess paces around the room, looking out her windows to the lake below in quiet contemplation. She doesn't say a word to us, and I have to assume we're waiting for something.

"What's she asking for?" Levi turns to me.

"I'm not sure. I only caught a few words. I think she was asking her assistant to get someone else. Another sister, maybe."

"Are we in trouble?" he asks, half concern and half amusement on his face. Leave it to him to be amused at the ire of the sisters.

"I guess we'll find out. I'm sure I am." I force a grimace when I almost reflect his grin.

"Or you could be the hero for bringing these back. They might make you a saint or something. You'll have your own relics." He ponders, the suppressed smile reaching his eyes as he looks me over.

"I doubt that—if they knew what I was up to when we found them."

There's a soft chuckle on his part, and I'm glad that he came with me. It makes me a little less terrified of the consequences I might be facing. If they're truly dire, holding his hand through it will make the blow a little less severe.

Another ten minutes pass, and then the abbess's assistant appears with another sister, Sister Agnes. She was the former abbess of the convent. I've only met her once and seen her maybe a handful of times. She's a retired nun, aging gracefully as she approaches one hundred years old in the retiree wing of the convent. She was always exceedingly quiet whenever I saw her, but also exceptionally kind the one time I met her. She welcomed me and told me how happy she was that I chose her beautiful little convent.

But the moment she comes into the room and sees the relics on the abbess's desk, her whole face lights up. She smiles brightly, her eyes darting from the relics to me and back again. Tears start to stream down her face as she presses her hand to her mouth in shock, and she inspects them more closely. The abbess joins her, and there's another exchange of excited Bavarian between the three of them. The abbess's assistant turns toward me and smiles, and blessedly starts explaining the situation.

"The relics were lost during the war. The nuns had to flee the convent and were hiding in homes hidden in the Alps to avoid being caught up in any of the crossfire. Sister Agnes hasn't seen them since then," she explains in English.

"Oh wow." My grandfather had been so close to uncovering the truth before he died. I wish he could be here.

We spend another hour chatting with the nuns and learning a little bit more about the history of the abbey during the war. Their happiness about the discovery of the relics dulls the abbess's anger toward me over what Corey's men did in the wake of my kidnapping, and she agrees to let me stay and return to my old room after Levi explains how pivotal I was in getting them back to the abbey. Only after she berates him thoroughly for pretending to be a priest, that is.

He only speaks in half-truths, focusing on the historical

research and paperwork that we found in my family home, and skipping over the complicated path we followed to get them back into their hands. That part I'll have to keep to myself in quiet atonement. The last thing I want is for anything to happen to Levi or his friends and family.

It's late when we finish our discussions, well after dinner, and the last boat has departed the island, so the abbess offers Levi a room in the guest wing of the convent for the evening. We say our goodnights and agree to meet for breakfast. A last chance for us to say our goodbyes, and hopefully, I can get through them without falling apart. It already feels odd to watch him walk away this late at night, to no longer be stuck in the same cabin or curled up at his side in the same bed—a place I'd started to think of as home.

But this is my real home, and I have so much work to finish here before I can even start to think about what comes next. So I'd have to let my already mended heart break one last time in hopes that the pieces I put back together are stronger than before. Enough to withstand losing the one man I'm not sure it's possible to forget, even for a moment.

FIFTY-THREE

Z ephyrine

I STEP out of the shower, wrapping the towel around me before I tread out into my room to find clothes. I've been spoiled by my time at Bull Rush Ranch, the lavish main ranch house with its large showers and soaking tubs, the endless hours of hot water. Even the little heater tank outside at the cabin was less chilly than what we have here in the convent.

It's a small sacrifice in the scheme of things. One I'll have to adapt to again, along with all the rest. It's a mounting list that weighs heavily on my heart. So much so that I sat up for three hours tonight, finishing some of the work I'd left behind on my desk when Levi took me from it. I figure it can't hurt to get on the abbess's good side on day one, especially if I can keep the goodwill momentum going from the relics.

But for now, I've got to try to get some sleep. At least a few hours before the sun comes up. Maybe then, I might not look like death warmed over when I say goodbye to Levi. A hopeful wish that disappears the second I feel a hand cover my mouth and another wrap around my waist.

"Don't scream," Levi whispers, his forehead falling to my shoulder. "I couldn't sleep."

I wrap my hand around his, and he drops it away from my mouth, letting it fall to our sides. I turn and look at him, wide-eyed and worried, a million thoughts racing through my head.

"No one saw me." He shakes his head. "And I installed a better lock while I waited for you to get out of the shower."

"You nearly gave me a heart attack."

"I'm sorry for that."

"You shouldn't be in here. If the abbess finds out—" I shake my head.

"She won't." He stands by my desk, carefully examining the items lying on top of it and smirking as he picks up the aspergillum. "But if she did, would it be the worst thing to happen?"

"I don't want a get-out-of-jail-free card. I need to make all of this up to them. They deserve more from me." I shake my head.

"All the reasons I love you are the same ones that mean I have to lose you." He sighs, rolling the metal rod in his hand. "Sometimes I wish you were a little less of an angel, you know?"

"You're not losing me. You're just putting me back where you found me." I close the distance between us and run my fingers down his forearm. "Plus, I think we both know I'm not an angel. Unless we're talking about the vengeful kind." I give him a sympathetic smile, hoping it quells his doubts.

"The vengeful kind is my favorite." His eyes drift over my face and land on my lips.

"You should go back to your room. Get some sleep," I whisper.

"I can't sleep without you, so there's no use." He leans down, his lips brushing over mine in soft strokes, giving me the briefest taste of him before he stops to look at me—a question in his eyes.

"You can't sleep in here either. Never know what you'll wake up to. Being tied up. Burned." I nod to the aspergillum in his hand, and his eyes flash bright with the memory.

"Don't tease me with a good time, sweetheart." He kisses the side of my throat, his fingers tracing along the edge of my towel and then twisting around the ends of my damp hair. "You're already half naked for me. Wet."

"We shouldn't. Not in here. It's wrong." I point out the obvious, like he doesn't already know.

"That's your favorite way to have it." He slips the aspergillum under my towel and between my thighs, the cool touch of the metal eliciting a gasp. He uses the wand to part me, sliding it through my wetness and letting it roll over my clit. Each rib and rung of the metal adds a new facet of friction.

"Lev." I say his name like a warning, trying and failing to say more.

I should list all the reasons this is a bad idea. Why he shouldn't be touching me in this room. Why this shouldn't feel as good as it does. But I don't. Instead, I let out a stuttered breath as he takes another pass over my clit. I find myself burying my face against his shoulder, muting my protests, when he nudges my entrance with the tip.

"It's okay to want it, Zeph." He coaxes my face free from his shoulder, kissing my lips softly and breathing the words against them when he speaks again. "Just tell me how bad you want to be fucked. How much you need it to ward off the lonely nights here."

"It's wrong. That's for holy water. It's—" I choke on my words as I feel him press it inside me. He works it in and out, taunting me with just enough that I want more, then taking it away again. My breathing's uneven, and I lick my lips as my fingers dig into his shoulders. My chin drops, and he kisses me again before I let out another soft gasp. He pulls it out and rolls it over my clit, daring me to ask for more.

"Oh. Levi..." I whimper. "Please."

"See? It feels good, doesn't it?"

"Yes," I cry out softly when he slips it inside again. He pulls the tucked towel free at my chest, and it falls, pooling at my feet. His hand goes to my breast, cupping it and thumbing over my nipple as I lean into his touch.

"I'll never get over how gorgeous you are." He leans down, sucking my nipple into his mouth, his tongue playing over the tip.

"Oh god." I run my fingers through his hair and down his neck, letting my nails sink into his traps. He works me up, switching from one breast to the other and alternating the pace of penetration until I'm rocking my hips, desperate for more friction.

He pulls back, my nipple glistening as he kisses a path up my chest to my neck and then takes my hand, threading his fingers through mine. He brings me to my desk, clearing a space on it and turning my chair backward before he pats the seat.

"Kneel on this and bend over the desk. Elbows here. Palms here." He points to where he wants me as I climb onto the low-back chair. I follow his lead, letting him put me into position until I'm prone and fully on display for him. He gives my ass a soft squeeze.

"What are we doing?" I breathe as I look back at him. It's rhetorical. I know exactly what we're doing.

We're breaking every vow I've ever taken. Crossing every

line I've sworn I would never touch. Giving away every chance I have at redemption.

"This is wrong," I whisper. But he won't let me think of it like that.

"Don't they always tell you your body is a temple?" He answers me with a soft kiss to my core, his tongue teasing me with the promise of more before he pulls away. "I'm just worshiping at the altar, like any good penitent would."

"You don't seem sorry," I argue as I hear the sound of his zipper dragging down, and his hand passing over his cock. He presses the head against my entrance, hesitating for a long moment like he's enjoying the bit of torture he's putting us through before he sinks inside. He groans, barely even trying to mute himself.

"You're right. I'm not." He drags the ridges of the aspergillum up my center, teasing my ass as he fucks me slowly. "Not when I've got you like this. How could I ever be sorry for this?"

"So wrong," I mutter as I rock my hips, grinding my clit over the rounded edge of the desk chair, desperate for more.

"But it feels good, doesn't it?" His hand follows the curve of my ass, and then I see him pick something up from the table. I hear the pop of a bottle topper, and a moment later, I feel a cool liquid dripping between my cheeks.

"What's that?" I ask, glancing back over my shoulder to see him eyeing the label as he straightens his glasses.

"Anointing oil." A wicked grin spreads over his face as he sets the bottle back down. "Perfect."

"Levi," I whisper his name in nervous anticipation as his thumb circles me.

"You trust me?"

"You know I do."

"You remember how you keep yourself safe from the wolf, little red?" Amusement seeps through his tone.

"Confess," I repeat the safe word I picked for us.

"That's my girl. Now relax for me." He dribbles a few more drops over me before the tip of his thumb slips in.

I curse. The intrusion feels new and tight. I tell myself to focus on his cock. How good it feels. How full I am. If I can take him there, I can take him here.

"Breathe." His voice is calm and soothing as he massages me, sliding his middle finger in and working it slowly in and out. He takes his time, slow thrusts of his dick in and out of me to keep me grounded while he helps me ease into the rest. "You're so fucking tight. I need time we don't have. You think you could take a little more?"

"Yes." I want to be brave for him, so I nod my agreement, trying to catch my breath as I slip my fingers between my legs. I need more than I can get in this position, and I want the distraction of pleasure as he tests my limits. I circle my clit as his cock stills inside me, his finger slipping free, and I mourn the loss of the fullness I'd felt with a muted curse.

I hear the pop of the little topper again and feel the oil drip down over me. I glance back and watch him slick the narrow end of the aspergillum up to the flared base of the guard that keeps it from slipping into the pail. It's much smaller than he is, but still more than I've ever taken.

"Levi. That's—" I swallow hard.

"Wrong?" A dark chuckle rumbles free from his chest. "It won't feel wrong. Not when we're working you so full you can't think straight."

"I trust you." I remind myself. He'd never ask me to do anything he didn't think I was more than capable of.

"Just focus on your breathing. Slow. Steady. I'll make it good for you," he promises.

I take a deep breath and slowly release it as he pushes it inside me. My heart pounds in my chest, but every inch he slips in sends a shiver of awareness down my spine. I tease my clit with the pads of my fingers and start to move again, rocking my hips forward and backward. I test my limits, and I hear a low groan of approval rumble out of his chest as he watches me.

"How's that feel?" He gently palms the curve of my cheek as he starts to move again.

"Good. Different but good." I breathe out the words in between soft little moans as I adjust to the feeling.

When he's sure I'm ready, he moves in earnest, countering his thrusts and alternating them with the thrust of the makeshift toy he's created for me. Slowly bringing us up to our normal rhythm.

"So good," I murmur.

"Fuck, sweetheart, look at you like this. Falling apart for me while you're spread out naked over your desk." He curses again, and I cry out as he picks up his pace. "So damn beautiful."

"I need more, please," I whimper, my fingers working my clit until I'm begging for him to put me out of my misery.

"Yeah? You need me to fuck this little cunt full? Beg me for it."

"Levi. Please. *Please.* Oh god..." My words fade into a mess of curses that alternate with me calling out his name.

I try to use the desk to brace myself as I feel him take me to the verge and hold me there. So close and so far. Another murmured curse from my lips, though, and he answers my prayers, giving me enough that I can barely hold it together. Before I know it, I'm coming hard, shattering into a million pieces that I might not ever be able to put back together again.

"See what I mean? Nothing is more sacred than this. The sound of you crying out like an angel—my angel." His steady tone and the reassuring stroke of his palm over my hip and cheek take me floating out into an ocean of pleasure.

"It's so good," I mumble into my forearm, bending low as I'm overwhelmed by another wave.

"That's my perfect girl. You're doing so good. Come all over my cock." He talks me through it. "Oh fuck. You should see how soaked you have me and your desk. I love it."

"Come inside me, please," I beg him. I want to be full in every way possible—marked and ruined, knowing I'm his completely even when he's gone. "Let me watch you."

The aspergillum is discarded, and he hauls me up into his arms, kicking the chair out of the way before he flips me over on the desk. He's not gentle when he spreads my legs wide and slams inside. He's unhinged, feral even, as he takes us both to the point of ruin.

"Holy hell. You're so deep." I have to catch my breath to speak, and he drags his lips down my throat. I bury my fingers in the hair at his nape.

"I have to be. The only chance I have of saving my soul is when I'm buried deep inside you," he whispers against my ear.

I wrap my legs around him, my fingernails dragging down his back as he fucks me senseless, speeding us toward our finish. I can feel the building wave of my third orgasm, holding me hostage as he wrecks me completely with the sounds he's making.

He comes hard, groaning so loudly I have to slap my hand over his mouth to muffle the noise. An act that only serves to make him more determined to fuck me harder, rattling the desk underneath us while I say a quick prayer that the sister next door doesn't wake up and come knocking, wondering if things have escalated from kidnapping to murder.

"Fucking hell, look at this tight little cunt. Fucked so full you're leaking," he mutters against my palm as I loosen my grip.

We both watch the evidence drip out onto the table in streams underneath us. My fingers are still lazily circling my clit as his eyes fall heavy on the sight.

"Did you come?"

"Twice."

"But?" He's still breathing heavy, the words coming out clipped but focused. His intense gaze makes me confess the truth.

"I think I could again."

"Fuck yes, you will. Tell me what to do." He's eager, his lip rolling between his teeth eagerly as he waits for my command.

"Get on your knees and clean up your mess." I try for a stern order, but the amusement breaks on my face. His eyes soften, the intensity making way for devotion before a grin flashes over his face, and he hits the ground.

"Anything you want," he murmurs against my skin before he swirls his tongue over my clit, sucking gently while I massage myself with the pads of my fingers—the two of us working in tandem.

"Oh my god…" I mumble. I dig my heel into his back, rocking against his face as I fall into the waves one last time. He draws it out for me, gently laving his tongue and lapping up every last drop of us while I run my fingers through his hair.

Finally, he looks up at me, nothing but admiration in his eyes, before he takes a deep breath and stands. He holds his hand out and pulls me to my feet, wrapping his arms around me and pressing me to his chest. The scent of his cologne and the feel of his skin on mine lure me into the calm again.

"How am I going to live without you?" I voice the thought that's been rolling through my head all evening.

"You're asking the wrong person because I'm praying you can't." He slips his hand under my jaw, cupping it and tilting my head up before he kisses me one last time.

We fall asleep together in my bed, me wrapped around him, naked and uncaring if we're caught like this or not. But in the wee hours of the morning, when I wake up, he's gone. The bed empty. The door locked. The sheet pulled back into place over me, and the room straightened like everything was a dream. Only the empty bottle of anointing oil reveals the truth.

When I get up in the morning, I find the phone he gifted me with a note:

I couldn't bear to hear you say goodbye, so I'm saving us both the trouble. I set up your phone so I can keep an eye on you, just like old times. You know where I stand. How I feel. You ever want to come home, you call me.

I press the phone to my chest and sob until it's finally time for my shift in the kitchen.

FIFTY-FOUR

L evi

"KNOCK, KNOCK." Charlotte's voice is at the door of my office.

"Come in," I call, my brows knitting together in confusion. "Didn't realize we had a meeting today."

"We don't. I was just in town on business with Hudson and figured I'd ask for this favor in person."

"What favor is that?"

"I have a potential contact I've set up a meeting with. She wants my help locating something she thinks might have ended up on the black market. She's a liaison for a much bigger client who doesn't want to wait. The problem is she needs a meeting this Friday, and Rowan and I have another appointment in Seattle that weekend already."

"They won't wait?"

"No, and I'd rather not have Hudson go. There's the potential for this one to be dangerous. Frankly, I'm not entirely sure it's not a trap, and he has several board meetings next week. They frown on him being full of bullet holes at those things. Apparently, it makes the investors nervous."

"If you need me to, I can," I offer, shrugging off the danger. I could use it to feel alive again. The casino has been wildly uneventful lately, and Zephyrine's brothers have been as quiet as their father. "There's an event at the casino, but I can see if Grant and the rest of the staff can handle it."

I need something to pull me out of this pit of despair. I've been wallowing in it for weeks—far too long. She'd be disappointed in me if she could see. Watching me sulk and eating up every morsel of the short messages she sends my way. But they're few and far between, just like she promised. Enough to know she's alive and well, but not enough that we can fall back into old habits. Not enough to give me hope that she's coming home. Not that I'm willing to accept an alternative.

"I thought you all might hire that Bishop guy. He seemed capable. Maybe you get a few weeks off for a vacation after this?" Charlotte scans me like she's seen roadkill in better condition.

"We're talking about it. He's not much for a nine-to-five."

"Neither are you, by the looks of it." She gives me a sympathetic look.

"It's just been a long few weeks. Months really."

"Well, if it's the reason I suspect, you might like where you're headed."

"Where's that?"

"Munich. That's not far from your nun, is it? Maybe you could see her?" Charlotte gives me hope.

My heart skips a beat at the thought of seeing her again. Her sweet smile. Her gorgeous blue eyes. Even if it were just in passing while I sat at the back of the church at the abbey for Mass, I'd take it. A glimpse of her to get me through a little longer. But then my heart falls.

"I shouldn't. She needs time to figure things out. Space to decide what she needs to do to make peace with everything."

"Well, I'm sorry for you both. Truly. I went through something like that once, and I wouldn't wish it on anyone." Charlotte offers a small smile of support.

"Neither would I." There's no sense in pretending to be fine around the people that know me best when it's obvious I'm not. "But maybe this job will be interesting enough to provide a distraction."

"I hope so. I'll have my assistant send over the details?"

"Sounds good," I agree, and with that, she's out of my office. And I'm left alone with my thoughts, doing my best to stop coming up with reasons I need to go to the abbey or the lake.

THE CAFÉ IS busy as hell this afternoon, tourists and locals alike bustling through the square, only pausing for their midday coffee break under the autumn sun. There's a perfect view of the old town hall from here, not that I can see it with the constant thrum of bodies back and forth over the cobblestones. It's probably why I don't even see her approach my table.

"Is this seat taken?" I'd recognize her voice anywhere, and I practically spill my coffee in my lap as I turn around.

I expect the nun—out of the sundresses and boots Dakota picked for her in Colorado and back into her convent uniform of wool skirts and blouses, no makeup, and a braid neatly tying back her long red hair. But instead, she's in a pale-pink tea-length dress, her gold cross necklace glimmering in the sun, and her long legs on display. She's cut her hair, and it's styled in loose curls, and the makeup she's wearing subtly highlights all my favorite features.

"Zephyrine," I say her name softly as I stand, and she smiles. "You look gorgeous."

"You too." She smiles and leans in to hug me. I wrap my arms around her and pull her close, the familiar scent of her wafting around me.

"I've missed you so damn much. What are you doing here?" I pull back and look her up and down again. "I can't imagine the abbess approves of this."

"She knows I'm here. Or theoretically she does." She squeezes me one more time and then moves to her chair. I pull it out for her and then remember I have an appointment. I curse before Charlotte's description of the new client replays in my mind, and I close my eyes, pinching the bridge of my nose and lifting my glasses as I process the trap she'd set for me.

"The abbey is the new client, and you're here on their behalf?" I raise a brow, realizing I've been tricked.

She settles into her chair, pulling the small blanket they've set out over her lap. I sink back into my own, still taking in the fact that I have her in front of me again. I wish I'd known it was her I was meeting. I'm still jet-lagged and only half awake. I was barely able to manage the black shirt and slacks, but Charlotte has a strict code about uniforms herself, so I'd grumbled my way through the shave and press before I left. She would have made an excellent abbess if she weren't in a relationship with three men.

"Close but not quite. The Vatican," she replies.

"The Vatican?" I nearly choke on the sip of coffee I'd just taken.

Before she can answer, the server appears to ask if Zephyrine wants anything.

"Sie hätte gerne... Einen Kaffee mit viel—viel—Sahne und

Zucker. Und... einen Kuchen. Erdbeerkuchen," I answer for Zephyrine, and the server's lips quirk at my description of her cream requirements, but she nods her understanding and takes off for the kitchen again. When I look back at Zephyrine, she's grinning brightly, her eyes raking over me as she takes in my appearance.

"Your German is getting better," she compliments me. I'm not sure it's that much better, but I'm trying.

"I figured that if you're staying at the convent permanently, I'd need to learn if I want to keep talking to you."

She shakes her head, glancing down and pressing her lips together in a sweet smile.

"I couldn't give up English completely. Have to be able to whisper conspiratorially with the other girls behind the abbess's back."

"How are you getting along there? Are you back in her good graces yet?"

"Oh, I'm in the best of them now that I'm not her problem anymore. How are you doing? Business back to normal at the Avarice now?"

"It's fine." I don't want to talk about life back home. I just want to talk about her. I want to know how she's doing and how they're treating her. "Not her problem? How so?"

"Well, I went to the Vatican with the small envoy the abbey sent along with the relics. Everyone agreed it would be best to take them to the museums there so they could undergo conservation and be reassessed. The abbey doesn't have funds for that, and one of their curators was very interested in delving more into their origins. They'd already been doing quite a bit of research by the time we got there, and we brought copies from our archives for them to look through." She talks animatedly as the server returns with her coffee and strawberry cake, with a large side pot of cream. She pauses to smile at the server and thank her profusely.

"Did they find anything new?" I ask, as she ladles several spoonfuls of cream into her coffee.

"Yes." She takes a sip, savoring it as she closes her eyes and sets it back down again. She leans back in her chair, the seriousness returning. "There's a missing relic."

"Another one?"

"Yes. There's one more besides the three we found in the vault. They were all part of a collection of items that Charlemagne was believed to have carried with him during his rule. Whether they were sacred or he was as superstitious as my father, there's disagreement, but there's a fourth. The abbey records were incomplete because the fourth piece wasn't kept with the other three. It was only brought there as the war intensified. They thought the abbey might be safe from the worst of it given how isolated it is."

"It probably would have been, if not for Schaefer."

"Right." Her fingers trace over her necklace, and then she sits forward. "So that's my new mission."

"Finding the last one?"

"Yes. I'm hoping that with Charlotte's help, I can find it and return it to be with the others. Put things right that my family made a mess of. Finish the work Grandad O'Leary started, and hopefully make some small amount of amends for all the harm my dad's family has caused over the years."

"The abbess is willing to let you leave to do that?"

She nods, taking a delicate bite of her cake and washing it down with another sip of her coffee-flavored cream.

"I told her the truth about everything. It felt like the right thing to do."

"Not all the details, I hope." I could only imagine the

abbess having a heart attack if she knew one of her precious nuns was tying men up and taking advantage of them in fields somewhere in the States, and that's before we even get to the convenient disappearance of her husband.

"I spared her that much." Zephyrine grins, and her blue eyes light with the thought.

"She threw you out then?"

"Surprisingly, no. She said we're all human, and we make mistakes. That it had been unusual circumstances, and she could understand, given the situation, how something like that might happen. She just asked that I spend time in prayer and reflection, make sure that becoming a nun was what I truly wanted. Reminded me that it's a lifetime of commitment," Zephyrine explains.

"What did you decide?" My heart is practically in my throat with hope.

"I thought about something Dakota said, about how I might be forcing myself into a box that wasn't of my own making. One that might not really exist if I took a step back. So I thought a lot about everything. I thought about you." She looks up at me. "I couldn't stop thinking about you, if I'm honest."

"Me either," I admit.

"I thought about the past. About Chase. My father. My mother. All the work my grandfather did. Everything we managed to accomplish in such a short amount of time. With Charlotte's help and your family's and the Kellys'. I compared that to what I could accomplish in the convent, and I realized I could probably do a lot more good outside of the convent than in it. And the abbess agreed with me when I spoke with her."

"So you're leaving?" My heart might explode in my chest while I wait for this woman to get to the words I want to hear.

She nods. "I'm leaving the convent, but I'm still working as a liaison of sorts. A way to make amends to them for leaving after so long there without joining the order. But I'm free to go where I need to. I just have to go back every so often to check in, and I'll still need to touch base with the curators at the Vatican."

"So where will you be living?"

She grins. "Well, when I messaged Dakota to thank her for the advice she gave me, she told me I needed to get my quote 'ass back to Purgatory Falls,' and sent me a slew of apartment rental listings in town."

"I can get you a place. Easy. Fuck, you can live at my place or the ranch. Wherever you want. I'll make it happen."

"Well, I actually have one. She picked one out with me and helped me put down a deposit." She looks to me for my reaction, and I bite my tongue. Charlotte and Dakota were conspiring both for and against me, it seems. I'm not sure how to feel about that. But she continues on, drowning out my thoughts. "I figured if I'm going to start over, I want to try it on my own. I went from my father to Corey to the convent. I only had a few months at university, so I've never really had the chance to stand on my own two feet. I think I need that. To figure out who I really am, you know?" she explains.

"I see." I swallow back an impulsive response before I speak again. "If that's what you need, I understand. I'm just glad you'll get a chance to be out from behind those walls."

"But I'm also really hoping for the chance to see where things might have gone between us. In a different life. Where we weren't stuck in a cabin and you weren't having to constantly follow me around and rescue me. And I was just a girl who lived in the same town who happened to develop a massive crush on you after meeting you at a café one day." She reaches across the table, her fingertips brushing over my knuckles.

My heart kick-starts in my chest again, rebounding from the pit of my stomach as my eyes lift to meet hers before they drop down to where we touch. I take a deep breath, letting my thoughts turn over before I speak.

"I mean, if there is a chance that you might be interested, of course. I understand things could have changed. I know how we left things, how I left things, and... Well, I wouldn't blame you if you've moved on," she adds quickly.

"I didn't move on, Zeph. How could I possibly move on knowing you're out here? You're everything I ever wanted and more that I didn't know I needed. I'm just trying to reconcile my greedy, jealous impulses with what you're offering." I push my glasses up and scrub a hand over my mouth, my eyes following the uneven masonry of the stone building in front of me. "I know you're right. It's the right way to do things. You need your freedom. I knew that when I left you at the convent, and I know it now. I respect it, but fuck, I hate the idea of you being alone like that. I worry, you know? He's still out there even if he is handcuffed by the investigations and inquiries."

"Dakota said you'd say that. Which is why we picked one of the apartments in the new residential wing of the Avarice. I'll have the extra security, and if you think I should have more, it will be easier to install there. Plus, I figured it'd make sleepovers at each other's places easier. Less baggage. Shorter commute. Assuming you're up for that, we could always negotiate how many nights a week that is." A wry smile forms as she watches my reaction.

"I think I'd be up for that, yeah." My voice cracks with the effort of trying to sound calm.

"Good, because I was hoping you'd give me a lift back to the States with you tomorrow." She takes another sip of her coffee, wiping the thin line of cream that formed on her cupid's bow with a napkin. "After you ravage me in my hotel room tonight, that is." Her lashes lift with the invitation.

"I think I can manage that for you."

"Perfect."

FIFTY-FIVE

Z ephyrine

"HOLY FUCK." Levi lets out a low whistle as he surveys the hotel room I'm staying in. We took a walk around the city and ate dinner at a quaint little Gasthaus down the street at his insistence. If it had been up to me, I might have just brought him back here and worried about room service later. "Is the Vatican paying for this?"

"No. This is Charlotte's doing." I do a quick twirl, grinning as I look back at him. "Isn't it gorgeous?" The hotel rises above one of the main squares in the city, and the floor-to-ceiling windows in the room have spectacular views of vintage roofs and cobblestone paths leading out between the churches and shops. "I think it might have been a setup though." I tap the champagne bottle that's on ice on the table and snatch one of the chocolate-dipped strawberries that sit next to it, offering it up to him.

He takes a bite and lets out a small hum of approval.

"Good?" I ask as he grabs my hips and pulls me close.

"Not as good as the ones in the woods, but they'll do for tonight." His hands slip around to my back and follow the curve of my butt as I step out of my flats and tuck them under the table.

"Do you want some champagne? Or I can see if room service has whisky?" I glance back to see if there's a menu. I feel oddly nervous at the thought of being with him again. He pauses abruptly and raises an eyebrow, studying my face.

"Did I misread what you meant about coming up for dessert? Are we slow-rolling this? Back to square one with the dating and chaste kisses?" He doesn't complain, but I can see the look of concern flash behind his eyes.

"Are you capable of chaste kisses?"

He presses his lips together, one eye closed and the other looking to the ceiling in contemplation, before he leans down to press a soft kiss to my cheek. Just that little touch has my heart thudding in my ears. He moves to break it, but his lips glide lower, kissing along my jaw and down my neck as he walks me backward, pinning me against the table. I let out a soft sigh when he finally lets me go.

"I don't think so." He breathes, his eyes heavy as he looks to me for permission.

"Good, because I was thinking more along the lines of making up for lost time." I wrap my arms around his neck and kiss him softly where his shoulder meets his neck, slowly working my way up. "The Late-Night Playlist you made me is good, but it doesn't live up to the real thing," I whisper when I reach the shell of his ear. "I need you to remind me what it's like. Can you do that for me? Please?"

"Fucking hell," he mutters under his breath.

He shoves the champagne and strawberries out of the way, one of them tumbling to the ground as he lifts me on top of the table. His hands are under my dress, wrenching my panties off as he kisses my throat again and again.

"I'll fuck you slow later. I promise. I'll let you ride my face as much as you want, but I need inside you."

"Yes, please." My hands slide down his back, digging into his shoulder blades for purchase as he slips his belt loose. I can't even think to help him. I'm just lost in how good he feels. The smell of his cologne wraps around me again, and the sounds of the city below are drowned out by his breathing and my heart racing as he works his zipper down.

"You thought I'd be that easy, huh?" he asks, pretending to be cross, but the smirk that forms gives him away.

"I hoped so."

"Well, you'd be right. And I'm not even remotely sorry about it."

He closes the distance between us, and I slip my hands around the waistband of his jeans, shoving them down with his boxer briefs. He grabs my hips and drags me to the edge of the table, slipping inside me where I'm already wet and ready for him. I cry out softly when he pulls out and slides back in again, moaning his approval against my cheek as his hands dig into my ass.

"Christ. You feel so fucking perfect." He lets out a shuddering breath as he starts to fuck me.

"You too." I don't have words right now. Just a flood of emotions that steal my breath and confirm that I made the right choice. This is exactly where I'm supposed to be.

He's uncharacteristically quiet as he concentrates, kissing me up one side and down the other as he fucks me like he's been deprived of it for years.

"You feel so good like this. Having you bare. I missed it." I talk since he won't, and the quiet is making me anxious all over again. "I thought about you every night. I couldn't stop listening to the recording we made." I run my hand down his back and use the leverage to shift our position slightly, taking him deeper while he keeps a steady pace. His thumb brushes over my clit, building the need for him. I bring my lips to his ear. "I waited until everyone went to sleep and put my headphones on. And I'd put that part where you're telling me what to do on a loop, imagining I was doing it again while I touched my—"

He cuts me off with a kiss. It's rough and claiming, his tongue tangling with mine for several long moments before he finally releases me to let me breathe again.

"You can't talk like that if I'm gonna make it last long enough for you. It's been too long without you, and I'm a weak fucking man right now," he confesses, his eyes brimming with concern as they meet mine.

"I don't care about it lasting." I kiss him softly before I meet his eyes. "Don't hold back. You're going to have plenty of nights to do that."

He gives me a doubtful look, and I run my hand around his neck, slipping my fingers into his nape, and bringing my lips back to his ear.

"Don't make me beg. Mark me. Make me yours," I plead, and it's all the encouragement he needs.

"Fuck me." He moans low as he starts to fuck me faster, his breathing heavy, and more broken curses flow from his lips as he comes inside me. I dig my nails into his back, begging for him and telling him over and over how good he is.

He pulls out, his cock still heavy and hard as he drips out of me onto the edge of the table. The sight of us nearly pushes me over. I'm so close to my own orgasm that I can barely stand it. His thumb circles my clit again to test me, and I whimper, spreading my legs to give him better access, before he drops to his knees in front of me.

"I've got you, sweetheart. Whatever you need," he promises as he keeps up the pressure on my clit and uses his free hand to drag me all the way to the edge. I slide my leg over his shoulder, and he spreads me wide. His tongue teases me as he laps up the mess we've made.

"Fuck, the taste of me on you like this. I needed this so fucking badly." He lets out a guttural sound from his chest and kisses my clit, wrapping his lips around and sucking until I see stars. The wave of pleasure rises so hard and so fast that I don't see it coming.

"Oh my god, I can't—" I start to murmur, but the moan I can't hold back cuts me off.

He slips two fingers inside me, working me from the inside and out as I rock my hips forward against his mouth. I take in a deep breath and cry out for him, running my fingers through his hair and begging him for more. He draws another wave out of me and then kisses me softly, tracing them slowly over the inside of my thigh to my knee as I come down from the high.

"Good?" he asks, glancing up at me as he continues his trail of kisses down my leg to my ankle.

"I might need you to come first every single time if that's how it ends for me." I laugh as I grab the edge of his collar and tug him up while he sets his clothes to rights.

"I've been so fucking desperate for you." He breathes the words against my skin as he bends over me, and I lean back. The confession echoes through my heart because he's all I've wanted since he left the convent.

I let him pin me to the table as he kisses me gently. The taste of us on my lips as I wrap my legs around his waist is perfection. He picks me up and carries me to the bed, laying me down before he climbs on next to me. He takes a lock of my hair, shorter now since I cut it, and winds it around his finger absently as he studies me.

"I missed you," he confesses.

"I missed you too."

"I'll walk any line you want me to. Whatever you need to make you feel confident about where your life is headed now, I'm here for it. I'm just happy to have you back." His eyes meet mine with the kind of sincerity I've only ever known from him.

"Do you hate the idea? The apartment and everything? I'm willing to negotiate."

"Not at all. Honestly, the more I think about it, the more I like it. It's a little bit like getting to start over on the right foot instead of me stealing you in the middle of the night." His warm smile puts me at ease.

"I mean, we can still reenact that part sometimes, though, right?" I run my fingers up his forearm, flashing him a playful grin.

"Yeah, I think we can make that work." He grins back.

FIFTY-SIX

L evi

"I NEED you to do something for me." Zephyrine turns to me as we're walking out to the barn on the far side of the stables. Hazel sent us on a mission to see if we can find some hay to decorate the front porch with, and Zephyrine's excited that she was invited to help with holiday preparations.

"What's that?" I ask.

"You won't like it, but it's important." There's a worried but determined look on her face, and I feel the slither of apprehension up my spine.

"I don't think I like the sound of that." I eye her warily. I don't know what she has in mind, but I've only barely gotten her back, and I'm not keen to do anything but enjoy every second I have her with me.

"But if I asked you for something, you'd do it? You did once tell me you'd do anything for me."

"There are a few caveats, but yes." I stop and turn my head, using the brim of my hat to keep the late fall sun out of my eyes as I try to read what she's up to on her pretty face. "It'll be easier if you just tell me instead of dealing in hypotheticals."

"I want you to brand me."

"No." I don't even have to think about my answer. I turn on my heel and start walking again.

"Levi!" she shouts after me.

"I have no idea where you got that idea in your head."

"You have one. Bishop has one," she argues with me.

"How do you know Bishop has one?" I frown at the idea that he's been encouraging her.

"He told me."

"Did he give you this idea?"

"No. You did."

"I did?" I stop short. "I have no damn clue when I ever said anything to encourage that, but let me be clear, that I have zero interest in marring any part of you like that. I shouldn't have done it myself. It was a dark time in my life."

"Will you just listen, please?" She crosses her arms, a stern look on her face.

I take a deep breath, turning my head away to give myself a moment to see reason enough to let her talk. I should hear her out. It's her life, her body. And if we're honest, I can't stop her from doing anything she really sets her mind to.

"Fine. Talk." I'm still terse as I try to rein in my frustration.

"I want you to put your brand over the tattoo Corey had them put on me. I think it would be healing for me not to have to catch glimpses of it in the mirror anymore, and not to hear that angry rumble thing you do whenever you see it."

"I—" I start to tell her I don't do that, but she cuts me off.

"Yes, you do. You think I don't hear you, but I do. Maybe you don't even realize it. And I understand. I know why you do it. You love me. You're protective of me. You wish you had a time machine. But it's there whether we like it or not."

"You could go to one of those tattoo removal places. Don't they do that at the doctor's office these days?"

"I could. But the ghost of it will still be there. It's not a magic eraser. I've looked into it."

"A brand isn't either. It'll still be there underneath."

"But the tattoo will be destroyed by it, and the brand will be yours."

I press my glasses up the bridge of my nose and shift on my feet. I still hate it, but I can see why she likes the idea. I might do the same in her shoes. Fuck, I hate when she has a point I can't argue with. I kick the heel of my boot against a rock as I contemplate my next words.

"And we'd match. Here." She presses her hand to my chest, where the scar of the Bull Rush Ranch brand is burned into my skin. "And more importantly, here." She touches the spot on my stomach where she burned me in the convent.

"I don't even think about that, you know?"

"But I do."

"I don't want you doing this out of guilt. You have nothing to feel guilty about. You were defending yourself."

"Not guilt. Love."

I let out a long, frustrated sigh, looking skyward for some sort of intervention, but getting none, I meet her eyes again. They're full of determination, daring me to tell her no.

"If it's what you really want..."

"It is."

"It hurts like hell. Takes weeks to heal. No hot springs or the pool at the Avarice while you wait. The nurse we see will bitch and moan about elective injuries."

"I'm okay with all of that."

AN HOUR LATER, we're out in the barn, the brand heated, and her bent over one of the rails while Dakota holds her hand. I'm not doing this like Bishop or I did, half drunk and without a damn care in the world. We prepped her skin and I have wound care and bandages sitting and waiting at the ready, but my heart is still pounding in my fucking chest at the thought of marking her like this.

"You're sure?" I ask her again.

"I'm sure."

"Fuck..." I curse under my breath and grab the brand.

I line it up with her tattoo and press it to her skin, closing my eyes as she lets out a blood-curdling whimper of pain and curses with every single four-letter word in her vocabulary. It only lasts a brief moment, and I toss it back into the fire, but tears come to my eyes all the same to hear her cry out like that.

"Oh fuck, that hurts like a son of bitch!" She stands and dances around, wincing and laughing as she squeezes Dakota's hand.

"Um, I wish I had half that kind of courage. That was hardcore." Dakota and Zeph exchange a mutual grin.

She looks at me then, and seeing the tears in my eyes, her smile falters. She throws her arms wide and closes the gap, wrapping me up and squeezing me.

"Thank you. I know that wasn't easy, but I love you for doing it."

"Let's just hope it heals okay. Let me see." I make her turn around, and I grimace at the sight of it.

"Did it do the job? On the tattoo, I mean?"

"Yeah. Yeah, I think it did." That much was evident

already, and Dakota nods along, reassuring Zephyrine that her makeshift tattoo removal has gone to plan. "We'll have to check as it heals. Let's get you bandaged up." I make her sit still while I perform my ministrations.

"Do you think I could get Grant to do this?" Dakota looks at me.

"I don't think he'd let you do this in a million fucking years. He'll kill me for giving you the idea."

"Fine." Dakota lets out a huff of frustration. "But it's sexy. You two have matching brands on each other. That's commitment."

"Right?" Zephyrine agrees with Dakota. "You'd think he'd be more excited about the fact that I want him forever."

"I'm plenty fucking excited about forever, sweetheart. But I already knew that. I didn't need a brand to prove it to me. I just have to look into those pretty blues." I spin her around, and she grins up at me, the hint of a blush on her cheeks that I'm saying all this in front of Dakota. "See, just like this. The way you look at me? I can see forever right there in your eyes. You've been looking at me like that since the night at the lake."

"And when did you know it was forever?" she asks, and I grin at the fact that she doesn't argue with me.

"When I jumped in after you. When you burned me. When you kissed me that day in the woods. Just now, when you trusted me to do this. It wasn't just once, sweetheart. It's been every single day since I met you."

Zephyrine

I'M CURLED up on the couch in the corner of the ranch house's living room, watching the chaos of the Stockton family Thanksgiving unfold, and grinning like an absolute fool that I have a front-row seat to all of it. It's been an adjustment to be back stateside and not have the constant worry about my family or Corey in the back of my mind, but I'm happy. I've never felt this safe or loved in my life, and it's definitely something to be grateful for today.

"Thanks for all of your help cooking and cleaning up after dinner." Hazel drops onto the couch next to me. "I couldn't have done it without you."

"Of course. I'm happy to help. Thank you for having me. It's been a long time since I've had an American Thanksgiving, and most of mine weren't nearly this fun."

"Well, buckle in. Because if you think Thanksgiving is a lot with this family, wait until you see Christmas." She grins. "Speaking of, did you see these photo albums? Ramsey and I were looking through them the other day. We want to get all the siblings framed photos of their parents' wedding day as part of their Christmas gift this year. But there are some cute ones of little Levi in here too. It's hard to believe any of these guys were cherubic-cheeked little angels, isn't it?"

She points out a couple of photos of Levi, and I have to smile at the one of him standing next to a horse and grinning in his oversized cowboy boots. There's another of all four of the siblings standing out in front of the ranch house, and one with teenage Grant and Levi, on a mountain with their arms around each other.

"Hazel! Can I have your help with this?" Dakota calls from the kitchen.

"I'll be right back." Hazel pats me on the knee. "But you should look through them. There are some good ones in there."

I flip the pages, turning back through the Stockton family history until I find some of the black-and-white photos of his grandparents. One of them sitting on the bed of an old Ford pickup truck. Another where they're embracing, his grandfather, who could be Levi's doppelgänger, looking sharp in his uniform, and his grandmother wearing a beautiful dark-colored dress and victory curls.

I turn the page, and my heart stops. I pull the album off my lap, bringing it closer to my face like I might not be seeing clearly. Sitting around a table are a group of servicemen in WWII uniforms. Two of them I recognize instantly. Another face I know from the archival photos Charlotte's shown me. The last one I'd have a harder time recognizing if he didn't look exactly like the man who's just walked into the room.

"Why do you look like you've seen a ghost?" Levi looks over me with concern.

"Look at this." I pull the photo out of the album and hand it to him as he stands over me. It gives me the perfect angle to see the handwriting in inky-blue penmanship on the back.

Schaefer, O'Leary, Kelly, Stockton. 1945.

Levi curses under his breath, the color draining from his face.

"When I saw my dad last, he said something about killing two birds with one stone here at the ranch. I thought it was a grotesque reference to your parents. But what if he meant something else?" I ask.

WANT MORE ZEPHYRINE AND LEVI? Read the Bonus Epilogue:

WHAT TO READ NEXT

THE QUIET HORSEMEN

Bull Rush - Hazel & Ramsey

Dark Horse - Grant & Dakota

QUEEN CITY CHAOS SERIES

Before the Chaos - Prequel Novella

Rival Hearts - Madison & Quentin

Mine to Gain - Beatrix & Cooper

SEATTLE PHANTOM FOOTBALL SERIES

Defensive End - Prequel Short Story

Pick Six - Alexander & Harper

Overtime - Colton & Joss

Wild Card - Tobias & Scarlett

NOVELLAS

Lords of Misrule - Charlotte, Hudson, Rowan, & Finn

GLOSSARY

abbess – A nun who is the head of an abbey of nuns.

abbey – A group of nuns in a community setting, which includes a church.

act of contrition/contrition – a prayer recited during confession, an expression of sorrow for your sins

aspergillum – A tool for sprinkling holy water.

Carolingian relics – Objects of religious significance relating to the Frankish dynasty formed by Charlemagne's family in the 8th and 9th centuries.

convent – A community of nuns.

habit – A distinctive religious dress worn by Roman Catholic nuns, which typically consists of a tunic and cowl, among other elements.

near occasion of sin – A theological concept that a situation, person, or place could make an individual more likely to commit a sin due to the proximity and inherent temptation.

novice – A nun in training who has not yet taken her final vows but lives as a member of the convent.

prie-dieu – A prayer desk or stand with a kneeler, which is used for the recitation of devotionals, prayers, and reflection.

reliquary – A container of relic(s).

sacrament of reconciliation – Another term for confession.

thurible – An incense burner that is suspended from chains and typically carried by an altar server. It can be burned during worship services and used symbolically for purification.

ACKNOWLEDGMENTS

To you, the reader, thank you so much for taking a chance on this book and on me! Your support means everything.

To Kat, Kara, and Vanessa, thanks isn't enough for all of your hard work. I'm so grateful to have such an amazing editing team.

To Jaime, Cassie, and Mackenzie thank you for everything you do to make it possible for me to have more time to write and for all of your encouragement and support. I couldn't do it without you!

To Thorunn and Ashley, thank you for answering all of my technical research questions, your thoughtful feedback, and for all of your words of support!

To my beta readers, Tiffany, Britt, Sarah, and Jess, for your unhinged reactions that keep me going when I have doubts and making sure I'm keeping the Stockton family living up to their reputation.

To Eva and Kelly, you keep me grounded and inspired in equal measure. I'm so incredibly grateful for your friendship. I wouldn't have made it this far without you in my corner.

To my Content Team, thank you so much for all the support you give my characters, my books, and me. I wouldn't be able to do this without you, and I'm so incredibly grateful for every single edit you create and recommendation you give. Whenever I write about my FMCs supporting each other, please know you're always part of that inspiration!

ABOUT THE AUTHOR

Maggie Rawdon is a romance author living in the Midwest. She writes jaw dropping romance featuring men with the kind of filthy mouths who will make you blush and swoon and the smart independent women who make them fall first. She has a weakness for writing frenemies whose fighting feels more like flirting and found families.

She loves real sports as much as the fictional kind and spends football season writing in front of the TV with her pups at her side. When she's not on editorial deadline you can find her bingeing epic historical dramas or fantasy series in between weekend hikes.

Join her readers' group on FB here:
https://www.facebook.com/groups/rawdonsromantics

facebook.com/maggierawdon

instagram.com/maggierawdonbooks

tiktok.com/maggierawdon